A Brilliant Deception

AB&T Novels by Kim Foster

A Beautiful Heist

A Magnificent Crime

A Brilliant Deception

Published by Kensington Publishing Corporation

A BRILLIANT DECEPTION

An AB&T Novel

Kim Foster

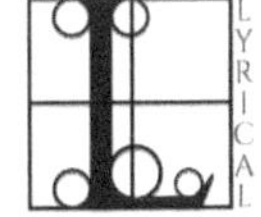

LYRICAL PRESS
Kensington Publishing Corp.
www.kensingtonbooks.com

To the extent that the image or images on the cover of this book depict a person or persons, such person or persons are merely models, and are not intended to portray any character or characters featured in the book.

LYRICAL PRESS BOOKS are published by

Kensington Publishing Corp.
119 West 40th Street
New York, NY 10018

All Kensington titles, imprints, and distributed lines are available at special quantity discounts for bulk purchases for sales promotion, premiums, fund-raising, educational, or institutional use.

Special book excerpts or customized printings can also be created to fit specific needs. For details, write or phone the office of the Kensington Sales Manager: Kensington Publishing Corp., 119 West 40th Street, New York, NY 10018. Attn. Sales Department. Phone: 1-800-221-2647.

Lyrical and the L logo are trademarks of Kensington Publishing Corp.

First Electronic Edition: June 2015
eISBN-13: 978-1-60183-066-1
eISBN-10: 1-60183-066-1

First Print Edition: June 2015
ISBN-13: 978-1-60183-485-0
ISBN-10: 1-60183-485-3

Printed in the United States of America

For my sisters, Deb and Vivi

Prologue

1192 AD, just outside Venice

Two galleys lay shipwrecked on the shore of the Adriatic Sea, a day's ride from the Venetian lagoon. The ships' sails hung in ragged strips, ravaged by the storm that had forced them ashore, still so far from home.

The twilit skies were calm now; the storm had receded as swiftly as it had begun. Only a mild, salty breeze remained, stirring the canvas flaps of the tents that had been hastily erected on the wet beach.

Cooking fires flickered among the clustered campaign tents, sending out warm sparks, filling the chilled autumn air with the smells of roasting meat. The men, the sailors, had abandoned the foundering ships and escaped by rowboat, bringing as many supplies as they could carry. Tonight, they would feast. Because although they had survived the tempest, the most dangerous part of their journey still lay ahead of them.

Sounds of singing and celebration rose into the darkening sky. God was on their side tonight. Most would say it was fitting for a band of Crusaders, returning home to England after a successful campaign in the Holy Land.

While most feasted and told tales around the fire, two men were huddled, discussing more serious matters in hushed tones within a candlelit tent—the grandest tent of the camp, set apart from the others.

"I have sent a small party into the city of Venice, in the cloak of night," said Thomas, the elder of the two. He had a trim gray beard and sharp green eyes, and looked older than his sixty-two years in his weathered chancellor's robes. "They will gather supplies, and most importantly, the items we will need if we are to go in disguise."

Traveling as a band of merchants would provide reasonable cover. The plan had merit. But the chancellor narrowed his eyes, watching the younger, taller man hovering over the map, studying the route and sipping his cup of wine. What was the likelihood they would be able to successfully disguise the king of England as a simple merchant?

Everything hinged on that. Of course, any king would have trouble pulling off such a disguise, but the one who stood before the chancellor's gaze would have particular difficulty. Besides the height—a head above most men—and the penetrating gray eyes, there was that hair: flame-red, like his father's, and a temper to match. And then there was the intangible, the aura in his very manner: the man was every inch a king.

It was one of the reasons they called him Lionheart.

The chancellor watched his king closely. Thomas knew Richard the Lionheart trusted him, considered him to be his closest adviser. Would he heed his advice now?

"Your Grace, I must advise you that the chances of capture are very high. We will be traveling through Leopold's territory, and coming dangerously close to Henry's." He indicated the parchment map. "The risks are grave indeed."

The king placed his cup on the table, sloshing the garnet-colored wine within, and turned his gaze on the chancellor. "What would you have me do, Thomas? After everything we have been through, I will not be thwarted on this last stretch." Candlelight flickered in the king's eyes.

Although the Third Crusade had been a success, the journey home had been less so. Foul weather had plagued the Crusaders all the way. They had been forced ashore on the island of Corfu, where they had changed to two new ships—the ships that now lay wrecked beside their camp.

There was no choice in the matter now—they had to make their way overland. Thomas knew the king would not leave his men, would not make a secret journey, saving himself and abandoning everyone else. He did not even suggest it. But there was another issue that needed to be raised.

Thomas smoothed his velvet robes. "I fear, Your Grace, if we do not return home quickly, there will be little left of your throne to reclaim."

King Richard's expression turned stony. They had discussed this many times, and the king was well aware of the whisperings about his brother John. Rumors said the prince was taking too many liberties, wielding too much power. There was a good chance Richard would have a battle for his own throne once he returned. And the longer he stayed away, the worse it would be. It may already be too late.

Thomas, however, had been formulating a plan ever since they'd put ashore. It was desperate and risky, but they had few choices.

"Your Grace, you should consider sending someone ahead. A small, clever group could reach England well ahead of our larger group. They can slip through enemy lines and travel efficiently."

The king tightened his mouth, listening. He looked down at the ring on his finger. A massive ring made of lustrous gold, holding a giant ruby like the heart of a lion. That had been the point, of course, and the reason for the peace offering from Saladin, the sultan they had battled throughout the Third Crusade.

It had been the gift to accompany the treaty signed by both leaders, the act that had ended the Crusade and signaled their return journey home. When Saladin had presented King Richard with the ring, he had explained its origin in a private audience with only the king and the chancellor in attendance. Thomas's eyes had opened wide while Saladin described the ancient roots of the precious object. It was a deep honor indeed. Thomas had known it, and so had the king.

In the weeks following that act, many songs had been sung of the battles, the success of the campaign, and the ring as the symbol of all that. There was but one ring like it, and it would now announce King Richard's identity as clearly as a trumpeting herald might.

King Richard considered Thomas's advice. At last, he nodded. "Send for the man they call Lox," he commanded.

Thomas opened the flap of canvas at the front of the tent. The smells of roasting meat and woodsmoke curled into the tent, and the candles flickered. He gave orders to the guard standing outside. A few minutes later, Lox entered the tent. He bowed deeply before the king.

Thomas looked closely at the man. He was not tall, but had broad shoulders and thick, curled hair. He was unshaven, like all the men in the troop. His keen eyes quickly marked everything inside the king's tent.

Yes, Lox was an excellent choice.

Thomas knew him to be a faithful, honest, and courageous man.

He had fought well throughout the Crusade, leading the yeomen archers well. But more than that, Thomas knew Lox had special talents. He was shadowy and could remain hidden, slip in where he wasn't permitted.

A sudden laugh rang outside by the campfire, the sounds muffled by the tent's canvas and the rich furnishings within. King Richard addressed Lox. "You will take three of your most trusted men, and you will take an alternate route home to England."

"Sire?"

"You will leave tonight. You must go quickly. We will be behind you, but we will be . . . slower."

Lox frowned slightly but continued to listen.

"Furthermore, you will take this with you." At this, King Richard removed the ruby ring from his middle finger and handed it to him. Thomas watched Lox's response closely as he accepted the ring. It was a wise decision. After all, there were many aspects of the king's person that would give him away, many things that would be difficult to disguise. But the ring would be a dead giveaway.

"Take the ring to my brother John and tell him what has happened," continued the king. "Take it to him and tell him the tale of our journey. If I have not returned within six weeks, something has happened to me. Death, possibly, capture almost certainly. The prince will know what to do."

Lox looked at him uncertainly. Doubtless he had heard the rumors of Prince John's treasonous acts.

"Your Grace," Thomas said quickly. "I must question the wisdom of putting so much faith—"

"*If* he is no longer on our side," King Richard said, turning from his adviser and placing a hand on Lox's shoulder, "well, you are a man of resources and intelligence, which is why I have chosen you for this task. I charge you with the power and the wisdom to know what to do."

"But, sire, I am just a—"

The king held up an imperial hand to stop him.

Thomas cleared his throat. "This ring, Lox, is a leader's ring. Men will follow you. It will assure your success."

Lox frowned. "You speak as though it's a talisman."

"Because that's exactly what it is."

Lox opened his palm and looked carefully at the ring that rested there. Then he closed his hand around it and lifted his head to face the king. "I will do this, sire. I will bring your ring, and your word, back to England. You can rest assured."

King Richard held the man's gaze. "I know you will."

Thomas stepped from the tent with Lox and watched as the man returned to the group, his new mission worn heavily about his shoulders. The chancellor turned to look out across the water. In the distance, the lights of Venice—the fabled city—shimmered over the sea's horizon.

He stepped back inside the tent, closing the canvas against the sounds of singing and feasting, returning to his king. "It is well, Your Grace. You have done everything you can."

Richard the Lionheart took a final sip of wine and nodded grimly. "I only pray it will be enough."

Chapter One

A famous bank robber was once asked why he robbed banks. "Because that's where the money is," he said.

It was for much the same reason that I stepped from a convertible Mercedes on a glittering sunny day, tossed the keys to a valet, and strolled up the plush red carpet into the Beverly Hills Hotel. The iconic green-and-white-striped awning arched overhead as I carried my Rodeo Drive shopping bags into the legendary Hollywood landmark, wearing a printed wrap dress, enormous Chanel sunglasses, and a golden blond wig.

The sunglasses weren't to hide my face from the paparazzi. They were to cover my line of sight. My gaze was not searching for a waiter from whom I might order a champagne cocktail and crab plate, but counting security staff, exits, and scanning for my mark. Yes, I was casing the Pink Palace.

I deposited my shopping bags with a helpful bellboy and swanned into the Polo Lounge.

This was where directors and A-list celebrities made deals over spinach salad, where Marlene Dietrich had been banned for wearing slacks, where Charlie Chaplin had maintained a standing reservation at Booth Number 1.

It was also where I was searching for a very specific target.

This particular disguise, in any other part of the world, would have garnered me an excessive amount of attention. But here, dressed and behaving like a diva starlet merely meant I blended into the scenery, much like the potted ferns in the lobby. I had considered disguising myself as hotel staff, but promptly dismissed the idea. Too much risk of being called upon to carry bags or fetch a drink or sweep a floor at some critical juncture of the job. This way I was free to move as I pleased, and since I was doing this job alone, complete freedom was a must.

Alone. My heart squeezed a little at that thought. Only two months ago I'd been in Paris, working closely with—and torn between—two of the most incredible men I'd ever known, and now . . . well, my solo status wasn't limited to professional activities, these days. My personal life was as dried up as half the Hollywood careers in this room. I straightened my shoulders. There was no time for self-pity today. Besides, it had been my choice.

I walked up to the bartender in the Polo Lounge. "Have you seen my agent? Miles Shapiro? I'm supposed to be meeting him here," I said irritably, tapping my glossy nails on the bar top.

Miles Shapiro, I knew full well, was ensconced in a high-end rehab facility in Malibu—a fact not yet publicly known, but one that had been helpfully provided by my trusty hacker, Gladys.

"Sorry, haven't seen him today, miss," the bartender said. He watched me with that look, the one that suggested he thought he might recognize me—had he seen me in a small movie role recently? But he couldn't quite place me, so he treated me like a celebrity anyway, just in case.

Exactly what I'd counted on.

I continued scanning the Polo Lounge—looking not for Miles Shapiro, but for my mark, Gretchen Plattman.

She was a horrendous woman, by all reports. The badly behaved trophy wife of a notorious LA gangster. She'd had a brief—and spectacularly mediocre—career in a few horrible films and then turned her attention to finding the richest son of a bitch she could. The fact that her husband continued to make his fortune on the broken backs of baby-faced inner city kids forced to do his dirty work made no difference to her. Not when it meant she could shop at Christian Dior and lunch at Spago.

It had been with no small amount of pleasure that I had accepted this assignment from my Agency. It always heightened my satisfaction quotient when I knew my efforts had an element of poetic justice to them.

I wasn't just looking to rob Mrs. Plattman of whatever she happened to have in her Birkin bag, however. I had a specific target: The Briolette of Kashmir. Somewhere out there, someone was very keen to possess this stone. But certain things in this world aren't for sale, no matter how great your means.

That's where my Agency usually comes in. They commission professional thieves on their roster to obtain the unobtainable.

For a fee, of course.

Not all Agency thieves have a code, but I had mine: I did not steal pieces that were uninsured, and I did not steal from people who couldn't afford it.

Happily, both those conditions were met in this instance at the Beverly Hills Hotel.

The Briolette was a spectacular diamond—worn as a pendant—that Gretchen Plattman reportedly never removed. According to all accounts, and confirmed by my surveillance, she slept, showered, and even had sex wearing it. The latter typically with younger, tanned, buff men paid for from her husband's offshore Bermuda account.

There was, however, one occasion during which Gretchen would remove the Briolette: her weekly Dead Sea mud wrap treatment at the spa in the Beverly Hills Hotel. During that treatment, which lasted ninety minutes, the diamond was locked away in a small safe behind the check-in counter at the spa, and was retrieved by Gretchen the moment her treatment was complete, to be returned to its place around her perfumed neck.

That small window, when the Briolette was to be nestled inside the safe—that would be my moment. Ninety minutes should be plenty of time, if everything went smoothly.

But first I needed to find her, because she was never on time for her appointment. She went up to the spa when she pleased—early, if she was bored (a sporadic occurrence); late, if she paused to woo a has-been producer (a frequent occurrence); or not at all, if she was drunk (a very frequent occurrence).

After failing to find her in the Polo Lounge, I went outside. The sun sparkled down like a spotlight on the Beverly Hills Hotel pool—the selfsame spot where Katharine Hepburn had once jumped in, fully clothed. Where Faye Dunaway had learned to swim freestyle for her role in *Mommie Dearest*. Green-and-white-striped lounge chairs fringed the water's edge, and behind those, a border of pink-walled cabanas, where stars and directors took full advantage of the single best placc in Hollywood to see and be seen.

And there, tanning her leathery hide, was Gretchen. Lounging on a chaise, inside the second cabana from the bar, preening herself and ordering a waiter to fetch some ice.

Perfect. I had her.

But there was a problem: the large bodyguard standing near her. My mouth twisted with bitter annoyance. He would be armed, which meant this job was going to be a little trickier than I'd hoped.

My skin baked in the sweltering sun. I pulled a giant floppy hat from my oversized Tory Burch bag and glided over to the poolside bar. Sliding onto a stool, I focused on a new plan. A white-jacketed bartender crushed endless daiquiris and poured fizzy flutes of Dom Pérignon as I watched Gretchen surreptitiously. To conceal my surveillance I pretended to gaze with admiration at the strapping young actor taking to the diving board. I felt my shoulders relax; there were perks to this assignment.

My gaze slid back to Gretchen and I spotted the Briolette. It was a truly huge diamond—a ridiculous thing to wear in the middle of the day.

Avert your eyes, Cat, I told myself. It would not be good to be seen paying too much attention to the stone.

The young woman seated next to me at the bar rudely snapped her fingers at the bartender. I glanced sideways at her. She was knocking back her margarita at an impressive rate. Her laughter pealed out and threatened to shatter the barware. She boasted to the bartender of her recent movie offer, and all the opportunities that were imminently, and assuredly, coming her way. My skin bristled with annoyance.

"But I wonder if I should change my hair. You know, something more dramatic, perhaps? People are always telling me I could pull it off . . ."

I imagined people's eyes were turning in our direction, and not in a positive way. I was in the perfect surveillance position at this point, but as for remaining subtle and under the radar, this loud starlet was impairing my ability to do so. I scoped out a different spot as she continued speaking to the bartender—who was also clearly wishing he, too, could be somewhere else.

"People like us, you know, we *feel* things so much more deeply than regular people. That's what draws us to this profession, you know."

I rolled my eyes, hidden behind my sunglasses. Then a couple dressed like tourists, wearing walking shorts and Eddie Bauer buttoned shirts and sandals, walked out to the pool. They looked starstruck, and also completely uncomfortable. The starlet glanced their way, and then snorted. "Oh my," she said loudly, pausing to sip her margarita. "Somebody took a wrong turn."

There were plenty of perfectly pleasant people here—why was I a magnet for all the ridiculous types?

At that moment Gretchen rose from her chaise, flapping her hand for her bodyguard to carry her things. She was on the move. But not quickly—she stumbled a little, tripping on her kitten-heeled deck sandals. I waited two beats, then slipped off the barstool and away from the pool. I made my way up to the promenade level, striding purposefully like I had somewhere to be.

I knew I would get there faster than she would. She was not walking steadily, and would be stopping multiple times to fawn over someone or other.

The spa reception area was an oasis of calm, with its bubbling fountain, soothing Spanish guitar music, and clouds of lavender essence. I strolled to the desk and asked the girl in a white lab coat to see a list of services. I kept my sunglasses on, as so many self-aware young starlets did. Just as I sat down in a plush chair in the waiting room to peruse the menu, Gretchen walked in.

Right on cue.

Unfortunately she arrived with her bodyguard in tow. He leaned down to pick up a magazine and I saw his firearm. A 9mm Glock.

I frowned and watched Gretchen remove her Briolette. The desk girl took it to the back room to presumably put it in the safe.

I was not going to get a better opportunity; I would have to take it. As an aesthetician led Gretchen to her treatment room, I slipped out of the reception area, back into the corridor. Around the corner, I ducked inside a linen closet where I had stashed a disguise—a spa uniform. I covered my wrap dress with a starched white lab coat, swapping my espadrilles for flats. I whipped off my blond wig and replaced it with a funkier look—a bright pink wig in a swingy bob.

I checked my reflection in my compact mirror. I looked completely different.

Back in the spa, I was annoyed to see the bodyguard still there—sitting on the sofa with a magazine on his lap. He was clearly not going anywhere. Even more unfortunate was the sight of a hotel security guard, chatting with the bodyguard.

Damn, what was he doing here?

This was a poor development, but the fact was I was there now, inside the spa, and dressed like I worked there. All three were looking at me. I had to continue.

I walked up to the front desk and talked to the girl there. "Hi, Olivia," I said, reading the name on her name tag. "I'm Macy. I started last week. Supervisor wants me to finish this shift—guess you're off the hook early."

The girl's eyes opened wide. "Really?" And then she hesitated. "Actually, I think I'll stay for the next half hour—I want to be here when Reese Witherspoon comes out—she always gives the best tips," she whispered.

"Ah. Okay," I said, brain churning to determine how I was going to get her out of there. I just needed a little alone time with the safe in the back room.

At that second, the security guard strolled up to the desk. Handsome, young, and eyes only for Olivia. My gaze slid back to Olivia, who looked like she could power a small condo she was burning so bright.

Okay, this could work to my advantage.

I would have preferred to be completely alone, but with them distracting each other at the front desk, that could leave me with the safe in the back room. I hoped the fully armed bodyguard remained engrossed in his magazine.

I cleared my throat. "So I'm just going to do some straightening up in the back room, okay? You've got the front desk, right, Olivia?" I asked.

She nodded absently and continued her conversation with the cute security guard. I went into the quiet back room, located the safe, and immediately got to business.

The safe was not particularly sophisticated, and it was the work of a few minutes to get into it. The door swung open. I spotted the Briolette, slid my hand toward it, and . . .

"What are you doing?" Olivia asked.

I froze and turned around. "Oh, I was putting something in here that belonged to a client . . ."

I looked at her, wondering if she'd buy it. I held my breath and watched the suspicion and doubt cloud over her eyes as she processed the scene.

Nope, she wasn't buying it.

Plan B. Without hesitation, I grabbed Olivia's arm, pulled her into the room, and executed a Krav Maga maneuver to knock her out cold with one go. I left her in the room lying on the floor, slipped out, and locked the door behind me. I slowed down and walked casually back to the front reception area.

Unfortunately, I walked straight into the questioning gaze of the security guard Olivia had been flirting with. He looked behind me, wondering where she was. I smiled. "She had to use the restroom for a sec. She'll be right back." He said nothing, watching me closely.

"Actually, I have to go get some more towels from downstairs—you don't mind watching the front desk for a minute, do you?" I said.

"Sure."

I flashed him my warmest smile and glided out the door. "Thanks a mil. Back in a jiffy."

The armed bodyguard hadn't moved, continuing to flip through his magazine. Out of the corner of my eye I could see the security guard's head turn back to the room behind the desk, where Olivia was unconscious. It would only be a matter of time before he went to check it out. I had to be fast.

I raced to the linen closet, pulling out my cell phone as I went. Inside the closet, I put the phone on speaker while quickly changing back to my previous disguise, keeping the Briolette tucked in my bra.

"Yes, hello, I need vehicle 356A right away," I said when the valet answered the phone, reading the number off my ticket.

I poked my head out of the closet and, seeing a clear path, flew down the corridor. Before turning the corner I glanced over my shoulder and saw both men come flying out of the spa, the security guard talking urgently into his walkie-talkie.

Damn. They hadn't spotted me yet, but they'd either discovered Olivia, or the breached safe, or both.

There would be more armed guards in the lobby, guards with walkie-talkies who would now be alert to the crime in progress. So the lobby was out; I needed an alternate escape route.

Attempting to reach the nearby stairwell would mean revealing myself to the guards. But I knew there was another stairwell, down the far end of this corridor. I set off for it at a sprint, and made it without being seen. The instant I lunged into the stairwell I heard thundering bootsteps coming up.

Nope, not that way.

I spun and reentered the corridor. There was nowhere to go.

Just then, the elevator bonged, halfway down the corridor. I raced for it, dashing inside before the doors slid closed. "Whew! Just in time," I said. I eyed the one other passenger inside—who had not made any effort to hold the door open for me, I noted. It was the bitchy starlet from the poolside bar, texting furiously on her cell phone.

As the elevator went down, I caught my reflection in the mirrored interior and realized something unfortunate: I still wore the pink wig.

I squeezed my eyes shut. I had no way to hide a wig—no bag or purse or anything, as I'd abandoned everything in the linen closet. I searched the elevator for somewhere I could stash the wig, and in doing so took another look at my elevator companion.

She smelled even more strongly of margaritas now. She flicked a glance at me without any sign of recognition in her face; I was not important to her in the least. Which gave me a glimmer of an idea.

I cleared my throat and said, "You know—your coloring is perfect for pink hair. Have you ever considered it?"

She shrugged, looking unimpressed and pouty. The elevator descended another floor and I kept talking. "My stylist sent me this wig and it looks terrible on me, washes me right out—but it would be perfect on you. You've got the right cheekbones and full lips to pull it off. Do you want to try?"

Three minutes later, the elevator doors slid open at the lobby and I exited the car. I slowed myself down, crossing the marble floor. Behind me I heard a ruckus. I looked back and watched as two guards tackled a girl wearing bright pink hair.

I suppressed a smile and kept walking, ever closer to the front door.

"Did you find your agent?" asked one of the doormen kindly, as I walked through.

"No, he never showed." I sighed and shook my head. "Oh well, time for some retail therapy. Ta-ta!" I lifted my head high and walked straight out the front door.

I scanned the driveway; the valet hadn't arrived with my car yet. My stomach tightened.

At that moment, an elderly woman called out, "Oh, someone please stop him!"

I spotted a little white dog darting away. The dog was headed for the driveway, chasing a squirrel. A Ferrari was coming up the driveway, driven by a valet who was roaring up the slope fast. He wasn't going to see the tiny dog in time.

Reflexively, I sprinted. I lunged and grabbed the dog and rolled out of the way.

When I stood up, a small cluster of stunned expressions greeted me. I smiled and brushed off my dress. "I, um, I've been training," I offered, clearing my throat. "Action movie. They want me to do my own stunts . . ."

I handed the fluffy little dog back to the woman. At that moment, a valet arrived in a convertible Mercedes—my car.

As I pulled away from the curb I squinted at the rearview mirror. The armed bodyguard and two security officers strode out of the hotel. Before they even glanced in my direction they beelined to the valet stand, presumably to shut down the exits while they searched for suspicious characters.

I reached the road and roared smoothly away, unheeded and unfollowed.

The convertible top to the Mercedes retracted at the push of a button and I drove away, fast, down the winding hills of Sunset Boulevard. The wind whipped my hair as I continued along palm tree–lined boulevards under the sparkling LA sun. An exhilarated grin threatened to split my face as relief washed over me, and the warm tingle of a job successfully done spread throughout my limbs.

Once again, it never ceased to amaze me how shockingly good it felt to behave so spectacularly bad.

Several minutes later my phone rang. I glanced down, still driving, and saw a familiar number flash on the screen—Templeton, my handler at AB&T, the Agency of Burglary and Theft. I answered the encrypted call and put it on speaker. "Templeton, you must be clairvoyant!" I said, laughing. "I just finished the job, you'll be happy to know. It's in hand, in all its sparkling glory."

There was a moment's hesitation. "I beg your pardon?" he said, then mumbled and answered his own question. "Oh, the Briolette. Yes, jolly good, my dear." My eyebrows knotted slightly. He sounded distracted, and—something else I couldn't place. "But that's not why I'm calling," he said.

A bristle of warning traced up my scalp.

"Petal, you need to come home right away. Your mother is in the hospital. She was hurt."

My chest collapsed inward as all the air left me. "What? How?"

"I'm not sure how to tell you this—"

"*Templeton.* Tell me. Now."

A moment's pause. Then, "She was shot. Because . . . well, you see, Catherine—she tried to stop a burglar."

Chapter Two

I got back to Seattle as fast as I possibly could. The flight was brief but agonizing, and I went to the hospital straight from the airport. I arrived just after 8 p.m.

The antiseptic environment of the hospital—smelling of industrial cleaner and vomit—slammed into me as soon as I walked in. The fluorescent lights didn't help my growing headache. But I ignored the pain. It didn't matter; I only cared about getting up to the trauma ward.

I arrived at the doorway to my mom's room. She was as white as the starched sheets that covered her. She gazed out the window at the darkening sky, the tubes and wires running out of her to various IV poles and monitors clustered around the bedside. It was all so—invasive-looking. One of the machines was bleeping. Another was making a whirring sound. A white-coated doctor—a resident, maybe?—stood by the bedside, making notes on Mom's chart. He looked impossibly young, as well as tired. The greens under his white coat were creased and rumpled, like he'd been sleeping in them. He looked up at me—through glasses with smudge marks on the lenses—forcing me to enter the room before I was ready.

A panicky feeling crawled up my throat as I crept in and stood by the foot of her bed. The room smelled of bleach. Her gaze turned to me, an oxygen tube under her nose. My heart squeezed at the sight of my mother like that.

As she saw me, her face softened into a weak smile. "Cat. Darling, I'm so glad you're here." Her voice was hoarse.

I wanted to say something but didn't know quite what. So I settled for smiling back at her and hoped I made it look convincing.

"It looks like your mother is going to be fine," the resident said, clicking his pen and sliding it back into the breast pocket of his white coat. "The surgery went well, there should be no permanent damage. Recovery will take some time, of course."

"How much time?" I asked. "Did you get the bullet out?" I peppered him with a million other questions, barely giving him time to answer, until my mom reached a cool hand out from under her sheets and gripped my hand.

"Sweetheart, *stop*. Everything will be fine. Let the doctor go see his other patients. There will be time to talk later."

She was right. I glanced apologetically at the resident.

"I'll be here in the morning," he said. "I can answer more of your questions then."

I nodded. "Thank you, Doctor."

"I'll leave you two alone," he said and strode out, his sneakers squeaking faintly on the polished floor.

"Do you need anything, Mom?" I asked, pulling up the blanket that was rumpled at the foot of her bed and tucking it around her. "Are you okay?" I wasn't talking about physically, and we both knew it. "How do you feel?"

She sighed and took a few deep breaths. "Well, I feel rather stupid, for one thing. I don't know what I was thinking."

"Templeton told me what happened," I said.

"I thought I could reason with the thief," she confessed.

I looked down at the bandage covering her left shoulder. I cringed, thinking of a bullet ripping through my mother's flesh. Templeton had filled me in on what had happened, exactly, as I'd raced to the airport in LA.

My mom had been at a museum after hours, helping clean up after a benefit dinner, when someone detected a break-in. Instead of calling the police, like normal people would do, she went to investigate, and see if she could stop it.

In the process, the perpetrator shot her.

"Who was it?" I demanded of Templeton. My first thought was someone with Caliga Rapio, the ruthless organization of unscrupulous, violent thieves. The thought of it made my stomach curdle.

But it was worse than that. Much worse.

"He was one of ours," Templeton said. "He works with AB&T."

"*What?*"

"Apparently it was self-defense. He was startled. You might have done the same thing, Catherine."

Those words echoed in my ears now, looking down at my mom in the hospital bed. It was a punch in the stomach. A small part of me wondered—was it true?

I was a criminal, too. I was part of the underground world that produced people who shot unarmed fifty-nine-year-old women who interrupted their crime-in-progress.

Being a thief was the one thing in the world that made me feel truly special. It was my unique talent in the world, and it made me feel alive. And I had always justified my choice of profession by keeping a set of ethics—my Thief's Credo. Besides, I was merely playing a role in what I call the Secret Sport of Kings. Stealing one another's goodies has long been a pastime of the überrich. Right or wrong, it's part of the fabric of our society.

But now—well, that justification felt rather thin.

"Why would you do it, Mom? Didn't you think of the danger?"

"No, Catherine. I didn't."

I was desperate to understand. Why would she take such a risk? One possibility had occurred to me, and it was gnawing away at my insides. Had she grown overconfident in the past year, because of her involvement in my line of work?

The trouble was, my mom considered herself my business manager, which probably made her feel overconfident, like she was part of the criminal world. I had allowed this little fiction because she seemed to get so much pleasure from it, and it gave her something to do. I imagine she felt like she knew criminals. She understood burglars, and how they worked.

But while *I'm* aware of the dangers in my chosen profession, I'm not sure if my mother is. Or was. Maybe I hadn't done enough to warn her of the very real risk. I didn't routinely carry a firearm, but there were many thieves and criminals who did. Had I neglected to make sure she knew that?

It all added up to one inescapable truth. This incident was my fault.

The world tilted and my head swam as the guilt threatened to overwhelm me. I hadn't protected my mom from this. I'd let her become involved with my little underworld. It was careless and stupid.

I gazed away from my mother to stare at the bleeping machines next to her, pretending to study the lights and the flow of fluid through the IV tubes.

"There's something more," my mother said. A cloud of worry and unhappiness moved across her face.

"It's okay, Mom, we don't need to talk about this stuff right now. You need some rest."

"No. This is important."

I put my hand on hers. Her skin felt cool, her bones delicate and thin underneath mine.

"When the shot went out, a terribly clichéd thing happened," she said. "My life flashed before my eyes. And it was a good life, Cat, very good. But there was something missing."

I had an unpleasant feeling I knew where this was headed.

"It was grandchildren," she said. "I wanted to see grandchildren there."

I closed my eyes. This was well-worn territory. Why did she have to bring it up now? I tightened my fists inside my pockets. My mother had almost died—and this was what she was thinking about? My mouth grew thin and hard. It was the last thing I wanted to discuss now.

"I want you to be happy, Catherine," she said. "You are my only child. And . . . I can't help feeling that my life will be left incomplete unless I see you happily married and with a gorgeous, healthy baby." A tear slipped down her face.

In spite of myself, my frown softened, just a little.

"I don't want you getting all upset about this," I said, squeezing her papery hand. "Let's talk about this later. You really should rest."

She was tired, obviously, because for once she didn't fight me on this. I settled my mom back down on her pillow and turned off the lights. I went to the window in her room and stared at the streetlights, the brake lights of the cars on the freeway.

Marriage. Children. For the first time, I actually rolled the idea around in my mind. A small ache centered in my chest. Maybe it was something I wanted, too, after all.

Once my mom was breathing steadily, asleep once more, I left the room. In the corridor my father was returning with coffee from the cafeteria.

"Is she asleep?" he asked, handing me a steaming Styrofoam cup. I nodded and we sat on the orange vinyl chairs in the small waiting area for families, and sipped the weak hospital coffee.

We didn't discuss the details of what had happened. I was afraid of what my dad would say. He was not in favor of my chosen profession. He had learned the truth much later than my mom had, and though she had been on board, he had decidedly not been. In fact, for a long time he really didn't want to have much to do with me, after he learned the truth. Penny, my sister, had always been his baby, but I was "Daddy's girl"—his partner in crime. We had been inseparable, until he learned my secret.

I wondered if things would ever be the same between us.

Somehow, I found myself telling him what my mom had said about grandchildren. For a long time he said nothing, staring into his coffee cup.

"Well, Kit Kat, maybe you need to think about it. When your mother was your age, we were already married. And you were on the way."

"Really?" I frowned into my own coffee cup, processing that.

Even if this *was* something I wanted, there was one big, glaring problem. No boyfriend. No viable candidates. It wasn't lost on me that as of a few months ago, there had been not only one highly qualified, exceptionally desirable contender, but two. Until I'd decided I needed some time to be alone to find the truth in my heart.

Now I'd lost them both. There would be no marriage on the horizon for me anytime soon.

My phone vibrated and gave a brief chime. I glanced down to check the message, relieved for the interruption. It was from Templeton. *Meet me at The Pacific Summer Fair for the handover. Ferris wheel.*

I sighed. This was normal procedure. After a theft, I always met Templeton in a public place to transfer the spoils and debrief. It was the last thing I felt like doing now, but I didn't have a choice. The Briolette was still on me.

"I, um, have to go, Dad."

He watched me with suspicion but said nothing.

"Something I have to do." I couldn't explain to my dad where I had to go. But he knew I was choosing my job over my family. I stood and walked away down the corridor before his look of suspicion could turn to one of disgust.

It is my job, I reminded myself. Right or wrong, it was the path I had chosen, and for now I had an obligation to see it through.

Trouble was, at that moment, I felt the same degree of disgust at myself that he did.

Chapter Three

It was dusk, a clear midsummer Friday night, which meant the carnival was busy. Smells of popcorn and cotton candy and axle grease from the rides filled the air. The sky sang with sounds of laughter and the rattling wheels of midway games and calliope music from the carousel.

I made my way to the Ferris wheel, stopping to buy a candy apple along the way, walking along the trampled and flattened grass. I gazed up at the giant spinning wheel in the sky, its lights blinking and flashing. In the lineup I spotted Templeton and slipped into the queue behind him, knowing we'd be paired up when we got to the front of the line.

The bar clunked into place, and we were lifted backward, swinging into the sky.

"Are you all right?" Templeton asked, keeping his gaze on the sky in front of us.

I said nothing for a minute, then nodded. "I will be, I think."

"And your mother?"

"She's doing okay. She's lucky."

Templeton nodded. "Indeed."

We said nothing for a moment as the ride climbed to the apex.

"I have something for you," I said. I pulled out a small padded envelope and held it in my right hand, the candy apple in my left. We were at the peak of the ride so no one on the ground could possibly see the package I handed to Templeton. He accepted it with a gleeful smile.

It made me happy to make Templeton happy, but that was the extent of my positivity. My success at the Briolette job felt as hollow and brittle as a scooped-out eggshell.

The Ferris wheel creaked and groaned as we rounded the top for the first time and started our descent. "Fabulous work, Petal," Templeton said, tucking the packet away. "However, there is no rest for the wicked."

I turned to him. "No?"

"I've got something very exciting for you—I think you're really going to love this next assignment."

My stomach twisted. Ordinarily the prospect of a new assignment brought nothing but eager anticipation. Now it was the last thing I wanted. I wasn't ready. I needed time to be sure my heart was still in it. And I wanted to make sure my mother was going to be okay.

"There's a ring. And we've been contacted by a client who wants you to retrieve it for them."

"Templeton, I—"

"I know, Catherine. But I think you're going to like the sound of this."

I sat back and looked at him doubtfully. "Go on."

"It's a man's ring, and it's from the Middle Ages—the twelfth century. It's the finest gold, set with a massive ruby."

My eyebrows knitted together. Something about this was tickling my memory. I took a bite of my candy apple, sweet and tart at the same time.

Templeton was working hard not to grin. "It's the legendary ring of Richard the Lionheart."

I almost choked on my apple. "But—I thought that ring was a myth. Nobody has actually seen it." Being a jewel thief, it was my business to be familiar with all notable pieces of jewelry and gems—real and legendary.

"Well, now they have. It was found in a grave that was recently unearthed by archaeologists in the north of England—in Yorkshire. They're calling it a very significant find, although they haven't yet released the information to the public. And they're not telling us any more details than that."

The Ferris wheel swung slowly back toward the earth, the chair tilting underneath us as we reached the lowest point. We swooped backward through the nadir and then climbed once more to the sky for our second go-around.

"Do we know who is hiring us? And why?"

"Well, things are a little need-to-know at the moment, and the information I have is pretty scant. All I know right now is that it looks like we've been hired by some branch of local government in England. Apparently it's not a theft for monetary gain, but to hide the very existence of the ring."

I licked my lips. It was odd, and not the usual motive for stealing a jewel.

He angled his head and looked at me carefully. "Does it matter?"

It did, actually. Everything about my job, my role in life, had been thrown around like the topsy-turvy ride at the carnival, and I needed something to feel grounded by. I needed a good reason to get involved. It was intriguing, but I wasn't sure it was a good enough reason.

"So—where is the ring located now? Where is this job to take place?"

"It's currently being held in a lab at the University of York. Under high security. National-level security, in fact."

"Surely they have professional thieves in England? Why me?"

"Well, that's an interesting little story. And . . . it's where there's a bit of a catch."

I groaned. Why was there always a catch?

"They came to hear of you because of the Louvre job you did in the spring," Templeton said.

Ah. So that was it. "They were incredibly impressed at that. Your name is being tossed around in European circles quite a bit," Templeton continued. "Something you should be very proud of."

I smiled in spite of myself. I *was* proud of that job.

"They say they can't leave this to chance—they can't risk the existence of this ring becoming public knowledge. In one week the archaeologists are going to release this information, and show the world what they've found. It has to happen before then. So, they say they need the best."

"Okay, well, that's very flattering. But—what's the catch you mentioned?"

"Well, they want you . . . but they also want Ethan Jones. They are, essentially, insisting that you work together. They know you worked together on the Louvre job, and they believe you are the perfect pair to do this job."

I was quiet a moment. "Oh," I said. "Well, that's awkward."

Things between Ethan and me were not terrific at the moment. Well, that wasn't accurate. It would be more correct to say they were . . . *nothing*, at the moment. Because I had no idea where Ethan was. I hadn't seen him in the past several months, and neither had anyone else.

After I had told him and Jack, on the banks of the Louvre, that I needed to be alone for a bit, it seemed he had taken me at my word. There were rumors he'd joined the Peace Corps or something. Which was pretty hard to believe, given that he was one of the most dedicated career criminals I'd ever met.

"They know it wasn't just me and Ethan doing that job, right? They know Jack helped, too?"

"They know. But, apparently, they're not interested in hiring someone with such deep connections to law enforcement as Jack. They don't want an FBI agent, even one who has been dismissed from the bureau. They only want you and Ethan."

I chewed my lip. I didn't think they'd be so committed to the idea if they knew about all the undercurrents between Ethan and me.

"Anyway, Catherine, I don't think it's something for you to worry about. It will only become an issue if they're actually able to find him. Which is doubtful. It shouldn't affect your acceptance of the assignment."

I nodded. He was right.

But there was still the larger reason why my stomach felt sour about this job. It had everything to do with my mother.

"So, my dear? What do you say? Are you up for it?"

"I don't know, Templeton. I'm not sure. I need a little time to think about it."

"Why? They're offering a very generous fee. It's a fabulous job. I thought you'd be thrilled."

"Maybe. But . . . I'm not sure I want *any* job right now."

He scowled. "Catherine, this would be a bad career move for you, to turn this down."

I looked out over the carnival, at the blinking lights from the arcade games. Bleeps and horns and ticking sounds from the Wheel of Fortune floated over to us on the warm breeze.

"Just give me a little time, okay?"

"I can hold them off for twenty-four hours. But you will need to give me an answer by this time tomorrow."

I fiddled with the remaining bit of candy apple, twirled the stick in my hand.

"I do have another bit of news," Templeton said. "AB&T has been incredibly pleased with your performance these days. So they are giving you a new, elevated set of responsibilities."

"Oh?"

"We need you to train a new recruit. There's an asset who has recently joined the Agency, and he's got raw talent. But he needs to be trained in the ways of the professional thief. We think you're the perfect person for this job."

I sighed. "Oh, Templeton, I don't know. I mean, it's flattering. But I don't know anything about how to teach this stuff. Or be a mentor or anything."

"Sure you do. You had a mentor when you started going pro, didn't you?"

Brooke Sinclair. Thinking about her gave me a bitter taste in my mouth. Brooke had been the most skilled teacher I could have asked for. Until she stabbed me in the back.

But this would be different. I would be the mentor. It was my opportunity, perhaps, to do right by a trainee, unlike what Brooke had done to me. Also . . . it could be fun, teaching a newbie, and a good distraction from thoughts about the deeper meaning of my job. And whether I could actually continue in it or not.

"Don't worry, it won't interfere with your regular work," Templeton said. "You just have to bring him along to work on a couple of skills. Polish his pickpocketing craft, etcetera."

I shrugged. "Okay, maybe." I shifted in the Ferris wheel chair and it creaked beneath us. "Templeton, I was wondering something."

"Yes?"

I fidgeted with the edge of my sweater. "Have you heard from Jack?"

He looked at me closely. "Not exactly. But I've heard . . . one or two things through the grapevine."

I waited. Jack Barlow and I had a long history. Not the smoothest of romantic rides, unfortunately. But we'd been through so much together. It gave me a cramp in my chest that I had lost touch with him in the past two months. It was still difficult for me to accept we were no longer a couple.

"You know Jack was dismissed from the FBI, yes?"

I nodded. This I knew.

Templeton sighed. "It seems he's also forgotten about the Fabergé quest, the Gifts of the Magi. He doesn't appear to care anymore."

My eyebrows raised. It wasn't like Jack. The quest was a legacy passed down to Jack from his father, as it had been passed through the generations.

Only a few people knew the truth about the Gifts of the Magi. Long ago, the Gifts had been secreted inside a Fabergé egg. Retrieving that Egg, and the lost Gold, Frankincense, and Myrrh contained within, was the only honorable goal Jack's father—an infamous thief, in life—had ever pursued. The trouble was, not only had Jack rejected his father's way of life and joined the FBI instead, he had become completely estranged from his father. It wasn't until after the man's death that Jack had learned of the quest. It hadn't been easy for Jack, but once he had wrestled with the demons of his criminal heritage, the quest had come to occupy a large and important—although secret—piece of his life. "Is that all you've heard? What's he doing instead?"

He glanced at me sideways and hesitated. "You're not going to like this, Petal. I've heard that Jack has been making some rather questionable lifestyle decisions lately. Throwing a lot of money around, drinking too much, and . . . dating everything that moves."

I developed a feeling of nausea that had nothing to do with the Ferris wheel.

Chapter Four

In spite of being exhausted, I couldn't sleep. Maybe I wasn't used to sleeping alone yet. It had only been three months since I'd moved out of Jack's place and back into my own apartment.

But it was more than my lonely bed. I had too many questions in my head. Too many things to worry about—my mother, this new job, Ethan . . .

I tossed and turned until my pajamas knotted in a sweaty mess around me. The LED numbers on the clock display stared at me. It was just past midnight. Was that all? I felt like I'd been lying awake for hours.

I got up, pulled on a pair of sweats, threw my hair into a ragged ponytail, and walked out of my apartment. A quick glance in the mirror of the elevator proved to be a mistake. I had neglected to take off my makeup before going to bed, so there was mascara smeared around my eyes and a generally shiny, smudgy look about my face.

It didn't matter. Who was I trying to impress? All I needed to do was walk a little. Clear my head, then get back to sleep.

If it were a more reasonable hour, I'd have called my girlfriends to meet for coffee or a glass of wine. I really could use some therapeutic girl talk. Or a distraction, at least. But neither Mel nor Sophie would appreciate me waking them up in the middle of the night to talk about my problems.

Cool night air tingled my nostrils as I stepped outside. At least the neighborhood was familiar. It was the same one Jack and I had lived in.

I strolled, hungry and wondering what would be open after midnight. But I wasn't going into a bar or restaurant looking like this. Corner store it was.

I stepped inside the fluorescently lit space that smelled of stale coffee and lemonade slushies. I shuffled down the aisles in search of suitable snacks. Chocolate—yes, I was definitely in need of some chocolate. I also grabbed a pint of Ben & Jerry's Chunky Monkey ice cream. And a huge bag of pork rinds. And a *People* magazine with a picture of the latest Bachelor. Then I noticed a sale on mega packs of tampons, and also toilet paper. Might as well stock up, right?

I felt sheepish putting all this stuff on the counter in front of the very young and quite cute guy with deep blue eyes working the cash register, but really, what did I care? I didn't know him. And I needed this stuff. Especially the pork rinds.

The door chime jangled and I heard a man and a woman enter. The woman laughed flirtatiously as the man finished the tail end of a story.

My heart stopped in its tracks. Even though I hadn't turned yet, I knew the man's voice. It was Jack.

My head turned on an irresistible swivel. Sure enough, Jack Barlow was entering the store with a woman on his arm. They were both in cocktail attire.

Jack looked drop-dead gorgeous, as always. Tall, dark, broad shoulders, great hair. Jack was the kind of man who would look perfectly at ease in lumberjack attire; he had the rugged look of an outdoorsman. But he cleaned up like nobody's business.

The woman I didn't know. She was young, early twenties. A slender, leggy blonde in a nude, sparkly cocktail dress that showed a lot of smooth, glowing skin. Jack's arm was around her waist as they walked in.

My chest pinched. Fortunately, they hadn't seen me as they entered. I had to get out of there, fast. I turned my face away from them, back to the clerk.

"That comes to eighteen sixty-one," the blue-eyed clerk said, tallying my purchases.

I rummaged in my wallet and quickly produced my debit card. He rang it through and I heard the woman's laughter from behind me, deep within the aisles of the store. I didn't turn to look.

As I stood at the counter I wondered if Templeton had been right about Jack. I hadn't fully believed him. It was so out of character for Jack. But it was harder to dispute now. The whole badly behaved playboy thing had never been Jack's scene, even though he certainly had the means.

A knot of guilt centered in my stomach. If he really had changed for the worse—was it my fault?

I heard their voices moving closer to the counter. I hastily punched in my PIN. The clerk looked down at the machine and said, "Nope, didn't work."

In my urgency I must have punched it in wrong. I tried again, on the edge of frantic. I had to get out of there.

"Sorry. Declined again."

I closed my eyes and tried to relax. Jack and his companion were right behind me now and I didn't have a lick of cash on me.

"Okay, never mind," I said quietly to the clerk. "I'll—um, come back." I would just leave, abandon my items on the counter.

"Cat?"

My heart sank into my tennis sneakers.

I steeled myself and turned, staring into the faces of Jack and his perfect date. There I was with my unwashed hair, smeared makeup, and grubby sweats attempting to buy a jumbo pack of tampons and pork rinds, but seemingly too broke to do so.

I wanted to crawl inside that jumbo pack of tampons and die. Instead, I applied a bright smile and said, "Oh! Jack! Didn't see you there. What a . . . coincidence."

New goal: extract myself from this situation as soon as possible, ideally with my self-respect somewhat intact.

"Yeah, small world," Jack said. He was holding a bottle of Prosecco. This corner store, surprisingly, had a decent selection of wine.

There was something different about Jack. Something less cautious, somehow. He'd always been the hero, the warrior, the guy you could count on to do the right thing. Now, here, he looked a little more rogue. A little more don't-give-a-shit. But perhaps it was my imagination.

I tried as hard as I could to keep looking in his eyes. But I was drawn to his companion, whom Jack hadn't introduced yet.

"Oh, I'm sorry," Jack said, seeing my gaze shift. "Let me introduce you. Cat, this is Madison. Madison is an undergrad at UW, in political science."

I briefly wondered if this was as uncomfortable for her as it was for me. I also wondered if Madison was someone he was dating casually—or was she a more serious girlfriend? They looked very familiar with each other, very comfortable. This whole line of thinking threatened to excise my heart with a dull spoon.

I grasped onto the only part of the conversation I could. "Oh, I'm a student at UW also," I said. "I'm doing my master's in French lit. But Jack probably told you about that."

As soon as the words were out, I wanted to take them back. It was a ridiculous thing to say. Why would he have told her that? Why would he have mentioned anything about me at all? An awkward silence blossomed.

"Oh, did you two used to date?" Madison asked, finally piecing it together. There was surprise and a certain amount of doubt in her voice.

This was a punch in the throat. I caught a glimpse of myself in the reflection of the door, which was like a mirror because it was dark outside. I looked like I hadn't showered in a week.

"So," I said, giving a small chuckle, "I was just out for a run." I glanced down at my outfit, and my generally disheveled appearance, by way of explanation. Not that they were asking for an explanation, but I couldn't help attempting to give one.

"You run at this hour of the night?" Madison asked. A hint of disbelief curled the edges of her tone.

"I didn't know you were a runner," Jack said. "When did you start doing that?"

Crap. I should have said hot yoga. That would have been much more believable. And fashionable.

I needed a way out of there.

The store clerk cleared his throat. "Miss, are you going to pay for these things?"

Oh God, the tampons and ice cream and pork rinds. "Um, that's okay, I don't really need that stuff," I said weakly.

"Here, do you need cash?" Jack asked, reaching into his wallet.

"No!" I said, more vigorously than was necessary, placing my hand on his arm to stop him. Then I quickly withdrew it, which Madison noted with a perfectly penciled, arched eyebrow. "Thank you, Jack—but I'm okay."

In truth, I was anything but okay. I quickly mumbled something vague about seeing them again sometime and bolted toward the exit.

Even before I reached the door, I knew there were stinging tears waiting to come out. I was a cautionary tale, an Aesop's fable about the dog with the bone. I had no right to be upset because the fact was . . . *I'd had him.* He had been mine. And I'd messed it up. In trying to figure out which man I loved the most, Ethan or Jack, I'd lost them both.

I burst out the door and the second I was out of view started sprinting down the street.

See? *There.* I was running, now, wasn't I?

Chapter Five

Jack's housekeeper, Evelyn, woke him a few minutes past noon. He was alone in his bed. After the corner store incident the night before, instead of bringing Madison back to his place to share the bottle of Prosecco like they'd planned, he'd dropped her off at home. He wanted to be alone.

Evelyn threw open the curtains, and harsh sunlight poured into his room. Jack groaned and covered his eyes with a down pillow. His head throbbed.

"It's the afternoon," Evelyn said plainly, a statement of fact, no judgment tucked inside.

It was a ridiculous hour of the day to be crawling out of bed, but Jack couldn't find it in himself to care. All he wanted to do was nurse his hangover. Just because he'd taken Madison home didn't mean he'd stopped drinking.

He dragged his sorry ass out of bed and into the bathroom. In the mirror, Jack barely recognized himself—face pale and slack, dark smudges under his eyes. He looked away in disgust and twisted the shower nozzle on.

After his shower, starting to feel more human, Jack dressed and went into the kitchen to find that Evelyn had food waiting for him—eggs and bacon and hot coffee. For the hundredth time he wondered what he would do without her. The thought triggered a pang of guilt. He knew the only reason he had the means to afford a housekeeper and this penthouse was because of his father. Or more specifically, his father's illicit and lucrative lifestyle. Jack had inherited a fortune because of it.

Evelyn bustled around the kitchen as he sipped coffee and left the food untouched. Then, she came over and stood in front of him. He looked up to see her glaring down at him, hands planted on her hips.

"You need help, Jack," she said to him flatly. Jack said nothing. He continued sipping his coffee.

But Evelyn wasn't to be deterred. "Ever since you came back from Paris you've been different."

He put his mug down on the table and looked up at her. "You mean ever since my career went down the drain? Yeah, you could say that's when things went to shit."

"It's not only about your career and you know it," she said.

He grumbled. He knew she was talking about Cat.

"This isn't you. This kind of lifestyle—it's not worthy of you."

Jack ignored her and pretended to read the newspaper. But he wasn't focusing on the words. He was thousands of miles away, back in Paris.

After Cat had left Jack on the banks of the Seine three months ago, crushing his heart into the cobblestones, he'd pretended to be okay with it all. Pretended he felt only respect for her decision.

After a week of moping around at home, brooding on the whole thing, he'd decided he was done with relationships. Never again would he let someone destroy his heart. From then on, he'd just have fun. Nothing complicated. So he started dating, with a vengeance. He soon discovered it was a great distraction.

Especially after everything else went to shit, too. Shortly after returning home from Paris, Jack had been dismissed from the FBI. Well, not exactly. His supervisor, Victoria Sullivan, had filed a formal report recommending his dismissal. Jack had known what would come next: a long and drawn-out procedure, during which they'd scrutinize Jack's behavior. His transgressions, his tendency to do things not exactly by the book.

Jack just didn't have the stomach for it. So he voluntarily surrendered his badge.

Evelyn's voice pulled him back to the present. "Wesley called again," she said pointedly.

Jack remained stony-faced. "I've already told you. I'm not calling him back."

He was not getting dragged back into all that again. Wesley was the AB&T operative who was heading up the search for the Fabergé egg that contained the Gifts of the Magi. For a long time the Fabergé quest had given Jack drive, supplying him with a purpose that made it worth getting out of bed in the morning. But Wesley and Jack had failed so far in every attempt to recapture the Fabergé egg. It had slipped through their fingers and now it was gone.

Wesley had tried to involve him in the search for the Gifts again and, more importantly, for the lost portion of gold that had become separated from the other two Gifts at some point. It was something they'd learned about from Esmerelda, a French agent with the enigmatic Department of Antiquities who had helped them with the Louvre job.

But after everything that had happened with Cat in Paris, Jack had turned his back on anything remotely connected with Cat's world. He didn't have the heart for it.

After that, he'd grown restless and idle. Rudderless. Not long afterward he'd started drinking. Gambling a little more than usual. But Jack would get all that under control . . . eventually.

"Just think about it, Jack," Evelyn said. "You need to find your direction again, or you're going to destroy yourself."

After breakfast, Jack left the apartment and went out for a walk. He stopped to get a coffee at Starbucks and then strolled downtown. The Seattle streets were the epitome of Northwest cool. Laid-back, nobody in a major rush to get anywhere, everyone carrying steaming paper cups. The sidewalks were unusually dry; it hadn't rained in days. A freshening sea breeze came in off Puget Sound.

Jack sipped his coffee as he walked past the Seattle Art Museum.

There was a delivery truck parked outside in the back lane, in the loading bay, with the back door rolled entirely open. Inside the truck lay paintings wrapped and packed for shipping. Two deliverymen were bringing them in one by one, and they looked like they were in a rush. As they worked in tandem, there was a moment, each time, when the precious cargo was left unattended, the back of the truck open. Jack overheard them arguing about it. It wasn't protocol to leave the truck unguarded, even for a second, but it sounded like the man in charge was keen to finish early.

Jack knew he could use those slivers of opportunity if he wanted. He could stroll over, pluck a painting from the truck, and walk away. He glanced around—he was having fun now, imagining, playing this game—and he mapped his escape route. Yes, that alley there. He could make it to that alley before they saw him. And from there, he could escape through the neighboring building.

He glanced up. No CCTV.

Definitely doable.

The art in the truck was not likely to be Rembrandt or anything. But it must have had value. The SAM wasn't some crummy local gallery. It would be so easy; it required just the right amount of panache. A large part of him was tempted to do it.

Jack thought of his father, John Robie. A career criminal, one of the best jewel thieves the world had seen. It might have been something to be proud of—if it hadn't ruined Jack's childhood. If it hadn't meant their estrangement, and his father's death before they'd had a chance to reconcile. Layers of complicated emotion pressed down on Jack, clouding his vision. He pushed it all away, shoved it back in the dark corner from whence it came.

Jack hovered. He waited by the truck for the next moment of opportunity, pretending to be reading a text and sipping his coffee.

The moment came. The truck was unattended again and Jack walked over. He knew nobody was watching as he climbed up easily into the cargo compartment and plucked the nearest canvas from the stack. It felt good in his hand.

The urge to take it right out of the truck was intense, like a powerful ocean current. Like a seductive beckoning.

Then Jack put the canvas down, returning it to exactly the same spot. He hopped down from the truck and strode quickly away. The delivery guy returned just as Jack rounded the corner out of the alley. He didn't cast Jack the slightest glance.

As Jack strolled away, he tossed his coffee cup in the trash. He turned south on Union Street toward the waterfront, catching glimpses of Puget Sound between the city's high-rises.

Jack had put the painting back because he didn't need it. What he did need, however, was to feel alive. And for a moment, when he had picked up that canvas, he had.

Chapter Six

Kenya

Ethan swung the hammer. The last nail. *There*. The frame was done. Now they could take a break. The schoolhouse would be finished before the end of the week.

The sun baked his neck, and blow flies hovered and buzzed around his sweaty bandanna. Ethan wiped his forehead and looked to the horizon, where the packed earth of the village gave way to the grassy savannah of the Maasai Mara. The hint of a dusky mountain range rose above it in the distance.

Ethan made his way to a nearby picnic table, grabbing a sandwich and a bottle of water from the cooler printed with the NGO's logo and name: Global Life. He sat down beside two other men. One of them was a new guy—a young hipster with muttonchop sideburns and long bow legs, like a cowboy. Gary was the other, older man. During the three months Ethan had been there, Gary had become his friend. He was balding, with droopy puppy-dog eyes and the hint of a beer belly, but he was sharp as an arrowhead.

The new guy, Ryan, was talking about where he'd been before this. He'd done a stint with Greenpeace in the Congo, and before that with the Peace Corps in Colombia. He wasn't the first such person—a lifer—Ethan had met, but it never ceased to amaze him that there were people who spent their whole lives nomadically volunteering.

Ryan asked Gary about his previous life. "Schoolteacher," Gary said.

Ethan knew the story. Gary had worked at a private school in a privileged neighborhood of New Hampshire. Until one day he got fed up with all the bratty, snotty kids—and their even worse parents—and signed up with Global Life. That had been three years ago. He had no intention of ever going back.

"So how about you?" Ryan asked Ethan. "What did you do before coming here?"

Ethan unwrapped his sandwich. "You know . . . a little of this, a little of that."

Ryan laughed. "Sounds suspicious. What? Were you a criminal or something?" He laughed even harder.

Ethan smiled but couldn't bring himself to laugh, much.

"So what are *you* running from?" Gary asked Ryan.

"What makes you think I'm running from something?"

Gary shrugged. "Most people who end up here are running from something. Something ugly in the past—bad family life, career failure, got fired or quit or whatever. So they end up here. Or places like this."

Ryan scoffed. "People can't volunteer out of a sense of the greater good?"

Gary took a bite of his sandwich. "Maybe. But usually there's something else, too."

Ethan squinted into the distance and sipped his water, saying nothing. After Paris, after successfully robbing the Louvre together with Cat, he'd stayed in France for a short while, wondering what to do next. The idea of going back to his old life had lost the appeal it once held.

And then, one day while he'd been poking around bookshops in the Latin Quarter, he'd come upon a protest underway. It was a peaceful protest—not an unusual sight for Paris. People were always rallying for some cause or other.

The protest was being run by Global Life. He'd started chatting to one of the canvassers and the next thing he knew, he was signing up and boarding a plane.

So here he was. Building a schoolhouse for orphans in Kenya with his bare hands.

He enjoyed the fieldwork. There was something deeply satisfying about rolling up his sleeves and helping people who were truly in need. It was something he never thought was in him.

Once the break ended and it was back to building, Ethan found himself working side by side with Gary, sawing boards. It was now the full, searing heat of the day, and they sipped water constantly. It felt like it was evaporating straight out of their skin as soon as it went in.

A young woman in shorts and work boots approached their workbench and Ethan looked up from his work. She wore sunglasses, and a golden braid swung down her back. "You boys okay for water?" she asked Ethan with a gleaming smile, holding up two frosty bottles of water.

Ethan squinted into the sun. "We're good," he said simply, inclining his head to the full cooler beside them. "Thanks."

She shrugged. "Okay, just say the word," she said with a lilt in her voice. "Whatever you need." She strolled away, gazing at Ethan over her shoulder.

"She's got a thing for you, dude," said Gary.

"Not interested."

The other man stood up straight and laughed. "Ah, there it is."

"What?"

"The thing you're running from. The reason you're here."

Ethan shook his head dismissively. "Right. Whatever."

"You got burned, golden boy. I can see it now."

Ethan ignored him, hoping he'd shut up eventually.

Gary laughed. "Yep, that's it. Burned by a woman. Shit, she really must have broken your heart."

Ethan scowled and bent his head to his work. Technically, Cat hadn't broken Ethan's heart. She'd just said . . . she needed some time alone. The exact same thing she'd said to Jack. But Ethan would be damned if he was going to sit around and wait for her to make a choice, only to watch her eventually ride off into the sunset with Jack.

No, thank you.

"Well, I hate to tell you, but you're going to have to come up with a new way of escaping your life, and the girl—whoever she is."

"I'm not escaping—" Ethan began. Then he straightened and narrowed his eyes at Gary. "Wait, why? What do you mean?"

"Because they're shutting us down," Gary said. "What—you hadn't heard?"

Ethan stared. "Are you serious?"

"Truth," Gary said. He put down his saw. "Word is, the funding ran out."

It was a kick in the stomach. “What about the schoolhouse? The villagers? Who’s going to help them?”

Gary shrugged. “It’s the shitty thing about NGOs. If somebody decides to pull the plug, it’s over.”

Ethan rubbed the back of his neck. There had to be something he could do. He’d have to find out more. For now, they had boards to finish cutting. They continued working for a while and then Ryan approached their work area. He looked at Ethan. “Jones—you’re wanted in the main office.”

“What about?”

Ryan shrugged. “I don’t know. Go see for yourself.”

Ethan put down his saw and walked a dirt path up the dusty hill, toward the camp. A cluster of semipermanent safari tents made a circle around a firepit. Smells of cooking—some kind of rice and bean dish, probably—emanated from the kitchen tent. Dinner wasn’t far off.

The hinged screen door of the office tent creaked when he pulled it open. Ethan’s boots clomped on the plywood floor. Inside the tent was Ethan’s field supervisor, a man in his early forties wearing khakis and a retro graphic Batman T-shirt, with a whiskered, leathery face and deep smile lines.

Ethan’s gaze slid automatically to the man beside him. It was someone Ethan knew on sight, and the last person he expected to see here.

Looking incredibly out of place, in his three-piece suit, sipping a cup of tea, was Templeton.

Chapter Seven

Seattle

I walked along the lawn of Emerald Downs, the horse racetrack, carrying a Starbucks coffee. Over my left shoulder, the rumble of horse hooves thundered on the dirt track. The air shimmered with cheering and hollering from the stands. I wasn't sure I was up to this—training someone for AB&T—but I was badly in need of some distraction. My mother was still in the hospital and I was powerless to do anything to help her. Indecision over the Lionheart job in Yorkshire sat like an undigested lump in my stomach.

I made my way to the rendezvous point. There, perched at the base of a bronze horse statue, was a young man wearing a San Francisco 49ers jacket. That was the signal. The 49ers were Seattle's rival; there was little chance anyone else around here would wear such a thing.

He had a small frame and a boyish haircut topping his sweet, innocent face, with ears that stuck out like doorknobs from the sides of his head. In truth, it was an excellent look for a thief. People wouldn't look twice at him, let alone suspect him of anything.

I sipped my coffee, sized him up for a minute, then walked over. "So you're the trainee," I said.

He grinned. "I am. And you're my teacher."

I nodded.

We walked to the stands and sat down on a cold aluminum bench. People around us were busy watching the race and scribbling in their betting books. The air smelled of beer and manure and fresh-cut grass.

He introduced himself as Felix Tucker, and we got down to business. "So how did you land in AB&T's lap?" I asked him.

"My stepfather put my name forward. He thought I'd be good at it. Lock picking is my specialty. But I guess I need some brushing up in other departments, like pickpocketing. Which is why I'm here today, right?"

I nodded. That was the goal. I was to teach him the finer points of pickpocketing. If I could focus, that was. I puffed out my cheeks and glanced at my watch, wondering what Templeton would consider an acceptable time investment. I'd promised him I would do this, but now that I was here my heart really wasn't in it. Maybe I could get out of this somehow. I could call it off, give Templeton some kind of excuse.

Felix cleared his throat. "Can I say how much of an honor it is, Ms. Montgomery, to have you training me? I've heard a lot about you and your work," he said. "I also heard about the LA job, the Briolette of Kashmir? Nice one, by the sounds of it."

I smiled a little, in spite of myself. "Call me Cat, okay?"

He nodded. "Anyway, I'm really looking forward to today," he said. "At AB&T they say you're one of the best pickpockets they've got."

I lifted my eyebrows. "They say that?"

Well, that was flattering. I supposed it was one of my more highly developed skills. It was certainly the one I cultivated first. It was how I'd started in this line of work, honing my craft in public places like Pike Place Market.

When I was an enterprising young crook, pickpocketing was the whole job. You'd take a watch, a bracelet, a billfold of cash. Job done. Now, for the high-stakes work, pickpocketing was just part of the skill set. But the value wasn't to be underestimated—all kinds of information can be gleaned with the expert application of swift fingers. ID. Hotel key card. Paystub with a signature. Lipstick with a set of fingerprints. Jewelry store receipts. Dinner reservations.

"Okay, let's get to work," I said. "Let's see where your skills are at."

It didn't take long for me to spot a prime target: a woman in her twenties among the crowd lingering by the bar. She carried too many things—a purse, a drink, a jacket on her arm—and she was distracted on a number of fronts. Not only was she ritually checking her appearance in windows and sundry reflective surfaces, she was also texting obsessively, taking photos with her phone, and repeatedly attempting to capture the attention of her older date—a man who displayed visible wealth in his Patek Philippe watch and his commanding posture.

I described the target to Felix and, keeping my gaze pinned on her, said in a low voice, "She's got a Louis Vuitton wallet in her purse." I had seen her remove it while hunting for lip gloss in the purse. "Get it for me."

He nodded. I sipped my coffee and watched him approach, evaluating his technique.

Not bad, I thought. A little stiff. A trifle too self-conscious. But we could work on that.

He sized up the situation proficiently, taking a few short glances at the target. He kept his eyes flicking, but subtly. Good. And then he allowed a long look when a cheer went up for the winner of the race.

Nicely timed.

He maintained good positioning. He was standing close, but not too close. Within striking distance. With the next major distraction—the start of the next race perhaps—he would go for it. I leaned forward to catch everything.

The woman turned unexpectedly. I nibbled a fingernail. Did she see him?

She did. But her eyes slid right over him. My lips curled in a smile. A forgettable appearance was the advantage I'd spotted on first seeing him.

Watching another thief at work suddenly reminded me of the last thief I'd worked with. Ethan. Of course, he would probably use an entirely different approach here, since his appearance was anything but forgettable. Ridiculously gorgeous and charismatic, Ethan used his looks as an asset, a weapon. He could charm and disarm anything. Men, women, babies, Mafia bosses . . . whoever.

There was more to him than that, though. My mind trailed off, spiraling away on thoughts of Ethan. He was a hero—even though he didn't know it. He'd saved me more than once. He liked to think of himself as a bad guy. But the truth? Even though he did bad things for a living—like I did—he was one of the good guys. Which probably wouldn't make sense to anyone but me.

I snapped out of my daydreaming and focused on Felix. He had regrouped, repositioned, and was going for it again.

I gripped the edge of the bench, watching closely, and . . . *success.* He had it. There had been the barest flash as he'd lifted the wallet, and he'd been a little clumsy in the dismount, but he'd stuck the landing.

He strolled through the crowd, making his way back over to me.

"Good work, Felix," I said to him casually, not looking at him yet. "Couple of tense moments, but you did it. I'm impressed. We can work to smooth out those rough spots, no problem. I can see why AB&T wanted you."

I turned to see him grinning like a kid on the last day of school before summer. I let him enjoy it for a moment. And then I said, "Now go put it back."

His face fell. "Seriously?"

I nodded.

He stared at me for a minute, then dutifully returned to the spot where our poor little victim stood. It's often trickier to do the return job, of course, and almost impossible if the mark has already noticed the theft. But I was impressed—I watched as he somewhat haltingly pulled it off.

She was, however, an easy target. Very naïve and very distracted. We'd need to hone his skills on more savvy targets. We spent the next hour angling various marks and I watched his skills improve, bit by bit. Even more significant—I could see his confidence growing.

Taking a break in the tiny café Felix thanked me again for taking the time to help him out.

"No sweat, Felix," I said as we stood in the coffee lineup. I realized I was telling the truth—it really wasn't as bad as I'd thought it would be. "Besides, I'm not that busy these days, so it's no problem."

"What? No big assignment coming up?" he asked.

I winced slightly. He raised an eyebrow and waited.

"Okay, there is an assignment," I confessed. "And it's a pretty big one. They want to fly me to England. But I'm not sure if I'm taking it."

"Why not?"

"I'm not sure I want any more assignments."

He choked. "What are you talking about?"

I fidgeted. "I don't know. It's just—I'm not sure this line of work is for me anymore." He stared at me with utter bewilderment. I looked around. Nobody was paying any attention to us. "It's like this, Felix. I have always justified this profession by calling it the Secret Sport of Kings. The überrich have always nicked each other's goodies. And they always will. It will go on without me."

He nodded. "Yeah, I get that."

"Well, I'm not sure if I believe that anymore. I'm starting to think I've been fooling myself all this time. And . . . I wonder if it's time to get out."

I wasn't sure it was a good idea to unload all this on an inexperienced kid—a virtual stranger, at that. But I had so few people I could talk to about this.

Felix was quiet. How could he understand my point of view? He was at the beginning of his career, and I was, perhaps, at the end. Then he brightened with an idea. "Okay, but what's this assignment? Maybe it would make a good last job. You know, a grand finale."

It wasn't a bad thought.

"Presumably they're paying well?" he asked. "If they're flying you all the way over there?"

I nodded. "Very well."

"Then that sounds like your ideal swan song. If that's what you want it to be."

He was making entirely too much sense. I could do this last job, then leave AB&T for good. Focus on my studies—that was where my future lay, right? Hadn't that always been my plan? I was close to being finished with my master's degree and then I could move forward, maybe get a PhD, find a nice academic position in a leafy college town.

If I took the Lionheart job there was the sticky issue of working with Ethan again. But maybe they wouldn't even be able to find him. He was off the grid, apparently. Perhaps they'd partner me with another thief. Either way, it wasn't enough of a reason to turn down the job.

I thought about it more as we ordered our coffee at the counter and took our cups to the cream and sugar stand. I turned the cream jug upside down and received the merest trickle. I looked down at the baskets and frowned. They were all out of sugar.

I tried the door of the cupboard under the counter, thinking they'd have spare supplies in there. The door was locked. I looked up for assistance, but the café was packed, the lineup was huge, and there were no staff people in sight. I pressed my lips together.

"Hang on," said Felix.

Before I knew what he was doing, he'd crouched down and I saw the flash of a lock pick produced from his sleeve. Then suddenly the cupboard door was open.

It was the fastest lock picking job I'd ever seen.

"That—um, that was impressive, Felix."

He grinned broadly. "Thanks. It's my best skill, I think."

I flicked a glance around. Nobody else appeared to have noticed a thing. "I'd say. Are you always that fast?"

He shrugged and nodded.

I was pretty swift with a lock pick, but this guy made me look like an amateur. My brain was churning. He could be useful . . . on a job. If the need should ever arise. *Interesting.*

I filed the thought away and kept moving forward with the task at hand. "Okay, let's keep going, shall we? You scan for a suitable candidate, I have to make a quick trip to the restroom."

When I came back, I surveyed the area, looking for Felix, but I couldn't see him anywhere. Where could he have gone? And then I spotted him. He was homing in on a new mark. I followed his line of sight to his target and my chest seized.

No. Not that one.

I had to get to Felix. I pushed through the crowd. But I got there a second too late. I saw Felix's hand slip, rather skillfully, inside the man's pocket.

The mark's hand snapped around Felix's wrist.

It was over; he was caught. The mark glared at Felix, then wrenched his arm behind his back, dragging Felix away, presumably to the nearest security officer.

"Atworthy, stop!" I shouted. Both men froze, staring at me.

"It's okay. This guy, he's with me."

The mark was none other than my professor from UW.

"You know him?" asked Felix, his face a mixture of shock and relief.

"He's my prof in the French lit department. My thesis supervisor, actually." I looked around and lowered my voice. "But it's okay—he's also a former assassin."

At that, Felix's eyes went even wider. "And that's supposed to make me feel better?" he whispered.

Atworthy still had a hand firmly wrapped around Felix's scrawny wrist.

"Catherine, what the hell? What are you doing? Who is this?" Atworthy demanded once we'd moved away to a more private spot.

"We—um, we're doing a little training exercise. You weren't supposed to be a mark. I didn't see him targeting you until it was too late."

Atworthy dropped Felix's bony wrist. He looked annoyed, but I was pretty sure he wasn't going to do anything about it. The three of us stood there awkwardly. The thunder of hooves momentarily made all conversation impossible, and a cheer rose up as the horses crossed the finish line.

In the beginning I hadn't known that Atworthy used to be an assassin. I'd only learned the truth a few months ago, when I'd broken into his house looking for clues about his identity and he'd subdued me with a frightening amount of skill and a balisong blade.

Not everyone in my life was secretly a criminal. I did have civilian friends.

Just not a lot of them.

Atworthy spoke again once the din quieted. He rubbed the back of his neck. "It's a lucky thing, actually, that I bumped into you here, Catherine. There's something I need to talk to you about. It has to do with your studies."

I raised my eyebrows. Not what I was expecting. "Oh. Um, maybe we could go somewhere else to discuss?" I turned to Felix. "Why don't we call it a day? That was a good first effort. Talk to AB&T and we'll set up another session, okay?"

A few minutes later I was sitting across from my professor in the lounge inside the clubhouse, where large plate-glass windows muffled the roar of the races. Waiters brought coffee and cocktails to patrons seated in leather armchairs around us.

A mild-mannered alter ego is a requirement for a successful thief, and I had mine. Luckily, my cover as a grad student also happened to be something I enjoyed. I wished I could devote a little more time to it, as it always suffered when I had to plan a job or case a museum or whatnot, but that was how it was. Not for long, though.

Felix's idea was a good one. I'd make the Lionheart job my last, then turn my full attention to my academic career. It was what Atworthy had been gunning for all along; I knew he'd be happy about it. I'd tell him as soon as he told me his piece of news.

Atworthy leaned back in his chair and cracked his knuckles. I couldn't help noticing that he looked somewhat uncomfortable, at whatever he was about to say. My stomach tightened.

"What is it?" I asked, not sure I wanted to hear the answer.

"The thing is, Catherine, the graduate board has voted," he said. "There was nothing I could do. There have been too many absences. Too many missed deadlines. You're on probation. Again."

"Why? What does that mean, exactly? What do I have to do?"

He sighed, and looked at me with sympathy in his eyes. "I think you need to take a long, hard look at things. The trouble when you've been put on academic probation twice is that you then need to reapply."

"Can't you explain to them somehow? Cover for me?"

"Catherine, I've been doing nothing *but* covering for you."

I liked Atworthy, and I had always trusted him. I could see he'd gone out on a limb for me. "So you're saying I've been kicked out of the program?"

"Well, I'm not sure it's quite as harsh as that . . . but, well, in a manner of speaking . . . yes."

I slumped in the chair. *Damn.* This wasn't good.

"I think maybe it's time for you to consider a different career path. Because I don't think the academic life is for you."

Later, I left the racetrack and returned to my car. Templeton called me on my phone as I crossed the parking lot.

"Listen, lamb, I've got a bit more information on the Lionheart job."

I kept walking, fumbling in my purse for the car keys. "Go ahead."

"Are you sitting down?"

"Not yet. Why?"

My hand closed around the cool, sharp keys, and I pulled them from my purse.

"You know the grave I mentioned—the one where they found the Lionheart ring?"

"Sure." I reached my car and extended my hand, pushing the keyless entry button on my fob. Nothing happened. I remembered then,

I'd forgotten to change the dead battery in the fob. I reached forward to put the key in the lock, the old-fashioned way.

"Well, I learned who the remains belonged to. They're saying the man in the grave, the man who was buried with Richard the Lion-heart's ring, was—are you ready?—none other than the man we know as Robin Hood."

The keys glanced off the door lock and clattered to the ground.

Chapter Eight

En route to London

I adjusted the overhead light on my seat, 22A on the British Airways overnighter to London. All around me people were sleeping or watching the movie that flickered in front of their faces. There was a steady hum of engines, and the faint scent of chicken parmigiana in the air from the dinner trays that were being cleared. The woman in 22B pulled her eye mask down in position and settled in for a snooze. Sleep would be impossible for me. I had too much going on in my head. Besides, I had work to do. I raised the plastic airline glass and took a sip of my wine, then powered on the tablet resting on the tray in front of me.

When Templeton had told me about the identity of the grave, about the Robin Hood connection . . . well, it had changed everything.

"Are you serious?" I had said, frozen beside my car at the racetrack parking lot.

"Completely serious."

"You're talking about the real man," I had said, struggling to get my head around what Templeton had told me. "The real Robin Hood. Not the cartoon version or the Errol Flynn one or anything. The living, breathing man who stole from the rich and gave to the poor. Yes?"

"Indeed."

The very thought of Robin Hood had twanged a whole cascade of emotion in me. For the general public, the idea of Robin Hood was a charming legend, a cute little tale you told children . . . but it was a different story for those of us who were professional thieves. Robin Hood was our patron saint, the demigod of burglars.

"So, the skeleton in this grave—what makes them think it was the real Robin Hood?" I asked.

"Well, evidently the ring itself provides a certain amount of proof. Then there are various other lines of archaeological evidence—I'm afraid it's a bit beyond me, but I believe you will be briefed on all that once you receive the documents from the client."

"Do you know anything more about who the client is? Who wants the ring?"

"Well, this is interesting, too. We were contacted by a representative from the City of Nottingham. They want you to take the ring, the Lionheart, because they don't want it to ever be discovered. They want it to have no association with the grave and the bones that were dug out of the earth at that spot."

"Why not?"

I could hear him stirring a cup of tea in the background. He sounded positively jolly. Templeton loved this kind of stuff.

"Two reasons," he started. "For one thing, the grave was located in Yorkshire. Not in Nottingham. Apparently there is a huge rivalry, and controversy, over whether the real Robin Hood had truly lived in Nottingham, or whether he had been a Yorkshireman instead. Over the years, the feud has become very nasty. I have a cousin who lives in a nearby county, by the way, and he's always recounting the latest developments and threats, etcetera. People feel very passionate—"

"Templeton? Stay on point, please."

"Right-o. As I was saying, the discovery of the Lionheart, on this body, provides more proof that Robin Hood was a Yorkshireman. Which, to the people of Nottingham, is a travesty. But even more importantly, the fact that Robin Hood had this ring in his possession makes him look like a different kind of thief than the man he was generally believed to be. It makes him look like the kind who would steal from a king, and *not* to give to the poor, but keep the spoils for himself. Robin Hood is beloved by the people of Nottingham, and they simply can't let that sort of thing come out, that sort of damage to his reputation."

I had frowned, hearing that. If the man in the grave was the real Robin Hood, why *did* he have the king's ring on him? Why would he have kept it for himself? The legend generally tells that he kept nothing for himself. It gave me a sour feeling, thinking that perhaps Robin Hood wasn't the hero we had all imagined him to be.

But I couldn't get caught up in that. If I were going to take this job, it would need to be for business reasons only.

I thought about everything Templeton had said. "Wait—are you telling me this is a job authorized by the government of Nottingham?"

"The representative was from the sheriff's office, to be precise."

My mouth twitched. "The . . . *sheriff of Nottingham* is giving me this assignment?"

"It would appear so."

I wouldn't have even guessed there was still a sheriff of Nottingham.

"So, Petal, what say you? Are you in?"

It was a game changer, to be sure. Robin Hood gave the ancient art of burglary honor. It felt poetic and deeply meaningful. The opportunity to hold a ring that Robin Hood himself wore, right to the grave . . . how could I pass that up? "Yes, Templeton, I'm in."

He'd told me then about the next steps I needed to take. At the stadium on my way to the airport, in locker #335, I was to obtain a bag that contained some key pieces of equipment. A GPS for when I got to England. Also, an encrypted iPad.

Sitting in seat 22A, I looked down at that very iPad now resting on the tray in front of me. It held documents and photographs and files. I hesitated before tapping the screen. I told myself that if there was anything in there I didn't like, I'd get out of it. I'd call Templeton when the plane landed and tell him I'd changed my mind. Do a little sightseeing in London, then come home.

Before heading to the airport, I had visited my mom in the hospital. I couldn't bring myself to tell her where I was going or what I was doing. Not exactly, anyway. I told her I had to go out of town for a job. Of course she'd known what I meant.

"Well, Catherine, you have to do what you have to do," she'd said with a sigh. She looked away out the window, but before doing so I'd seen the disappointment in her eyes.

And it had crushed me. If my resolve hadn't been firm before, it was now. Like Felix had suggested, this would be my last job.

I put down my glass of wine, swept the pointer over the folder, and tapped twice.

A dialogue box popped up with a warning that I was about to pass through an encrypted barrier. To go any further, I needed to sign a document of secrecy.

Well, this was different. Unorthodox. I flipped on my phone and placed a quick call to Templeton. "What's with this agreement?" I asked him.

"I have no idea. I don't know anything about it."

I read it out to him, and he was quiet. "I suppose this is what happens when you are commissioned by a government agency," he said. "The British, they love their bureaucracy."

"Am I signing this, Templeton?"

"I don't see how you can move forward without it."

I stared at it for a few moments. Then I signed it.

Dire warnings were issued the moment I pressed SAVE. Were I to back out now, there was a case built to prosecute me. The British Government would be notified and I would be tracked down and arrested for conspiracy, among other charges. The officials of Nottingham wouldn't go down—I would.

I swallowed. Well, I was all in now.

I flipped through the documents and stared at a fuzzy photograph of the Lionheart ring itself. My skin tingled at the sight of it. Normally the jewelry I stole had a distinctive female flavor. This was all male. All-powerful male. And that was fascinating. The next photograph was of the grave in Yorkshire, where they had found the remains and the ring.

I searched the files and found some information about Robin Hood, the man. Or, Robin of the Hode, as he was called in some original sources. There were newspaper clippings about the feud, the dispute between Nottinghamshire and Yorkshire. This was the heart of the thing—the reason I'd been hired in the first place.

At times, the feud had spurred some terrible violence. I sipped my wine and flipped to another article, a report of the suspicious death of a Yorkshire man who had been researching the history of Robin Hood.

I shivered. Yes, this was a far cry from the charming bedtime stories of a band of merry men. I had entered something much more serious, much more dangerous.

But there was no backing out now.

Chapter Nine

Kenya

Ethan sat in the passenger's seat of the Jeep as Gary maneuvered and bumped the vehicle around potholes in the packed dirt road. They were headed toward a small village, the back of the truck filled with fresh supplies for the local villagers, including water, medication, and food stores. It was part of their regular routine, their weekly rounds. Neither man was speaking. Ethan squinted out over the dusty, sun-baked road ahead of them. They both knew they wouldn't be doing this much longer. Global Life would soon be shutting down.

"So where are you going to go after we're done here?" Gary asked.

Ethan shrugged. "No idea. You?"

"I guess I'll find another NGO. Or maybe I'll go home. Haven't been back for a while."

Ethan watched the passing scenery. The savannah with its rolling grassy hills, punctuated by spreading acacia trees, overlooked by the mountains in the background. A small cluster of giraffes paraded near the acacia trees, walking in slow motion, a majestic gait. A flock of larks rose up, taking to the African skies. The roar of the Jeep's engine drowned out the sounds of wildlife.

But although Ethan was seeing the dusty plains of Kenya, his mind was far away, mulling over the offer that had been presented to him yesterday.

"It'll be a doddle for you, Jones," Templeton had said in the Global Life field tent as he sipped his Earl Grey tea. "A very straightforward job. And do I need to repeat the amount of money they're offering?"

It was a lot of money, for him to fly to England and do what he did best. And the job itself sounded tempting. The legendary Lionheart Ring. Richard the Lionheart. And the connection to Robin Hood—it was difficult not to feel inspired by that.

It was a little outside his area of specialization, however. Ethan was an art thief. But it would be a mere week or two of work. Like Templeton had said, it sounded like an easy job. An easy buck. But there was one big problem. It would involve working side by side with Cat Montgomery. Something he swore he wouldn't do again.

The Jeep bumped through divots and ruts in the dirt road, pulling Ethan's attention back to the moment. The village came into view on the horizon.

Gary took a swig of water from his bottle, then shifted gears. "It's such a load of crap that they're shutting us down," he said.

Ethan grunted his agreement.

"I'm still holding out hope, though," Gary said.

"Hope for what?"

"A benefactor. A donation. Something like that."

Ethan turned to look at Gary, shielding his eyes against the sun. "How likely is that?"

"Not very. That's why I call it hope."

Ethan squinted ahead. A small ember of an idea began to flicker in his mind. "What's going to happen when we stop coming?"

Gary shrugged. "I guess they'll have to find some way to survive. Or not."

They arrived at the village. It was little more than a cluster of circular mud huts topped with pointed thatched roofs. It was the way these proud, strong people had been living for centuries: simply, and connected with the land. Living and dying at the whim of nature. Small fires burned and the smell of woodsmoke crept up Ethan's nostrils. The moment the Jeep's wheels crunched on the dirt road and came to a stop, villagers began to emerge from their huts and hearths to greet them. Children sprinted to them, grimy faces brightening with full openmouthed smiles.

Ethan leapt out of the Jeep with a huge grin and was immediately swarmed by kids. They knew him well, and were eager to tell him all their stories, and to see what Ethan had brought. Ethan crouched down low and removed his sunglasses. He handed out the trinkets and pocket candies he'd brought for them. The children watched, mesmerized as he performed a magic trick with a scarf and a coin, and then they dissolved in shrieks and giggles. Ethan grinned even more widely.

Back home, he had never really had many kids in his life. He didn't know anything about them. Ethan realized now what a mistake that had been.

The kids flitted around him like groupies to a rock star. Ethan made his way to the back of the Jeep to help Gary haul out the water and supplies. As he heaved a jug of water onto his shoulder, Gary said, "Those kids sure do love you. They're gonna miss you."

The children disappeared in a flurry as the chief of the village came over to Ethan and Gary, standing tall in his plaid blanket wrap and carrying the chief's staff. Ethan knew he was only in his forties but he looked much older, deep wrinkles around his eyes and grizzled gray in his hair. He reached out and shook Ethan's hand, thanking him personally—a firm grip from a wiry arm.

The chief then invited them into the schoolhouse, explaining that the children had been preparing a surprise for the men.

The schoolhouse was dark and cool, in contrast to the searing sun outside. It was a simple room, but Ethan knew it to be one that had been built by Global Life last year. Donated wooden desks were arranged in neat rows. A simple blackboard adorned the front of the room. Art supplies were tucked in a back corner.

The teacher, a stout woman with a colorful head scarf, welcomed them. The schoolchildren stood shoulder to shoulder at the front of the classroom. Ethan and Gary stood to the side and watched. Then the children began to sing.

An amazing sound reached Ethan's ears—sweet and rhythmic. As the earthy, lovely music and the voices of the children reverberated in Ethan's head, he blinked furiously. His eyes stung, and it had nothing to do with the dust from the road.

The truth hit him like a sledgehammer. It was within his power to do something more to help these people. At once, Ethan knew what he had to do.

When they returned to Global Life headquarters, Ethan went straight to his bunk and started packing.

Chapter Ten

Seattle

Jack stared at his hand of cards in the high-stakes poker room at Stardust Casino, under moody spot lighting and glittering chandeliers. He wore his tux with ease. He sat back in the plush full-grain leather chair. Women in shimmering cocktail dresses lingered nearby, watching his every move, but he barely noticed them.

In fact, he wasn't really noticing much. He looked up, searching for a waiter who might bring him another single malt.

Then he changed his mind and decided to get it himself from the bar. He certainly didn't need to; the staff was more than happy to serve him endlessly all night. But he needed a brief stretch and a break.

While he waited for the bartender to pour his drink, someone came to stand beside Jack.

"Hello, Templeton. What's up?" Jack said, without turning around.

A smooth British voice answered. "I could ask you the same thing, Jack."

"I'm enjoying myself, what does it look like?" The bartender placed his drink on a napkin and Jack picked up the cool glass.

"Is that what you call it?" Templeton replied with a faint snort. "Well, if 'enjoying oneself' entails total self-destruction, then I suppose that's what it looks like." He stood with a closed umbrella at his side, watching Jack carefully.

Jack took a sip of his whiskey. "Templeton, you don't know me. You have no fucking idea," he said in a low voice.

"Well, why don't you tell me? I believe you left the FBI—"

Jack interrupted him with a short laugh. "If by 'left,' you mean I was forced out for bad behavior, then yes."

"And you're doing what, now?"

Jack shrugged and glanced around the room, at the glamour, the superficial excess, the beautiful women. "Pretty much this. Not too shabby, right?"

Templeton looked at Jack and his mouth twisted with a mixture of pity and disgust. "Jack, you can do better. You *are* better than this."

Jack kept his face blank. "What do you know about it? You're just Cat's handler."

"'Tis true. And one of the reasons I'm here is to arrange a further meeting with you. I want to get to know you better. There are some people at AB&T who have expressed interest in recruiting you. They seem to be under the impression that you are a talented field agent. And with your pedigree . . ."

"Do *not* bring up my father," Jack warned in a low voice. That was a subject he most definitely did not want to discuss. He did not want to hear the name John Robie. Would he ever escape his father's ghost?

Not likely, he thought. When Hitchcock makes a movie about your father's life, people don't tend to forget that sort of thing. If Templeton even breathed the words "To catch a thief . . ." Jack really couldn't be held responsible for what would come next.

"What about the Fabergé quest?" Templeton asked. "Have you stopped caring about that? Jack, you had an honorable cause once. I know it's in you. Caliga is still out there, you know."

The Fabergé quest. *Caliga*. Jack took another sip of his whiskey to wash away the sudden bitterness that flooded his mouth. Last time he had seen anyone connected with Caliga Rapio was when one of their agents had been speeding away from a villa in Monaco, the stolen Fabergé in his possession.

At the time, Jack had been sure it meant the Gifts of the Magi were now in the hands of Caliga. And that was bad news for everyone. The Gifts contained power, and the last thing the world needed was a ruthless organization like Caliga Rapio wielding even more power than they already possessed. Of course, Jack and Wesley had later learned that the Fabergé only contained two of the three Gifts, that the Gold was missing. Which meant they still had a chance.

"I'm sure Wesley has things under control. He doesn't need me."

"Listen, Jack," said Templeton, "we can see you're floundering. You have been for quite a while. It's time you joined us. It's your destiny—surely you can see that?"

"I don't know who you think you're talking to, but I'm perfectly fine. I don't need to join you, or any other criminal underworld organization. Hell, I don't even need the FBI."

"You need *purpose*," Templeton said, standing at the bar. "We can help with that."

Jack barked, "Ha. Purpose. Says the man who works for a thief agency."

"There's honor in it. You know there is."

Jack said nothing but glanced sidelong at Templeton. The older man stared into his eyes, assessing, and then nodded once.

"I see they have misjudged the situation," Templeton said. "You are not the man you used to be, Jack. Or—more accurately, you are not the man I know you can be. I don't think you have anything to offer AB&T now."

Jack said nothing but held the man's gaze. Templeton's face softened into something that resembled pity. "You appear to have lost the plot, Jack."

Jack nodded. "Fine. Then that sounds like an end to this conversation. Is that all?"

Templeton picked up his umbrella. "If you get yourself straightened out, when you return to who you are, consider looking us up."

Jack ran his tongue over his teeth and scooped up his whiskey, turning away from Templeton and heading back to the poker table.

Chapter Eleven

Heathrow Airport, London

The flight was uneventful, and I yawned as we landed at Heathrow, stretching the airplane kinks out of my neck. Muffled announcements sounded overhead as I stood in the concourse waiting for my luggage to come down the carousel. As I tried to shake off the sleepy feeling, someone walked up behind me.

"Well, well. Miss Montgomery. Fancy seeing you here." The accent placed him instantly. Not to mention the tone: pure hatred.

I turned, trying to conceal my alarm, and stared into the face of Ludolf Hendrickx. Interpol agent.

"Hello, Hendrickx," I said mildly. "How nice to see you again."

"Is it? Hmm."

I tried for a smile. "Forgive me, but I need to keep watch for my suitcase," I said, turning back to face the carousel.

My brain was churning. Was he here for me? Did he somehow know what I was up to? This couldn't possibly be coincidence.

"So what brings you to the UK, Miss Montgomery? Holiday? Business?"

"Oh, visiting some old relatives."

"Really? I didn't know you had family here." His tone stretched taut.

The last time I saw Hendrickx we were standing beside the Seine in Paris. And not one but two official agents—one French Secret Service, the other FBI—had provided me with a rock-solid alibi to explain my behavior.

And the behavior in question was the successful pilfering of the Hope Diamond from the Louvre.

Hendrickx knew I was guilty, and the look on his face at the time had been unforgettable: a toxic cocktail of rage and frustration at having his prize kept from him. Like a dog on a chain that was a few inches too short.

"Oh, I think I see my bag over there," I lied, desperate to get away. "It was nice seeing you again, Hendrickx." I moved to the other side of the carousel, deliberately positioning myself behind a large post, out of his line of sight.

My stomach flip-flopped. I stared at the slowly rotating baggage carousel, thinking things through.

A man cleared his throat. "Oh, there you are," he said. Hendrickx again. "Not your suitcase after all, I suppose?" I turned my head to smile at him.

"My mistake."

He smiled back—a foreign expression on his usually stone-cold face. "You know, Miss Montgomery, I was wondering—have you seen Esmerelda lately?" he asked, feigning innocence. "I would be curious to hear if you two are working on any interesting cases together. Perhaps Interpol can be of assistance?"

Esmerelda was the French secret service agent who had bailed me out in Paris. Last I'd seen her, we'd been talking about the Fabergé egg and the long-lost Gifts of the Magi. More specifically, the missing Gold. She'd said she would be in touch if my assistance was needed, if the Gifts or the Gold or the Fabergé had been located. But Esmerelda hadn't only been French Secret Service. She also worked for an even more covert organization: the DOA. The Department of Antiquities.

That had been three months ago; I'd heard nothing from her since. "No, I haven't been in contact with Esmerelda lately. I'm sure she's quite busy."

He nodded. "Yes, I'm sure."

I turned back to the carousel and did my best to keep my face smooth as I scanned the bags. I tightened my leg muscles so hard I developed leg cramps. Where was that damn suitcase? I needed to get out of there.

At that moment, Hendrickx leaned in closer. "Cut the shit, Montgomery," he hissed in my ear. "I know you are a crook." His tone was as warm and pleasant as a junkyard dog. "Why everyone keeps covering for you, I have no idea. I *know you*, though. And I am going to be watching you very carefully. You will eventually make a mistake. And I'll be right there when you do."

I took a second to gather myself. "Hendrickx, you are confusing me," I said in a calm, smooth voice. "I really have no idea what you're talking about. I think you've been misinformed in some way. But I can assure you, I'm no crook."

He stared at me, eyes smoldering. He was taking this personally. But I was sure he didn't have anything concrete on me. He wouldn't be issuing vague threats if he had any cause to arrest me right now. He was just trying to intimidate me.

It was working.

This was going to be a big problem, and I needed to deal with it. But first, I had to ditch him. I spotted my navy blue suitcase coming down the carousel but I remained motionless, waiting for it to come to me and formulating a plan.

I looked at my phone, but really I was looking all around me using my peripherals. I didn't see anyone else who seemed interested in what I was doing. Hendrickx must be working alone.

I swiftly grabbed my suitcase off the carousel and started walking away.

"Good luck with everything, Hendrickx. I wish you well," I said over my shoulder, striding in the opposite direction. Would he let me walk away? Not likely.

It was time to enact a fourth-degree shake-off.

We were on the ground floor, arrivals level. I walked toward the elevators. I knew Hendrickx was hovering several feet behind, following me. I paused near an elevator, not pushing the button, but pretending to search in my purse for something. I was close enough to the elevator to make it a possibility that I would get on, but not so close that he'd be sure. I was holding him off, making him wait and watch for my next move.

When the elevator doors opened, I didn't get in right away. I let everyone else go first, pretending to be absorbed hunting deep within my purse. I counted silently in my head, waiting for the last possible second.

The instant before the doors closed, I darted in. As they slid shut, I caught a glimpse of Hendrickx, on the move, surprised and annoyed at my sudden maneuver.

As soon as I was inside the elevator, I started changing my appearance. I slipped on the wig that I always carried in my purse. I took off my jacket and stuffed it inside my bag. I ignored the peculiar looks darting my way from my fellow passengers. Possibly they might give a report to Security later, but that wouldn't matter, once I was far from here.

I grabbed a pair of running shoes from my suitcase and swapped them for my Jimmy Choos, jamming my feet into them without tying the laces, and stuffing the pumps into my carry-on. Finally, I transformed my convertible suitcase. I quickly retracted the wheels and unzipped the compartment that held the backpack straps. I heaved it onto my back. I glanced at my appearance in the elevator mirror. Totally transformed.

I rode the elevator all the way up to the top, the third floor. No doubt Hendrickx had grabbed the next elevator going up, so I didn't have much time.

The doors binged and opened to the top floor. But I didn't get off. Instead I kept riding it all the way back down to the ground floor. This would only buy me a short amount of time. But with a little luck, that's all I would need.

On the ground floor there was no sign of Hendrickx. He must have gone up the other elevator, as I'd hoped.

I walked quickly out of the airport without making it look like I was hurrying. The key was to not move your legs faster, but to lengthen your stride. Even a small increase in stride length will move you across a room much faster, without looking like you're in a rush.

Glass doors parted with a *swish*, leading to the exit. Outside, in the gray London drizzle, horns honked and shiny black cabs jostled for position. My heart sank at the length of the taxi queue. It would only be a matter of time before Hendrickx figured out I wasn't on the upper floor.

I scanned the possible targets, and my gaze landed on the perfect candidate. Second in line was a young woman of eighteen or nineteen looking every inch the gap year neophyte. She sported a brand-new backpack with a Canadian flag stitched onto it, a London guidebook, and a terrified expression. *Perfect.*

I quickly adjusted my appearance, pulling the hair of my wig into a more youthful ponytail, and adjusted the pitch of my voice slightly higher, slightly younger-sounding, and then approached her. "Hi—you're from Canada? Me, too!"

She was stunned a moment, staring at me, and then grinned widely, like we were long-lost cousins.

"Do you know where you're going?" I continued, in a bewildered and confidential tone. "I just landed in London, and I've never been here before."

Relief washed over her face. "Same here!" she breathed. "I have no idea."

"I'm kinda terrified, to be honest," I said.

As I spoke I watched her closely and mimicked her body language—a technique well-known within confidence circles to be one of the best ways to get someone to trust you. Show them what they see in the mirror.

I gradually moved closer, inching my way into the taxi lineup. "Listen, I have the name of a hostel my sister's boyfriend gave me," I said. "He told me it's a great base for backpackers so I thought I'd head there, but I'm not sure how to get there . . ."

"Do you want to share a cab?" she said quickly.

I smiled and joined the queue beside her.

Within three minutes, we were climbing into a large, glossy cab. As I slid into the seat, I glanced over my shoulder inside the airport. On the other side of the sliding glass doors I caught a glimpse of Hendrickx. Hissing into a cell phone, looking furious, savagely scanning the foyer. Before he could look out to the cab queue, we were gone.

Now I needed to get myself to Yorkshire, somehow.

A flight would be way too high-profile, too trackable. Ground transport was less regulated, less closely monitored. The train was the obvious choice.

I pulled out my phone and glanced at my new Canadian friend, feeling a twinge of guilt. With one quick message I booked her a room at the Savoy in London and paid for it on my scrambled, untrackable account. I'd make an excuse and hop out at King's Cross train station, and give the cabbie instructions. Treating her to a couple of nights in a swank hotel was the least I could do.

I leaned back into the slippery seat of the cab and exhaled. My relief only lasted a few moments before an uncomfortable twist settled in my stomach. I'd evaded Hendrickx this time. Would I be able to repeat the feat next time?

Chapter Twelve

York, England

I stepped off the train onto the platform in the city of York. It had taken me just over two hours to get here from London's King's Cross Station. I prayed I could continue to stay under the radar, well away from Hendrickx, until I got to the safe haven of the country manor.

Outside the station, double-decker buses rumbled along under waterlogged skies. An old brick hotel with glossy black signage sat majestically across the street and, beyond that, a green hill rose away from the road, topped with an ancient, crenellated stone wall. I knew York had been a medieval walled city—maybe this was the fortified wall. Unfortunately, I didn't have time for sightseeing.

I walked briskly away from the train station. I rented a MINI Cooper under a false name and drove to the countryside. Medieval walls and cobbled streets soon gave way to rolling hills of every shade of green, thick forests, and farmland with stone cottages. This was *Downton Abbey* territory. My friends would love this; we watched the show religiously.

I was headed to a country manor hotel outside town, not far from the university campus where the Lionheart was being held in the Department of Archaeology's secure vault. This was where Templeton had insisted I stay.

"Be sure to check out the pub on the ground floor," he'd said. "I think you'll find it especially to your liking."

I pulled the car into the gravel parking lot of Harrow Hall. It was a sprawling manor nestled into the rolling Yorkshire hills. The grand central building of honey-colored stone, ornamented with turrets and ivy, graced a broad swath of green lawn and manicured gardens. I gazed at row upon row of leaded-glass windows. It was more a castle than a hotel.

I had to hand it to Templeton. Not only was it divine, it was also smart; staying in the countryside was a good way to remain incognito. Even if Hendrickx somehow figured out my destination, he'd likely be looking for me in a larger hotel in the city.

Taking Templeton's advice, I went directly to the pub. After that journey I was sorely in need of a drink.

I walked into the darkened, cozy room and breathed in the smell of hops and sizzling bacon and the faint but sweet aroma of pipe smoke. I hopped onto a wooden bar stool and ordered a pint from the long-aproned bartender. Sipping the frothy ale, I looked around the pub.

I immediately recognized what Templeton had been referring to. There was an old mural on the wall depicting a forest scene with a man carrying a bow and arrows. Scattered around the room were various other paraphernalia: a brass rubbing of an old forest, an antique arrow quiver, a gilded frame displaying an illuminated manuscript of an old ballad: *Gest of Robyn Hode*. Also in frames were cuttings of newspaper articles that followed the quest to find the real Robin Hood. In the corner was a woodcut of Richard the Lionheart.

None of this memorabilia had the flavor of the modern interpretations of Robin Hood. No stills of Kevin Costner or Russell Crowe anywhere in sight. This was vintage Robin Hood territory—the real deal. My nerves hummed.

I looked around at the locals in the pub. I knew in small towns like this, people never strayed far, generation after generation. So were any of these people remote descendants of Robin Hood? I was halfway through my sweet, frothy ale when I heard a very familiar voice ordering a pint from the other end of the bar.

I turned with a start, and watched as Ethan Jones nodded to the bartender and lifted his freshly poured pint off the bar. He began strolling in my direction.

My heart gave a juddering double step. *He has come.*

He looked good. His skin was golden brown—he'd obviously been spending a lot of time outdoors—and he was a little bigger, maybe, in the chest and shoulders. Like he'd been working out more or something. Maybe the rumors about him being overseas were right. He'd always been in great shape, but it seemed like he'd stepped things up a notch. His pretty-boy look carried an edge of ruggedness now.

I couldn't stop the smile as he came closer. But then I hesitated—should I hug him? Shake his hand? Neither? I found myself in a very unfamiliar, and uncomfortable, position of being on uncertain footing with Ethan.

He smiled. I wasn't sure—was it a rather perfunctory expression? "Cat," he said, nodding, and sat down beside me at the bar.

Cat? He'd never called me that. Always Montgomery. I felt a pinch in my chest.

He was dressed in a plain T-shirt and jeans. Even if he had been working in the great outdoors, he'd certainly cleaned up well. He smelled amazing. I noticed a distinct swiveling of heads from the other women in the pub.

"I'm glad you're here, Ethan," I said. "I wasn't sure you'd come." My heart fluttered a little at the idea that he'd come here to work with me.

"I wasn't sure I'd come, either." He took a sip of his pint. "To be honest, I couldn't pass up the money. It was an offer I couldn't refuse."

Oh. He made no mention of working with me as a factor in his decision.

Ethan was friendly enough in his tone, but he was a little formal, a little too distanced. I'd never known him to have a formal bone in his body. Even though I had no right to expect a different reaction, his demeanor gave me a sick feeling in my stomach.

I sipped my pint, attempting to conceal my disappointment. It looked like Mel and Sophie, my best girlfriends, had been right. Sophie had said I would end up regretting what I'd done on the banks of the Seine, letting two amazing men slip through my fingers. "Are you nuts?" had been her exact words, as we'd discussed it at our favorite wine bar when I'd returned home from Paris. "Jack and Ethan are crazy about you. And you rejected them *both?* What were you thinking?"

Mel had supported a somewhat different point of view. "You go, girl," she'd said, raising her glass to mine. "You don't need a man. You take all the time you need."

I'd nodded at her. "Thank you. That's what I thought. They'll each understand when I'm ready, right?"

Mel had knocked back a swig of her drink and laughed. "That? No. Not in the least. Ethan and Jack . . . they're not the kind of guys to sit around and wait. I mean, maybe. But—you can't count on it, no."

"So where have you been hiding yourself, Ethan?" I asked, as brightly as I could. "There are all kinds of rumors. People are saying you went off with the Peace Corps."

He smiled. "I didn't join the Peace Corps."

"I knew it!" I said, plunking my beer down on the bar. I started to laugh. "I didn't believe that one for a second—"

"It was Global Life," he said, interrupting me. He took a long sip as I stared at him with surprise. "I was volunteering in a village in Kenya."

At that moment, a large man in a flannel shirt with a red bulbous nose approached the bar and flagged down the bartender. While he waited he turned to face us. "So—how are you two going to vote?" he said, a slight slur to his words. He waved toward the TV behind the bar. The BBC was broadcasting their evening news report. The caption underneath read "Succession vote to take place this week . . ."

"Er . . ." I started, not having the slightest clue what he was talking about.

He took a great swig of his pint as soon as the bartender placed it on the bar. "Well, *I* won't be voting for it, that's for sure," he continued.

"Nobody would," said the man on our other side, a short, balding man with a comb-over. "But that's why it's not up to us, you gormless git. It's happening in the House of Lords."

The debate became rather heated at this point, and others joined in. I looked apprehensively between the men. Getting in the middle of a bar brawl was not on my list of things to do tonight.

"It's come up before, it'll get shot down again," somebody else said—a scrawny, birdlike fellow with eyes spaced very close together.

"What's the issue, gentlemen?" Ethan asked, leaning over me to address the man on my left with the comb-over. The scent of Ethan's skin—a scrumptious combination of soap and leather and maleness—rolled over me. I tried to ignore the weakness in my knees.

"Well, it's all about who would succeed the prime minister if he dies," said Comb-over.

"Why, is the PM going to die?" I asked.

"No, he's healthy as a horse. But there's no clear line of succession. We've never had it spelled out."

"Exactly!" said the birdlike man. "Why do we need a law that says the deputy PM has to take over? Like the Yanks? Ugh. We've been fine in the past, we'd be fine now."

"No, we need a clear leader, not just left to chance. Her Highness needs to hear about this. I'm faxing a petition to Buckingham Palace this very week—"

"The queen has . . . a fax machine?" I asked.

"She most certainly does." The man withdrew a small card printed with the royal insignia and a variety of contact information including a Twitter handle—@BritishMonarchy—and a fax number: 01234-QUEEN1.

I suppressed a smile as the bickering continued. I decided it was time to leave the Brits to their political debates. I turned to Ethan. "Should we go check in?"

"Sure."

There was no entrance to the main part of the house through the pub, so we went outside and walked along a gravel pathway to the main entrance. Every inch of the entry hall was covered in chintz. And every wooden surface was polished to a mahogany shine. It smelled of homemade bread and lilac and strawberry jam and wood polish, and there was something fairly . . . romantic about it. I glanced uncertainly at Ethan as he rang the bell at the front desk. The person who responded was none other than the man who had been sitting beside us at the bar, Mr. Comb-over.

This was the opposite of being anonymous. And that made my skin crawl.

But there was nothing to be done now. The man called back to someone in an inner office, and a friendly-looking woman came bustling forward to check us in. I watched Ethan as he handed his credit card to our hostess. I hoped he would start to relax soon. I'd never known Ethan to hold a grudge.

Maybe I was imagining his coolness. If he wasn't over it, he wouldn't have come to Yorkshire prepared to pose as husband and wife in this romantic country manor as a cover for our job, would he? Maybe he was just tired from the trip.

"Welcome to Harrow Hall, Mr. and Mrs. Jones, it's a pleasure to have you. I'm Mrs. Weatherby. Now, would you prefer a room on the second or third floor?"

I opened my mouth to voice my preference when Ethan jumped in. "Oh, you misunderstand. We're not a married couple. We're brother and sister. And we're going to need two separate rooms."

I shut my mouth.

Oh. So maybe he wasn't quite over everything.

Fine. I didn't need anything complicating this job anyway. This was good. Better, in fact. Keep it simple, keep it professional. Right?

I grabbed my suitcase and tried to ignore the messy maelstrom of emotions that swirled through me as we climbed the curving mahogany staircase to our rooms.

Chapter Thirteen

The next day, it was time to get to work.

After a full English breakfast served by Mrs. Weatherby, Ethan and I drove to the high-security lab on the university campus. "So what do we know?" Ethan asked as we drove along thick hedgerows and tight twists.

"The ring is inside the lab, in the Archaeology vault. There's national-level security all over it. They're taking it pretty seriously."

Ethan was quiet a moment as the sunlight flickered through the windshield. He glanced over at me as I sat in the passenger's seat. "Do you believe it? All this stuff about Robin Hood?"

"I'm not sure. Do you?"

He nodded. "There's way too much written about this guy for it to be a fairy tale. There had to have been a real man."

"And you think this is the real thing? That they actually found his remains?"

"That, I don't know. But there are some important people who do believe it. Look at the measures they're taking to protect it."

We entered a roundabout and I squinted at the road signs, giving Ethan directions. "Did you see all the Robin Hood paraphernalia in the pub last night?" I asked. "These people are pretty passionate about ownership of the real Robin Hood."

"It's a heated debate here. If you believe the stories, they're willing to kill over it." He laughed. "That, and their politics."

I smiled, remembering the previous evening at the pub.

"Why do you think they loved him so much?" I asked.

Ethan slid a hand over the steering wheel, thinking as he drove. "Well, he stood for something admirable, didn't he?"

"Even though he stole?"

"Robin Hood was looking out for the common man. He was fighting oppression. He was David against the Goliath of the aristocracy. That's why they love him. He was their champion."

"So . . . if Robin Hood was standing up against the oppression of the aristocracy, why had he kept Richard the Lionheart's ring for himself?"

Ethan kept his gaze forward. "Now, that's an excellent question."

We arrived at the lab and parked in a small lot near the building. Far enough away to be unnoticed—tucked in with a couple of other cars—close enough to be able to watch the building. The lab was a low structure, four stories, ultra-modern. The Brits loved their history and their heritage buildings, but they also loved their modern architecture, too.

It would work to our advantage that the discovery of Robin Hood's bones had been kept very quiet. We didn't have to worry about avoiding a phalanx of press and local crowds—our only job was to outmaneuver the official security.

On my tablet, I pulled up the digital file Gladys had sent containing blueprints and schematics, the spoils of her hacking efforts. Now we just needed to find a few seams and gaps, and find a way in.

I studied the documents while Ethan staked out the entrances. An hour later, I was trying very hard to focus on the job and ignore the presence of the man seated two feet from me in an enclosed space. Every time he shifted in his seat, I became acutely aware of the muscles in his forearms, his legs . . .

And why did he always have to smell so damn good?

I scraped a hand through my hair and stared at my files. There were two choices, as far as I could see. We could break in during the middle of the night, or we could attempt entry during the day, posed in disguise. I laid out the options to Ethan.

"There's less automated security during the day. They won't have all their systems on," he said.

"But there are also more people around."

"What? You're not keen on an audience when you do your naughty deeds?" he asked, winking.

My heart fluttered. It was the first crack in his cool façade, the first sign of life. This was the old, lighthearted Ethan I knew. But he seemed to immediately regret his innuendo. He turned away quickly and returned his focus to the doorway.

The silence grew awkward and the tension thickened. I needed a change of topic, something we had in common. I grasped at the first thing that sprang to mind.

"So, Ethan, have you heard anything about what Caliga is up to lately?"

"I haven't heard anything about anything. I've been in Kenya, remember?"

I nodded. I had meant to make small talk, but mentioning Caliga set me on edge. Were they any closer to finding the complete Gifts? Was Jack on their trail? It was unsettling, not knowing what Caliga was up to. But, truly, I had quite enough to worry about at the moment. I pushed all those thoughts away.

After two more hours of surveillance and plotting, Ethan and I managed to put together a plan. Other than that one lapse, Ethan had kept all our interactions strictly business. A hollow feeling settled in my insides.

At least we had gotten our work done. From what we observed, the people who got a free pass, an easy entry to the lab, were the academics. The scientists. If we could pose as one of them, we'd be golden.

It was time to call it a day. I was ready for a comforting pub dinner at Harrow Hall and an early night.

When we entered the manor, I was grateful for the crackling fire in the giant hearth and the smell of roast beef and Yorkshire pudding. The perfect antidote to spending the better part of the day cramped in a car with someone who probably wanted to be anywhere but. We were headed toward the main staircase when Mrs. Weatherby spotted us. "Ooh, Ms. Jones, someone is looking for you!"

"Sorry?" My instincts prickled.

"Somebody came by, and asked if you were staying here. He used a different name for you, my dear, but I assumed that was your maiden name. Montgomery, was it? I have a cousin who's a Montgomery. Lovely family. Bit too heavy on the drink, unfortunately. Anyway, he described you to a tee."

I flicked a glance at Ethan. He was as alarmed as I was; I could tell by the flex in his jaw.

"Who could it be?" I said to him in a low voice.

"Did he say anything else?" Ethan asked Mrs. Weatherby. "Can you describe him?"

She chuckled. "No need for all that. I told him you were staying here, and sent him up to your room. He's there now."

Chapter Fourteen

We both looked up the broad staircase. *Up there now.*

This, right here, was one of the main reasons I hated non-anonymous inns. This would never happen in a big hotel. Mrs. Weatherby stood beside the desk, expectantly, idly dusting a lamp shade. I turned to her. "Mrs. Weatherby, do you think you could do us a favor? I haven't been able to get my mind off those delicious currant scones you served earlier, at breakfast. I wonder if there's any chance you have more? I'd love some with a nice cup of tea."

"Why, certainly!" She beamed at the compliment and bustled off to the kitchen.

Which left us free to strategize unobserved.

"Do you think it's Hendrickx?" Ethan asked.

"Who else knows I'm here?"

"If he's hunted you down, and he's up there, you're going to have to confront him. You can't just run."

"What if he's here to arrest me?"

"Arrest you for what? You haven't done anything," he said. "Yet."

I chewed a fingernail. "And what if it isn't Hendrickx? What if it's somebody robbing us?" We had a lot of valuable gear up there. We were strangers in this tiny village, and many people knew it. Our arrival must have been noted.

I knew that newcomers were often the best marks. Out-of-towners who didn't understand local rhythms or customs. And, apparently, it was acceptable local custom to let any old person who said they knew you go walking up to your room and paw through your suitcase.

Although, from what Mrs. Weatherby had said, it sounded like this was someone who did know me. He'd used my real name. My stomach tightened.

"I'll go up another way," Ethan said. "Give me a five-minute head start."

Ethan slipped away outside. I knew by "another way" he meant scaling the building on the outside. I waited five, then crept up the staircase, muscles coiled. I was ready to attack, or bolt, or whatever.

I unlocked the door to my suite and walked in. The room was empty. Where was the mystery man? I spotted Ethan just outside the open window.

The en suite door opened and a man walked out, whistling and rubbing his hands on a towel, looking perfectly at home. He looked up and saw me.

My face must have registered shock, because in that instant, Ethan burst through the window and attacked the other man.

I yelled "No!" but it was too late. It was all a blur, and at the end of it, Ethan had the man pinned to the ground, ready to start the interrogation.

I leapt over and grabbed Ethan by the shoulder. "Ethan, let him go! It's okay, I know him."

"What?" demanded Ethan. "You do?"

From the ground, trapped on his back, Felix Tucker stared up at us with terrified eyes.

Ethan released him immediately and stood back.

"His name is Felix and I've been training him at AB&T." I lowered my voice to a whisper. "He's one of us."

Felix sat up. "Well, that was a nice welcome. Is this how they do it in Yorkshire?"

Ethan shrugged. "You break into the room of a pro, this is what you're going to get."

"I didn't break in," Felix said, scowling. "I was let in. By a very nice lady who offered me tea. And currant scones."

Right on cue, I heard Mrs. Weatherby's voice outside the bedroom door. "Helloo? Is everything all right? I heard some rather loud thumps."

I opened the door to see her holding the tray of currant scones and craning her neck to see inside the room. I silently cursed. Now we would need to come up with a suitable alias for Felix.

"Oh, hello, Mrs. Weatherby. Yes, everything is fine. I believe you met Felix, our cousin?"

Her eyes twinkled. "Oh, I had no idea you were cousins! You should have said . . ."

"Yes, well, it's been a long time, and we've got a lot of catching up to do. Thank you very kindly for the scones, Mrs. Weatherby."

After she left, we locked and latched the door, and I turned on Felix with my hands on my hips. "You have to go home, Felix. You realize that, right?" I glared at him. "What on earth are you doing here, anyway?"

"I came to help with this job."

"What? I don't need any help. I've got Ethan, and we're doing fine. Wait—did Templeton send you?"

"Not exactly. I mean, he mentioned it. Thought it might be a good learning experience . . ."

I scowled. Templeton was worried Ethan and I wouldn't be able to get along professionally. Did he think Felix would act as a buffer?

"Maybe I could tag along?" Felix suggested. "You could show me the ropes?"

"Totally out of the question. Felix, I'm sorry you came all this way, but I really need you to go home now," I said.

"Come on, can't you use me? You know I've got skills. Maybe you need to get in someplace really fast?"

"What's he talking about?" Ethan asked.

I crossed my arms and glared. "Lock picking. He's . . . approximately the best lock picker I've ever seen," I said. "Like lightning."

Ethan looked at him again, this time appraisingly. "You don't say."

"Stop, Ethan. Don't even think it."

Ethan pulled me to the side and lowered his voice. Felix was making quick work of the currant scones. "Montgomery, you know we could use another pair of hands. And if he's as fast as you say—"

"He's a trainee! He's not fully ready." Although my arguments were emerging less forcefully now, because of what I'd noticed. Ethan had just called me Montgomery. Like usual. A warm little spark ignited in my chest.

We debated a little longer, but I eventually gave in. I didn't have the strength to argue with them both. And besides, I could see the positive side of having an extra assistant.

"Fine. You can stay," I said to Felix at last. "But your role is going to be limited. And you have to do exactly as we say."

Chapter Fifteen

Ethan sat back in a plush armchair in Cat's suite and popped a piping hot sausage roll in his mouth. It was a dramatic change from the field camp in Kenya with Global Life. The room was warm and comfortable, if a bit flowery, and smelled of the delicious tray of food Mrs. Weatherby had brought up—the sausage rolls, plus pork pie, Yorkshire pudding, and lamb stew. They had requested supper in their rooms, explaining they had much to catch up on.

In truth, they were plotting the finer details of the heist.

Felix was bent over a deep bowl of lamb stew, while Cat spread out all their materials on the coffee table. "So, Montgomery, what's the plan?" Ethan asked. "How are we going to pull this off?"

In spite of everything, Ethan was starting to enjoy himself. The entire journey here he'd psyched himself to play it cool, hold back. But once he'd seen Cat again, once they'd started spending time in such close proximity . . . well, it wasn't going to be quite so easy.

But the sting of Paris was still fresh. He turned his attention to the blueprints and paged through a stack of security detail.

"Masquerading as academics—with lab coats and ID badges and everything—will help us gain entry," Cat said. "But I'm not sure it's going to be enough. I think we need to create entire academic identities."

"How?"

She leaned back in her armchair, thinking, and stretched her legs out. Her leg brushed against Ethan's. His pulse kicked. Cat quickly sat up again and crossed her legs, avoiding eye contact with Ethan. "We could be visiting professors from another university. Which means we'd need to plant an introductory e-mail." She tapped a pencil against her lips, thinking. "And maybe we could get Gladys to upload our photos and academic bios on some university site or something . . . in case someone decides to get smart and check up on our credentials."

"Montgomery, you really do have a devilish little mind inside that head, don't you?" He sat back and gazed at her with admiration. "And I mean that as a compliment."

A grin tugged at the corner of her mouth.

He was about to say something even more charming about her angelic looks . . . but stopped himself in time. *Shit.* Was it impossible for him to not flirt? Keep things professional, Jones.

It was helpful having Felix there, Ethan decided. Felix could be the third wheel, the cushion between them. Ethan stood and moved away from Cat, around to the other corner of the table, keeping Felix in the middle.

They turned their attention to plotting out contingency exits, should the job go sour. Every good thief needed backup exit plans.

"This spot here. This looks the most vulnerable. We could get out there," Cat said, putting her fingertip on the blueprint. Ethan nodded. She was right. As usual, her instincts were dead-on.

Was it wrong of him to be turned on by a thief being really good at her job? He nodded again. "But what about here?" he said. "There's a weak spot right here—the CCTV can't properly cover that zone, there are blind spots."

Cat paused, looking at the area he was indicating. "You're right. We have to take that into consideration." She smiled at Ethan. The room brightened significantly.

The next task was poring over academic texts, briefing themselves on the basic lexicon of archaeology, should they be cornered into a conversation.

Ethan exhaled loudly. This was going to be the trickiest part of the plan.

An hour later, after all the food was gone, Cat flopped back with a sigh. "Shit, how the hell am I going to memorize all this stuff before we go in? There's a reason I study French lit at school, not science or archaeology. How does carbon dating even work? Am I going to need to know that?"

Cat leaned across Ethan to reach for a file on the other side of the coffee table. Her hair left a clean, springtime smell in the air when she leaned back in her chair. Ethan felt momentarily intoxicated by the familiarity of the scent, and from Cat being close enough to . . .

No. Do not get drawn in, he scolded himself.

Felix looked at the empty food tray with dismay and cleared his throat. "Anyone hungry? I think I'm going to go down to Mrs. Weatherby's kitchen and see what I can find."

"Good idea," Cat said.

After Felix headed downstairs, Cat and Ethan stood at the breakfast bar, where they had spread the blueprint out to get a complete look at all the factors. Cat moved around to Ethan's side of the bar, and her side touched his. It instantly kindled a memory of being physically connected to her entire body, with decidedly less clothing than they had on now.

Stop it. He tried to scrub that memory from his brain. And failed.

"Are you okay, Ethan?"

He clicked back to reality. She was looking at him with mild concern. "You seem a million miles away," she said.

"No, I'm here. I'm definitely right here."

She must have sensed the electric spark between them, too, or maybe it was the heat coming off his body, because she suddenly began fidgeting with her sleeve. An awkward silence followed. She looked up into his eyes.

Then, Felix returned through the door. "Okay, I've got biscuits and cheese, and some kind of pickle thing. The English really do like their pickles, don't they?" he said, strolling into the room.

He placed the platter on the table, and then looked first at Cat, then at Ethan.

"What? What's going on? Is something wrong?"

Ethan knew they looked guilty, like a pair of amorous teens being walked in on by a parent. Except they weren't doing anything half as interesting. But then Ethan was flooded with another visual.

Get it together, man. *Professional.* Keep it professional.

This was clearly a mistake, flying here for this job. He tried to remember the reason he was here: to help Global Life. They needed him. He had to keep that in mind.

There was a sound outside in the hallway, like some kind of motor starting. Both Cat and Ethan's heads snapped up. "What's that?"

Felix looked back toward the door that he hadn't entirely shut, as his arms were laden with food. "Oh, that's just the housekeeping doing the vacuuming. I passed her on the way up, although I hardly noticed her at first. Almost tripped over her, actually. You know how cleaning staff manage to make themselves virtually invisible . . . *what?*"

Ethan exchanged a glance with Cat.

It was a great disguise. Scientists would need to do science-y things, and would get too much attention. But custodial staff . . . well, the people who were sweeping the floors were typically overlooked.

They would need to figure out a few logistics, like obtaining uniforms, and a truck. And preventing the regular staff from turning up at the same time. But all that would be the work of a single day. They had a plan.

And tomorrow night, they'd do the job.

Chapter Sixteen

I walked into the Harrow Hall pub where Ethan and Felix each sat in front of a frosty pint, and tried to plaster a smile on my face. We had spent the better part of the day gathering supplies and taking care of bits and pieces for the job. Then, after they had gone down to the pub, I had made a quick call to my mother.

The conversation had left me with a tangled coil in my stomach.

"We're ready to go," Ethan said as I slid into the booth. "Tonight's the night." He paused, taking in my fake smile and body language. "You feeling good, Montgomery?"

"I don't know." I fidgeted with my hands under the table. "There's something that doesn't feel right about tonight. Is it supposed to rain? Not good for climbing buildings—that's one of our getaway contingencies."

Ethan craned his neck to look out the window. The sky was perfectly clear with no clouds in sight. "It looks pretty good to me," he said.

"Yes, but this is England. That can change," I said.

"That will be true no matter what night we choose. We're going to have to do it independent of the weather."

I shook my head. "It's no good. Not tonight. I need a little more time to feel ready."

I could still hear my mother's voice in my ear. She was doing better. Physically, anyway, I knew she was making a good recovery. Emotionally, I wasn't so sure. She sounded different. She didn't utter one single reminder or "helpful" suggestion—to bring an umbrella, or a jacket, or a clean pair of underwear. Nothing.

When she asked me where I was, I lied. I said I was studying, doing field research overseas for my degree. I hadn't even told her I'd been kicked out of the program yet.

She liked the idea I was doing academic work, I could tell. Her voice brightened. "That's good, Cat. That makes me happy. That's your future, sweetie. But you know that, I'm sure."

Guilt twisted inside me.

"Montgomery, we need to do it tonight," Ethan said, pulling my focus back to the pub. He looked at me closely. "Is there a problem?"

I pressed my lips together. "Give me an hour. I need . . . a little time. To get my head straight."

He lowered his voice and turned his back to Felix. "What's going on?" he asked. His eyes had softened with concern. His all-business approach was crumbling. "Is there something I can do to help you?"

"I think I need some air. I'll be okay." I stood and pulled my coat around me.

He placed a hand on my arm. "Do you want company?"

I shook my head. "Thanks, Ethan. I just need to clear my head."

Ethan nodded. "Don't take too long. Not to pressure you, Montgomery, but every minute matters."

I stepped out and walked briskly into the countryside, scanning the horizon. Surely there had to be some moors around here somewhere. There was a long tradition of people walking for miles in this region to think deep thoughts—sundry Brontë sisters, for example. Between the woods and the hills there had to be enough legend and magic and atmosphere to get me in the right mood, surely.

But after an hour of freshening breezes and heather-scented fields, I felt no better.

There was no good answer. If I backed away from the job, I'd be shirking my commitments. If I went ahead with it . . . would I be able to live with myself?

What was going on—was this just last-minute jitters? Or were my instincts telling me something? I ran a hand through my hair and tried to make peace between my head and my heart, but it was impossible. And now I was out of time. I turned my feet back in the direction of Harrow Hall.

"Okay, I'm ready," I said. It was partially true, anyway.

Ethan looked at me carefully and nodded. "Let's get moving."

Back in our rooms we gathered our gear. "You're sure you'll be able to open those locks?" I asked Felix, watching him tuck his lock picks into his pack. I hoped it wasn't a mistake, bringing a trainee along.

"Positive," he said. "But I think the question you should be asking is: are *you* going to be able to focus on your job with him around?" Felix asked, jerking his head in Ethan's direction.

I glanced at Ethan, who was busy checking our equipment and oblivious to Felix's words. "What do you mean?"

He rolled his eyes. "Come on, Cat. There's obviously stuff going on between you two. The tension is so thick I could cut it into big old slices and serve it with ice cream."

"Let's stick to the job, okay?"

An hour later, everything was going according to plan. Felix's voice came over our earpieces, "Okay, I'm in hallway B. I just picked the locks for the entry doors. They're open."

Excellent. Our way was clear. If anyone glanced at the CCTV they would merely see two custodians making their way through the corridors.

Felix would be making his way to the control room next. He'd lock pick his way in there, and turn off the internal security systems.

In hallway B, Ethan shot the security camera with a small pellet gun, tucked under his arm. A direct hit popped the glass on the lens. Perfect. He moved carefully, staying in the blind spots of the remaining cameras, and repeated his shooting twice more.

Then Ethan stood guard, pretending to mop a floor, while I disabled the intruder alarm, quickly and efficiently. We opened the door to enter the secure zone. The ring was located on the third floor, in a safe within a climate-controlled vault, behind bulletproof-tempered glass.

We slipped along the corridor, then walked into the central office where the safe was located. Unexpectedly, the sliding glass doors to the inner stronghold were wide open.

The hairs on my arms lifted. But after a quick survey nothing else appeared amiss, and we had no time to hesitate. I had to get going and crack this safe.

Ethan watched my back, guarding the room, as I moved to the safe. I managed to block all my other warring emotions and cracked the safe quickly, and smoothly. I let the door swing open, and . . .

Empty.

Ethan and I stared at the open safe in disbelief. "It's gone," I said into my earpiece to Felix, staring at the barren space. "No ring. No nothing."

"What?" came Felix's incredulous voice from his station in the control room.

I turned, and looked again at the open glass doors. I then saw what I had missed the first time: a tiny metal card, wedging the doors open.

"Somebody broke in here right before us," I said.

Ethan's head turned sharply to where I was looking. "When?"

And then, over the earpiece, I heard Felix urgently whisper, "Holy shit, they're still here! On the CCTV—two men. Heading to the atrium."

"Okay, stand down, Felix. Do *not* go there. Leave it to us." I was quickly trying to figure out what the hell to do next.

"Too late—I'm going," Felix said. "I'm close. I can get there. A security guard and one of the scientists are just ahead of me."

"Shit," Ethan said.

"Felix, stop," I said. "Go to the exit, like we planned." Ethan and I moved quickly but silently through the lab. We had to get out of there. My heart pounded with a shot of adrenaline.

And then, a gunshot. And another.

The sounds ripped through me. Ethan and I immediately, wordlessly, changed direction and raced to the atrium.

"Felix, are you there? Are you okay?" I hissed. There was no response.

In the atrium, one scientist was dead on the ground, blood pooling under him. The security guard was three feet away, also shot, unseeing eyes staring at the ceiling.

But there was no sign of Felix. Where was he? My head spun. We raced to the empty control room, down the hall from the atrium. "Look!" Ethan shouted. "I see them."

On the CCTV screens, two figures were hustling Felix at gunpoint into a van. One of the men I didn't recognize. The other, I most definitely did.

Sean Reilly. Rival thief, cold-blooded murderer, all around son of a bitch.

Chapter Seventeen

Ethan's vision went to pinpoint sharpness. He had to get Cat out of there, and he had to try to save Felix. They raced outside in time to see the black van peeling off. Ethan darted to their getaway vehicle.

He stopped abruptly, staring at viciously slashed tires. His hopes dropped into his stomach.

There had to be another vehicle they could take. But there were no cars left. It was the end of the day, and almost everyone had gone home. Only one rickety old bicycle was leaning against a wall. Shit. They would be able to run faster.

In the distance, the sound of approaching sirens wailed over the hills. Cat stood staring helplessly after the disappearing van, an anguished expression on her face. "Cat—come! *Now*." Ethan dragged her away.

There was no other option; they started running for it. They were surrounded by countryside and undulating hills, but there was a forest not far away. They sprinted, flat-out, for the cover of the trees.

As they entered the edge of the woods, Ethan glanced back and saw three police vehicles pull into the parking lot of the lab. He turned and disappeared into the darkness of the forest.

It was shadowy and cool. The forest floor was covered with ferns. Tall trees soared high above their heads.

They moved silently through dappled shadows; every sound seemed to be absorbed by thick layers of moss. They couldn't stop there; they had to keep going and get as far away as they could from the lab and the university campus.

They ran past streams and down into little valleys, putting distance between them and danger, going deeper into the safe haven, the refuge of the forest. As they got deeper, Ethan allowed himself to think of something beyond mere escape and survival.

He'd recognized the man who had killed the scientists and taken Felix, just like Cat had. Sean Reilly was the worst type of thief. He was a ruthless, violent sociopath who didn't play by the rules and had no code of honor. He'd been expelled from his own agency long ago, and now he did mercenary work.

So whom was he working with this time?

And—more worrisome—why the hell wasn't he locked up? Last he'd heard, Reilly had been sentenced to a nice long stint in prison, because of his involvement in the conspiracy to steal the Hope Diamond and, most importantly, his murder of Albert Faulkner III and three other innocent people.

After several more minutes running and splashing through shallow streams, and scrabbling up leaf-covered hills, there was no sign they were being followed. Ethan put his hand up, signaling Cat to stop, and they listened. Nothing.

They walked a long way, not speaking, and when they came out on the other side, they found themselves on a country road.

"Should we go back to Harrow Hall?" Cat said, walking beside him.

"All our gear is there. We have to."

"We need a vehicle. It's going to be a long walk."

"Maybe we can hitchhike."

They began walking along the road, saying little. Ethan glanced at Cat. Her face was grim, her eyes clouded.

"We'll get him back," he said. "And we'll be fine. There's no reason to think we're suspects yet."

"Maybe not, but it won't be long before we are. What are the chances we got out of there without our faces showing up on CCTV somewhere?"

Ethan flexed his jaw. She was right about that.

They had to get somewhere safe. But where was that, exactly?

Chapter Eighteen

When we emerged from the woods, a pub appeared after a bend in the road. No surprise—every crossroads and roundabout in England contained a pub. The Golden Arrow shone out of the gloom like a beacon, gilded letters on a glossy black sign, lanterns glowing against the gray stone exterior. It was twilight.

The pub was a beautiful sight for us, exhausted and freezing as we were. It had started raining about twenty minutes before. We needed shelter, and I needed to contact Templeton.

We entered the dark pub, ducking under the doorway's low lintel, and slid into a booth. The tavern smelled of moss and ale and roast lamb. Ethan went up to the bar to order.

"Templeton, it's me," I said through the encrypted line on my cell phone. "We lost it. Ethan and I were doing everything right. But when we got to the safe, someone else had been there just before us."

"Who?"

I took a deep breath. "Reilly."

There was silence on the line.

"But there's something else. Something worse. They have Felix. They kidnapped him."

"What? *He was with you?*" Templeton didn't bother keeping the alarm out of his tone. "I suggested he tag along to learn, not to go on the actual job—"

My voice caught. "He managed to talk me into it. I don't know if they thought he was a scientist, an employee, or what—but they stuffed him in a van."

"Do you know where they took him?"

"I'm going to find out," I said with determination. "Somehow."

"I may be able to help with that. I think I know who Reilly is working with," he said.

"Who?"

Templeton hesitated a moment. "Caliga."

All the air left my lungs.

Templeton told me the rest of the story. Reilly had been busted out of prison a while ago. It wasn't a jailbreak, more a loophole that his lawyers had exploited. Someone must have been blackmailed along the way, was Templeton's assessment. Caliga was widely considered to be behind it. Which meant they owned him now.

I thought about the likelihood of this. It was a good fit. Reilly was ruthless; Caliga was ruthless.

Templeton grew quiet again. He had something else to tell me, I could feel it. "You're going to need help, Petal," he said.

"Not the police."

"Not exactly. Listen," he said, hesitating, "there's someone I need to talk to about this. Someone who is in a position to assist you."

"Who?"

"Well, I'm going to have to talk to him first, and I'll get back to you. Sit tight." He disconnected the call.

Sit tight, my ass. I was going to find Felix. He was my responsibility.

Ethan returned to the booth with two pints and slid into the seat beside me. We sat side by side so we could both keep an eye on the TV but not have our backs to the door. It meant he was very close to me. I felt the heat coming off his body, sensed the tension in all those muscles, caught the faint scent of sweat on him. And in spite of myself, as inappropriate as it was, I felt my skin tingle as a result.

I kept a firm eye on the TV in the corner of the pub, looking for any news about us, or the break-in at the archaeology lab, or anything.

On the news, there was a story about the deputy prime minister. "Duncan Wakefield is a well-liked and admired man, very pro-British," the reporter was saying, of the deputy PM. "He is a strong leader with an impressive military background. Most people here feel this was a key factor in the result of the vote in the House of Lords earlier today . . ."

So that bill passed. It seemed a year ago—not three days ago—

that Ethan and I had been sitting in Harrow Hall Pub listening to the locals debate the merits of the Succession vote, before things had gone so terribly wrong . . .

The next story on the BBC, however, pulled me right out of my reverie about Harrow Hall. A crime scene flashed onto the screen, and the image was chillingly familiar: emergency response vehicles parked in front of the archaeology lab surrounded with yellow police tape, our car with the slashed tires in the background, Scotland Yard investigators swarming all over the place.

Breaking news on the BBC flashed along the ticker underneath. I read the words with growing panic. *University of York archaeology facility: Two men dead, safe breached—unknown contents stolen.*

Grainy images of the thieves making their escape from the lab then flashed up on the screen. I made out Reilly, and whoever his associate was, but they would be unidentifiable to anyone who hadn't been there in person.

Unfortunately, the next set of images were much more clear. Crystalline shots of Ethan and me popped up on-screen. We were in our custodial disguises, but nonetheless highly recognizable. I shrank down in the booth. The shot flashed back to the crime scene, where a reporter was interviewing one of the plainclothes officers. Unfortunately, that officer was none other than Ludolf Hendrickx.

Shit.

"We have some good leads," Hendrickx said to the reporter with a grave face. "Some very active suspects that I will personally be tracking down."

"Why is Interpol involved?" the interviewer asked.

"We have reason to believe that the contents of the safe were of international interest. And we have reason to believe that the criminal behind this operation is a repeat offender we have been tracking for a while."

When he said "criminal" I had little doubt he was talking about me. I curled my fingers into a fist, driving my nails into my palm. How did he get there so fast? He must have already been in town. Which means I hadn't been quite as adept as I'd thought at staying under his radar.

This was bad. Hendrickx now thought I was the thief in a job I had attempted, but had failed at. Worse, I was a suspect for murder.

More than ever, I needed to find Reilly, rescue Felix, get the ring, and then disappear.

Ethan's voice cut through my thoughts. "Montgomery, we need to get moving. Our faces were just shown on TV. We need to make ourselves scarce." I glanced around the cozy interior of the pub. Nobody appeared to be looking our way or paying us any attention. Yet.

"We're not going back to Harrow Hall," he said in a low voice as we both stood and pulled our coats around us. "All the important stuff is on us anyway. Let's go."

I popped on my sunglasses, even though the sky was rapidly darkening, and Ethan pulled his hat way down low as we walked out the front door. We had no idea where we were headed, only that we needed to get as far away from there as possible.

Chapter Nineteen

Seattle

The sun glimmered in a crisp blue sky as Jack walked downtown along Seneca Street. He was in the financial district after a meeting with his investment adviser, and there was a bounce in his step. Things weren't perfect, far from it. But, generally, he was having a good day. And there hadn't been too many of those lately.

He passed a vintage shoe-shine stand with two seats. *Why not?* He was in no rush. He stepped up onto one of the seats and greeted the aproned man who was lingering by the stand, polishing the brass handrail.

The man grinned at him and soon began shining his shoes. Jack took a deep breath; the waxy smell of shoe polish almost overpowered the ubiquitous Seattle aroma of roasting coffee. He gazed all the way down the street to the harbor, and caught a glimpse of blue water.

Someone climbed into the seat beside him. Jack turned to glance at the newcomer and groaned.

The shoe shiner appeared momentarily distressed at the sudden rush of business, at the idea of having to make a customer wait.

"No hurry, my good man," Templeton said to the shoe shiner, snapping open a newspaper.

Jack made a fist. "Templeton, please. Not again. I've already given you my answer."

"I require but a moment of your attention. This is something new."

Jack considered walking away, but the man had only polished one shoe so far. He sighed. Fine, he would listen to Templeton. Just until his other shoe was polished.

"Have you heard of the Lionheart Ring, Jack?" Templeton asked.

Jack frowned. "Nope."

Templeton nodded thoughtfully. "Yes, most people haven't."

Templeton went on to describe the Lionheart, its heritage, the mystery. And the fact that it had recently been found in Yorkshire, England. Jack listened and pretended to look disinterested. He looked forward at the traffic in the street, the people on the sidewalk. A truck rumbled by, drowning out all other sound for a moment. "So what does this have to do with me?" Jack asked once Templeton finished.

"It's Cat, Jack. She went to retrieve the ring. It was her assignment."

Jack's stomach tightened at the sound of Cat's name. He nodded. "Sounds like the kind of thing she would enjoy."

"Yes, well, I'm not sure she's enjoying it all that much now. She needs your help. Things are quickly going south over there."

A spasm of worry centered in Jack's chest. He reminded himself they were not a couple. She was in a world that he needed to stay away from. She was a grown-up and she had made her choices. "That's too bad, for her, it really is. I hope she's okay. But—I don't see how this involves me." He worked hard to maintain a neutral tone.

"Well, it's about more than failure, I'm afraid. People are in danger. The people who took the ring also kidnapped a member of her team."

Jack tightened his jaw. "Oh. Well, that's not good. But maybe you should be calling the authorities. Someone who can actually do something about it. It still doesn't involve me."

"Oh, but it does, my good man."

"How's that?"

Templeton took a deep breath in through his nose. "Because the person who was kidnapped is your half brother."

Jack looked sharply at Templeton. "What the hell are you talking about? I don't have a half brother."

Templeton gave him a crooked, sympathetic smile. "In fact, you do. His father was the same as yours—John Robie. And now, well, he's in big trouble, Jack."

Chapter Twenty

I checked the side-view mirror for the hundredth time as we sped along the motorway, clenching my hands onto my knees, looking to see if we were being followed. Ethan and I were making our way back to London in a car we had rented using false ID. We needed to get as far away from Yorkshire, and as close to an extraction point, as we could.

"Why would Caliga even want the Lionheart Ring?" I asked, staring out the window as Ethan drove. "It makes no sense. In terms of value, it's not the most precious thing out there. I mean, it has some worth. It's a ruby from the Middle Ages with legends attached to it. But even still."

"I don't know," Ethan said. "But there has to be some reason. The last time they crawled out of their hole for something and got this aggressive, they were after the Fabergé egg and the Gifts of the Magi."

"Maybe it's more valuable than we realize," I said, thinking it through. "When it's revealed that this legendary ring even exists, there's going to be a huge uproar. That's the kind of thing that pushes the value of an item sky-high."

I glanced in the side mirror, scanning the road behind me. There were a number of cars behind us, but none that raised my Spidey sense.

"So you think it's for money?" Ethan asked.

I shrugged. "Caliga is a huge operation. They need a constant source of income."

We knew Caliga was—besides being huge—a very old operation. They were formed by the descendants of that original theft, the Gifts of the Magi. But over the years they had branched out into other projects, just like AB&T had.

I pulled out my phone.

"Who are you calling?" Ethan asked.

"Gladys. I need to know where Sean Reilly has gone, where they've taken Felix. She may be able to find out."

Ethan tightened his hand around the steering wheel. "Listen, Montgomery. I want you to think about this. I know this was our assignment, but . . . well, the game has changed. The danger factor is on a whole other level now."

"What are you saying?"

"I'm not sure going after them is smart."

"It may not be smart, Ethan, but it's our job. What would AB&T say if we dropped out now?"

Silence.

"And Hendrickx? Is he going to stop trying to hunt me down just because I stop pursuing the actual Lionheart? Is he going to believe me if he catches me and I say I don't have it?"

He shrugged, conceding the point. "Not likely."

"And the fact that they've kidnapped Felix? We should not worry about that?"

"Well, that's the thing that concerns me the most. Think about it for a second. Why did they take Felix alive? Why didn't they kill him, like the guard and the scientist? It's suspicious. And I don't know what it means."

He was right. It didn't make any sense. Was it a trap?

I thought about it for a long time. But I kept coming back to the same answer. "Ethan, I don't know what it means, either. But how can I not go after him? I can't leave him. If you don't want to do it, I understand. I'll go alone."

"Montgomery—I'm not saying I don't want to do this. I do. It's just—I need to make sure you're fully aware of the risks. And that your head is totally in it."

"I am. And it is. Plus, I really have no choice. I have to go after them." For all those reasons. And more, to be honest. My pride was wounded, being so thoroughly—and easily—bested in a job. And now that I knew Caliga was involved, I knew it must mean there was something more to this case. "But why would you even ask me that?" I said.

Ethan looked straight ahead. He shifted in the driver's seat. "Montgomery, you hesitated. When you went out for that walk on the moors.

I'm not trying to be cruel, but you gotta know that if you hadn't done that, we would have the ring, and Felix would be fine. They were one step behind us. You know that, right?"

This was a kick in the stomach. But a part of me knew he was exactly right.

"You have to be ready to go, to make your move," he continued. "Hesitation in this business can be very dangerous. And . . . I'm worried about you."

A warmth curled in my chest at these last words. *Ethan is concerned for my safety.* It made sense. He'd seen me at my worst. In Paris, when I'd been rocked by panic attacks, trapped on a rooftop . . .

A prickly feeling crept in. Did he doubt my abilities? Did he think I'd lost the knack?

"Ethan, there are a few things I'm not completely sure about, I'll admit it. But there's one thing I am dead-certain about. We have to get that ring back, and more importantly, we have to save Felix."

Ethan nodded grimly. And then a crooked smile snuck across his mouth. "Good. I was hoping you'd say that."

I dialed Gladys's encrypted number.

She answered immediately and I quickly explained what I needed to know. Keeping my eyes pinned to the side mirror, I stayed on the line as she got to work.

"All right, here we are," Gladys said, after several minutes and much clacking of keys. "I've got an airport manifest from York airstrip showing a private jet registered under the name of Sean Reilly bound for Venice."

"Venice, Italy? Is that where they've taken Felix?"

I glanced at Ethan. He winced. "Venice is where Caliga's headquarters is reported to be," he said. "Templeton was saying something about that a few months ago. We'd be going into the hornets' nest."

"Thank you, Gladys," I said. "We'll be in touch."

I disconnected and looked at Ethan carefully. "I'm up for it, if you are."

His jaw flexed and he looked straight ahead at the road.

"Okay," he said. "Venice it is."

Chapter Twenty-One

The Venice Simplon-Orient-Express departed from London Victoria train station at ten o'clock in the morning. On the platform, stewards in crisp blue uniforms with gold braid assisted people with their bags and finding their reserved cabins. The first leg of the journey, before we changed trains on the other side of the English Channel, would be on a Belmond British Pullman: black-lacquered train cars with gilded lettering, pulled by a crimson engine.

Ethan and I climbed on board, and within minutes the train departed with a sharp hiss of releasing brakes, and the squeal and clang of iron on steel.

The train had been the logical choice of transportation. Flying to Venice would be too trackable; we needed to stay invisible not only to Caliga, but to Hendrickx and Interpol, too. The Orient Express would take one night, and we'd be in Venice the following afternoon.

We settled into our seats and I checked the messages on my phone. An e-mail popped up from Professor Atworthy. "I've managed to get a meeting with the dean next week. All hope may not be lost."

My heart quickened. My way out. *My future.*

Grasping on to the thread of optimism, I sent him a quick text back. "The later next week, the better. May be tied up with one or two commitments for the next several days."

I pressed SEND and looked up to see Ethan glancing at my phone. "Anything I need to know about?" he asked.

"It's fine. Just my prof. You know, Atworthy."

His brow furrowed. "Did you encrypt your text?"

I took in a sharp breath. "No—oh my God. I forgot." I had been so focused on the idea of academic salvation. I cursed myself for being so careless. "Do you think it'll cause a problem?"

"I don't know. Sending that message could reveal your location. They can triangulate from a sent text."

I chewed my lip. It was too late now. I'd already sent the message.

Ethan caught my worried look. "It will probably be fine. It was a two-second interchange. Somebody would have to be locked right on, to get your data."

I nodded, feeling slightly better. Then a waiter brought us mimosas, which made me feel much better.

I sat back in the seat and did my best to enjoy the ride. The interior of our compartment was filled with plush furnishings in deep colors of burgundy and navy, trimmed with mahogany and brass. I was comforted by the smells of sizzling butter and garlic—the food I knew was being prepared by the French chef. Brunch would soon be served.

Ethan said he needed to stretch his legs. While he went to explore the train, I gazed out the window at the passing scenery as the train rolled through the Kentish countryside of farms and villages and the occasional castle. I remembered the last time Ethan and I had taken a rail journey together: the train from Paris to Geneva. We had been in the middle of a job then, too.

But that time, there were no hard feelings between us. We hadn't gone through hell and back in the Louvre—yet—and I hadn't said those fateful words on the banks of the Seine.

We were in a different place now.

My phone chimed. An incoming call from Templeton. *Good.* I had a lot of questions. This time I took care to answer using an encrypted code.

"What's your status, Catherine?" he asked.

"We're en route to Venice."

"Good. That's good. And you're safe? You've not been followed?"

"We're fine." *So far*, I thought. "So what's up with this ring? Can you tell me anything more? Why does Caliga want it?"

"It's the Robin Hood connection, my dear."

Of course it was. Caliga believed themselves to be the true ancient order of thieves, I knew that. Naturally they would want a Robin Hood token. But was that all it was?

"And then . . . there are also the rumors," he said.

"What rumors?"

"Well, some people believe the ring has powers. The power of leadership. Why do you think Richard the Lionheart was so universally revered?"

I *knew* there had to be more to it, a reason Caliga was desperate to possess it.

"They say that ring was the reason Richard was so successful," Templeton said. "There's magic in the ruby. The gift of charisma and influence. Some say it explains why a man who was not born in England and barely spent any time in the country was so beloved by the people. Even today, there's a bronze statue of Richard the Lionheart outside Westminster. Many historians can't really account for that degree of adoration."

I thought about that statue. I was all too familiar with it; Westminster was the fortress from which I stole the Fabergé egg, so many months ago.

"Caliga wants that power, Cat. The power of charisma, the power of leadership. The power of the Lionheart himself. That's what they want."

"And they're willing to kill for it," I said. I thought of the dead archaeologist, the dead security guard, both on the floor of the lab. Then I thought of Felix.

"Listen, Catherine, there's someone who may be able to help you. If everything works out, he will meet you in Venice."

"Good," I said, although I wasn't really listening. I was far away, back in that lab, looking at that horrible scene. I hung up with Templeton and shook my head, trying to focus on my present circumstances.

"Here, Montgomery," Ethan said, returning. He handed me a bottle of water, then sat down and pulled out an iPad. "Also, I found out some more information about the Lionheart ring."

"Where did you get this from?" I asked, looking at the iPad. Our tablet was on the list of things we'd had to leave behind at Harrow Hall.

He raised an eyebrow. "I believe you've forgotten my profession."

I smiled.

"I'll return it, don't worry," he said.

I watched him flip through pages on the screen. "Here. Stop there."

It was an academic paper on important jewels of the Middle Ages. I scanned down to the brief section on the Lionheart Ring. *Some say the ring was given to Richard the Lionheart by the Sultan Saladin, as part of the peace agreement, during the Third Crusade.*

The description given of the ring was unmistakable. It then listed a bibliography, mentions of the ring in primary sources: various ballads about Robin Hood and ballads about King Richard. We clicked on links to each of the ballads, and indeed, the Lionheart Ring was mentioned in several of them. But nothing about how it came to be in Robin Hood's possession.

Richard the Lionheart had been captured on his return journey from the Crusades, after he'd been shipwrecked near Venice. He'd been held prisoner for over a year by his mortal enemy, Leopold V, duke of Austria.

I shuddered at the thought of prison. As a career criminal, I sympathized with the man. It must have been awful. The only thing worse than a year in a prison, as far as I was concerned, was a year in a *medieval* prison.

"Templeton says this ring has some sort of special power," I said, glancing at Ethan to gauge his reaction. "What do you think of that? Do you believe it?" I asked him.

"No. But that doesn't matter. Caliga believes it. And if it drives them to do their worst, that's what we have to focus on."

We passed through the Chunnel then, and the windows went black with darkness. We'd be on the other side soon, in continental Europe. We were getting closer to Caliga with every passing hour.

I thought about how we were going to tackle Caliga. How to get past their defenses, to rescue Felix and retrieve the ring. "I wish we had more people on our team," I said. "I wonder if there are more people to call in." I looked up at him uncertainly. "What about . . . getting Brooke's help?"

"I'm going to stop you right there. Brooke abandoned you the last time you needed her. Remember Paris? Even if you could convince her this time around, she's not going to be loyal. You'd never know if she was going to bail on you again."

He was right. I dropped it. Brunch was served then—eggs and Belgian waffles and good coffee. And another round of mimosas.

I became aware of how close I was sitting to Ethan. We were side by side, alone in our cabin, poring over our documents. I could feel the warmth of his body, the firm muscle of the leg that was touching mine. My abdomen contracted with a pleasant flutter.

If I had any hope of keeping this professional, of not letting things get messy with Ethan like they had in the past, I was going to have to ignore every sensation that was surging inside. Two and a half mimosas had probably been a mistake. I pushed the half-empty glass away, and attempted to focus on the page in front of me.

Ethan followed my sight line down to the picture, a drawing of the Lionheart Ring. "I've noticed you don't wear a lot of jewelry, Montgomery. For a jewel thief."

It was true. I used to wear my sister's ring, but that hadn't even been a real jewel. Ever since dealing with the deeper reasons I had worn Penny's ring, since exorcising the demons that had haunted me over her death, my hands and wrists had gone unadorned.

I grasped at the new topic, however. Talking was good. If I kept talking, I might stop thinking about how close Ethan was sitting to me. "You're right, I don't. I guess I'm pretty particular about jewelry."

"Ah, high standards. I see. Occupational hazard."

I nodded. "The only thing I'd wear now—if I was going to wear any jewelry—would be a single ring. One perfect ring." Now why had I said that? The champagne in the mimosas must have loosened my tongue.

He sat back and crossed his arms over his chest. "And what would make it perfect?"

"It's funny, but the stone would look a lot like this," I said, pointing at the picture of the Lionheart. "Well, not exactly, but close. Not a ruby, but a red diamond."

"Why?"

Before I could stop myself, the words came bubbling out of me. "White diamonds are beautiful, but they're somewhat . . . cold, you know? But a red diamond is different. It's like fire. Not only is it the rarest color for diamonds, it's pure passion."

Ethan was quiet, simply listening.

"Penny's ring was pink," I continued. "That had suited her. She was sweet. But for me, I'd want red."

"What about the rest of the ring?"

I replied automatically, describing the image in my head. "The stone would be cushion-cut with a white pavé halo and a platinum band. The white halo for the good in the world, the red diamond for the passion. A ring like that would symbolize everything about life, love, me, and the man I would want to marry. All in one perfect piece of jewelry."

I suddenly stopped, realizing what I had just said. Things grew very awkward.

"Well, Montgomery, I truly hope you get your ring one day."

Ethan's face was unreadable.

Chapter Twenty-Two

For the next hour I silently chastised myself as the train moved farther into Europe, closer to Venice. How I wished I'd kept my mouth shut and stayed focused on the job, like the pro I was supposed to be. For the rest of the day's journey, I was careful to steer clear of uncomfortable personal topics.

When it came time for supper, we opted to dine in our cabin. There was no need for any more witnesses to our faces than was strictly necessary. Outside, the skies were thickening, darkening quickly over the tiny stone villages we flew past.

The cabin was set up for dinner with a small table in the middle, and I sat on the long plush bench that would eventually double as one of the beds. Ethan sat across from me in a chair. As the white-jacketed waiter laid the sumptuous meal in front of us, I felt a pang of guilt. How could I enjoy myself while Felix was a prisoner?

Ethan noticed my hesitation. "You have to keep up your strength, Montgomery. There's nothing more we can do right now. We're on our way. You need to eat."

"And the wine?"

He shrugged, then smiled.

"Having a meal like this without a good bottle of wine would be a crime in itself. We have to draw the line on our misdeeds somewhere."

I smiled in spite of myself. I picked up my glass, and after a heady sip, dove into a forkful of filet mignon that melted in my mouth.

At this point, we were traveling deep into continental Europe. The train was taking the Gotthard route through Switzerland, which meant we would soon be in Northern Italy. The skies were very dark now. After we finished eating I stared at the window, but all I could really see was my own reflection—my pale, worried face.

Ethan leaned forward and put a hand on my knee. "It's going to be okay. We'll get him back. Felix will be fine."

I looked into his concerned green eyes. I wanted to believe him. "It's just—if someone else in my life gets hurt because of me . . . I don't think I could stand it."

He paused. "Who else has been hurt?"

I frowned and stared hard out the window again. He slid across to my side of the table, tucking in close to me on the bench. His voice grew gentle. "Montgomery, what happened? You can tell me."

I exhaled a shaky breath. "My mother. She was shot."

Ethan clenched his jaw. "*Shit.* Is she okay—"

"She is now."

I told Ethan the whole story. When I finished, he said, "That's awful. I can't even imagine." He paused. "But . . . you know it wasn't your fault, right?"

"No, I don't know that."

"It was a random incident. If you were an investment banker, it would have happened all the same."

"What about karma?"

He shrugged. "Not something I believe in."

I looked at him in surprise. "I think people want to believe in karma," he continued. "But the fact is . . . sometimes bad shit happens to good people. Sometimes good shit happens to bad people. There's no justice. There's no karma. And if there is—she doesn't clock in to work every day."

I thought about his words for a long while. "Is that how you live with yourself? You know, doing this kind of work?"

He took a sip of wine. "We all rationalize it in different ways. But yes, I sleep at night because I don't believe in universal justice. If I want justice, I have to make it happen myself."

I nodded. That was why he took this assignment. To help the NGO, Global Life.

"You know," I said, "you've changed, Ethan Jones. When I first met you, the only person you cared about was yourself."

He laughed. I liked his laugh. I hadn't realized how much I'd missed it.

"But there's way more hero in there than you realized." I poked his chest, and through the fine knit of his T-shirt I felt taut muscle under my finger. I probably lingered there a little too long.

"You sure about that?"

"Positive," I said, withdrawing my hand. "Anyway, I always suspected you were a good guy, deep down. You're just proving me right." I arched an eyebrow and smiled smugly.

He groaned. "Oh, this is not good. You're going to be impossible to live with now."

"You'll get used to it."

"What?"

"Me, being right about stuff."

Ethan reached up and brushed my hair back away from my face. "I bet I will," he said.

The edges of the train compartment grew blurry as I focused on Ethan's face. I couldn't think of a thing to say. I wanted a clever comeback. But all I could think about was falling into those eyes. My gaze traced the chiseled edges of his face. His jaw, his mouth . . .

He reached his hand up again, but this time it curved around the back of my neck. My skin tingled where he touched me. It was cool in the cabin, but I was reaching a molten temperature.

Part of me wanted to resist. This was a bad idea. We needed to keep things professional. And yet, I couldn't stop myself leaning toward him, drawn to his warmth like iron filings to a magnet.

Then we were kissing.

His hands moved up, his fingers entwining in my hair and pulling me closer. I melted under his touch and he pressed me back against the seat, kissing me more deeply.

Burning fire spread throughout my body. I stopped fighting it and gave in altogether. We were alone. We had all night here. There was nobody to interrupt us.

I reached up and began tugging at his shirt, suddenly desperate to feel his skin against mine. He pulled back from me, for a moment, like he was sizing up my intentions, making sure I knew what I was doing. In that instant, I yanked his shirt right up and over his head, and threw it to the side.

His face registered surprise, briefly, and then he gave a wicked grin that made everything inside me turn to complete jelly. "Naughty girl," he said, now hovering over me, bare chested, hair tousled. "So that's how it's going to be, is it?"

He took hold of my shirt and ripped it off, revealing the black lace bra I wore underneath. He groaned and gently bit my lip. We tumbled backward to lie down on the bench and Ethan slid his body over mine. The length of him was deliciously heavy as he pressed into me. His hands traced up my sides, burning my skin under his touch.

And then, something changed. I realized the train was slowing down. We both sat straight up, alert. Something was wrong.

Were we coming to a stop? There was no reason for a scheduled stop at this point.

We quickly put our clothes back on, and Ethan curved his hands on the window, peering outside. "I can't see a thing. We're in the middle of the countryside."

Within a minute the train had fully stopped. A tingle of warning traced up my neck. I long ago learned to take these hunches seriously.

Almost as fast as the train stopped, it was rolling again. I pulled on my shoes, crept out toward the cocktail car, and peeked through the door separating the cars. There, I saw two passport control officers making their way through the car, checking passports, heading in our direction.

I squeezed out of sight and crept back to our compartment. I yanked the door open as the train gave a small lurch. We were picking up speed quickly.

"We have to get off this train," I said to Ethan.

He was in motion immediately. "They don't usually bother with passport checks once you're inside the EU, right?" he said, packing his bag.

"They still retain the right to make random spot checks."

"Random, my ass."

My thoughts exactly. This was Hendrickx's doing.

We packed our stuff up in less than a minute. Now we just had the small problem of getting off a moving train.

Chapter Twenty-Three

Ethan swung the backpack onto his back and followed Cat out of the train compartment. They needed a way off this train and they needed it now. It wasn't going to be easy. They didn't have parachute packs so a BASE jump was impossible. Pulling the emergency stop cord would be incredibly suspicious, shining a spotlight on their escape.

There was only one decent option: they would have to jump off the back of the train.

He agreed with Cat that this must have been Hendrickx's doing. But how Interpol had figured out they were on board he had no idea. Ethan pushed the questions away—he'd have to think about it later. For now, they had a job to do.

Cat knew what they had to do, too, clearly, because without discussing it, she began heading to the back of the train. Once the train slowed to go around a curve in the tracks, they could make a well-timed jump. The key was in the landing.

Ethan tightened his jaw as they made their way through a car of lounge seats. People were relaxing after dinner, reading or talking and sipping cognac. Mellow jazz music played softly. In spite of his pounding heart, Ethan moved casually, like he was in no hurry, pretending to look for an open seat. Drawing attention would be a bad move at this point.

They reached the back of the lounge car and glided the doors open to the rearmost section of the train, a storage car, filled with boxes and refrigerated supplies and unfortunately, two men, waiting for them.

Caligu.

It was as obvious to Ethan as if they'd been wearing name tags. In the next second he recognized them specifically—these two had been working with Sandor last year, when Cat had been in a race for the Fabergé egg. And now, they were blocking the way out.

The door slid shut behind Ethan and Cat, sealing all four of them in.

One of the men, with a shaved head like a cue ball, glared at Ethan with an unpleasant curl to his lip. The other, with eerie pale eyes, sported a faint smile. What did they want? To warn them? Block their exodus so Interpol would snatch them? Or were they there to kill them?

Ethan knew he could take down one of the men. He flicked a glance at Cat, standing on high alert beside him. She was a good fighter. But these guys were huge, and mean-looking. Ethan tried to quickly assess their weaknesses. He couldn't see too many.

"Cat Montgomery. Ethan Jones," said the one with the pale eyes. "It looks like you two think you're going somewhere. Too bad, this is a very nice train."

Ordinarily, Ethan would have opted to stall for time, giving himself a few moments to size them up further. In this scenario, that wouldn't work. Passport control was behind them, making their way through the train, and they'd be there any minute.

"If you're thinking of going to Venice," the other man said, "you should reconsider."

"Oh, is that where this train is going?" asked Ethan. The smart-ass comment triggered an angry flare in both mens' eyes.

"You can't win, and you can't get the ring back. And if you try anything stupid, Felix Tucker will pay the price."

Ethan cringed, and he felt Cat stumble slightly beside him. So Caliga knew who Felix was; they hadn't been fooled by his disguise. Which meant they must have taken him hostage for a reason, like Ethan had suspected. But what was the reason? Ethan still needed to know. The Caliga men had revealed one useful fact, however: Felix was still alive.

"Ring?" Ethan said innocently. "No idea what you're talking about." Ethan could sense Cat's tension as she stood very close on his left. She'd recovered, and he knew she was ready. Her muscles coiled.

The bald man, the bigger of the two, narrowed his eyes. "Oh right. You're going to Venice for—what—the romance?"

The men laughed, a nasty sound. Then all eyes slid to Cat. "Can't blame you, though," the pale-eyed man said, looking meaningfully at Cat. "Still, there's a message our boss wanted us to pass on to you."

A second later, Ethan dropped down low as the larger man launched himself at him, and Cat leapt to the opposite side, evading the attack of the other man. Luckily Ethan was ready for the impact, which was like a freight train. He pivoted to the side, preventing a full frontal take-down, and instead kicked the man's legs out from under him as he churned past.

Ethan had to assume they would kill if they got the chance.

He reached down, disabling the man with an arm twist, pulling up, pummeling him with a kick and a sharp blow. Ethan was stronger than he'd ever been before, and it felt good. But the man was up again, not to be subdued that easily; he kicked into Ethan's stomach, taking his breath for a second, then punched him in the face. The pain sheared into Ethan's brain. The man drove Ethan backward into a pile of boxes. Ethan fought to stay in control. He brought a fist up, catching the man on the side of the jaw. He felt the man go momentarily limp. He took that opportunity to flip the man away, then deliver one sharp jab to the throat. The man dropped, unconscious.

Ethan looked sharply toward Cat. At that moment, she was rolling out of the way as the other man launched himself at her. She was using her size as an advantage by letting her attacker do the work. She kicked up as he flew through the air, carrying him right over top of her, and sending him headfirst into a refrigerator.

The man dropped down in a crumpled heap.

Ethan allowed a small, grim smile. He knew neither man would be unconscious for long, but they would be dazed enough to not be able to stop their escape from the train. He reached out to Cat and helped her up.

Through the window between the cars Ethan glimpsed the passport control officers entering the last lounge car. They would reach the storage car in a minute. "Let's go!" Ethan shouted to Cat.

They dashed to the very back of the car and Ethan ripped open the back door. The sound of the train on the tracks was deafening. Wind rushed in Ethan's ears. The late evening sky was a deep indigo, pricked by a few stars and a silver crescent moon.

Ideally, Ethan would have chosen to wait until the train took a bend to leap off, but they didn't have that luxury anymore.

Ethan squinted outside for a soft spot to land. They were in Italy, not yet Venice, but growing closer. They were through the Alps, on the other side, in Northern Italy, the Lombardy region of foothills and rolling grassy farmland and small villages. They would have to take a leap of faith. Literally.

"I'll go first," Ethan said. "If I don't make it, don't try it. Just find somewhere to hide. Okay?"

Cat nodded.

Ethan got as low to the floor of the train as possible, and bent his knees so he could leap away from the train car. His stomach flip-flopped like mad. He jumped perpendicular to the train, as far away from the train car as possible. His first goal was to not get sucked under the train.

His second goal was to land without breaking every bone in his body—most importantly his neck.

He covered his head protectively with his arms, and felt the ground come up fast. He stretched out to get all his body parts hitting the ground at the same time, knowing if any one bone hit first, it would likely break. He smashed into the ground with a grunt, and all the air left his lungs. He rolled like a log, bumping and crashing. He squeezed his eyes tight and prayed.

After several seconds of rolling along, Ethan came to a rest.

He forced his eyes open in time to see Cat flying off the train—same formation, same technique. He remained motionless, scanning his body for the sharp pain of a severe injury. His tissues screamed and throbbed in many areas, but no one particular place more than the others. No vital areas seemed to be hurt.

He would have been happy to lie there for a while, but urgency to go help Cat forced him up to a crouch, and then an agonizing stand. The train was clacking away in the distance now, growing farther and farther away.

He found Cat after several minutes of hunting. Lying in a field, not moving. His heart spasmed. "Montgomery!" he shouted, rushing to her side, eyes raking her body for signs of blood, injuries, broken bones. "Oh God. Cat! Can you hear me? Are you okay?"

Chapter Twenty-Four

My eyes opened and I stared up at Ethan's face, gazing down at mine with extreme concern. I groaned and shifted a little. "I'm okay. I think." Where were we? I couldn't seem to remember anything. The ground felt cool and hard, and covered with something grassy. Were we in a field? The black sky told me it was nighttime. "What happened?"

He sat back and exhaled. "Thank God you're awake. You had me worried there, Montgomery."

I attempted to sit up, and everything swam. The world tilted and I felt a wave of nausea. I lay back down. "How long was I unconscious?"

"After the train jump, I think you were out for about a minute."

Train jump?

Ethan checked me for injuries. When he reached the back of my head, he winced. "You've got a big bump here. Do you remember hitting your head?"

Fragments of the fall were starting to come back to me. I remembered flying through the night air, then hitting the ground, then rolling out of control . . .

"I must have hit my head as I rolled. Maybe a rock or something."

Ethan shone the light of his cell phone in my eyes. "Your pupils are okay. Can you feel everything? Your hands and feet?"

I wiggled my fingers and toes. He nodded and kept checking me, feeling the back of my neck. I tried for a smile. "Do you know what you're doing, Ethan, or are you making this up as you go?"

"I learned a little first aid when I was in Kenya, working in the field." His normally lighthearted tone was gone. A deep frown creased his forehead.

My head was pounding now, throbbing like a toothache.

"I think you have a concussion," Ethan said. I closed my eyes as another pulse of nausea surged over me. When I opened them, Ethan sat back on his heels and looked around, jaw flexing. I knew we couldn't stay there. We had to get moving.

"Can you stand?" he asked.

"I can try."

He helped me up and I gritted my teeth through the dizziness. "We need to get you to a doctor," he said.

I tightened my mouth. I knew we didn't have time for that.

"I'll be fine. I've had a concussion before—it'll wear off." When I was a kid, in gymnastics, I'd smacked my head on the balance beam. The concussion from that had laid me low for three days. But we didn't have three days for me to be out of commission now.

All we could do, for now, was keep moving.

Ethan helped me with each step, and slowly, I was able to walk a little more easily. The throbbing and the dizziness remained unchanged, but I pushed through it. The midnight sky arched overhead, its velvety curtain concealing our movements. We spent the night pressing on, journeying through Northern Italy to get to Venice, in the easternmost part of the country.

Ethan wanted to stop but I insisted we keep going. He checked me periodically to make sure I wasn't worsening, and the look of concern in his eyes remained fixed.

We hitchhiked a little, with an old Italian farmer in a falling-apart truck, then took a bus from a tiny town we stumbled upon. By the time we reached the Veneto region we were cold and exhausted and I felt terrible. But I wasn't about to admit that to Ethan because we were almost there. We just had the task of getting ourselves into the city of Venice itself. Being built upon a lagoon, there were only a couple of ways on and off the island, and that list didn't include cars. I was not keen to get on another train, and it wouldn't have been smart, anyway. They would be monitoring all trains now.

So we opted for the water route, chartering a powerboat.

It was sunrise as we approached Venice from the sea, the air smelling of fish and salt. As we crossed the choppy water, Venice rose up like a mirage. Hazy sunlight bathed the glittering city in a lemony glow. I blinked, gazing at the miraculous sight: the spire of

Saint Mark's Campanile, the Doge's Palace like a frothy wedding cake.

Ethan steered the boat right into the city, mooring it in a small canal off Piazza San Marco. Palazzos and houses in shades of ocher and clay and cream lined every canal, rising up in a stately manner, their ornately carved front doors opening directly onto the water.

I shivered. Somewhere in this tangled maze of canals and piazzas lay Caliga's headquarters, where they were keeping the Lionheart Ring and where Felix was a prisoner. At the thought, the tall Gothic windows took on a more sinister feeling. Were we being watched, even now?

We had no idea where Caliga was hiding. Truthfully, there was a great deal we didn't know about Caliga. The identity of their leader, for example. Who had taken the helm after Sandor had fallen from Big Ben to his death? Although I had to admit I had never felt fully convinced that Sandor had been the top man anyway. He was too young; there must have been someone above him.

I pulled out my phone and scrolled to the photograph Templeton had forwarded me, the only clue we had to the leader's identity. It was a grainy, nondescript photo of a man with his head turned and partially obscured by a telephone box. It was not helpful.

"This is the best we have?" I'd asked Templeton.

"Unfortunately," he'd said.

Ethan and I left the chartered boat tied to the moorings and entered the streets of Venice, making our way to our lodgings—a small, inconspicuous hotel overlooking a tiny *campo*, very discreet and off the beaten track. We briefly stopped to pick up a few essentials, water and clean clothes topping the list.

I swayed as we entered the lobby, and Ethan helped me to a soft armchair, worry creasing his face. "Stay here. I'll go check us in."

I lost track of time, sitting in the lobby, and things grew somewhat fuzzy. Then Ethan approached, holding up a key card. "Our room is ready—number three-fourteen. Let's get you to bed."

Our room?

Ethan noted my reaction. "Montgomery, I'm not letting you out of my sight. The most critical phase after a head injury is the first twenty-four hours. I have to keep an eye on you, make sure you don't slip into a coma or anything."

In the room, while Ethan ordered room service, I showered and then pulled a fluffy hotel robe around me. I took a deep breath. The therapeutic value of a hot shower is not to be underestimated. The cloudlike bed beckoned me irresistibly, heaped with feather pillows and white linens. I lay down; I would just close my eyes for a moment . . .

Several hours later I woke with a start. Ethan was standing over me, gazing at me worriedly. "Hey, Sleeping Beauty . . . how do you feel?"

I slowly sat up and rubbed my eyes, attempting to clear the cobwebs from my brain. It took me several minutes to remember where I was.

Venice. We had to find Felix. I sat up more fully and my head spun. The pain had lessened, but the dizziness and fog were still there.

"I asked Templeton for the name of a discreet doctor in Venice," Ethan said. "Someone AB&T uses. Unfortunately, the only one he had on record is out of town right now. Templeton is working on finding a substitute."

I knew we couldn't go to a regular hospital. It would broadcast our presence to everyone who was hunting us.

"I'll be fine," I said. "If it's a concussion, it will have to get better on its own. There's not much a doctor can do anyway."

Ethan didn't look convinced. But he also looked like he had something else to say.

"What is it?" I asked.

"We have a meeting in Piazza San Marco," Ethan said. "Are you up for it?" He explained that while I'd been sleeping, Templeton had also told Ethan about a rendezvous he'd set up. We were to meet a contact in the Piazza San Marco. Someone who could help us with our quest.

I dressed as quickly as I could. When we walked out of the hotel, I was surprised to see it was already dusk. I had slept most of the day? Well, it was probably a good thing.

We strolled the labyrinthine streets of Venice, matching our pace to everyone around us to avoid attracting unwanted attention. Fortunately for me in my current state, people sauntered slowly here. Usually with gelato in hand.

"Why the mystery about this meeting?" I asked Ethan as we walked. "Why can't we know who it is?"

"No idea."

We walked alongside the Grand Canal, past the Rialto Bridge that arched across the water. The waters of the canal shifted in the dusky purple sky of twilight, turning reflective, looking like mercury. Barbershop poles speared out of the water as mooring posts. Lanterns reflected their light into the canal. Somewhere near the bridge, someone was playing an accordion; the romantic notes floated their way to my ears.

As we walked, Ethan periodically glanced at me, attempting to conceal his concern but not doing a very good job. And though I struggled to appear fine, worry gnawed away at my belly. If this concussion didn't pass quickly, how was I going to do the job? How could I possibly get the ring and rescue Felix?

Beautiful, carved palazzos rose up from the waters, and bridges arched across tiny canals. We passed cafés and restaurants, alongside the canal. Smells of garlic and grilled seafood curled up my nose. Shop windows glowed, filled with glittering displays of carnival masks and colored glass made into fanciful sculpted shapes.

It was a magical city, trapped in time. Without the presence of cars, you easily forgot you were part of the modern world. A warm summer breeze stirred my hair as we crossed a bridge.

At last, we reached the Piazza San Marco, a huge expanse of open space framed with restaurants and cafés with their rows of alfresco tables where people sipped cappuccino, nibbled pastries, or enjoyed a meal. String quartets on small stages filled the square with Vivaldi. In the center of the piazza, people strolled arm in arm, savoring gelato, while flocks of pigeons fluttered about them like confetti.

It was undeniably romantic. I glanced at Ethan. He was pointedly avoiding my gaze.

A lot of the previous night's events were fuzzy in my mind—the head injury messing with my memory—but one thing stood out in sharp detail: kissing Ethan in the train car, undressing each other . . .

Heat flushed up my face. Nothing had been said about it between us, which left me feeling uncertain and vaguely uncomfortable. I struggled to focus on the task at hand.

"How are we to recognize the person we're supposed to be meeting?" I asked Ethan. Templeton had not provided a pass phrase. No secret handshake. No photo or file. Just an instruction to meet our contact underneath the winged lion column, the *Lion of Venice*.

"Don't know," Ethan said. "I'm hoping it will be obvious."

As we moved to the far end of the square, the winged lion column came into sight. My gaze slid down, and I instantly knew why we didn't need a secret handshake.

Chapter Twenty-Five

Jack had known who would be meeting him in Saint Mark's Square. He'd also known Cat and Ethan were working on this assignment together. The knowledge didn't stop his stomach from curling unpleasantly at the sight of them. Not that they had been walking hand in hand or anything. It was just that they looked . . . like a pair, somehow.

He wasn't sure this had been the right decision. Although what choice did he have? Now that Jack knew about his half brother, he could hardly leave the kid at the mercy of Caliga.

During the flight over here, Jack had thought a lot about Templeton's revelation. He'd demanded to know when Felix Tucker had been born and then tried to calculate where his father might have been at the time. But it was a futile exercise. John Robie had maintained a jet-set lifestyle when Jack had been young; he was constantly away from home. Jack would never know the whole story now, of course. His father had been dead for years.

"Oh my God. I can't believe it's you," Cat said in a low voice as she approached him. "What are you doing here? What do you know? Why—"

Ethan interrupted, speaking directly to Cat. "What if this is a trap? An FBI sting? How do we know we can trust Jack?"

Cat scoffed. "It's not a trap."

Ethan didn't look convinced. Jack crossed his arms and waited; he didn't owe the man any explanations.

He watched Ethan conduct a visual sweep of the area. Jack followed his gaze. Ethan looked to all the places Jack would have, for signs of surveillance or an ambush. The art thief was as sharp as ever, he'd grant him that much.

"Fine. Let's go somewhere we can talk," Ethan said, marginally less suspicious.

A few minutes later, all three of them tucked inside a dimly lit café a block away from Saint Mark's. As Cat took her seat, Jack noticed she stumbled a little before sitting down. "Are you okay?" he asked sharply. For her to be anything other than perfectly agile was unusual.

"I'm fine."

Jack peered into her eyes carefully. Her gaze was slightly unfocused. Jack sat bolt upright and turned on Ethan. "What the hell happened?"

Ethan winced, then quickly schooled it. "She hit her head," he confessed. "She seems to have a concussion."

"A concussion! *How?*"

Both Cat and Ethan remained quiet. Jack gripped the arms of his chair. "Jesus Christ, somebody better tell me what happened—"

"We were on a train," Cat began. Between them, Cat and Ethan told him the full story, although Jack got the distinct feeling Cat was downplaying it for his benefit. *Typical.*

Jack looked to Ethan. "I need to hear it from you, Jones. Is she okay? How bad was it? Do we need to take her to the hospital?"

Cat let out a strangled sound. "What the hell? Since when do you two team up against me?"

Ethan ignored her, and addressed Jack's question. "It was a bad fall. But . . . I think she's going to be okay. We'll need to keep a close eye on her."

Jack glanced at Cat, who was glaring at them both, and nodded. Fine. He could do that.

His insides twisted at the thought of her being hurt. Jumping from a train? It could have been so much worse.

And then, with a tinge of sadness, he reminded himself: *she wasn't his to worry about anymore.*

The waiter brought out three espressos, dark and rich. "All right, let's get down to business," Jack said. If he was going to get involved in this job, he was going to do it his way. "I know you two are on assignment to retrieve the Lionheart Ring. I know the job went sour in England. And I know you're now hunting Caliga's headquarters, the Lionheart, and the hostage they took."

"And how do you know all that?"

"Templeton. He gave me information that sent me over here to help."

"And that's all it took, to get you to come over here?" Cat said. Jack heard the surprise and gratitude in her voice, with possibly a tinge of admiration. Jack sipped his coffee and glanced at Ethan.

The man was looking at him with narrowed eyes. To gain his trust, Jack would need to prove himself in some way, and this idea truly pissed Jack off. The guy was a crook, and Jack was an FBI agent. *At least I used to be.*

His gaze flicked between Ethan and Cat. What was going on between them? There was obviously a lot of tension. They'd been working together for a few days, so maybe . . . ? The thought made Jack's ears pound as blood rushed to them.

At that moment, Cat stood. "I'll be right back."

Instantly, both Jack and Ethan stood, too. "Are you okay? Do you need someone to go with you?" Jack said. Ethan watched her with concern and held her elbow protectively.

Cat flicked her eyes between the two of them. "Um . . . I'm just going to the restroom. I think I can handle it."

She disappeared down the corridor, leaving the two men staring at each other as they sat back down.

"Okay, Jack, we get it. You're a goddamn hero," Ethan said. "It was a nice move, showing up here to help Cat with a job gone south. But some of us have been here right from the start."

Jack opened his mouth, about to correct Ethan, and tell him the real reason he was there.

But then he reconsidered, and bolted down his coffee instead. Why not let Ethan think he'd come here for Cat? Ethan didn't need to know that Felix was his half brother. Neither did Cat, for that matter. It didn't change anything, in terms of their objective, and if it got under Ethan's skin, that was just a bonus.

If it changed his status in Cat's eyes? Well, Jack wasn't sure he wanted to go there. He frowned, the feeling of being left on the chilly bank of the Seine too fresh in his mind. Even so, Jack decided to keep the truth about Felix to himself, for now.

When Cat returned, Jack started grilling them about what they knew about Caliga, who was in charge, and where they thought the ring might be. He was surprised they didn't have a lot of information.

"What do you mean you don't have surveillance records? What about background checks?"

Ethan scowled. "Jack, this isn't some FBI operation. The rules are different." Then he crossed his arms and added, "Not that you'd be welcome at an FBI op, from what I hear."

"Whereas you'd be plenty welcome," Jack shot back. "The guest of honor, no doubt. Should I make a call?"

"You're not insulting me by calling me a criminal." Ethan's eyes flashed.

"Does it insult you if I call you an asshole?"

"Whoa, stand down, you two," Cat said, holding her hands up. "You know we all worked well together in Paris. We can do it again. Do I need to remind you what's at stake? Smarten up, both of you."

Both men glowered like sullen teenagers. There was silence for a few minutes, then Ethan said, "All right, Jack, since you're here, you must have some information on the whereabouts of the Lionheart." His tone was challenging. "Where's Caliga's headquarters?"

Jack looked between them with genuine surprise. "You two don't know? Well, *I* don't know where it is. I assumed you would."

At that moment, a woman's voice said, "They have no idea. But, fortunately, I do."

All three turned. Approaching their table was a petite woman with a massive amount of dark curly hair, and a faint scar over her left cheek. Esmerelda.

Chapter Twenty-Six

I blinked, making sure it really was Esmerelda. She was French Secret Service, and she'd helped me during the Hope Diamond heist in the spring. More importantly, though, she was a member of the enigmatic DOA. The Department of Antiquities.

Ethan swiftly stood and retrieved a chair for her. Jack called a waiter over and she ordered a cappuccino.

"I've been tailing you since this morning," she explained, taking the seat.

My eyebrows lifted. She was good. I was normally proficient at detecting a tail. It made me uncomfortable knowing this had happened without me being aware. I could see the same thoughts on Ethan's and Jack's faces. And then it occurred to me—was this a symptom of my concussion? Were my senses that dulled?

My next thought was even more uncomfortable—if she had been following us, undetected, might someone else have been, also?

As if reading my mind, she said, "I've been watching your backs. Nobody else is following you."

"So what are you doing here?" Jack asked. "Is the Fabergé egg here somewhere in Venice?" The last time we had seen Esmerelda, in Paris, we knew Caliga had the Fabergé, which contained two of the Gifts of the Magi—the Frankincense and Myrrh. The third, the Gold, was still missing.

"No, not that we can tell," Esmerelda said. "Caliga has it somewhere, but that somewhere could be anywhere. We don't think it's here in Venice."

"So why are you here?" Ethan asked.

"I've been reassigned. I'm in charge of protecting the Lionheart now."

Jack's eyes flicked around the café. "Where's your team?"

Esmerelda sipped her cappuccino. "I'm it. The DOA wants the Lionheart protected, but most of their manpower is being funneled into finding the Fabergé."

"Just you on the Lionheart?" I asked. "That sounds like an impossible assignment." I winced as my head gave a painful throb. I attempted to cover it by lifting my espresso cup to my lips, and wished I'd ordered a drink that came in something larger than a thimble.

She shrugged. "Remember, the DOA isn't necessarily concerned with ownership. We make sure precious objects are protected." She pushed her hair back, away from her face, revealing fine-boned features. "Anyway, now that I'm here, *you* are my team." She smiled.

Ethan, Jack, and I exchanged looks. As far as I was concerned, one more person assisting was fine with me. The more people, the better. Both men appeared to feel the same, and possibly for the first time that day, there was silent agreement. I wondered how long it would last.

I glanced sidelong at Jack. I understood now why Templeton hadn't told us who we were meeting in Saint Mark's Square—I might have avoided the rendezvous altogether had I known. The messiness of this current situation was almost too much to bear. Jack was, simultaneously, the single best addition to our team, and the single worst. He was sharp and strong and skilled . . . but whose side was he on, exactly? Did he still have loyalty to the FBI? And then there was the reopening of the old wound. The three of us working together again, with me feeling the familiar pull between them, confused as ever.

"I should mention," Esmerelda continued, "although there's nobody on your immediate trail, you should know that Hendrickx is coming after you, fast," she said. "We have monitors on Interpol's activity." She looked at Ethan and me. "And you two are lighting up all over the place."

I chewed the inside of my cheek. "That means we need to speed up even more," I said. "Find their headquarters fast, get Felix, get the Lionheart, and get out."

Jack leaned forward. "You said you know where Caliga's headquarters is?"

Esmerelda nodded. "I do," she said.

Ethan grinned. "Perfect. Let's get to work then."

Before leaving the café, I sent Gladys a quick message with the name of the building supplied by Esmerelda. By the time we got back to the hotel, she had sent through all the schematics, blueprints, and security details.

At the check-in desk in the hotel lobby, Jack and Esmerelda booked their own rooms. "Let's all meet in one of your rooms in ten minutes," Jack suggested, looking at me, and then Ethan. "Who has the larger suite?"

"Oh, we're . . . in the same room," I said, trying to make it sound as innocent as possible. Jack's eyebrows raised, just a flicker, before he applied a neutral mask. I stared at the checkerboard marble floor and pointedly avoided looking at Ethan.

"I insisted," Ethan added. "So I could monitor her concussion."

"Concussion?" Esmerelda asked.

"A minor one. I'll be better soon," I added quickly. I hoped it was true. My stomach tightened with worry—we needed to get moving with this job. Every minute of delay left Felix in further danger. How long could he hang on? But . . . how useful would I be to him, in my current state? I could barely walk a straight line. I wondered if the others had recognized just how off I was.

Ten minutes later, we gathered in the suite Ethan and I shared. "Okay, so let's see where Caliga is hiding out," Ethan said eagerly as I pulled up the files with all our intel. His eagerness matched mine—we needed to come up with a solid plan, and fast.

"Looks like an old palazzo in Venice, in the San Polo neighborhood, off the Grand Canal," I said.

"But that's right in the heart of Venice," Jack said, frowning. "It's not very discreet."

It was true. But in a way, it made sense. Caliga was nothing if not arrogant. Why would they bother to disguise themselves? They were powerful and they knew it.

"Here's what I still don't understand," Ethan said. "Why are they keeping Felix hostage? Why didn't they just kill him?"

Bile rose to my throat again at the thought of Felix being killed. But Ethan was right. We needed an answer to that.

"There are only a couple of reasons to keep someone prisoner," Jack said. "Either they're using him as leverage, to get someone to do something or pay ransom, or they're trying to get information out of him. And since they don't seem to be demanding ransom from anyone, I'd say it's the second one."

"But what information does Felix have? He's just a trainee," I said.

"They might not know that," Esmerelda pointed out. "They saw him working with you two. Maybe they're seeing this as their chance to find out about the inner workings of their most irritating enemy, AB&T."

That made sense. It didn't make me feel better, however. Every minute that Felix remained a captive worried me more.

"Let's go," I blurted out. "We know where they are now. We know where they're keeping Felix. Let's get in there and get him out." It was everything I could do to keep from jumping out of my chair. Then a wave of nausea hit me and I closed my eyes tight, waiting for it to pass.

When I opened them, everyone was staring at me.

"Montgomery, slow down," Ethan said gently. "I know you want to get Felix out . . . we all do. But if we go in there unprepared, we could *all* be killed. Felix included. We have to be ready."

I knew he was right. I also knew that by "ready" he wasn't only talking about a plan. He was also talking about me, and my current state of impairment. I dug my nails into my palms, and we got back to business.

This had to work. We had to get Felix out, and we had to get the Lionheart away from Caliga. I looked across the table at Ethan and Jack, who were both poring over security blueprints on a tablet. I pressed my lips together at the sight of them like that, and wondered how long it would last. The last time I had worked together with both Ethan and Jack was in Paris, planning to break into the Louvre.

That operation had ultimately been a success. Hard-won, sure, but a success nonetheless. I hoped we would work as well together this time.

I stood and paced over to the window. A wave of dizziness washed through me, and I had to grip the back of a chair for support. I glanced at the others to see if they'd noticed, and caught Jack watching me with concern.

"Cat, are you okay?" he asked. "Do you need to rest or something?"

The others turned sharply in my direction.

"I'm fine. I don't need to rest," I said, letting go of the chair back and hoping I didn't need it again. "What I need is a couple of aspirin and for us to keep going."

"You sure?" Ethan said. "You could lie down for a minute—"

"I *said* I'm fine."

Ethan held up his hands in mock surrender and everyone turned back to the work in front of us.

Over the next hour we drank many cups of coffee and ordered food from the café downstairs. As we devoured a platter of olives, cheese, and bread, Esmerelda sketched out an attack plan. Thank goodness she was there. Why Esmerelda was helping us, I understood. It was her job, her life's work.

What I couldn't figure out was why Jack was helping us. My gaze slid to him as he sat on a dining chair, frowning at a blueprint. The last time I'd seen him, he was enjoying himself thoroughly at home in Seattle. What had possessed him to fly across the globe to help us, to help me, with an assignment that was falling apart?

He shifted in the chair and I noticed the flex of his forearm muscles, the ease with which he moved. My heart sped up a little, remembering the feeling of his body near mine. Remembering all the intimate moments we'd shared together. It seemed like a lifetime ago.

The truth was, I was relieved he was here. Having Jack on our team made it a hell of a lot more likely we'd succeed, and I desperately needed this to be a success. But I wondered if it was possible . . . had he come here for me?

No was the answer that immediately came into my head. Not possible. In spite of all our history together, he'd made it quite clear that he was over me. The question was: would I ever be completely over him?

We continued working on our plan as the sky grew dark outside. The later we pushed, the more difficulty I had concentrating. I knew it was more than just being tired. Documents began swimming before my eyes.

"Okay, well, what about an escape from the rooftop?" Ethan suggested as we brainstormed exit strategies. "Any chance we could get a helicopter, last-minute?"

Jack stared at him a moment before speaking. "Please. There are a million ways that could go wrong. Does anyone have a serious suggestion?"

"Hey, no need to get cranky," Ethan said, glaring at Jack. "You haven't come up with anything, I've noticed. What are you doing here, again? Oh, that's right, playing the knight, sweeping in to save us all—"

"Do you want to step outside, Jones?"

"Enough," I said sharply, turning on them both. "Listen, you two need to *play nice.*"

And then the floor tilted and the edges of my vision went black and fuzzy. The room grew incredibly hot. I felt like I was suffocating . . .

The next thing I knew I was on the floor, my cheek pressed against the scratchy wool rug. My eyes fluttered open. Jack and Ethan were close, in my face, gazing at me worriedly and snarling at each other.

"I knew you should have taken her to a doctor—" Jack said.

"Not helping, Jack," Ethan spat back.

My head felt thick. I tried to sit up but failed.

"Would you two give the woman some room?" Esmerelda said, pulling them away, clearing some space for me.

Esmerelda helped me up to the couch, and my mind started to clear. My first emotion was anger at myself for looking so weak. How were they going to trust me to be effective in this operation? A sinking feeling of dread settled in my stomach. How was I going to trust *myself?*

At least there was one benefit to my little fainting episode. I noticed Jack and Ethan were now working together—they were in the kitchenette fetching me a glass of water and a cool cloth.

I grimaced; it was not the way I wanted to get them to cooperate.

I closed my eyes and sank back in the couch, racked with anxiety and guilt and frustration. When was I going to be back to normal? And, more importantly, would it be soon enough for Felix?

Chapter Twenty-Seven

The next morning I left the hotel early. It had been a fitful, restless night, filled with shadowy nightmares about my mom. I awoke with an ache in my chest and a desperate need for fresh air. I walked out onto the streets of Venice in search of coffee.

Venice, in the morning, had a dreamlike quality. The air was hazy and had a pleasant, salty heaviness to it. The sounds of the canals lapping the lower walls of the buildings, lazy and peaceful, reached my ears at every bridge and waterside path. Gondolas sliced through smooth water, gondoliers pointing out the sights to their passengers in rolling Italian, only occasionally bursting into a few notes of song—to the delight of their passengers.

I strolled along a small canal and took a sip of coffee, a quick burst of delicious espresso topped with heavenly foam. The barista had given me a peculiar look when I asked to take my coffee with me. It wasn't something people did here, but I very much wanted to walk.

It wasn't until I'd been walking for at least twenty minutes that I realized something: I hadn't had any dizzy spells yet. I wondered how long it would last. I didn't dare hope they were gone for good.

I glanced at my watch. It was almost eight o'clock. I knew I should be getting back to the hotel to continue making plans with the team . . . but there was something therapeutic about this fresh Venetian morning. I was desperate to feel like my old self again; I would be no help to Felix unless I did. I'd give myself ten more minutes, then head back.

I crossed the majestically arching Rialto Bridge and arrived in the heart of an outdoor market. It bustled with the early rush of people shopping, picking up bread and fresh vegetables for the day. All around me were the sounds of shoppers haggling and old friends greeting one another, as bent Italian *nonnas* inspected tomatoes and filled string bags with lemons and lettuces.

As I wandered, I passed a bookseller's tiny stall. A book titled *Crociate* stopped me. *Crociate* was the Italian word for the Crusades. That had been Richard the Lionheart's quest, I was pretty sure. My history was fuzzy, but I was reasonably certain of that.

The merchant saw me looking at the book. "*Vuoi guardare?*" he said, asking me if I'd like to look at the book. Since being in Venice, I'd surprised myself by how quickly my Italian was coming back to me.

"*Posso?*" *May I?*

He nodded. I reached forward and took the book in my hands, flipping through the first few pages. The book was old and the pages carried a musty smell.

He watched me carefully. "*Se siete interesati alle Crociate, si dovrebbe guardare a questo libro*," he said. The bookseller held up another book—this was the one I should really look at, if I was interested in the Crusades.

"*Grazie*." I put down the first one and picked this one up. It had a plainer cover, true, but as I flipped through, the images, the depth of the detail was much richer, I could see that straightaway.

As I paged through the book, we shared small talk about the weather, and the cost of gas in Italy—there were many grave remarks made about the recent price spike. Then I told him I was curious about Richard the Lionheart. Did he know anything about the history?

The book merchant's eyes twinkled. "Ah, yes, King Richard," he said, in Italian. "Venice is part of his story. A very important part. Did you know this?"

I looked up, and responded in Italian. "No, actually. I didn't know that."

He nodded. "But . . . it is not talked about much in books. And I am not really the expert."

I felt a twinge of disappointment and looked down at the book I was holding.

"But I know someone who is," he added.

My head lifted.

He smiled. "You would like to speak to him? Come with me." He told his assistant to mind the stall for a moment, and then brought me to a neighboring stall, two down.

I walked into the tiny space filled with glass vases and ornaments and bottles in candy colors of crimson and turquoise, curled like frozen honey into fanciful shapes, glittering like jewels. I knew glass-blowing was an ancient skill in Venice, the city's most famous artistry. Even so, my breath was taken at the magic of the glass.

The bookseller greeted the glassblower with the double-cheek kiss of familiar Italian locals.

"Giuseppe, I have someone here who has an interest in the Lionheart," he said, indicating me. The glassblower looked at me appraisingly. The bookseller smiled and nodded to me, then excused himself and returned to his stall of old books.

"You are interested in the story of King Richard, when he was here in Venice?"

"Yes."

He shrugged. "Well, there are books. You can read those," he said, turning back to his work polishing his glass pieces.

My shoulders dropped. It was a test. I would need to prove my worthiness in some way. "I wonder—do you know anything about this?" I pulled out a photograph of the Lionheart Ring—the one I had folded inside my purse.

His face changed, his eyes sparkling like the ruby in the picture. "Of course. It has been a very long time. And I've never seen an actual photograph . . . but I have read descriptions. This was the Lionheart Ring. He was wearing it when he was shipwrecked."

"How do you know that? Is that in here somewhere?" I pointed to the cover of the book.

He shook his head. "The truth of that is barely mentioned in any books. But I know because my family has always lived in Venice. And this is the story I have always been told. It was passed down through the generations. My ancestors owned the home where part of the crew hid, while they gathered supplies."

He told me the story of how they camped near here while they prepared for their overland journey. The journey had ended in disaster—it had not been long before Richard the Lionheart had been captured by his enemy, Leopold V, duke of Austria. He was held prisoner for over a year, until the ransom was paid and he was released.

"But when they captured the king, they did not capture the Lionheart Ring," he said.

"How did they keep it safe?"

"King Richard gave the ring to a trusted man—someone who went on his own way to England, secretly, and carried the ring home."

"Do you know who this man was?"

A knowing smile curled over his leathery face. "A trustworthy man who had been by his side during the Crusades: his most skillful archer, and a man with a great talent for stealth. They called him Lox."

" 'Lox'? Who was he?"

"You perhaps know him by the more complete name he used in his home in England."

"Which was?"

"Robin of Loxley."

Robin Hood.

Chapter Twenty-Eight

"Well, that certainly explains things," Jack said, once I told everyone what I'd learned. I had raced back to the hotel and found them all gathered in Jack's room. "If Richard gave the ring to Robin Hood, then he didn't steal it at all."

Esmerelda nodded thoughtfully. "It would explain why the description and story of the ring, and its location, were obscure and lost to history. And it would explain why the existence of the Lionheart Ring is not well-known in modern times."

I had lost track of time in the market and stayed too long. My insides squirmed with anxiety over Felix—a prisoner of his enemies, just like Richard the Lionheart. We had to get in there—ready or not—and get him out.

Ethan cleared his throat. "Well, it's all very interesting, but it doesn't help us much. We need to get to work if we're going to do this job tonight." He turned to me. "Montgomery, how are you feeling? You seem . . . a little better."

I was a lot better. The fuzziness, the difficulty concentrating, it had all settled to a low hum now. My balance felt solid again. I wasn't perfect, but I was pretty sure I could do my job again, and it was perhaps as good as it was going to get . . .

"Wait—did you say tonight?" I said, snapping out of my reverie. We had planned to take at least another day to do surveillance and map our approach. We had to get this right.

Ethan nodded grimly.

"Why?" I asked, feeling anxious. "Why tonight?"

"Because of this," Ethan said, turning to Esmerelda. "Show her what you saw when you went out to get bread this morning."

Esmerelda handed her phone to me. I stared at a photograph of Hendrickx stepping off a vaporetto, the Venetian water taxis.

"He's here," she said.

Shit.

Several hours later I was sitting among silk and wool blankets on the seat of a gleaming black gondola as it glided through the water. Jack stood at the back of the boat wearing a gondolier's uniform. I wore the disguise of a woman on her way to the opera, a full-length formal gown.

Venice in the evening was washed with violet and indigo. Lanterns perched on top of spindly posts cast sparkles into the glittering canals. Shadowy buildings lined tiny alleys and even tinier waterways.

Under my gold silk, long-sleeved Alexander McQueen gown I wore a wet suit. Under the red and gold brocade blanket in the gondola was a scuba tank.

We turned a corner, gliding gently around a building, and found ourselves in a tiny side canal, out of sight. Jack kept silent watch while I slipped off the dress, strapped on the scuba tank, and prepared to go in the water. We knew where the Lionheart was being kept in the palazzo. There was only one secure vault in the place, and that had to be where they were keeping it. It had a large amount of steel, and electronic signatures of a laser grid inside the vault.

I was going after the Lionheart Ring, while Ethan and Jack were going to rescue Felix.

When we'd been hammering out the plan, I had fought them over that part. "I have to go and get him," I'd protested. "He was my responsibility in Yorkshire."

"Cat, you are a jewel thief," Jack had said. "Not a rescue specialist, not an operative. Do what you do best. We need both parts of the plan to come together, right? We need to retrieve both Felix and the ring for this to be a success."

"From what we can see," Esmerelda had said, "there's much more security guarding Felix than the ring. It's a two-man job, Cat. I understand your impulse—but it will really work better this way."

Esmerelda's role in this op was simple: she would function as the lookout, for everyone, from her vantage point of a neighboring palazzo with a pair of computers and surveillance equipment.

"Why are you helping us take the ring, anyway, Esmerelda? I thought you didn't care about ownership," I'd asked her.

She'd smiled. "No, the DOA doesn't care. I care very much." It didn't surprise me. She was a woman with a strong sense of right and wrong. It was why she'd come to my rescue in Paris, why she'd put herself at risk to help me in a moment of great need.

I'd looked down at the plan, all our surveillance data. They were right. There was far more security and personnel attached to Felix. The ring theft was a solo job. If things went south with the rescue, Ethan and Jack would have to take out a lot of people to get to Felix. Something they would be much better equipped to do than me.

"I guess they don't trust him," Ethan had said. "They think he'll try to escape. They're not worried about the ring doing the same."

Both Ethan and I—the professional thieves in the room—had scoffed at that. It was typical naïveté—throw up some technology to protect it, and assume it would be fine. It was said that Caliga had lost the finer points of burglary. Here was more evidence of the truth in that. Sure, they could storm into a lab, shooting whoever stood in their way and retrieve something valuable. But as for understanding the thief's art? They didn't seem to put much stock in that.

I finally consented to the plan, because in the end, I knew if anyone could pull it off it was Jack and Ethan. Not that they wouldn't be at each other's throats the whole time. They were like chalk and cheese. Ethan, the crook, never took anything seriously; Jack, the lawman, took everything seriously. Though I had to admit, those lines were blurring lately. I hoped they would be able to put their differences aside for a couple of hours.

I dropped into the chilly water of the canal, the surface quickly swallowing me up, and then calmly descended toward the underwater hatch beneath Caliga's palazzo. At least I hoped it was there. It had been an ancient hatch, faintly scratched out within the old blueprints.

Bubbles fizzed upward like champagne, and spears of silvery moonlight shimmered through the indigo water around me. I made my way through the wood piles the city was built on, using an underwater GPS for navigation. Soon, I was directly underneath the palazzo. I turned on a high-power flashlight.

This palazzo had once belonged to the Venetian Mafia, and a secret underwater entrance would have no doubt come in handy for their smuggling enterprises. Or body disposal.

The hatch had been cemented shut long ago, however. I would need to drill through it with a plasma cutter to gain entry.

I cut the hole in the floor and pushed the door up, swinging it open on ancient hinges. I pulled myself up and into the antechamber. It was a large, empty room, dark and damp.

I removed my oxygen tank and left it by the hatch.

Creeping across the stone-walled room, at last I stood in front of the safe. I took a deep breath and started to crack into it, knowing the Lionheart Ring was just on the other side. I briefly wondered what else they might have stashed in this safe. The Fabergé egg? I couldn't think about it, I had to focus on safecracking. I wanted to be quick about it and get out of there in case things got ugly upstairs with the rescue effort.

I focused my vision to a pinpoint, blocking out the sounds of water dripping, shutting out all thoughts other than this safe. Three of the four tumblers gave way to my coaxing. I started on the fourth and final one, not letting myself get too excited.

A soft sound scuffed on the floor behind me. I froze, hand on the lock.

"Hello, Cat. I knew you'd be here sooner or later," a woman said calmly. Brooke Sinclair.

One word stuck out in that sentence: *here.*

Slowly, I turned toward her. "Brooke. I suppose you're here for the Lionheart, too?"

Her mouth twitched. "It's worse than that, actually. I work for Caliga now."

Chapter Twenty-Nine

Ethan nimbly climbed across clay roof tiles, the luminous Venetian waters far below.

"I'm on the roof," he whispered into his earpiece. "You in position, Barlow?"

Jack's voice rumbled in Ethan's ear. "Almost there."

Ethan looked down. The faint outline of Jack's gondola had reached the water's edge of the small *campo*. Ethan jumped down to the third-floor loggia—a columned, partially enclosed balcony, just below the roof. It was furnished with chaise lounges and a small mosaic table, potted ferns and climbing vines.

"Okay, I'm lowering the rope," Ethan said. The climbing rope dropped silently down and unfurled at Jack's feet.

Without wasting a second, Jack grabbed it and began to climb. "If I hear one crack about Rapunzel . . ."

"You said it, not me," Ethan replied. He could hear, through his earpiece, the efforts of Jack's climb. He was doing a good job being silent, only making an occasional grunt.

It irked Ethan to be working with Jack, but at the same time he had confidence in the man. Jack was competent—strong, fast, intelligent. Of course, even thinking those things annoyed Ethan.

Jack climbed over the edge and gave Ethan the food he had carried up in a backpack. Ethan spread it all out on a tray.

"You ready?" Ethan asked.

"You bet."

Jack nodded to Ethan, then pulled his ski mask down over his face. He continued climbing from there, up to the roof and over, in the direction of the room where Felix was being held, on the top floor.

Ethan wore a different kind of disguise; his features were covered by a fake mustache, a bushy brown wig, and horn-rimmed glasses.

They knew Felix's location because late last night, Gladys had been able to hack into and control a surveillance satellite. Infrared showed the one figure that wasn't moving throughout the house like the others. A figure that must have been tied down.

They also knew two guards were stationed outside the room. It was the guards Ethan would be dealing with tonight.

Ethan crept in through the main corridor and climbed one flight of stairs, carrying the food-laden tray. Applying his persona like a stage actor, he strolled toward the guards, who were playing poker. They weren't in uniform but wore jeans and T-shirts that clearly showed why they had been hired for the job—muscle power.

The guards immediately looked up as Ethan came into view. The larger one had icy blue eyes. Unusual for an Italian. "Who are you?" the larger one asked—in English. *Good*, Ethan thought, *they're not local.* That would help.

Ethan put on a heavy Italian accent. "I am with Italian branch of Caliga. They let me in downstairs."

Their suspicion immediately fell away at the sight of the bread and cheese and cured meats. Ethan put the tray down on the table in front of them.

As the guards began to eat, Ethan scanned for CCTV. There was only one camera. He would need to take that one down.

While the guards chewed and laughed noisily, Ethan surreptitiously folded a pellet gun underneath his arm and shot at the CCTV camera. Ethan coughed at the moment the lead pellet went *ping*, smashing the glass. The guards didn't notice, digging into the food as they were.

He tried not to smile. His next task was to get the keys. Then he would have to get out, before the guards started to go down from the tranquilizer in the food. The inherent problem with knocking out two guards was that one would go down first. The one with the faster metabolism, the smaller one, whatever. But it was impossible for them to both go out simultaneously.

Ethan spotted the keys resting on the belt of the smaller guard, the less alert-looking one. Ethan reached forward to pour coffee for the man, and flubbed it, dribbling coffee on the man's shirt.

"Oh, *merda*, I am sorry—" Ethan dabbed at the guard's shirt with a napkin. That was the moment he lifted the keys.

The guard looked pissed about the coffee, but there was no flicker of anything else. He hadn't detected the lift. Ethan looked at his watch. He knew Jack would be in position at the window right outside Felix's room, would be breaking in any second. Ethan would let him know once the guards had been neutralized. Only a minute more—

The smaller guard began to sway. The larger guard gave him an odd look. "What's wrong with you?"

And then, the larger guard, as predicted, looked at Ethan with suspicion. "Did you put something in this?" he said through his teeth. "Who are you?" The man stood, narrowed his eyes, and put a hand on his gun holster.

Ethan needed to stall. He had to delay the inevitable physical confrontation as long as possible. "What are you talking about?"

The first guard slumped forward, face-first onto the table. The larger guard looked at him at first with surprise, then with rage before lunging toward Ethan. Ethan backed up. He held his hands up, placating the approaching guard. "It wasn't me. I just brought the tray they gave me. I have no idea what's going on." Shit, it was taking an awfully long time for the tranq to take effect on this one.

A second later, someone was thundering up the stairs. There was no time for Ethan to do anything other than turn, as the newcomer appeared on the landing: *Sean Reilly.* The son of a bitch thief who'd taken the Lionheart and Felix.

Ethan's heart dropped into his stomach. Reilly would see the truth in Ethan's disguise in a second. Not to mention the unconscious guard slumped on the table. The standing guard grabbed his weapon and pointed it at Ethan. "Who are you?" he repeated.

Ethan had no choice but to raise his hands while the guard searched him and removed the gun Ethan had tucked in his waistband.

Reilly's eyes flicked around the scene, absorbing everything. "Get the keys," he hissed. "Somebody must be in there, extracting the prisoner."

Ethan clenched his teeth, thinking fast. Reilly was always two steps ahead. It was what made him a notable adversary.

The guard reached for the keys that were supposed to be hanging on the other man's belt. He then looked at Ethan with cold murder in his eyes, his gun pointed at Ethan's head. "Keys. *Now.*"

Through his earpiece, Jack had heard Ethan making small talk with the guards. He climbed silently through the window, hoping Ethan's charm would give Jack a few minutes to get Felix out of there. Now it seemed like things had hit a snag. A major snag. He needed to move fast.

The room consisted of crumbling, bare plaster walls and scoured hardwood parquet floors, and it smelled of sweat, salt, and mildew. In the center was Felix, handcuffed to a chair. His face bore bruises, and there was dried blood around his nose. His head flopped to the side but his chest rose and fell.

Jack's throat constricted at the sight of Felix, chained and beaten. Had he been drugged? How was it possible Jack hadn't even known of his own half brother's existence until a few days ago?

He approached Felix. There was a chance he was only sleeping, in which case he could wake at any second and holler. When Jack was close enough he pushed his ski mask off his own face and crouched right in front of Felix. He covered the man's mouth.

Felix immediately gave a muffled shout through Jack's hand, and his eyes popped open—instant recognition flooded through Jack. *His father's eyes.* It almost threw him off his game entirely.

"It's okay," Jack hissed. "I'm with Cat and I'm getting you out of here. Be quiet."

Felix nodded and Jack released his mouth. Jack untied the ropes that bound Felix's feet and arms. His wrists remained linked with handcuffs. Jack scanned the room for a ring of keys left somewhere, but he saw nothing. He'd have to pick the lock. As he worked, Felix watched him carefully, eyes wide. "I can't believe you're here," Felix said in a low voice.

Jack looked up. There was something in Felix's tone. "You know who I am," Jack said. It was more of a statement than a question. Felix nodded.

Jack got the handcuffs loose and they dashed for the window, just as shouting came from the corridor and hammering reverberated on the door. Jack couldn't quite make out what was being said, but it didn't matter. They had to get out now.

* * *

Ethan dove away, ready to feel a bullet smash through him. But there was no shot, no sound. The next sound was the guard hitting the floor, unconscious. At last, the tranq had taken effect.

Ethan used that as his window of opportunity to get away. He turned and sprinted up the staircase, as Reilly shouted into his walkie-talkie: "There's an intruder. The prisoner is making a getaway attempt . . ."

A few seconds later, shots rang out as Reilly fired after him.

Ethan flew up the staircase. At the top, a window was open, its shutters flung wide due to the summer heat. He climbed through it in a heartbeat, hearing Reilly thundering up the staircase after him.

Ethan swung himself outside, scaled a short distance upward, and hauled his body onto the roof. If he were lucky, Reilly wouldn't have seen him slip out this way.

"Barlow—do you have Felix? Is he secure?" Ethan whispered.

"Yes, we're out the window. Heading toward the boat. You?"

"Got a little trouble. But I'm going to make my way to the extraction point. It may take me a few extra minutes, so you two go ahead, get Felix out of here."

Ethan deftly leapt from roof to roof, feet searching for steadiness on the clay tiles. He moved as quickly as possible, moonlight lighting his way, heart pounding, eager to get as much distance as possible from Reilly. He focused on his breathing. Almost there.

A shot zinged by his head, barely missing him. He dropped low and glanced over his shoulder. Reilly was closing in on him.

Chapter Thirty

I stared at Brooke in disbelief, trapped in the vault room. How could she? Caliga was the *enemy.*

"Why, Brooke?"

She shrugged. "They are a different organization than when Sandor was in charge. They've really cleaned house, Cat. They're not so bad—"

"Stop. I don't want to hear it. You sound like you've been brainwashed."

She smiled. "I'm not surprised you feel that way."

I flicked a glance behind her. I needed to find a way out of here. "Are you really telling me the reason you're working for Caliga is because they're 'not so bad'?"

"You're right. The most important reason? I like to be on the winning team."

My mouth curled in distaste. "Even if it means that people get hurt?"

"Cat, we operate in the criminal underground. Sometimes people are going to get hurt." A hint of disgust flickered across her face. "You're a criminal, too. You're delusional if you think you can function in this world and still have lily white hands. You can't have your cake and eat it, too."

I clenched and opened my fingers. I didn't like how much sense that made.

I needed to stall so I could figure out how far she would go to stop me. "Why does Caliga want this ring so badly?"

"You know I can't tell you that. Suffice it to say, however, we have big plans. It's really exciting, Cat. You would love it."

I narrowed my eyes. "Why is it only you here, anyway? Where's your whole 'winning team'?" I asked.

"They didn't think you would be down here already." Brooke shrugged. "They underestimated you. I was the only one who knew you'd be here."

In spite of myself, I felt a small glow of pride at that. And discomfort that she knew me so well.

"Anyway, here's the deal. You can't have this ring, Cat."

"Because you're going to stop me?"

"Yes." And then Brooke pulled a gun on me. "This is your chance to join us."

"You know I'm not going to do that."

She nodded, expecting my answer. I took stock of the distances. I could make it to the open hatch—it was just a few feet to my left. But I wouldn't have time to put on the oxygen tank and connect it to my breathing mask. Plus, if I made a move, there was a good chance Brooke would shoot me, despite our history.

"So what are you going to do? If you let them capture me, you know they'll probably kill me."

I could see a flicker of hesitation in Brooke's eyes. Maybe she hadn't thought this through. Maybe she didn't know what her next move should be.

But I knew what mine would be.

I sprinted toward the hatch and immediately dove straight into the open square, plunging into the icy water without my oxygen tank.

I could make it. I had to. I'd needed the tanks because I had to hover for a while, cutting through the floor. But all I had to do now was swim straight out to the surface.

I swam hard, legs kicking powerfully. I knew the adrenaline blast from my escape would only last so long, and I had farther to swim. I prayed I wouldn't experience a dizzy spell or get disoriented before reaching the surface. My legs tired and my lungs felt like they were going to implode. I tried to keep calm, to preserve energy and oxygen. At last my head broke the water's surface and I gasped for air. I had made it.

But there was a big problem.

The alarms were clanging in Caliga's palazzo. Lookouts carrying semiautomatics ran along the upper edges of the building, scanning the canal. I floated in the water, like a bobbing cork for target practice. I was about to take another breath and duck down under the water's surface when, out of nowhere, a speedboat appeared. It roared up beside me. *Shit.* I was caught.

But then I heard a voice I recognized. "Get in!" Atworthy—my professor—hollered. He tossed me a line and reached his hand down.

I scrambled onto the boat. The ruckus continued on the roof, but it seemed they weren't looking for me. Which meant they were probably looking for Jack, Ethan, and Felix.

In an instant Atworthy maneuvered the boat away, and worked on getting us lost down canals.

"How did you get here?" I shouted over the engine.

"Remember, I still have a lot of connections. There was chatter about a thief getting herself into some trouble with Caliga. I tried to get in touch with you on your cell, but I kept getting a message about the number being unavailable."

"And so you came to *Italy?*" I said in disbelief.

"I happened to be here for a conference on European Literature this week," he said. "I've known Venice was Caliga headquarters for quite some time," he said.

I heard his words, muffled as they were through my waterlogged ears. But it was too much to process. And I was too exhausted to question it.

I needed to know what was happening with Ethan and Jack. I pulled my earpiece out of my waterproof pack, and fitted it into my ear. "Ethan, Jack—can you hear me? Do you have Felix?" I barked.

There was no answer for a long time. I started to panic. And then, I got a crackly response. "Affirmative! I have him." It was Jack. "We're heading to the safe house. Jones is still on the rooftops, trying to shake a tail."

I bit my thumbnail, trying not to worry about Ethan. The relief over Felix caused me to slump back in the seat and exhale.

"Do you have the ring, Cat?" Jack asked.

I closed my eyes against the crush of defeat.

"No," I said, hating the way it sounded.

Jack was quiet a moment, then said, "Never mind. You'll get another shot."

We disconnected after agreeing to meet at the safe house.

Atworthy slowed now, gliding through the tangle of canals, switching back and forth. The engine came to a low rumble, to attract a minimum of attention. But we kept moving, which improved my comfort level.

"Where am I taking you?" Atworthy asked.

I gave him directions to the safe house. At the next crossing, he steered the boat in the new heading.

Chapter Thirty-One

Ethan wasn't surprised Reilly could leap the roof tiles as deftly as he could. Of course—the man was a burglar, first and foremost. Rooftops were his office, as they were for Ethan.

"Esmerelda, you there?" Ethan said into his earpiece. "I need an extraction." He changed direction, sliding halfway down the rooftop, to a lower building abutting the palazzo.

He imagined the blueprint of the palazzo, steering clear of the room where Felix was being held. He needed to draw Reilly away from Felix and Jack making their escape.

There was silence except for Ethan's breathing, loud in his ears, as he tried to put distance between himself and Reilly. Where the hell was Esmerelda?

Then came a crackle in his earpiece. "Get to the Grand Canal," Esmerelda's voice burst through the static. "Anywhere near the Scalzi Bridge. I can pick you up there."

Okay, he could do that. Meanwhile, he would continue heading in the opposite direction from Jack and Felix. If he could lead Reilly off for a while, that would help them get away.

He raced along the spine of a rooftop. He stayed light on his feet like a cat. One slip the wrong way and he'd go sliding down the tiles into the water.

He ran and leapt across a small canal, landing on a rooftop on the other side. He almost lost his balance; the tiles on this roof were crumbling and wobbly. He slid halfway down, then regained his footing. He swung down quickly onto a lower rooftop, sprinted along it for a few minutes, then climbed back to the upper level. He caught a glimpse of the shimmering water of the Grand Canal. He was getting close.

And then he saw Reilly, running at him from a different rooftop, at an angle designed to cut him off, to stop his route to the Grand Canal. The man was perfectly designed for this kind of activity: lean, aggressive, and agile.

Ethan jumped across another tiny canal, heart thundering, and pulled himself down into a loggia, out of view. In a few steps he lunged across the open-air loggia and out through the other side. Where to go now? He needed to get away from the last point where Reilly had seen him, then he could surface at another location.

If he went down to street level, would he be able to find his way to the Grand Canal? Venetian streets and canals were a rabbit warren—he couldn't be sure his sense of direction wouldn't fail him.

He ran along another low balcony ledge for several feet, then leapt across to a neighboring villa, staying low. After another block like this, Ethan peered over the roof's edge and hauled himself onto the rooftop.

Reilly was nowhere to be seen, and neither were any of the other men Ethan knew had been following along on street level. He then realized he wasn't hearing any gunshots, either. And—now that he thought about it—Reilly hadn't fired at him once since leaving the palazzo, even when he'd been within range.

Had Reilly changed tactics? Perhaps now he wanted to capture him, if he could. For information, or whatever else they could get out of him.

But the idea of being merely captured by Reilly and his team, and not killed, offered very little comfort. Ethan ran across the rooftop spines, sprinting now, trying to get as far away as possible. Then Reilly popped up in view, much too close.

Ethan made an abrupt turn and sprang to a neighboring roof. Reilly followed, made the leap. Ethan saw his face: pure, snarling hatred.

Reilly followed the same path as Ethan now, and he was gaining on him. The shouts from the other members of Caliga down below on the streets filtered up to Ethan's ears. They were fanning out, covering the area. Ethan's mouth went dry as he faced the fact that his window for escape was narrowing.

He raced up an exterior staircase and back onto the rooftop, Reilly uncomfortably close behind.

Two rooftops lay before him—a choice. One was perfect for parkour, new tiles in a tight pattern, but it was a less direct route to the Canal; the other roof's tiles were old and fragile-looking. But it was a direct path to the Grand Canal and the Scalzi Bridge. Ethan took a deep breath and vaulted onto the old rooftop. He struggled to keep his balance then started sprinting.

Reilly didn't hesitate. He leapt the divide.

Shit. Ethan would have to turn and face him. Fine. He was bigger and stronger than Reilly. He could take him down. As long as he was right in his guess that Reilly wouldn't actually shoot him. Ethan turned abruptly to face his pursuer.

Reilly's eyes went wide—he hadn't been expecting that. There was a slight wobble as he pulled up to a stop and readjusted his footing. The tile under Reilly's feet, instead of merely wobbling, cracked and gave way completely. Then all the tiles underneath Reilly collapsed like sliding cards, folding into a pack and taking Reilly with them. He slid straight down the rooftop and all the way into the cold canal below.

Ethan wasted no time. He turned and fled across the lone rooftop that stood in the way of the Grand Canal. When he reached the edge, he glanced down and saw Esmerelda in the powerboat, far below. She stood and signaled to him.

And then he spotted Reilly, again, dripping wet and climbing onto a lower balcony. Did the man *ever* give up? He pulled out a gun from his waistband and pointed it directly at Ethan.

Okay, maybe he'd changed his mind about the capturing-him-alive thing.

It was a long shot; Ethan wasn't sure he'd take it. And then, Reilly's glance moved toward the canal, locking on Esmerelda, who was waiting in the boat far below. He readjusted his aim.

A shot rang out. Esmerelda's head snapped to the side as blood and tissue spurted out of her skull. She slumped and her body flopped, lifelessly, over the side of the boat and into the water.

"No!" Ethan roared.

He ran straight down the rooftop toward the water and leaped into the air.

Chapter Thirty-Two

Jack and Felix slipped through the lanes and side streets of the Castello region of Venice, sticking to the shadows, moving quickly. As far as Jack could tell, nobody was pursuing them. He glanced with concern at Felix, breathing heavily beside him. They needed to get to the safe house.

He heard muffled sounds coming from far away—an urgent shout, perhaps—but nothing specific. His earpiece, unfortunately, had come loose and fallen out when they were making their escape through the window.

Now he had no idea what was going on with the others, and that worried him. One thing he did know, however: it was because of Ethan's actions that he and Felix had managed to get away.

Jack heard a gunshot. The sound ricocheted through the misty air from far away, closer to the Grand Canal. Jack closed his eyes as dread clamped around his gut—could that have been Cat? Or . . . Ethan? He didn't care for Ethan Jones, but that didn't mean he wanted him shot. Especially not after he'd taken additional risk to draw Caliga away from Jack and Felix.

Lanterns glimmered in the dark waters of the canals. The smell of fish and salt was less potent at night than in the full heat of the day. Jack took a sidelong glance at Felix's beaten face.

They had to keep moving. Jack couldn't do anything to help Ethan or Cat right now. The most important thing was getting Felix to safety. They made a sharp left turn and after a few more minutes were nearly at the safe house. Almost clear.

They entered a small alley. In the shadows of the tall buildings, Jack spun and faced Felix. His burning questions would not wait one minute longer. It was time for some answers.

"Why?" Jack demanded. "Why didn't anyone tell me I had a brother?"

Felix's eyes popped wide with shock. He said nothing. Then he looked away for a long time, and when he looked back, his eyes had grown dark. "You already had everything. Do you really think you deserved to have even more?"

"What the hell are you talking about?"

"Our father chose *you.* He chose to be with you. Me and my mother—we were tossed aside."

Jack opened his mouth in retort, then quickly closed it.

Felix spat into the gutter beside them. "Sure, he visited once in a while. Maybe you remember him being away from time to time."

Jack did remember that. All those times Jack's father, the great John Robie, had been away on "business." He'd later learned that business typically involved the execution of high-stakes burglaries. But . . . maybe that hadn't been the case every time.

"And sure, he taught me one or two cool things," Felix said. "Enough to pique my interest in his line of work. When I got old enough, I did my own detective work and figured out where his real home was. We were living in New Jersey at the time. It sure wasn't the South of France, I'll tell you that."

Jack's father had moved the family to Saint-Tropez on the French Riviera. That was where Jack had grown up, attending exclusive American schools for ex-pats.

Felix's voice cracked with emotion. "Do you have any idea how devastating it is for a kid to realize his father has a whole other life? And one that he prefers?"

Jack felt renewed disgust for his father. How could he have abandoned Felix? There were so many questions that would remain unanswered. Felix stood in front of him, with fists in tight balls at his sides. Jack's chest ached.

"By the time I figured out the truth, your mother had been dead for years," Felix said. "But our dad had remarried. I overheard a conversation with my mother once. He said you were going through a difficult stage. That you wouldn't be able to share him with anyone else. He needed to fix things with you, first, before bringing another kid into the family."

"But that never happened," Jack said in a low voice, looking down.

"No. It never did."

In a blinding flash, Jack remembered a fragment of conversation with his father, years ago. His father had said something about "growing" their family. Jack hadn't wanted to hear anything he had to say at that time. He was in such a dark place with his father at that point, having just learned about his secret profession. The betrayal of that had been fresh and raw, and Jack would have been damned before he let John Robie get something he seemed to want.

And then, another memory surged. John Robie's will being read as Jack sat in an expensive leather chair in the lawyer's office. The solicitor had mentioned a small amount going to somebody or other in New Jersey. Everything else had gone to Jack. He had assumed the person in the States was some kind of old friend, or shady colleague or something. He'd been so shaken up by the sudden death of his father, and the unwanted inheritance, he hadn't bothered to look into it any further.

Jack's gut twisted. It looked like John Robie hadn't been the only monster in his family. A selfish adolescent boy had hurt people, too. Because of his rage and angst, Jack had ensured Felix's rejection. It was, at least in part, his fault.

"Felix, I can't change any of that. I wish I could, but I can't." But maybe he could still make up for it, somehow. "You're getting home safe. I'm going to see to that."

Chapter Thirty-Three

I gripped the seat as Atworthy took the speedboat around a corner. We were almost at the Grand Canal. Once we got to the bigger waterway, the artery of the city, it would be much easier to move quickly and get away.

As we arrived at the mouth of the canal, however, something caught my eye: movement, on the rooftop of a building that overlooked the canal.

It was Ethan.

I jolted upright with alarm. What was going on? He was supposed to be far away from here.

I followed Ethan's line of sight. Down in the Grand Canal was a speedboat with Esmerelda at the wheel. She was looking up at him, waiting for him to . . . jump?

A shot rang out, shattering the peace. Esmerelda's head snapped back and blood spurted out of it. It was a direct hit. In slow motion I saw her body collapse and fall over the boat's edge into the water with a splash.

"NO!" I screamed, and heard an echo of the same sound coming from the rooftops. The air left my lungs. In the next instant Ethan leaped into the air, jumping off the rooftop. He hit the water and swam several quick strokes to the side of the boat. He was up on board in a second. My heart slammed against my rib cage, expecting him to be shot also, any moment. But there was no second shot. Where was the shooter?

A boat rounded the bend, coming fast. Caliga. It was like staring at a terrifying movie. Ethan was scanning the water, frantically searching for Esmerelda's body.

"Ethan, just go," I hissed into my earpiece. "There's nothing you can do."

There was no response. But I knew Esmerelda was dead. She had been shot in the head, an unsurvivable hit.

At last Ethan grasped the steering wheel and the boat roared forward. He sped off, away from Caliga and away from us.

I spotted a familiar figure standing beside a motorcycle on the bridge Ethan sped underneath. Raven hair flapped in the breeze coming off the canal.

Brooke had seen everything. She must have grabbed that motorcycle and raced straight here from Caliga's palazzo. She stepped forward, and the lanterns on the bridge illuminated her face. Her expression was one of unmistakable horror.

"We have to get out of here, Catherine," Atworthy said. I nodded, wordlessly. He pushed the throttle forward and we moved swiftly away. He quickly got us lost in the canals.

Once I found my voice, I gave him directions to our safe house. As we made our way, the scene of Esmerelda getting shot replayed in my mind, like a grisly loop.

I couldn't help thinking about my mother.

"It was my fault," I mumbled. "Esmerelda was helping us—helping me." I turned away, hot tears burning my eyes. "How many more people are going to get hurt because of me?"

Atworthy glanced over his shoulder at me. He hesitated a moment before speaking. "Esmerelda knew what she was doing. You didn't force her into anything. She was here in Venice because she wanted to help. Plus, it was part of her job."

I said nothing, staring behind us at the rippling wake from our boat. Within minutes, we arrived at the safe house.

On my instruction, Atworthy brought me to the secret entrance. It was a gate, a glassblower's studio, deserted and dark. The boat pulled up to the tiny *campo*. "It's this way," I said.

"I'm not coming in," he said. "I've stretched the bounds of my cover too much as it is. It would be difficult to explain if I didn't show up to give my lecture at the conference tomorrow."

I nodded numbly. I couldn't ask him to risk any more. And for Atworthy, simply being in Europe was dicey. He was in the witness protection program, having fled from France years ago and the people who wanted retribution for his desertion as an assassin.

A minute later he was off again, steering the boat through the darkened waters, heading back toward the Grand Canal.

I slipped through the gate and into our safe house.

Jack and Felix were inside. I felt a small ripple of relief when I saw Felix, rescued and safe. But it was not enough to overpower the tremendous feeling of despair over Esmerelda.

At the sight of me, Jack knew something horrible had happened. His eyes took me in, scanning over my body quickly, and he looked relieved to see I wasn't injured. He immediately grabbed me and held me in a very strong embrace. "It's over. You're safe," he said. And then, "What happened?"

I squeezed my eyes tight. He put a hand on my head, stroked my hair, but said nothing for a moment. Then he pulled back and looked in my eyes. "Tell me."

He watched me steadily, holding me up with that rock-solid gaze, as I described what had happened to Esmerelda. He remained quiet, but I saw sadness and fury cloud his eyes.

Ethan wasn't there yet. He'd be arriving any second. I hoped he would, anyway. I knew he would have to take a more circuitous route to shake off Caliga. I prayed he would be able to do that. The image of Esmerelda being shot, her body dropping into the deep, dark Venetian waters, flashed in my mind again.

But my despair soon turned to a cold, hard determination.

Caliga. They had to be stopped.

Chapter Thirty-Four

In the safe house, Jack forced himself to watch Cat's eyes steadily as she told him about Esmerelda's murder. He knew she needed him to be strong, and the sight of her so distraught, wet and shaking in her scuba suit, flared every protective urge he possessed.

And then her expression slowly changed—he could see it happening in her eyes, as she gazed back at him. He watched her anguish compress into something fierce.

"I need to contact Gladys," Cat said abruptly. "And Templeton. We need to plan our next move—"

"Cat," Jack interrupted gently. "Just breathe. It's been a hell of a night. Why don't you take a minute for yourself, okay? We'll figure everything out soon enough."

Cat hesitated and then nodded. She excused herself to the washroom. Jack watched her walk away and raked a hand through his hair.

A minute later, Ethan arrived. "Were you followed?" Jack demanded sharply.

Ethan shook his head. He was still damp from his swim in the canal, and his eyes looked haunted. There was no need to discuss Esmerelda's death. They all knew the situation by now.

Cat returned to the main room, and Ethan looked quickly at her, suddenly hopeful. "The ring?"

Jack flinched. Cat swallowed and shook her head, then told them the whole story of what had happened in the vault. Jack's eyebrows lifted when she got to the part about Brooke. "So Brooke Sinclair is fully Caliga now?"

Cat nodded. And then hesitated. "Well, I'm not sure about fully. After Esmerelda was shot—I saw her face. She was there, she'd raced to the Grand Canal, probably in pursuit of me . . . and she saw what happened to Esmerelda. And there was no mistaking her revulsion."

Everyone was silent a moment.

"I don't think she knows what she signed up for, joining them," Cat said.

"Well, perhaps she didn't," Jack said, "but she does now."

Ethan turned to Felix. "Who's in charge? Is it Reilly?"

Felix shook his head. "Reilly is high up, but he's not the man at the top."

"So who is?" Jack asked.

"I don't know," Felix admitted. "They spoke of him, but they didn't use his name. And I never saw him. I don't even know if he's here, in Venice."

Ethan pursed his mouth and exhaled hard. "So what now?" he asked. "Do we try again?"

Felix shook his head. "You won't be able to try in Venice again. They're taking the ring out of here tonight."

"To where?" Cat asked.

"Singapore," Felix said.

Cat's forehead furrowed. "Why Singapore? What's their plan? And how did you learn all this stuff, anyway?"

"They assumed I didn't speak Italian," Felix said, shrugging. "They were wrong."

"So what do we do now?" Cat asked, looking around at everyone.

"We have to go," Ethan said, with a determined set to his jaw. "Esmerelda would want us to continue."

Jack, who had been merely listening to all this, sat back in his chair and looked pointedly at Felix. "Well, *you* are not going anywhere."

"Like hell I'm not," Felix blustered.

Jack crossed his arms firmly. "I didn't fly across the globe to rescue you, only to have you put yourself in the exact same goddamn position."

The room went silent.

"Wait—what?" Cat said after a moment, looking between the two of them with astonishment. "You came to rescue . . . *him*?"

Ethan and Cat exchanged a bewildered glance.

Jack said nothing. Felix glared at him. "He's my brother," Felix said.

Cat's head spun to face her trainee. "He's *what?*"

Jack shrugged. "Half brother, technically."

"And I am going to Singapore," Felix said.

"Fine. Then I guess I'm going, too," Jack said. "We'll go to Singapore. Just to assess the situation. And then we'll walk away, if we have to. That's the deal. Take it or leave it."

At that point, Cat's phone beeped. She tore her eyes away from the standoff and glanced down.

"Hang on, Gladys," she said, answering the call. "We're sorting something out." She looked questioningly at everyone. "So, am I safe in saying . . . we need four tickets to Singapore?"

Jack and Felix continued glaring at each other.

"Wait," said Ethan. "Is there any chance we can stop them before they leave Venice? Before they even go to Singapore?" He looked to Felix for an answer.

"Maybe. If we act fast—"

"It's going to have to be really fast," Cat interrupted. "You might want to look at this." Cat turned the screen to face everyone and it flickered to a real-time CCTV shot of a helicopter landing on the *campo* outside Caliga's palazzo. Everyone watched as the Caliga team loaded into the chopper. There was little doubt they were decamping right then and there. But Jack noticed Brooke was not among them.

"There's no way we can catch them," Cat said, her voice tense. Jack knew she was frustrated. She was never good at hiding that.

"They must be taking the helicopter to the airport," Ethan said.

Jack nodded. It would be Marco Polo Airport, on the mainland, about four miles north.

"So, Gladys, can you get us four tickets on the next flight to Singapore?" Cat asked.

"Not a problem," she chirped. The sound of computer keys clicking came over the line. "It's not a frequent flight path, though. There might be a delay of a day or two . . ."

Jack ran his tongue along his teeth as he struggled with the idea that had occurred to him. "Belay that," he said suddenly. "It's fine, we don't need the tickets. We'll take my ride." Jack had traveled to Venice on his private jet, and it was still waiting for him at the airport.

He hazarded a glance at Cat. She was grinning.

"Gladys, can you follow them, and find out where they're going?" Ethan asked.

"Of course, dear. Once they land, I'll be able to monitor their movements."

Cat sat back and chewed her thumbnail. "I still have a lot of questions," she said. "There's so much we don't know. We don't even really know what Caliga has planned, and why they want the Lionheart Ring."

"Actually, we do," Felix said.

All eyes shifted to him.

"The Lionheart was made with the Gold."

Chapter Thirty-Five

Jack's private jet, en route to Singapore

Despite Jack's jet being a fully stocked, luxuriously appointed, five-star hotel on wings, I couldn't sleep a wink. My mind swirled and churned like a whirlpool, processing the fact that the Lionheart Ring had been fashioned with the long-lost Gold of the Gifts of the Magi. I had known the Lionheart was an extraordinary piece of jewelry; I hadn't realized *how* extraordinary.

The story of the Gifts of the Magi was becoming clearer now. In the course of history, the three Gifts had been broken up—the Gold taken and crafted into the Lionheart Ring in the twelfth century, the Frankincense and Myrrh locked inside a Fabergé egg several centuries later.

We had found the long-lost Fabergé last autumn, after generations of searching . . . only to have it spirited away by Caliga. And just as we'd learned the secret location of the Gold, Caliga—once again—had beaten us to it.

I shifted in the leather seat I was stretched out on while jazz music tinkled in the background. In spite of the physical comfort, I couldn't clear my head. The stakes of this job were so much higher now, and more people were getting involved. And more than that—people were sacrificing their very lives for the cause. A hard lump formed in my throat thinking about Esmerelda.

I couldn't quit, though. If for no other reason, I had to keep going for her. She had believed in this mission. I would see it through, for Esmerelda.

Gladys popped up on a video call. I sat up straight at the sound of the video feed coming through, as did Jack. He moved over to sit beside me so we could both hear what Gladys had to say.

I glanced behind me to where Felix and Ethan were still sleeping. I thought about waking them up, but they looked peaceful and relaxed. And, as a group, we needed to get as much rest as we could. Jack and I could get the details and relay it to them later.

"Okay, so tell us, Gladys. What have you learned?"

I glanced at Jack, wondering what he was thinking. On our way to the airstrip, Jack had made a call. All he'd said was, "If the Lionheart is actually made of the Gold, the gold from the Gifts . . . I know somebody who would be very interested in hearing about that." I asked him if it was Wesley he'd called, but he'd refused to tell me.

As we sat side by side, I realized it was the closest I'd been to Jack in ages. I could tell by his rumpled appearance that he'd tried to sleep, too, but had obviously been unsuccessful, as well. It was a look I was familiar with. How many times had I woken up next to Jack, with him looking exactly that way?

"There's an Australian businessman in Singapore," Gladys was saying on the video screen. "A rather powerful fellow, name of Chips Walker, he retired in Singapore because it's a marvelous tax haven. He happens to be a billionaire, and he's involved with Caliga. In fact, he appears to be funding their plan."

"What's their plan?"

"It's hard to say. But I must tell you, it feels like something big. Eastern power appears to be getting involved, somehow. Chips Walker has a lot of contacts in North Korea, and China, and they seem to be positioning themselves for something."

I frowned, considering that. Gladys kept speaking. "I did hack into an e-mail from Walker. He was talking about the power of the Lionheart. A power that straddles East and West. Because of the fact that it belonged to a Western king, but was given to him by an Eastern sultan, Saladin."

Plus, I thought, the fact that it had been fashioned from the Gold that was part of the original Gifts of the Magi—a gift from Eastern kings.

Gladys was right. This *did* feel big. But what did it all mean?

She signed off then, saying she was going to keep digging and would tell us more once she learned it. Also, that she needed to attend to her pineapple upside-down cake or it would burn.

I glanced at Jack. He was deep in thought. My eyes traced his face. He was starting to get some scruff; he hadn't shaved in a couple of days. It suited him. In fact, even rumpled and scruffy, he looked amazing. He was wearing a T-shirt and jeans and he smelled great—like soap and fresh pine needles.

I cleared my throat and straightened my cardigan, then got up to use the restroom. I needed to stop this. In the tiny restroom I looked at myself sternly in the mirror. *Do* not *get pulled in, Cat. Do not fall for him again. Jack is not yours, and he never will be.*

I walked out of the washroom, still completely lost in thought, not paying attention, and walked right into Jack, who was standing right outside the door.

He put out an arm to steady me. I looked up at him in a daze. "Whoa there," he said. "Somebody need a coffee?"

I smiled. "Yeah. Definitely. It's been a tiring couple of days."

The space outside the restroom was tiny. Standing so close to Jack suddenly, being held by him, touched, feeling his warmth, smelling his skin—it made me feel even more light-headed than I had before. His touch was so familiar. It brought back, in an instant, all the memories of being physical with him—in bed, in the shower, on the kitchen counter . . . my face flushed, burning—where had *that* memory come from?

I cleared my throat again and broke away from Jack, quickly returning to my seat. Within minutes, everyone else had woken up. Once the flight attendant had brought fresh coffee and breakfast, and we had updated Ethan and Felix about Caliga and Chips Walker, we got to business. We needed a plan.

"Okay, so Singapore is tiny, as far as countries go," Ethan said, digging in to the omelet in front of him. "But I think we need a few more specifics on location." He looked to the video screen, where Gladys had popped up again, in a real-time feed.

"There's only one place they could be taking it," Gladys said. "It's Walker's most secure location. Here, I'll show you."

A picture flashed on the screen. It was a super-modern high-rise, one of these architectural marvels with three towers and an enormous platform stretching between all three, like a space age Stonehenge.

"The Marina Bay Sands," Gladys was saying. "One of the most iconic buildings on Singapore's waterfront, a luxury resort and casino. It also has the honor of being the world's most expensive building. The towers are fifty-five stories high, and the platform on the top is called the SkyPark. It contains gardens and restaurants and an enormous vanishing-edge pool."

The idea of swimming and viewing the skyline two hundred meters above the city sent shivers down my spine. It would be incredible. Two months ago, that height would have seen me panicking. I was thankful I'd gotten over that brief spell of fear.

"Walker has more than one high-tech vault contained within the complex. The Lionheart Ring will be inside one of them. Here are the possibilities." Gladys went on to produce files and schematics and blueprints of the Marina Bay Sands. For the next hour, over several rounds of coffee, we sketched out a plan for entry.

Ethan was grimacing at the blueprint in front of him. "What about the getaway?" he said. "This place is a fortress. Getting out is going to be even harder than getting in." He was right. Every good thief always needs several ways of getting out of a building, should things go sour.

Jack nodded. "We'll need a few solid extraction plans. Can't always count on ex-professors turning up in speedboats, can we?" He glanced at me with a crooked smile. My heart thumped.

"Or being able to hand a pink wig off to an unsuspecting decoy," Felix said, looking at me with a grin.

I smiled back, knowing he was talking about my recent Beverly Hills heist. The others looked confused. "Inside joke," I said to them. "A little thing about my last job."

We turned our attention to devising a few breakout plans. But as we worked, I felt a growing discomfort deep in my stomach. There was something about what Felix had said that didn't sit right with me.

When Felix got up to use the restroom, I watched him go, then stared out the window, frowning. My insides flip-flopped. I didn't typically get squeamish on airplanes, but at that moment I was very uncomfortable. And then I realized why.

I had never told anyone about the pink wig.

It was a detail I'd neglected to mention to Templeton. After all the stuff that happened after that job, with my mother, I didn't do my usual debriefing. So the question was, if I never told anyone about the pink wig, how could Felix possibly know about it?

Unless he had been following me. Or, maybe, talking to someone else who'd been watching me. But why would he keep that a secret?

Panicky questions crowded into my brain. How did he know about the wig? Who was Felix, really? And the stickiest question of all: could he be working for the other side? Was there a chance Felix was actually Caliga?

Chapter Thirty-Six

Singapore

In the small executive airport where private charters came and went, there was a surprise waiting for us: Templeton, in the flesh, at the arrivals gate. He wore a linen suit and was sitting in the colonial airport underneath fans circling lazily overhead, surrounded by potted ferns and sipping tea from a china cup.

At the sight of him, my heart squeezed. He was a warm, welcome sight in a foreign land. After a round of hugs and handshakes, Templeton got down to business. "All right, darlings, I have a hotel reservation for us. Here, Catherine, give this to the driver." He handed me a card.

I looked at the small rectangle of heavy card stock. My eyebrows lifted. "Raffles? Not exactly low-key, is it, Templeton?"

He grinned like the cat who'd eaten a canary. "When you're a group of film producers, you don't need to be low-key."

"Ah."

"Besides, no self-respecting Englishman would stay anywhere else when in Singapore."

We gathered our bags and made our way to the shiny black Bentleys waiting outside. The tropical heat of Singapore hit me immediately, wrapping around me like a warm blanket.

My stomach tightened as I watched Felix. If he made even the slightest slip, I wanted to see it. I needed to know what was going on with him, what his secrets were, what his agenda was.

Our car pulled up to Raffles: precise rows of windows and carved pillars decorated the gleaming white building, topped by gracefully curved terra-cotta roof tiles. The hotel was surrounded by lush green gardens, perfectly manicured lawns, and softly rippling palms. The air, heavy with the fragrance of blossoming rhododendrons, was like thick honey, late-afternoon sunlight warming everything to a golden glow.

Once we were settled in our individual rooms, we gathered in the bar downstairs as the sun was setting. The iconic Raffles Hotel Long Bar was every inch gleaming mahogany and graceful rattan; bamboo ceiling fans gently stirred the air, creating a pleasant breeze.

"Have a Singapore Sling," said Ethan as I slid onto a bar stool beside him. "This is where it was invented. At this very bar."

I ordered, then sipped the cold, sweet cocktail. "Where's Felix?" I asked, looking around, attempting to maintain a casual tone, although I felt anything but. I glanced at Jack, who looked unconcerned.

"He said he had to go out," Jack said. "Wanted to get some supplies in town or something."

I nodded, keeping my face neutral. But the cocktail soured in my stomach.

"Oh, there he goes now," Ethan said, gazing out the windows that overlooked the front lawns. I turned my head quickly, squinting out at the twilit outdoors, to see Felix walking briskly away from the hotel. "Did you want to talk to him?" Ethan asked.

I glanced at Ethan, Jack, and Templeton, who were looking at me with curiosity. My eyes shifted to Jack, in particular. Felix was Jack's brother. Was there a chance Jack was in on it, whatever Felix was up to? Even if he wasn't, how would he feel about me making wild accusations about his only brother? The brother he'd flown across the globe to save?

No, I had absolutely nothing firm to say, no real reason to suspect Felix of anything. I needed to learn a little more first before I started slandering members of our team.

I shook my head. "Nope, it's fine. Just wondering." I sipped my frosty drink and stared ahead, silently counting to ten.

As the three of them discussed the cricket match playing on the television behind the bar, I excused myself to find the restroom. But in the lobby, instead of turning left to the restrooms, I turned right and slipped out the back entrance. I doubled around to the front in the direction Felix had gone, taking care to stay hidden from the Long Bar's windows.

I moved fast and spotted Felix in short order. He was headed on foot toward the city center, and I tailed him. I reached for my phone in case I needed to call for backup, and then . . . *shit.* I'd left my purse at the bar. No cell phone, no wallet.

I liberated a pair of oversized sunglasses from a sidewalk kiosk and slid them on my face, doing my best to stay incognito. Felix paused outside a small city park and pulled out a cell phone. I moved close while he was distracted with dialing and tucked in behind a large palm tree, close enough to overhear.

I missed the first part of the conversation as I positioned myself closer. But then I heard him say, "Yes, everything is fine. It's all a go."

Alarm bells reverberated through my head. *What* was all a go? And more importantly—*who* was he talking to?

I made sure I was completely out of sight as he listened intently on the line, and then I heard him say, "Well, I can make it to Station Q, if that helps." *Station Q?*

I chastised myself for leaving the hotel without my phone or any other way of communicating with the rest of my team. This was a huge development—I had to keep following. Felix turned off his phone and kept walking, farther away from the hotel. I chewed my lip, trying to decide if I should go back for reinforcements and tell them what I'd witnessed, or continue following him.

There wasn't really a choice. I had to find out exactly what Felix was up to. I would have to find a way to communicate with the team later.

I followed him as he made his way through a few downtown blocks and right into the train station. I tried to steal a glance at a map in the station, but I had to keep my eye on Felix. I couldn't let him get out of view. My fists tightened as I watched him step onto a train. One car farther down, I slipped on board, too. The train car smelled of wheel grease and vinyl upholstery. I found a seat and positioned myself so I could keep Felix in view through the window between the cars.

For three hours we traveled on that train. We were headed north, I assumed. It was the only direction to go in, really, as Singapore was at the bottom of the peninsula.

I glanced at the person seated beside me. "Do you have a phone?" I asked politely. I had to get in touch with the others. The elderly Asian woman looked at me warily. I mimed my request and tried to think of a few words she might understand. In the end it was futile, she either didn't have a phone or didn't understand. She glared at me with suspicion and moved away. There was nobody else seated anywhere near me, and I was loath to leave my post, lest Felix slip away to a different car or off the train altogether.

Fine. I was on my own here.

The scenery outside, at this point, had faded to black; we must have been going through Malaysian countryside. If this had been an ordinary train ride, I might have slept—the gentle rocking movement of trains always made me drowsy. There was far too much adrenaline in my system to allow for that now, and I had to watch Felix.

After a long stretch with nothing but blackness, the bright lights of a city began to flicker into view. I glanced out, and immediately spotted the recognizable twin Petronas Towers looming over the shimmering city of Kuala Lumpur.

We were in the capital of Malaysia. My eyes went wide with surprise. We'd come all this distance? I clenched my teeth. Okay, fine. I'd come this far. I would see this through. Wherever Felix was going, I was going.

I thought of Ethan, Jack, and Templeton, back in Singapore at Raffles Hotel. It had been about four hours since I'd disappeared from the bar. They must be concerned; they must know something was going on. I wished I'd been more strategic about this so they wouldn't worry. But I'd have to deal with that issue later.

The train deposited us in the heart of the downtown core. Being careful to avoid ticket checkers, I tailed Felix right off the train and into the streets of the city. It was past midnight, yet the sidewalks still bustled and buzzed with people. Tinny music played on a street corner among a collection of homeless people. The city smelled of gasoline and steamed rice and the heady fragrance of orchids.

After following Felix through the streets for several minutes, he tucked into an alley. He paused then, looking around to see if anyone was following him. But he clearly wasn't expecting a tail; it was a halfhearted effort. I watched as he disappeared through an unmarked steel door, beneath a lone blue lightbulb that hung crookedly above the doorway. The door, and the building it was within, had a shabby look. Litter and scraps had gathered against the wall as though they huddled there for safety.

I weighed my options. I had no idea who, or what, was through that door. My heart thumped thinking of all the potential dangers.

Then I pulled the door open and crept in after him.

There was a concrete staircase leading down into the darkness. I tiptoed down it as quickly as I could, my breathing loud in my ears. At the base was a damp, low-ceilinged corridor. I crept along and peeked my head into the first doorway I reached.

The room was lit up like Christmas. Electronic lights and displays blinked on computers and video screens. At least a dozen people bustled about, monitoring stations and moving between screens, pulling out files and consulting with one another. I stared, frozen a moment, trying to process what I was seeing.

It was some kind of underground operation. And it was organized.

The thing was, I didn't recognize any of it—it wasn't CIA, or FBI, or Interpol. It didn't have the look of Caliga. I didn't see any official uniforms or badges or seals, nothing to suggest this was local Asian police or Intelligence . . .

I had no clue what I was seeing, but one thing I knew for sure: I had to get out of there. I turned to slip away, and walked straight into a massive, immovable object: the hard chest of a security guard.

Chapter Thirty-Seven

"Well. What are you doing here?" the guard said with a toothy smile, speaking in perfect English.

My mouth went dry. Not good.

He stood me up from my crouched position and pushed me forward, into the room. "Look what I found," he announced, and everyone's heads turned our way.

I briefly considered fighting my way out of there. But it was too late. Too many armed men. Still, I had to try—

Felix stepped forward, staring at me with wide eyes. "Cat! How did you—" He noted my fighting posture, I'm sure, because he put his hands out in a calming gesture. "Relax," he said. "It's okay. You're safe. We're not the bad guys."

"Then who are you?" I hissed. I looked around me. "What is this?"

Felix glanced at someone beside him, a balding man he'd been speaking to when I'd been pushed in by the security guard. The man shrugged. "Go ahead. You have to tell her."

Felix worked his jaw. "It wasn't supposed to happen until after this job. If at all," he said to the man in a commanding tone that was very un-Felix-like.

The man shrugged. "Well, she's here now. You can't pretend she hasn't seen this. They'll understand."

"Who will understand?" I demanded.

Felix looked back at me, pinched the bridge of his nose, and sighed. "Okay. But what I'm about to tell you—it's highly classified. You cannot discuss it with anyone. Breaching that promise will mean your immediate cancellation as a candidate."

"Candidate? What the hell are you talking about, Felix?"

"Cat—just promise. The secrecy. Okay?"

"Fine. I won't tell anyone. Now, please, will you—"

"Come with me."

He pulled me by the arm and led me into a small inner office, away from the workings of the control room. He indicated a swiveling leather chair and took a seat behind a desk.

Once I was seated, he rubbed the side of his face and watched me carefully. "Why did you follow me?" he asked. "I didn't think you'd suspected anything."

I crossed my arms. "The pink wig, Felix. I didn't tell Templeton about that part of the job. I didn't tell anyone about that. The only way you could have known about it was if *you* had been following *me*."

Various emotions flashed across his face as he registered this. He finally said, "Oh shit." He was clearly annoyed at himself.

"So that's my story. What's *yours?*" I said, folding my arms, ready to hear. I was still guarded, but not quite as on edge. There was nothing about him that betrayed danger—at least not for now. My hackles were down. The fear, however, had been replaced by an industrial-grade curiosity. What on *earth* was going on here?

"I am actually a member of an organization called the Global Protection League. We call ourselves simply the League. I am their representative. And we have been watching you for a while."

I struggled to maintain a neutral expression. Felix went on to explain that the League was an independent international organization, with a mandate to protect world order and stop any threats to that.

"Like a military black ops?" I asked, trying to make sense of it all.

"Kind of, but not associated with a single nation."

"Like the UN?"

"Yes, only a little more—covert."

"Or a lot more covert," I said. I'd never heard of the League, and there was no way it was public knowledge. "What's all this?" I waved my hand, indicating the room we occupied and the control room we'd just left.

"It's Station Q—one of our nerve centers. There are many such places, outposts and safe houses like this one, all over the globe."

"And everybody who works here works for the League?"

"Well, yes. But there are various branches. Like—the Department of Antiquities. The DOA?"

I almost choked. He was talking about the covert organization Esmerelda had been working for. "They're part of the League?"

He gave me a wry look. "Didn't you wonder what they were a department *of?*"

I scowled. "So when were you planning to tell me? And—what do you mean, you've been watching me for a while?" I suddenly had a spasm of panic. "Are you investigating me? Am I considered one of the threats?"

"Not quite." He laughed a little, then his face became serious again. "No, the reason why we're monitoring you, Cat, why you are a person of interest to us, is because we want you to work for us."

This time I couldn't maintain my composure. My mouth dropped open.

"Well, I should say—we're *considering* you," Felix added quickly. "There's a little bit of dissension on the board. They're not sure if you're trustworthy enough, if your motives are honorable enough."

I pressed my lips together. Felix continued, "We've been monitoring your skills through this job. I wasn't supposed to reveal the truth to you quite this early. You're not supposed to know yet."

"And the fact that you were kidnapped by Caliga in Yorkshire? Was that all part of your plan?" I raised an eyebrow.

Here, he blushed through to his ears. "Er, no. That wasn't exactly part of the plan. I'm a recruiter. Not a field agent, per se."

He then went on to describe the various missions the League was involved in. All the ways they were monitoring, and neutralizing, global threats. Their work was extensive. And it was good.

"How do I know what you're telling me is the truth?" I asked.

"You need proof?"

"I'm afraid so." I'd been burned in the past by trusting too quickly. After Brooke I had promised myself I'd be more careful. "How do I know this isn't a mess of lies to cover something else up?"

"Fair enough," he said. He then showed me files. Documents of cases they'd been involved in. Videos of surveillance missions and past operations. There were corroborating documents, and files containing highly sensitive information. I spent a long time poring over everything he showed me. It all checked out. They were the real deal.

I said nothing for a moment, churning it all through. I looked down at my hands.

Felix kept speaking. "I've been in close communication with the board, with my supervisors. And they've said if you can pull off the Lionheart heist and secure the ring successfully—well, that's when they wanted me to reveal the truth to you and invite you to join us."

I looked up at him. A final test.

Felix leaned forward, closer to me. His voice lowered. "If you joined us, Cat, it would be an opportunity to use your skills for real good."

His words were unnecessary. I had already been having the exact same thought.

If I wanted it, this would be my way to a more honorable life. I could still keep doing what I was good at—but for the other side. I thought about my mother, the image of her lying in that hospital bed. Although I hadn't pulled the trigger, I might as well have. I was on that side. I was contributing to that culture. But this way—with Felix and the League—I actually had a shot at making the world a better place. I could be a real modern-day Robin Hood, not just a pretender.

And suddenly, I wanted it. I could taste it. I could see a way out. One I needed more than I cared to admit.

"It all hinges on this job, Cat. If you can do it, if you can pull it off, my case to admit you is going to be rock-solid. They will definitely extend an invitation. You rescued me and retrieved the target. They will want you for sure."

"And if I can't do it? If I fail?"

"Well . . ." He looked down at his feet, and the Felix I knew—the awkward and earnest kid—was back. "You have to understand, the stuff we deal with is incredibly sensitive. They have to be assured of getting the best people. They want the most competent, with minimal chances of failure. They've got a short list of candidates right now. If you fail, they'll go with someone else."

"Does Jack know?" I asked. "He's your brother, after all."

"No. Jack doesn't know. And he can't know. We have to keep very tight limits on who knows."

I paged through the files again, and came upon a document about Caliga. I stopped.

Felix glanced down to see the page I was frowning over. "Yes," he said. "We need to talk about Caliga."

"They have all three Gifts now," I said.

"They do," he said, voice grim. "The League is very concerned. The trouble isn't that there actually *is* power contained in the Gifts, but because now Caliga will consider themselves unstoppable, and will put into play whatever evil plans they have."

I nodded. "Is this one of the reasons stealing the Lionheart is my test?"

"Yes."

"Okay, but where is the Fabergé?" I asked.

"We don't know."

"So all I can do now is take the Lionheart Ring."

"Doing that will mess with their plans enough while we're still searching for the Fabergé."

I tugged on my earlobe, thinking it through. Would I be able to do it? I had never dreamed of having an opportunity like this. It wasn't going to be easy.

But it could be my chance to change . . . everything.

Chapter Thirty-Eight

Felix and I took the train back from Kuala Lumpur to Singapore. During the three-hour journey, through the wee hours of the night, we did very little talking. The only time we spoke was to create our cover story. We needed something credible to explain both our disappearances. We wouldn't be able to tell them the truth; we were both sworn to secrecy.

The rest of the time I was lost in thought, staring out the window into the inky blackness of the Malaysian countryside at night.

A band of chalky sky began to lighten the horizon as we grew closer to Singapore. Morning was on its way.

When we returned to Raffles, the others were breakfasting on eggs and toast points and mimosas on the sunny veranda of the hotel, lush lawns spread out before them. The exotic calls of tropical birds filled the air.

"There you are!" Templeton said, the minute I strolled onto the veranda. "Where did you disappear off to last night?" He then looked at me more intently and frowned. "Catherine, you look exhausted. Like you didn't sleep a wink."

I picked up a croissant from a basket on the table. "Do I?" I nibbled innocently on the croissant. I didn't want to resort to our cover story unless we had to.

Jack looked at me. "You do, in fact."

Templeton dipped a spoon into a soft-boiled egg and watched me thoughtfully. Ethan looked up from his plate of eggs and narrowed his eyes a little. And then he took a quick sideways glance at Jack, sizing him up.

Jack sipped his coffee and briefly peered at Ethan when he wasn't looking. The tension was thicker than the marmalade resting on the breakfast table.

It hit me, then, what they each must have thought. How this looked. Did Ethan suspect I'd been up all night with Jack? And Jack—did he think I had been up all night with Ethan?

I cringed. Okay, fine. I had no choice.

"All right, I'll tell you. But I don't want you to worry, okay?" I said. "When I went to the restroom last night I got another dizzy spell. I must have passed out as I left the restroom, because Felix found me when he came back through the hotel lobby to grab his wallet. He insisted on taking me to the hospital, and we went straight there. I didn't want to worry any of you so I made Felix promise not to say anything."

Felix, standing at my side, chimed in at this point. "It was a long wait but I stayed with her while they checked her out thoroughly. The doctor said everything was fine."

"Felix brought me back to the hotel safely," I said. "And here we are."

There was silence for a moment. "Well, I'm glad to hear nothing is wrong," Templeton said, looking concerned. "But are you going to be quite all right to continue today, Petal?"

"Of course," I said, waving a dismissive hand.

"It sounds like you need to rest," Jack said. "I don't think you're up to anything strenuous today, Cat."

"That's ridiculous," I said. "I told you I'm *fine*."

I was beginning to regret the cover story we'd concocted.

"You're anything but fine," Jack said.

"The problem is," Ethan began, "we really can't afford a day off."

Jack whipped his head to face Ethan. "You would risk her health for this job?"

"Montgomery is a pro," Ethan said between his teeth. "If she says she's fine, I say we trust her on that."

At that moment, I heard a familiar voice behind me. "Well, isn't *this* lovely?"

I turned. "Gladys!"

"That was quite a journey," she said, flopping into a chair and dropping her carry-on bag. A bellboy had followed her out, carrying her other luggage. "Shall I take the rest of your bags to your room, ma'am?" he asked.

"That would be wonderful, thank you."

I smiled; the interruption was highly welcome. And having Gladys here gave me a warm and cozy feeling—she always had that effect. Plus, having my hacker on site made me feel better when we were heading into a complicated job. And everything about this job was going to be complicated.

Jack eventually relented and stopped pushing for me to take a day off—he was outnumbered anyway. We got down to business.

Today, we were casing the Marina Bay Sands. We needed to lay the groundwork for the heist. And it was not going to be easy. We knew the Lionheart Ring was secured somewhere within the complex. Today we needed to find out exactly where.

Two hours later, I was walking through the lobby of the Marina Bay Sands. My first stop was in the shopping arcade, in a swimsuit store, to buy a bikini. I tried not to scowl as I paid for the tiny garment. I resented that this would be my uniform for this segment of the job.

When we had been devising this plan, we knew Chips Walker liked to linger by the SkyPark pool in the late-morning hours before lunch.

"So, Cat, you're also going to hang out by the pool," Ethan had said.

"Sure. I can pretend to be working at the poolside bar," I had suggested.

"Nope, that's not going to work," Jack had said. It wasn't a big enough staff, he explained. Other staff members would be suspicious, and as a new hire I'd have to actually show myself to be a good worker. I'd be too busy running drinks to watch Walker properly. I needed something with more freedom of movement.

"Fine. I can be a security guard."

"Sorry, darling," Templeton had said. "Singapore is rather old school. They don't hire women for that role."

"Montgomery, you're going to be the socialite in the bikini," Ethan said. He went on to explain that while I kept Walker distracted, Ethan would steal the man's phone, smuggle it to Gladys so she could download all his data, then slip it back to him unnoticed.

"The key is going to be keeping his interest," Jack said. "If you know what I mean."

"What?" I said, eyes wide. "No. I'm no good at that role. I can't do the femme fatale thing. I'll mess it up. Brooke is good at that kind of thing—not me."

"Yes, well, Brooke isn't here. And she isn't on our side, even if she were. So you are it, my dear," Templeton said.

I dug my nails into my palms. "Fine. But when we do the actual job, I want to do the good stuff." I scowled. "So can anyone tell me how I'm supposed to capture this guy's attention?"

"Montgomery, you won't have to do anything in particular to keep his interest. If you turn up in a bikini, you'll have him hooked," Ethan said. "Trust me."

I looked at him sharply, then immediately blushed. The others swiveled toward him, too, and Templeton raised an eyebrow. Ethan shrugged, showing no shame. "It's true," he said. My chest felt warm and bubbly.

After buying the bikini I headed to the elevator bank. The SkyPark pool and lounge area was only open to guests so I would need to finagle a key card somehow. I walked on to a crowded elevator, and sized up the most likely mark. He revealed himself almost immediately: a young man in his twenties, cocky, wearing a Hugo Boss suit, distracted and yammering on his cell phone. I assessed the level of fitness he possessed under that suit and frowned slightly; he was maybe a little too strong for my liking. He was possibly into martial arts, judging from the posture. But as he'd entered the elevator he'd bumped into someone, which showed his lack of physical awareness.

Then he pushed the button for floor seventeen and neglected to ask anyone else which floor they needed. Perfect. Totally oblivious of other people.

He would work. He was my best candidate.

I let the elevator ride up a few floors, then, at the next stop, I readied myself. I uttered a breathless "Oh wait—this is my floor!" at the last second, and jostled forward. I bumped into him, fairly hard, and knocked him forward a bit. I spun and clutched on to him to prevent him from falling into me completely, and as I did so I slipped a hand into his breast pocket and pulled out his room key.

"I'm so sorry," I mumbled, wearing my sunglasses, not letting him get a look at my face. And then strode straight out the elevator doors. His face showed zero expression of alarm.

Grinning, I tucked the key card into my purse. I now had full access to Marina Bay Sands resort.

I changed into the bikini in the restroom and arrived at the SkyPark poolside a few minutes later, walking out onto the sun-baked deck. This was the pool on the very top of the entire complex, on the platform that sat two hundred meters up in the sky, straddling all three towers.

I spotted Chips Walker immediately. I recognized him from the photograph: middle-aged, deeply tanned, yellowish-blond hair. Right after that, my eye landed on Ethan, over by the bar. He was disguised as a waiter at the poolside bar, wearing a black shirt and a long white apron.

I set my sights on my objective. I needed to distract Walker long enough to give Ethan a chance to swipe his phone. Then we'd need to slip his phone back to him—all without him realizing what we had done.

I considered my possible tactics. I quickly realized the best way to separate Walker from his phone was to get him into the water. My heart thumped as I quickly approached the pool. I wanted to get this done.

"Montgomery, slow down," Ethan said into my earpiece. "Be cool."

I slowed my walk to a casual sashay. From the corner of my eye, I saw Walker's head turn.

"You got him," Ethan said. "Now keep walking, keep his attention. Nice and slow, over to the bar."

I strolled to the bar to get a cocktail. Once I had a frosty Bellini in my hand, I strolled back to the lounge chairs by the poolside, right where Walker was sitting.

"Can I find you a lounge chair, miss?" Ethan said to me, holding a towel and a tray.

I flashed him a smile. "That would be lovely."

He had kept the lounge chair next to Walker folded and unoccupied. He now unfolded it and helped me settle in.

I was aware that on the other side of the palm tree, Walker was watching me. Now I had to start talking to him. And—most importantly—I needed to get him in the pool.

The talking thing proved to be no problem. He started chatting me up the second I sat down.

"That looks refreshing," he said.

I turned and looked at him through my overlarge sunglasses, over the rim of my drink. "It is. Bellinis are perfect for a sweltering day like this." I flipped my hair away from my neck, feeling utterly ridiculous.

He didn't seem to find anything I was doing ridiculous in any way. So I kept going, making a big deal over the heat, fanning myself with the magazine I'd brought. I felt self-conscious in the pitiful coverage offered by my black bikini.

Of course, in my next move, I knocked my glass over with the magazine. The drink went flying and Bellini spilled all over the place. "Oops!"

I could hear a snort of laughter from Ethan in my earpiece. *Damn.* Had I messed it up completely?

I flicked a glance in Walker's direction as another pool attendant bustled over to clean up the mess.

"It's okay, Montgomery," Ethan said. "He's not going to write you off completely because of that. He'll probably think it's cute. I would."

"Looks like I might have had one Bellini too many," I said, trying for a recovery. Walker laughed, clearly not put off. Ethan was right.

With that, I started to enjoy myself. I had Walker hooked. The power felt . . . exhilarating. And now, it was time to get into the pool. "Oh no, I'm all sticky now," I said in mock dismay, glancing down at my bare stomach, where I'd spilled the Bellini. I watched as Walker's eyes went to my skin. "I think I'll go in for a dip."

I slipped off the lounge chair and slid into the silken water.

I had to admit—it was an incredible experience. The infinity pool was two hundred meters aboveground, with the edge looking like it dropped off into midair, with the ultra-urban skyline of Singapore in the background.

I turned around to see Walker watching me closely. I felt my cheeks go warm and I tried not to squirm with discomfort.

"Nice blush, Montgomery. Perfectly timed," Ethan said.

"Why don't you come in?" I said to Walker. "The water is gorgeous."

Fortunately, he took the invitation. As he plunged into the water and moved toward me, I now had the small matter of keeping him away from me—but still in the water—long enough to give Ethan a chance to swipe the phone.

I could see Ethan walking toward us with a tray, ready to "tidy up." Partway there, he got called away by someone demanding more towels.

Damn.

Walker approached me in the water, moving in very close. "So where are you from, gorgeous? And—are you enjoying your stay in my hotel?"

I opened my eyes wide and let out a small gasp. "This is *your* hotel?" This was getting easier and easier. Nothing I said or did seemed to be absurd to this guy.

He smiled and waded even closer. "Maybe later I can show you some of the more exclusive parts of my hotel?"

I steeled myself to do whatever it took to keep him distracted. If I had to, I would make out with this guy, right here. There was too much at stake. But . . . I hoped it wouldn't come to that.

The quicker Ethan could get that phone and get out of here, the better. Nearby, a few kids jumped in the water and started splashing. The cool water drops from their splashing sizzled on my skin.

Through my peripheral vision I saw Ethan reach Walker's lounge chair, clearing glassware. I turned away and focused on Walker, who was boasting about various buildings he'd built.

Ethan straightened and walked briskly away. "Got it," he said, in my earpiece.

I breathed a sigh of relief. Walker had seen nothing. Ethan had been super-smooth about the lift.

Was it wrong of me to find that sexy?

I knew Ethan would now take the phone to Gladys, who was sequestered in one of the hotel rooms, and once she'd downloaded all his information, we'd have to find a way to return it.

One step at a time. What I needed to do now was hold Walker's attention just a little longer, while Gladys got the data we badly needed.

Chapter Thirty-Nine

Ethan had Walker's phone tucked in his jacket pocket. He moved quickly through the back hallways of the resort and down the service elevator, to the suite where Gladys and Templeton were eagerly awaiting him.

Cat had been amazing, he thought as he strode down a long corridor. Impressive. Professional. And . . . she had looked just as good in that bikini as he'd imagined.

"Here it is," he said, handing the phone to Gladys once Templeton had granted him entrance. The hotel suite was luxurious: sleek and modern furnishings, thick pile carpet, incredible view over the Singapore waterfront.

Templeton strode back to the other room where he was assisting Felix with his disguise—putting the finishing touches on his security guard uniform. In spite of Templeton's fussing, it was an easy disguise to pull off. There were hundreds of guards, nobody knew them all.

Felix's task was to go to the area where the Lionheart Ring was being held—once Gladys had figured out which one it was—and take photographs of the security features that protected it. They were keeping themselves busy with the uniform, but really, they were in a holding pattern, too.

Ethan waited, pacing, while Gladys hacked in and downloaded all the information she could get. "This should take me less than fifteen minutes," she said. Ethan checked his watch. It was everything he could do not to jump right out of his skin. He tried not to think about Cat, left alone in that pool with the ultra-sleazy Chips Walker. The sooner he could get back to her, the sooner she could make her getaway. But he knew they had to do the job properly.

Ethan paced over to the window. He squinted out, gazing over the skyline, and took a few deep breaths.

He thought back to the morning, when Cat had suddenly appeared at breakfast. That moment when he'd thought she'd spent the night with Jack . . . that had not been a good moment. He'd felt relieved about the hospital, and then immediately guilty about that. The fact she'd spent the night in an emergency department should not have made him feel better.

A tight feeling centered in Ethan's chest. This was exactly why he'd been reluctant to work with Cat again, to join her team. The idea of competing with Jack Barlow for her affections made him want to snarl. The easier thing to do would be to stop caring, stop even trying to compete.

But how could he stop himself from wanting to be near her? Ever since their ride on the Orient Express, he had been having difficulty thinking of anything else. He was drawn to her like a moth to a flame. Just as toxic, just as destructive.

He'd been trying to keep her at arm's length since then, attempting to maintain professional boundaries, but he wasn't sure how successful he'd been. Ethan needed to find a way to walk away. He hated wondering where Cat's heart belonged. Ever since he'd turned his life around, years ago, his impulse had always been to bail before his heart could be broken again. Always be the one to do the leaving and the rejecting. Impossible to get hurt that way.

Shit. I should have stayed in Kenya.

He glanced at his watch again. Gladys should be finishing any second.

"Oh dear," Gladys said, staring at her screen.

"What?"

"A small hitch, dear. Nothing dreadful. There's an extra security layer. It'll take me a few minutes to get through . . ."

Ethan squeezed his fists. More time for Cat to be in a highly vulnerable position. He took a deep breath. She would be fine; Cat could handle herself. And there was no real danger.

Right?

Chapter Forty

Jack stood in the heart of the security control room. He was disguised as an insurance underwriter, which meant the brownest, most ordinary suit on the planet, steel-rimmed glasses, and a plain briefcase full of files.

Jack was connected to the rest of the team through their earpieces. He knew Cat and Ethan had succeeded in grabbing Walker's cell phone, and that Gladys was, at that moment, downloading the billionaire's passwords and data. Everyone else was doing his or her part; now he needed to do his.

He stood before the chief of security and channeled his driest, most monotone voice. "We received a report that you've upgraded the system," Jack said to the security man. He pushed his glasses up higher on his nose. "In order to measure the risk exposure and recalculate the premiums, we need to know about the increased measures. I need to know about the security upgrades."

Jack waited, holding his breath, keeping his features smooth. He desperately needed this man to comply. The team needed this information—without it, they wouldn't know exactly where the Lionheart was being held, and they wouldn't have nearly enough detail on the security features that protected it. Gladys had attempted to obtain the information online, but the details about the upgrades hadn't been recorded in the system yet. Jack would need to get that intel in person.

The chief of security narrowed his eyes at Jack. "I haven't heard anything about this. I'm going to call your head office for verification."

"By all means," Jack said, keeping a level gaze and handing the man his business card with a phone number printed on it.

The security man dialed and put the phone to his ear. Once the call connected, Jack overheard a British voice coming through the receiver. "Eastern Shield Insurance, Albert Max speaking, how can I help you?"

Jack kept his breathing steady. He knew Gladys had intercepted and redirected the call; this was Templeton speaking.

The security chief exchanged a few short sentences of inquiry with Templeton and glanced over at Jack. The man listened, nodded, and finally hung up. "You check out. Okay, what do you need to know?"

A few minutes later, Jack was poring over paper files that contained details on the security systems. And though he wanted the details, he was also looking to confirm the exact location of the Lionheart. As he took photographs with the spy camera located in his tie clip, he experienced a thrill along the back of his neck. See, he could do the James Bond thing.

He immediately chastised himself for being so ridiculous. *Head in the game, Barlow.*

It quickly became obvious where the Lionheart was likely being held. There was one vault with much more security than the others. That had to be it.

"I have to make a quick phone call to the head office," Jack said to the security man, and stood. "And I'm going to get more coffee."

He moved to the corner of the room, by the coffee machine, and put his phone to his ear, pretending to make a call. "Okay, it's in the vault in the Singapura Wing, top floor of the middle tower. I think," he whispered, knowing the earpiece would pick up his words. He looked back at the chief of security, who was engrossed in a conversation with one of his managers.

"Right, Jack, got it. Singapura Wing," Gladys said.

"Felix, you got that?" Jack said. "Go there, get your photos, and get out." Jack knew Felix needed to go in person to the vault for on-the-ground assessment of the security measures.

Then Ethan's voice came on the line. "Barlow, are you sure that's the one?"

Jack exhaled through his nose. "Yes. I'm sure."

"Because you said 'I think' . . ."

He closed his eyes. Fine. He would try to get further confirmation. "Felix, just go. I'll try to confirm."

He poured a cup of stale coffee, then returned to the security chief.

"Right, they're wondering, in particular, about the upgrades to this"—he looked down at the files and ran his finger down the page, pretending to look for the name—"this vault. In the Singapura Wing. Can you tell me what you've got there right now?"

The security chief gave him an immovable stare. "Valuables."

Jack tried for a smile. "Obviously. But, for insurance purposes, we need to know the nature of those valuables. The replacement cost, for starters."

The security chief, at that moment, looked up toward the door. Someone new had entered the office. Jack's eyes flicked in the same direction, and his chest collapsed inward.

It was someone Jack recognized, and it was about the last person he wanted to see.

Hendrickx. *Interpol.*

Jack quickly pretended to drop his file, letting the pages fall so he could crouch down to the ground and stay hidden, collecting his papers. The security chief walked away, in Hendrickx's direction.

Jack kept his head down, but swiveled his eyes up, to see if Hendrickx had spotted him. He was speaking with one of the managers at a work station; there was no sign he'd seen Jack.

Jack's stomach flipped over. He had to get out of there. But he also needed to warn everybody else. He pretended to make another phone call, but really he was speaking into his earpiece, communicating with everyone. "Big problem," he said in a low voice. "Hendrickx is here. He just walked in."

"*What?*" Templeton said with alarm.

"Oh dear," said Gladys. "I'm finishing up. I have everything off Walker's phone now."

"I'll run the phone back up to the pool right now," Ethan said.

There was quiet on the line after that.

"Cat?" Jack said. There was nothing, only some faint crackling. "Cat, answer! You need to get out of there." They all knew Cat was still up at the pool, keeping Walker distracted.

Jack dared another glance over to Hendrickx, who was in heated conversation with the security chief. They were standing close enough that Jack could hear a few words. And what he heard was Hendrickx asking the chief of security for the current location of Chips Walker.

The security man shrugged. He called out to the room, in general, "Anyone know where Walker is?"

Shit. Hendrickx was looking for Walker? If he found him, he'd find Cat, too. And that would be bad.

A woman seated in front of a bank of security cameras said, "Yeah, I think I saw him up at the pool a little while ago." She squinted at the screens. "There he is—I can see him there now."

Hendrickx abruptly turned and stalked out, clearly on a mission. Jack's stomach dropped.

"Cat," he whispered into his earpiece. "Pick *up*. Do you copy? You have to get out of there. Hendrickx is on his way to you."

There was nothing but static.

Chapter Forty-One

Brilliant sunlight glanced off the pool's surface and into my eyes as I laughed at yet another of Walker's horrible jokes. I subtly waded two steps away from him—and his wandering hands. For the past fifteen minutes I'd been putting on an excellent show, flirting and keeping him very interested. It was a fine line I walked, between holding his attention . . . and encouraging him to sweep me straight up to his penthouse suite. At the same time, I was also trying to keep from being drowned by the kids who were playing right next to us.

Only a few minutes ago, one kid had taken a flying leap into the pool, cannonball-style. He'd splashed water all over me, including directly into my left ear, where my earpiece was inserted. I couldn't hear a thing through it. I hoped it would come back to life soon.

In the meantime, I needed to focus on keeping Walker from returning to his deck chair and retrieving his things. And subsequently discovering his cell phone was missing.

Last I'd heard Ethan and Gladys had almost finished downloading everything. It wouldn't be long now. At least that was what I was praying for. The way Walker was eyeing me hungrily, it was going to be difficult enough, even now, to discreetly slip away.

And then, things got a whole lot worse, because Hendrickx appeared.

I watched in horror as the tall, red-haired Interpol agent entered the pool area, scanning the crowd, looking for someone. Panic spasmed through my chest. I knew exactly who he was looking for. Me.

I lunged for my sunglasses, sitting on the edge of the pool, and pushed them on my face. It was a scanty disguise, but it was a start. I turned my face partially away.

Shit. How is he always so close?

I moved in the water so a palm tree was in the middle of the sight line between us. And then, I saw him lock on to a target and start moving. He was beelining for Walker. I breathed a small sigh of relief.

Hendrickx reached the edge of the pool where Walker floated. He looked directly at the man. "Sir, we need to talk."

I let my eyes flick around, searching. Where was Ethan? I needed to get away. But I needed to get that cell phone back in position even more. If Walker detected its absence, he'd be suspicious and change all his passwords and stored information. Everything we'd done today would have been wasted effort.

No, we had to get it back to him without either Walker or Hendrickx seeing it happen. But I was trapped in the pool, and Ethan was nowhere to be seen.

My earpiece crackled to life. "Cat—come in! . . . urgent!" I could make out Jack's voice. "Hendrickx . . . on his way . . . pool . . . looking for Walker . . ."

I bent my head down and spoke quietly. "I know. He's already here."

At that moment Ethan burst out of a service stairwell, looking out of breath and flushed—which, for him, meant he'd run hell for leather to get here. But he was too far away.

His eyes went immediately to Hendrickx. Concerned, but not surprised. He'd known. Which made sense. *His* earpiece hadn't been compromised by water.

Nothing had changed. We still needed to get Walker's phone smuggled back to him. This was going to take some fancy footwork.

While Walker was distracted, speaking with Hendrickx, I slipped out of the water. Hendrickx's gaze didn't turn in my direction; he was too focused on his urgent conversation with Walker. A curious urge overtook me. What were they discussing anyway?

I climbed nimbly from the pool and pulled on my large sunhat and a wrap. I withdrew a magazine from my bag and opened it, covering the rest of my face.

"Cat! . . . have to get out of there!" came the crackly directive from Jack.

"No. I need to hear what he's going to say," I said quietly. "I need to know how much of this op is compromised." I glanced at Ethan, who was hovering by the bar, watching me uncertainly. He was ready to bolt. He was ready to take me with him.

Walker climbed out of the pool, still deep in conversation with Hendrickx, and grabbed a towel. Mercifully, he seemed to have forgotten about me. In fact, both men were paying me absolutely zero attention. Walker sat back on his lounge chair and Hendrickx hovered nearby, still speaking.

Ethan grabbed a tray of drinks from the bar and walked toward me with it. I knew he must have had the cell phone. "I can't get close enough now," Ethan said in a low voice when he reached me, holding out the tray. I took two of the frosty cocktails.

My eyes, behind the sunglasses, flicked to Hendrickx and Walker. "It's okay—I can. Give it to me."

"We should just go."

"I can do it."

He stared into my eyes another moment, and I stared back at him over the rims of my sunglasses. He must have seen the look of determination in my gaze. Quick as silver, he slipped me the phone. I tucked it into the folds of my wrap. Ethan straightened and strode away.

A loud group of tourists moved away then, which allowed me to hear some of the conversation between Hendrickx and Walker.

"Fine. I will have some people look into it," Walker was saying.

Hendrickx scowled at this. "That's not a particularly satisfactory answer," he said. "We should really discuss this in private."

"No, I'm perfectly happy here."

Hendrickx's jaw flexed. "Very well. I am concerned about the contents of your vault."

"Concerned? In what way?"

"Concerned that they may include a stolen item."

"That's ridiculous."

Hendrickx paused, then spoke calmly but with authority. "I'm asking you to kindly allow me to inspect the vault."

"Do you have a warrant?"

Hendrickx hesitated, then produced a piece of paper. Walker inspected it. "This is an application for a warrant. Not an actual warrant."

Hendrickx's face flushed and my eyebrows raised momentarily. It was unlike Hendrickx to be so sloppy. He must have been truly desperate. I was also surprised at Walker's acumen, his resistance to being cowed by an aggressive Interpol agent. Perhaps Walker wasn't quite as boorish as he appeared. He wasn't an idiot. You didn't get to the position he did by being stupid. Cocky, maybe, but not stupid.

"Come back with a proper warrant and I will be happy to show you the contents of the vault," Walker said with an easy smile. Hendrickx had to know there would be no more discussion on the topic. He stalked away, casting not a glance in my direction.

Once he was gone, and well out of sight, I stood from my lounge chair and strolled back over to Walker, carrying the two cocktail glasses. "That didn't look like a fun chat," I said. "Here." I held out a chilled drink for him, flashing a warm smile. "You look like you could use this."

I held my breath. Was this going to be too much, too soon? He didn't really know me, after all. Was I being too pushy?

Walker looked deep in thought, considering Hendrickx's words, perhaps.

He turned to me, and my stomach flipped. But then, a small smile curled his lips. "That is exactly what I need." He took the glass.

"Everything all right?" I asked as he drank.

He nodded and crunched ice cubes. "Fine. I have something new to deal with. But I'll tackle it tomorrow. For now, I have much more interesting things to attend to . . ." He winked and clamped that predatory look on me again. I smiled and felt the phone under the fold of my wrap. I prayed I would have a window of opportunity soon.

There was a loud crash behind us. A tray of drinks had been dropped to the pool deck. Walker's head turned and in that instant I leaned down and slid the phone on the ground under his lounge chair.

"Oh, is this your phone?" I said, with a surprised, helpful tone. *Channel your inner Girl Scout, Cat.* "It was under the chair." I plucked the phone from the ground and held it up for him.

This was the moment of truth.

He looked at it, and looked at me. "Indeed, that *is* my phone," he said. And then he smiled. His tone told me everything as he said, "Why, thank you, gorgeous."

Not even a little bit suspicious.

I flashed him a coy expression and let him take the phone out of my hand, his fingers brushing mine as he did so.

Now I needed an exit strategy. I wasn't quite in the clear; it was all in the finish. I needed to get out of there without raising even a hair of suspicion. If he decided to get cautious and change his data, we'd be back to square one.

"Listen, I have an appointment at the spa," I said. "A girl has to take care of business, you know?" I pulled out a card and wrote a number on it. "But if you like, you could call me later."

It was a fake number, naturally.

My excuse seemed acceptable to him, and my bold offer seemed to appease his ego. "I'm playing in a poker tournament tonight," he said, "and I plan to celebrate my winnings afterward. I need to see you there." There was no question what he meant by his plan to "celebrate." He handed me an invitation and I promised to be there. I gathered my things and strolled away from the pool, commanding myself to walk slowly. Inside, I was jumping out of my skin with the feeling of triumph—*we had done it.*

Once I was out and safely within the elevator, I slumped against the wall and breathed a huge sigh of relief.

It didn't last long, of course, because I now knew we had a very big problem. We were going to have to do the job much sooner than we'd planned.

We were going to have to do it tonight.

Chapter Forty-Two

"Tonight? Are you crazy?" Jack said, staring at me in disbelief. "We're not ready to do the job tonight!"

I shrugged. "Well, it's now or never. Hendrickx warned him, so he's going to move it tomorrow."

We were all back at Raffles, gathered in Templeton's suite.

"How can you be sure he's not going to move it tonight, my dear?" Templeton asked.

"He said he was going to deal with it in the morning. He's got a poker tournament and then he's throwing some kind of party tonight."

There was protracted quiet as everyone on the team processed this.

"If we don't go in and get it tonight," I said, "we may never have another chance."

They knew I was right. There was further silence.

At last, Ethan raised his head. "All right, I say tonight it is. I think it's possible."

Felix nodded. "Let's do this."

I swiveled my head to look at Jack. Reluctantly, he dragged his eyes back up to mine. He shrugged. "You're all insane. But all right. Tonight it is."

I grinned and we set to work, concocting a detailed plan of attack. And the plan we came up with? Well, if we could pull it off—it would be nothing short of spectacular.

I'm not sure why I called them that night. I told myself it was because I wanted to check in and see how my mom was doing. Today was the day she was supposed to be discharged from the hospital.

"Dad? How is Mom? Is she back home now?"

"She's right here."

He handed the phone to her. "Darling!" she said. "It's so nice to hear your voice. Listen—while you're in Yorkshire, you should really look up the Petticoat family. You know, Thomas and Susan?"

"Oh, Mom, I'm not—"

"Don't protest, Cat. This is your cousin. Have you never looked at your family tree? Your father took ages putting it together a few years ago. We have plenty of family in the North. Anyway, I'm sure they could introduce you to someone. I'm *positive* there are many eligible men in North England—"

"Mom," I interrupted. "I'm not in Yorkshire anymore." Extended family in England was not going to be much assistance to me now.

"Oh." She paused and sniffed. "Next time, then."

"Any chance I have some well-connected relatives in Singapore, Mom?"

"I'm afraid not," she said. Then she asked, more quietly, "Is that where you are?"

"Yes."

My chest tightened; she asked no further questions about what I was doing in Singapore. Of course she knew.

"Sweetheart, I want to be sure you're trying to be safe."

Define "safe," I thought. I resisted the temptation to say it, staying quiet instead.

My mom filled the silence. "So, Singapore?" she said brightly. "That's exciting. A lot of suitable men, there, I'm sure—"

"Mom," I warned.

"What? It's simply an observation. Besides, you know your ovaries aren't getting any younger . . ."

I pinched the bridge of my nose. "I can see you're back to normal, Mom. Did they expect you to recover quite this quickly?"

As much as it irritated me, the truth was, she was right about my biological clock. It was the thing she'd always nagged me about, always wanting me to find a man and settle down and, most importantly, produce babies. And I'd always protested and resisted.

But just then, I really couldn't find it in me to protest. Because . . . it was a future that didn't sound all that horrible anymore.

"Listen, darling, do be careful, all right?"

"Yes, Mom, I'll try."

I disconnected the call and sat back. There had been something different about our conversation. Our talks usually had a certain cadence: she nagged and pushed her agenda; I brushed her off and dismissed her issues. It was a dance we did. This time however, there had been something different in her voice—a little more concern, maybe. And in my voice, a little more sincerity. Something more than lip service.

For the first time, I wondered if she was right. What kind of future was I creating for myself, flitting around the globe, all tangled up with the criminal underworld? It was no kind of future at all. Something needed to change.

As soon as I completed this mission.

Chapter Forty-Three

We were supposed to be getting an hour's rest before the job. We were ready, and there was nothing more to do but wait for our go time—midnight. So Templeton had ordered us all back to our respective rooms for a brief catnap before leaving.

Trouble was, I couldn't sleep. My brain felt like a hamster wheel, continuously rotating at a furious pace.

I stared out my suite's window at the slowly sinking sun and ran through the job in my head. I thought of everything that could go wrong. And, in particular, I thought about all the people I cared about who might get hurt in the next few hours.

I had to prevent that if I could.

Maybe it was talking to my mother that had triggered these feelings. Maybe it was the awareness that Templeton and Gladys and Felix—none of them field agents—were all here, ready to risk everything. Undoubtedly it was the memory of what had happened to Esmerelda, only a few days ago.

I knew what I needed to do, whom I needed to talk to. And it had to happen before the job started. I climbed from bed and pulled on a pair of jeans and crept down the long hallway to Jack's suite.

To my surprise he answered my knock right away. "Can't sleep?" I said.

He shook his head. "You neither?"

I shrugged.

"So . . . what's up, Cat?" Jack was one of the few people I knew who looked good when sleep-deprived. His shirtsleeves were rolled up, and his hair rumpled, like he'd been running his hands through it. The scruff on his face from a couple of days without shaving . . . well, the whole picture was a red-blooded look for him.

"I need to talk to you about something," I said, unsure exactly how to say it. "It's about the job."

"Okay, well, come in." He stood back to let me in.

I walked in quickly, head full of the things I needed to tell him. Once inside, however, with the door closed, I became acutely aware of the fact that Jack and I were alone, together, in a hotel suite.

I went to sit on the bed, then decided that was the wrong way to go, and settled for an armchair.

"Are you feeling okay?" he asked, looking at me with concern. "Your head—is it giving you trouble?"

"No, it's fine."

"Feeling ready, then?"

I frowned slightly. "I think so. I mean, I know everything is in place. I just . . . have to get my mind wrapped around a few things."

"You know what I think?" he said, walking over to the mini-fridge. "You need to relax." He brought out a bottle of Shiraz, already opened, and poured two glasses. "Here, have this."

"No, Jack, I'm okay—"

He pressed the drink into my hand. "You need it."

I nodded and took the glass.

"You're putting too much pressure on yourself," he said as I sipped. It was a really good wine—dark and full-bodied. "You've got this, Cat. You've done this kind of thing a hundred times."

"Yes, but usually it's just me. If I get caught, that's my own damn fault. I've never worked with such a large team before. If anything happens to anyone, it'll be my fault—"

"Hey, we're all grown-ups. And nobody is being forced into anything. Things happen. There's risk. We all know that."

I sipped again, thinking about what he said. The wine started to soak into my insides, softening my bones.

"Well, that's what I came here to talk to you about."

He raised an eyebrow. "Oh?"

"I need you to promise to do whatever it takes to keep people safe. Even if it means compromising the job." As I said it, I knew I was doing the right thing. Jack was FBI; he was uniquely positioned to help whoever needed it. "I mean—I know I need this job to succeed. But, in fact, it's more important to me that everyone gets out of there in one piece."

He looked at me carefully for a long time. And then he nodded. "If that's what you want, Cat, I can do that." He took a sip of his wine. "But tell me—what's going on with you? Why is this such a thing for you right now?"

I shrugged and shifted in the armchair.

"Does it have something to do with what happened to your mother?"

I looked at him sharply. "You know about that?" I fiddled with the glass in my hands and gazed down. Of course he knew about that. Jack always seemed to have the inside scoop when it came to me and my life. "My mother has always supported me in my career choice; she's never questioned it. But after she got shot . . . I guess *I* was the one to start questioning it." I laughed. It felt good to talk about it; I'd been keeping it inside far too long. "And you know what's even crazier than that? For the first time in my life, I'm starting to think all my mother's nagging about me getting married, having babies . . . well, you know, it's not all that off base. I think I actually want all that in my future—"

I stopped, realizing in that moment exactly who I was talking to. I glanced around awkwardly. "The point is, I don't want anyone else getting hurt because of me."

Jack's eyes were gentle. "You have my word on it, Cat. I will be looking out for everyone. And . . . that includes you."

I covered my mouth with the wineglass and took a large sip. My stomach tightened and I cast about for a change of subject. "Did I mention how amazing your suite is?" I said brightly and stood up. "Look at this balcony!" I walked out into the warm Singapore air prepared to feign admiration, but then quieted at the sight of the sunset: blazing pink clouds amid an aquamarine sky. A cashmere blanket lay rumpled on a plush chaise lounge, an empty coffee cup resting on a small table beside it. Jack had been sitting out here earlier. I wondered—what had he been thinking about, as he sat out here, alone?

The balcony overlooked the courtyard, lush with palms and ferns. I took a deep breath; the air was soft and full of the nectar of flowers.

I turned and looked at Jack, who had followed me out. There wasn't any of the cold detachment I'd seen in his eyes in recent days. He looked like the old Jack. My Jack. The one who truly cared about me, against his better judgment.

His eyes grew even more tender as he moved closer to me.

"Cat, I—"

My breathing quickened. Electricity sparked between us.

We had so much history together. Being on opposite sides of the law had always been the only thing keeping us apart. And now here we were, working together on the same side . . . Jack no longer FBI . . .

In an instant, he closed the distance.

His hands went up to my face and he pulled me into a deep kiss. His lips felt soft and warm on mine. A shiver traced down my spine. His embrace was an exquisite combination of familiar and exciting.

His kisses grew increasingly hungry. Our bodies pressed even closer together, and his hands worked their way through my hair. We both wanted the same thing. He picked me up with one smooth movement, carrying me easily, and moved over to the chaise lounge.

I sank into the cushions as he lay on top of me. I breathed deeply, and my head filled with the smell of his skin—intoxicating and alive with memories.

Jack was a big man, six feet three inches of muscle and sinew, and he was focusing every inch of that body on me. His chest against my chest, his heart beating into mine.

He kissed my neck and I leaned back. A delicious chill surged through me, and I arched into him. His hand went under the edge of my top, and in an instant pulled my sweater over my head. His shirt came off immediately after. I traced my hands over his bare chest, enjoying the taut muscles.

God, how I had missed him.

I slid my hands up and around his broad shoulders as he kissed me again. There was a little more urgency to his kisses now. He moved my legs apart with his thigh, still clad in jeans, and pressed against me. I moaned softly and bit his lip.

For a moment I forgot about everything else. All my worries and thoughts melted away.

Except one.

Ethan.

A little hook of guilt tugged at my brain. I tried to shut it down. It was ridiculous. We weren't a couple. I did my best to ignore those thoughts. I focused on Jack. His body, his breathing, his kisses. And then . . .

Jack's phone rang.

He ignored it and continued his work undressing me. But the phone kept ringing, sitting on a table inside the balcony doors.

"Um, do you think you should get that?" I asked reluctantly.

"Nope," he said, tugging at my jeans. His voice was husky and low. The ringing stopped after a minute, and I promptly forgot about it.

Jack had removed both of our jeans; the feeling of being nearly naked with him sent chills through me. A warm breeze slid over my skin as Jack lifted himself up, looking into my face. "Cat, I—" he began.

Then his phone rang again.

He squeezed his eyes shut and emitted a soft curse. "Just a sec. I'll tell whoever it is to leave me alone."

He climbed off the chaise and took three swift steps inside his suite. I propped myself up to enjoy the view of Jack standing at the glowing threshold with the phone to his ear, wearing only his boxer briefs, in all his finely chiseled glory.

Within a second, however, I could tell it wasn't going to be so easy for him to get rid of this call. His face changed. I sat up fully, my near-naked state forgotten. Something was wrong.

He disconnected the call and returned to me. I pulled the blanket over myself, suddenly feeling incredibly awkward.

"Listen, there's a bit of a complication," he said.

"Tell me."

"Brooke was spotted landing at the Singapore Changi Airport."

Shit. This could ruin everything.

Brooke was a pro. She was an excellent thief. It took a good thief to know exactly how to stop a theft from happening. But the worst part, perhaps, was that Brooke knew as much about me, and my modus operandi, as I did. As evidenced by her mangling of my Venice attempt. If anyone had a shot at blowing this thing apart, it was Brooke.

"We're going to have to rework the plan," he said. He recognized how much of a threat she was. "Someone is going to need to be assigned to Brooke, to make sure she doesn't kill this for us."

Jack started dressing again, without discussion. He paused, and looked at me. "Are you—um, I'm sorry, Cat, I just assumed . . ."

"No, you're right. We should, ah, stop." My skin crawled with the discomfort of the situation. I quickly stood and started getting dressed also.

"Call the others?" he said. "I'll get out the files. Let's have everyone meet in Templeton's room in five."

I nodded. I pulled on my sweater and rubbed my arms; the warm breeze on the balcony had suddenly turned chilly.

Chapter Forty-Four

Midnight, Singapore

Ethan stepped out of the elevator on the fifty-fifth floor of the middle pillar of the Marina Bay Sands and strolled down the corridor. He walked straight up to the security guard who was seated at the counter, keeping a pleasant expression on his face and one hand in his pocket. He sized the guard up as he approached. Tall, but not overly muscular. Eyes sharpish, but not laser.

"Okay, Ethan, you're dark," Gladys said, in his ear. "You've got one minute, then the cameras are back on."

Ethan knew any longer than that and people would investigate. A minute of lost connection, especially one that spontaneously went back online with nothing amiss, would be quickly forgotten.

"I'm looking for the bar," Ethan said. "Is it around here somewhere?"

"Buddy, you're way off," the guard said. "What you have to do is go back the way you came, take the elevator back down to—"

The instant the guard looked away to point down the hallway, Ethan fired a silent tranq gun into the man's neck. It took about 1.2 seconds to do it. The guard stopped talking, and put a hand to his neck, turning on Ethan. But Ethan had already put the tranq gun back in his pocket.

The guard's eyes narrowed. "Did you—"

Ethan knew there would be nothing for the man to feel on his skin. No blood or bullet hole. The tranq was contained within a tiny pellet lodged in his skin. Ethan gazed at him innocently. The guard's eyes clouded with confusion, not sure if he'd felt what he thought he'd felt.

And then, just as he seemed to be on the verge of contacting someone for backup, the guard's eyes rolled into his head, and he slumped forward on the desk.

Forty-five seconds to go. Ethan bolted down the hall and opened up a pop-up screen. He slid a flash drive into the side of the projector and pushed a few buttons in a precise order.

A perfectly reflected version of the hallway flickered into view.

"A little to the left," Gladys said. Ethan made the adjustment. "Okay, that's perfect."

He'd created a false wall—but only from the point of view of the CCTV camera. If you were there in person, you'd see immediately that it was fake. To a camera, however, it would look like nothing was wrong.

With twenty-five seconds to go, Ethan hopped over the desk in a single leap. He dragged the guard into the small room to the side. It was a brief tranquilizer that would wear off after thirty minutes, with total amnesia for the few minutes before he went down. The guard would assume he simply fell asleep.

Ethan removed his own clothes to reveal a guard's uniform underneath. He grabbed the guard's glasses and hat and popped them on, then tied the guard up—in case he were to wake early—locked the door, and slid into the desk chair.

"Okay, Ethan, back in four seconds . . ." Gladys counted down. "Three, two, one, you're on."

Ethan slowed his breathing and did his best impression of a bored security guard. He'd done his part. Next, Montgomery would have to do hers.

Chapter Forty-Five

I sat in the surveillance van with Gladys, parked in front of the Marina Bay Sands. We were glued to our bank of CCTV feeds, watching Templeton on one of our screens as he strode down a hallway with ramrod posture, carrying a tray of coffee cups. He knocked on a door, and was promptly admitted entry.

He disappeared from that screen, but reappeared in the next—within the security offices.

"Sir? Your coffee," he said to the night security supervisor, with the perfect smoothness of an experienced waiter. Our audio feed came from the mike he wore under his uniform. We had managed to pull some strings and get Templeton registered with the dining staff.

We knew the core alarms and doors were calibrated to whichever supervisor was on duty that night. Tonight the supervisor was a man named Thomas Lum. We needed his prints.

Mr. Lum looked at Templeton and took the proffered coffee, waving away the cream and sugar.

Templeton walked through the control room, tidying dishware. He stalled, taking coffee orders from the staff and wiping down counters. I saw him check his watch subtly once or twice.

And then he returned to Mr. Lum's desk. As he arrived, Mr. Lum's assistant started to reach for the empty coffee cup.

"Stop!" he shouted, perhaps too stridently for the situation. I cringed but Templeton covered quickly. "Don't trouble yourself," he said, grabbing the mug with a white-gloved hand. "It's my job, after all."

He placed the mug on his tray and walked briskly from the office. In the service elevator, Templeton turned with his back to the CCTV but I knew he was tucking the precious mug into a Baggie and sliding it inside his jacket. Five minutes later, he arrived beside the van, swinging the door open and climbing in with a grin that covered his face.

"Well, that was highly satisfying," he said. "It's been years since I've been in the field. I hadn't realized how much I'd missed it."

While Templeton mused about the delights of active duty, I grabbed the mug and quickly brushed for prints. Within minutes I had replicated them using a fingerprint kit and created a reproduction hand film with fake prints.

Just like that, we were through the first layer of security.

Felix came through my earpiece. "Got a problem here, Cat."

Gladys pointed to the CCTV screen that showed the room where Felix was stationed: the high-stakes poker room. Felix's task in our operation was to monitor Chips Walker. The man was supposed to be in the middle of his late-night poker tournament, and all Felix needed to do was make sure Walker didn't leave, say to spontaneously do a spot check of the fifty-fifth floor of the middle pillar, the location of the vault.

We knew his habit was to play poker in the late evening and drink single malt, his little bedtime routine. But we also knew he occasionally strolled around the resort complex before tucking himself into bed.

"What is it?" I said to Felix through the communicator.

"He seems to be getting bored."

I frowned. To keep him well away from the vault I was about to break into, we needed to know he was occupied with a riveting game of poker. "What? Why?"

"He doesn't have any worthy adversaries."

Shit. "He has to stay there. If he leaves, he might very well come up to do a check on the vault." This exact activity had been recorded in the security log Gladys had hacked into, once last week, twice the week before. Usually, it wasn't until much later, after he'd played poker for a nice length of time.

We needed some way to keep him there.

"I predict he'll stay for another hand and then he'll be out," Felix said.

We needed to find him a better opponent. Someone to keep things interesting.

"Felix, can you play poker?" I asked.

After a brief hesitation, Felix said, "Well, yes. Although remind me: which is higher, full house or four of a kind?"

I clenched my jaw. That was not a good question.

I ran through the options in my head. Jack was a very good player, but I couldn't pull him from his task. Same for Ethan. I wasn't stellar at poker, but I couldn't do it anyway because I had to crack into the safe.

I looked at Templeton and opened my mouth to ask the question. He straightened himself to his full height. "I have many talents, Petal. Poker is not one of them."

"Can you operate a computer?" Gladys suddenly chirped, looking at Templeton.

"Madam! Of course."

"Good," she said, nodding briskly. She pushed him down to sit in the chair she'd previously occupied. "Do this, this, and this." She showed him a few items on the screen in front of him, and scribbled a note on a piece of paper. "Most importantly, this is how you block the CCTV for one minute, in Ethan's wing. When he goes to collapse the screen, you'll need to do this."

I watched Gladys stand, straighten her velour hoodie tracksuit, and move toward the van door.

"Gladys, what the hell are you doing?"

"I happen to be a fairly decent poker player, if I do say so myself." She snapped open her sewing purse and pulled out a card. A laminated wallet-sized certificate: *Gladys Fitzsimmons, Silver Aces Poker Club Member—Seattle Chapter.*

My mouth dropped open. With that, she swiped on some lipstick and pinched her cheeks, left the van, and strode into the casino.

Why I continued to be surprised about the various talents Gladys had tucked up her sleeve, I had no idea. She might have looked like a banana bread–baking grandmother who enjoyed shuffleboard at the beach, but her skills were in a whole other class. Templeton and I stared at the screens as she walked in. She showed the same card to the guard at the high-stakes entry. It seemed Gladys was quite literally a card-carrying poker player.

They granted her entry, and within minutes had seated her at the table with Chips Walker. The others glanced at her. One man raised an eyebrow; another hid a smirk. Walker stayed, perhaps just for the entertainment value.

Twelve minutes later, she'd won the first hand.

Chapter Forty-Six

Jack sat in the Moluccas Room lounge, amid dark wood and gilded lanterns, his drink—an amber Manhattan in an old-fashioned glass—resting on a napkin on the table in front of him. Brooke Sinclair sat opposite him, sipping a dirty martini. Jack kept his eyes forward, resisting the urge to glance over his left shoulder, where he knew a lone figure was stationed, watching and listening to them from the other side of a thick bamboo border. Hendrickx.

Truth was, it was a three-way standoff.

Brooke, presumably, thought she was keeping an eye on Jack for her employer, Caliga. Hendrickx almost certainly thought he was the one in control, staking them both out. And they were each right in a sense. But the greater truth was that as long as Jack didn't make a move, he was keeping both Brooke and Hendrickx pinned in one spot, as surely as if he'd bound and gagged them.

And that, for the next hour, was Jack's entire goal in this enterprise.

Immediately after meeting with the team, as soon as Jack had learned of Brooke's arrival, he'd called her. He'd said they had some business to discuss. He'd chosen his words carefully, making it sound as though he needed her expert help in some way.

Stroking Brooke's ego was always a sure way to get her to cooperate.

To get Hendrickx to bite, he'd made the "rookie" mistake of calling Brooke on an unsecure line. Dropping a few key words into the conversation—*Lionheart*, *vault*, *operation*—ensured the call would get picked up by Interpol. He set the meet time with enough of an interval to allow Interpol to flag it, process the identification of the caller, and contact Hendrickx.

Brooke would have assumed Jack had used an encrypted line, of course. Keeping her unaware of the surveillance was the key to keeping her neutralized in the Moluccas Room. But really, Hendrickx was doing all the work on that front.

The Interpol agent's surveillance technique was excellent—subtle, seamless, and accomplished. Jack had let Hendrickx catch a glimpse of him, just enough to hook him. And then he'd allowed Hendrickx to follow him here. Hendrickx had selected the perfect stakeout spot and now he wasn't missing a thing. Jack was impressed. Hendrickx was a seasoned investigator.

Too bad he had latched on to the wrong suspect, though, for the evening.

Because while the three of them were locked in their little stalemate game, Cat would soon be high above them, breaking into the vault that contained the Lionheart.

Tonight, Jack was acting as a decoy, taking a rival thief out of play, and canceling Interpol's effect. Not too shabby for merely sitting in a restaurant having a drink or two. Maybe this job—working with the crooks—wasn't so bad, after all.

Jack lifted his Manhattan and took a sip. The perfect mingling of sweet, bitter, and smoky tingled his tongue.

"So, Brooke, listen. We're working on this assignment, I know you know that. But the reason I called you is because . . . well, I've got my doubts. I'm not sure Cat is up for it. She doesn't know I'm asking you this, but . . . would you consider joining the team? We've got a few days to pull it all together. With your help and expertise, we'll be ready."

He had worked hard to make it sound, subtly, like he was in charge. Like he was calling the shots on this op. One reason for that was to keep Hendrickx's interest.

Brooke rolled the stem of her glass between her fingers and watched him carefully.

"What's your time frame?" she asked. "When are you planning to do it?"

"In three days."

It sounded plausible, Jack thought. Neither Caliga nor Interpol would even dream that they might be going in *tonight*. And truly, it was a ridiculous thing they were attempting. But *ridiculous* seemed to be Cat's standard operating mode.

A waiter came by and took their order. It was late, almost midnight, so Jack ordered nibbles for them from the late supper menu: steamed dumplings and chicken satay. Things were going well, as far as Jack could tell, with his little game. He hoped he could keep it up.

"So, Brooke, are you interested in joining us?"

Brooke paused and sighed, slightly. "I don't know," she said, looking away. "I'm going to need to think about it."

Jack's eyebrows lifted momentarily, but he neutralized his expression before she looked back at him. Jack had expected Brooke to flat-out refuse to join them. But she hadn't said no. Was she playing him in some way?

He gazed more closely into her eyes. There was something new there. Doubt? Was she having second thoughts about her decision to join Caliga's side? Jack had never known Brooke to have qualms when it came to morality. But . . . perhaps there was a first time for everything.

"Are they treating you well over there, Brooke? Caliga, I mean?"

It was a stupid question, and Jack knew it. Caliga was a ruthless organization, everyone knew that. But he needed to tread carefully here.

Brooke said nothing. She took another sip of her drink. "They're paying me well, if that's what you mean."

Jack shrugged. "It's not."

Then he remembered Cat had said she'd seen Brooke's face right after they killed Esmerelda. Brooke had witnessed the cruelty of Caliga with her own eyes. Maybe that had changed things. Surely she knew Caliga killed people if they got in the way. But knowing something and seeing it firsthand were entirely different things.

Jack watched Brooke thoughtfully. He could tell nothing was certain in her mind. She wasn't ready to leave Caliga, but she wasn't completely on board with them, either. Her commitment was wavering.

Then she said, "I can't help you, Jack. But . . . I won't work against you. This conversation won't leave this table."

Again, Jack forced his face into a neutral mask. If he looked too shocked at her response, he'd reveal that this was all a ploy. That he never really expected her to go along with it.

The trouble, now, was that she had effectively sealed off that line of discussion. Which was way ahead of schedule. He needed to keep both Brooke and Hendrickx's attention awhile longer. They would need something new to talk about.

But it was Brooke who raised a new subject. "So, Jack, tell me. Are you . . . attached to anyone, now that you and Cat are no longer together?"

Shit. That wasn't the subject he'd have chosen. He really didn't want to talk to Brooke about his personal life.

"No," he said. "Not attached."

She sipped her drink and raised an eyebrow. "Interesting."

He plucked his glass off the table and took a swig.

Brooke said, "And you're not still . . . how should I say this . . . emotionally invested in her?"

He swirled his drink, staring into it. "Cat? Nope. It's over."

"You're not much of a liar, Jack."

He frowned. Brooke was grinning, entirely comfortable in their new topic, and Jack was itching to get out of there. Which wouldn't help anyone, of course. "Brooke, can we discuss something else?"

She smiled. "Yes, there it is. A bit too touchy. Your heart still belongs to her. Clearly."

"It doesn't."

"So you're either lying to me, or lying to yourself. Either way, it doesn't really help your cause."

"I don't have a cause."

"Here's an idea—why don't you just propose? Ask her to marry you."

Jack cast her a bewildered look. Was she insane? "What the hell are you talking about?"

Brooke rolled her eyes. "Cat. Ask her to marry you. Women love that stuff. If you could get the cojones to ask her, she'd be yours."

"Forgive me, Brooke, but I don't particularly feel like taking dating advice from you."

"It's not dating advice. It's more than that. And—trust me. You only have to ask her. It will change everything."

He tried to ignore her words; she was obviously trying to throw him off his game. But goddamn it, he was supposed to be in charge of this conversation, not Brooke.

And she was not supposed to be planting fool ideas in his head about proposing. It was ridiculous. It was the sort of crazy thing that only happened in movies.

And then, against his best intentions, he found himself visualizing it, like he was watching it on a big screen. He was there in grainy black and white, on a beach somewhere, down on one knee, waves crashing in the background, proposing to Cat.

A full, bright feeling entered his heart. Maybe . . . was Brooke right? He wondered . . .

No. That was not where they were going in this head game. He had to gain control of this conversation again. Jack glanced at his watch and was relieved when the waiter came by with their food. He still had forty-five minutes to go.

Chapter Forty-Seven

I glanced at the screen that showed the interior of the Moluccas Room. Jack and Brooke had just sat down but already appeared deeply involved in their tête-à-tête. A stab of jealousy hit me in the chest. They looked rather cozy. She touched his arm. He flashed her one of his most dazzling smiles.

I looked away, frowning. Whose idea was this part of the plan, again?

I shook it off; it was time to go.

"You ready, Cat?" Felix asked, nodding at me. He was in the van now, having switched places with Gladys, the ace poker player. Templeton had left the van a few minutes prior, returning to his post in the kitchen. There were to be no disappearances or suspicious acts from anyone from this point forward, until the job was done.

If I was going to make a move on this vault, it was going to have to be now. And I was as ready as I'd ever be.

I had the replicated fingerprints, the fake wall, and security codes. Everything was in place. But something was bothering me, like I was forgetting a key piece, or not taking something into account. However, I couldn't wait any longer. It was probably last-minute jitters, or the remnants of my annoyance at watching Jack and Brooke.

I strolled through the casino floor, heavily disguised in a glossy black wig and dark, bloodred lipstick. I wore a silvery cocktail dress and carried an overly large Louis Vuitton tote that contained all my gear. The goal was to look like someone who was staying on the subpenthouse floor, because that was the button I pushed in the elevator and I didn't need anyone questioning it.

All the way up to the fifty-fourth floor the elevator whisked me. It was one floor below the vault level.

There was a small, private lounge on the fifty-fourth floor, and beside that, a restroom. I walked inside and tucked myself into the middle stall, where I quickly changed into my more comfortable black Lycra suit. The stalls had full-height walls and floor-to-ceiling doors, which was good because I was going to be climbing up through that ceiling. It tends to get awkward if people see you doing that kind of thing.

Above the middle stall a vent traveled up through the ceiling and opened on the story above. The area where it opened was inside the hallway behind Ethan's fake wall, concealed from CCTV. I wrapped the straps of my Louis Vuitton tote around me and began to climb.

"Are you in position, Montgomery?" Ethan said in a low voice through the communicator as I clambered out and replaced the grill.

"Sure am."

"Perfect. Can't see you at all."

"Confirming that," said Felix, in my ear, from his position in the van. "I'm looking at the security feeds. No sign of you."

This made me smile. I pulled out the hand film containing the fake fingerprints, positioned it over my own palm, and placed my hand against the wall panel.

The scanner slid over my fingertips. A green light and a beep. The door unlocked, and I stepped through.

I pulled night-vision goggles over my eyes and crept through two layers of swiveling doors. As long as everything stayed dark, my movements wouldn't be picked up by the CCTV here.

I got inside and located the panel to disable the microwave system layer. Microwave sensors are among the most difficult to bypass, but fortunately we had an advantage. I entered the code we had stolen from Walker's phone, and I stood stock-still, waiting for the sensor to turn off. I stared at the panel, frozen, waiting.

Any minute now.

But it didn't turn off. "The microwave sensor isn't shutting down," I hissed.

"Did you use the code?" Ethan asked.

"It didn't work."

"Did you use the fingerprints?" Ethan said.

"Yes, of course. How else would I have unlocked the door?"

There was silence.

Why didn't the codes work? We had just retrieved them from

Walker's phone that afternoon. I looked at my watch. Ten minutes past midnight. And then I remembered, with a sickening thud in my stomach, why they hadn't worked.

It was Saturday. And there was a small line, fine print in the security schematics, that said the codes were automatically reset every week, midnight on Saturday. We had downloaded the codes from the previous week. Walker would probably be receiving his automatic e-mail with new codes, perhaps sent only a few minutes ago. Little good that would do us now. Bitterness flooded into my mouth. All that work today at the pool for nothing.

"The codes won't work," I said. "Is there any other way?"

There was a pause, then Ethan said, "There's one other way. If you cross the room at a normal speed the sensor will pick you up. But you can hack the system. To do it, you'll have to go at super slow speed," Ethan said.

"How slow?"

"Two inches per second."

That really was slow.

"There's one other thing you should do that might help a little, as backup," Ethan said.

"What?"

"You can cover the CCTV lens with something."

"Something—like what?"

"It has to be opaque."

I looked around for something I could use that would work. I took a close look at the camera on the wall beside me through my night-vision goggles. If I were MacGyver I'd have a roll of duct tape on me. But I wasn't, and I didn't.

But then I thought about something I did have.

Lipstick.

I smeared the dark red lipstick all over the lens, blocking it out. I could only hope it would work. It was the best I could do.

Turning, I faced the vault, on the far end of a very long corridor. I took a deep breath and started walking slowly. My heart pounded and my breathing was loud. Good thing there weren't noise sensors included in this security network—I was sure they would pick up my heartbeat.

I counted out my steps so they could hear my pace and let me know if I was going slowly enough.

"Okay, that's a good pace, Cat," Felix said. I exhaled and kept going.

"You can do it, Montgomery. You're the best," Ethan said.

My stomach fluttered at the compliment. Then I reminded myself he was probably just encouraging me, to help me get through this.

Damn. I cared about what Ethan thought of my skills, sure, but realized as I crept slowly across the floor that it wasn't only about his admiration on a professional level. Our moment on the train came flooding back to me. I could still feel his hands on my skin. Still feel his mouth on mine, his weight on me . . .

But then I thought of earlier. *Jack.* What had I been thinking? Here I was again, ruminating over a choice I'd already proven I was incapable of making.

Okay, Cat. Stop. Not the time.

I focused again on my steps, on walking slowly, on my breathing.

Somehow, I made it across the room and stood in front of the vault at last. It was a square door to an enormous safe, state of the art. I inspected the locking mechanisms, the control panel that needed to be cracked.

"Okay, I'm at the safe," I said. "It's going to take some time. But I think I can do it."

I pushed aside all the thoughts of Ethan and Jack, locked them up with a key, and turned my attention to the safe. I started working on the tumblers, clearing my mind and entering the safecracking zone.

I lost all track of time as I turned the wheel pack in a precise rhythm, feeling for notches, visualizing the inside of the lock. It might have been five minutes, it might have been fifty, but after a lot of concentration and a great deal of sweating . . . I was in.

The safe released its mechanism with a beautiful metallic clunk, and smoothly glided open. A chill traveled up my arms.

I stepped into the vault, still moving like I was in slow motion, like I was in a dream. I knew the same microwave sensor existed within the vault itself.

Inside, I found myself within a seamless square steel vault, the size of a large walk-in closet. It contained countless treasures, gleaming in cubbyholes and boxes, and in clear, ultra-strong acrylic cases. I had no doubt many of them were stolen. It wasn't that Chips Walker was short on means. It was just that you can't buy what isn't for sale.

It didn't take long to find the case containing the Lionheart Ring. Being the most recent addition to his collection, it occupied a position front and center, on top of a stack of cash boxes.

It was held within an old wooden box with iron hinges. I wondered if it was the one they'd found in the coffin itself—Robin Hood's grave—buried deep in the Yorkshire earth. I opened the box and stared at the ring.

After all this time, chasing this jewel across continents, I was finally staring at it. The ruby was the first thing I noticed. Enormous, especially for a ring, it was the size and shape of an acorn. The red fire smoldered within, like a hot, burning coal. The heart of a lion.

I lifted it up and held it in my gloved hand. This was the ring worn by Richard the Lionheart himself. The ring given by the king to Robin of Loxley. *Robin Hood.*

But I knew, now, it was a gift even older than the twelfth century. I looked at the gold it was fashioned with—lustrous, rich yellow gold. It was the gold of the Gifts of the Magi. My skin felt covered in sparks, tiny electric shocks.

This ring had been buried with the man who had forged the way for thieves and provided legend for centuries to come. My breath came quicker as I stared at it. The connection I felt was deeper than just the kinship of thieves, more profound than that. It wasn't the first time I'd held an incredible treasure in my hand. The Fabergé egg, last fall. The Hope Diamond, only two months ago. But this ring, it felt even more . . . personal, somehow.

But I didn't have time to stare and get lost in thought. I needed to get out of there.

With reluctance I tucked the ring into the pouch inside my suit, next to my body. I closed the box, replaced it, and retraced my steps—ever so slowly, moving through molasses—back out of the vault.

I closed and locked the vault door. As I began the long return journey across the floor, I heard Jack's voice. "Not to put even more pressure on you, Cat, but I need you to get out of there fast."

I froze. "Why?"

"Because Hendrickx is on his way to you."

Chapter Forty-Eight

"What?" I snapped. My stomach dropped. I was only partway back to the exit; I had a long way to go down the corridor. The door seemed impossibly far away and I had to keep walking in slow motion. I glanced down at my suit, thinking of what was zipped inside the pouch at my waistband. I would be caught, trapped in flypaper in the vault antechamber, carrying the ring. "What happened, Jack?"

Jack's voice was tight. "I had him in my sights. He wasn't going anywhere. And then he got a call. I don't know what he was told, exactly, but I did manage to overhear him say something about a vault. Within a minute he got a lackey to replace his post in the restaurant. Then he left."

I bit down on the inside of my cheek. "Can you follow him?"

"Already on it." I could hear him breathing faster. He was on the move. And it was impossible to miss the concern in his voice.

"Try to do something to slow him down," I said. "And I'll go as fast as I can."

But fast, of course, in this situation, could be nothing but inexorably slow.

"Hang in there, Montgomery, we'll get you out of there," Ethan said. Although what he was going to do, exactly, I had no idea. "What's your progress like?" he asked.

"I still have about thirty feet to go." I did quick mental arithmetic. I knew it would take about three minutes for me to cross the space. And then I still had to get out and lock all the doors, removing evidence of a break-in, to get away cleanly.

"Right," Ethan said. "Felix, do you still have the CCTV feeds?"

"Sure do," said Felix. "And . . . let's see . . . *oh crap.* Hendrickx is coming. He's heading to the elevators right now. He just pushed the call button."

I cringed and squeezed my eyes tight. And then, an idea. "Gladys, can you override whichever elevator Hendrickx gets on?" I said quickly in a hopeful rush. "Lock it up, or something?"

There was a pause and a faint rustle on the line, and then Gladys said, "Er, well, I would, dear, if I weren't right in the middle of a poker game with Walker."

The air left my lungs. I'd forgotten. She was trapped in the casino. There was no way she could get back to the van in time.

"Felix, is there any chance—"

"Oh Cat, I wish I could, but I don't have the first clue how to do that . . ."

Never mind. I steeled my jaw and kept moving ever forward toward the door. I mentally judged how long it would take me to cross the floor, and how long it would take Hendrickx to get there. I only needed a couple of extra minutes. But I knew I wasn't going to get it.

There was also the fact that Ethan needed to collapse the fake wall and get out of there before Hendrickx made it up the elevator. If he didn't, he'd be caught, too.

"Ethan, you have to get out of there." I wasn't going to make it, but there wasn't any reason for Ethan to get caught, too.

"No way. I'm not leaving you," Ethan said. His voice was firm.

"Ethan—"

"I'm serious, Montgomery. We're getting you out of there, or we're not. But either way, I'm not going anywhere."

My eyes started to sting and a rueful smile grew on my face. And I kept putting one foot slowly in front of the other, hoping for a miracle.

Chapter Forty-Nine

Jack stayed as close as he dared to Hendrickx, keeping the man on a tractor beam with an unwavering gaze. He had to do something, or it would be all over for Cat. He'd ditched Brooke when she went to the restroom, but he couldn't worry about her now. A small crowd of people waited in front of the bank of elevators. Jack stood two people off Hendrickx's right shoulder, as everyone waited, staring forward. Sweat dripped down the back of his collar.

Jack spotted a security guard. The guard's key card, the device that opened the slot machines, was hanging loose from his pocket. The guard was standing right in front of Hendrickx.

Jack cobbled together a hasty plan. Pickpocketing wasn't Jack's strength, but in this situation, that was okay.

"I have an idea," Jack said, thinking it through rapidly, knowing his words would be picked up by his earpiece.

"Jack—don't do anything stupid," said Cat, hissing urgently. She must have sensed something in his tone.

"It's okay. Me getting in trouble for a minor crime is better than you getting caught in the middle of a major one."

Jack moved forward in the crowd to stand beside the security guard, right in front of Hendrickx. He carefully avoided making eye contact with the Interpol agent. That would be too bold and far too suspicious. Hendrickx must have been watching him, though.

When the guard turned his head, Jack reached his hand forward and slid the key card out of the guard's pocket, just as the elevator chimed and the doors opened. Jack winced as he palmed the card; it felt so obvious to him, the guard must have noticed. But that would be fine. When you were committing hara-kiri, people were supposed to notice.

Jack flicked a glance at the guard's eyes as he dropped the key card into his pocket and moved away.

Nothing. No reaction.

The guard hadn't noticed. Jack frowned slightly, but it didn't matter. The guard wasn't the important one. Jack snapped his head back toward Hendrickx, expecting to see the man bearing down on him. It meant Jack would have to bolt, and that would be the tricky bit. But at this moment, he didn't have any time to consider the downside. He knew he had to prevent Hendrickx from getting on that elevator.

Instead, he watched as Hendrickx took a few steps forward to the open elevator at the end of the row, and disappeared through the doors.

"*No!*" Jack whispered hoarsely, darting to the elevator. The doors sealed the moment he got there.

"He missed it, Jack," Felix said miserably; he must have seen the whole thing on the CCTV thread. "Hendrickx turned his head at the last minute, looking at the elevator instead of at you."

A sickening pit opened in Jack's stomach. Hendrickx was on his way to the vault.

Standing alone in front of the bank of elevators, Jack stared in disbelief. Nobody approached him about the key card. No one had even seen his little crime. He stuffed a hand in his pocket but it was not the victory he wanted or needed.

His last-ditch effort had failed. Cat was about to get busted. And he was helpless to stop it.

Chapter Fifty

Ethan cursed silently. Moments ago he'd watched, on the CCTV screen in front of him at the guard's desk, Jack's attempted play at drawing Hendrickx off. And then he'd watched Hendrickx step inside the elevator, oblivious to Jack's effort.

Now the Interpol agent was headed straight to him.

"I can see him in the elevator," Ethan said quietly into his earpiece. "He'll be here in less than a minute." The elevator was going slowly, stopping at almost every floor to let various people off. "Montgomery, how much time do you need? How close are you?"

Silence. Then, "I'm getting there," she said, breathing heavily. "I still need about two and a half minutes. And a few extra seconds to get away."

Ethan stared at the CCTV screen. Hendrickx would be there before then. It wouldn't be enough.

He couldn't just sit there; there had to be something he could do. He'd said he wasn't going to leave Cat and he was going to hold to that. But the trouble was, Hendrickx would reach Ethan first. He'd see the fake wall, would probably even recognize Ethan if he stayed there.

His gaze shifted back to the CCTV monitor. Now it was just Hendricks and one other man inside the elevator.

Ethan would have to attack Hendrickx when he arrived. There would be no other way. He lifted his head to assess the space, the foyer outside the elevator where the desk was stationed. He had a weapon and he had the element of surprise. He could subdue Hendrickx. The fallout of that would not be pretty, but there was nothing else for it. He glanced back at the screen.

"They're stopping one last time, the other guy is getting out." He breathed. "Montgomery, are you anywhere close?"

"Not close enough. Two minutes."

He stood, felt the adrenaline surge and blood rush to his muscles, ready for a physical fight. It was time to position himself to attack Hendrickx the moment he walked off the elevator.

But something changed on the CCTV screen. The guy on the elevator, the only other person in there besides Hendrickx, was stopping at the threshold of the elevator car. Something was wrong. Ethan described what he was looking at. "He looks like he's having a heart attack or something . . ." Ethan couldn't believe what he was seeing. The man had collapsed. He was blocking the elevator doors. "Felix, are you seeing this?"

"I sure am."

Ethan watched, eyes wide, as Hendrickx crouched down to attend to the stranger. He was shaking him, speaking to him urgently. For a moment he appeared to hesitate, unsure what to do, but then he dragged the fallen man back inside the elevator. The doors slid closed. Hendrickx reached up, commandeered the elevator by pressing the Door Close button and the Lobby button at the same time, and rode the elevator all the way down. He pulled out his phone, presumably to call for an ambulance.

Then Felix made a strangled sound on the communication line. "Oh my God, Cat, I think that's—that's *your professor,*" he said. "I couldn't place him at first, but I remember him from the racetrack . . ."

Ethan squinted hard at the screen.

Felix was right. It was Cat's Professor Atworthy.

Suddenly, Ethan understood what was going on. Cat's prof was here, rescuing her yet again. Atworthy was faking a heart attack. Ethan had no idea how the man knew what was going on, but he did know Atworthy had skills; Ethan knew all about his past history as an assassin.

And he wasn't about to look a gift horse in the mouth.

"You've got your extra two minutes, Montgomery."

"That's all I need."

Silence hung heavily then through the communication line as they all held their breath, waiting for Cat to cross the remaining expanse of the vault room floor. Ethan's hands were tightly clenched on his knees as he watched the CCTV images of Hendrickx getting assistance down in the lobby for Atworthy. It wouldn't be long before he left the security and emergency crews to their job and he returned to his. In a second, Ethan realized what a clever move it had been—collapsing across the door like that, forcing Hendrickx to do something about it. If his body hadn't been blocking the door, he wondered if Hendrickx might very well have left the man for dead.

"Are you clear yet?" Ethan asked Cat. He wasn't moving until he knew she was.

Sure enough, Hendrickx was striding purposefully back to the elevator bank. He pushed the call button. Here they went again.

"Almost there," Cat said. "Just locking the door mechanisms . . ." Another several seconds passed. "Okay, I'm out," she said, with a heavy exhale.

"You can't go down the elevator, Cat," Felix said quickly. "Hendrickx is on his way back up. There's too much chance you'll cross paths. And you don't want to be anywhere near the lobby. Looks like Hendrickx has called in troops. They're flooding into the main entrance as we speak."

It was true. Ethan watched as the Interpol agent walked once more into the elevator. Cat would need an alternate escape route. He glanced toward the fake wall he'd placed in the middle of the corridor, knowing she was on the other side of it. He heard nothing from the other side—no surprise. She was a pro.

"No problem," Cat whispered through the communicator. "I'll slip through the stairwell door and go up to the rooftop. Ethan, I'll meet you on the ground as planned." There was a pause. Ethan heard the faintest *click* of a door latch. "Okay, I'm out of view," she said.

"Right, I'm blocking the CCTV for one minute," Felix said. "Ethan, get ready to go. Three, two, one . . . *now.*"

Ethan darted to the back room where the guard was tied up, still unconscious. He removed the ropes and hauled the guard out of there, sitting him down at the station and leaning him forward so his head was resting on the desk.

Ethan gave him a shot of the tranq antidote. In about forty-five seconds, he'd be waking up. A quick glance at the CCTV screen told him that was about the length of time they had before Hendrickx arrived on the scene. It should be more than enough time to collapse the screen and get the hell out of there.

He quickly threw his own shirt on over the uniform he wore. The rest of his costume change would have to wait—he left on the uniform trousers and tucked his own pair, rolled up, under his arm. Then he leaped over the desk to collapse the screen.

Ethan tried not to rush, tried not to panic. But he desperately wanted to meet Cat at their rendezvous spot, to help her escape, to make sure she was safe.

"You've got about forty seconds now, Ethan," Felix said. Ethan flexed his jaw and unlatched the screen, pulling on the handle with one hand to collapse it.

But it didn't collapse.

Ethan tugged at it, crouched there with his rolled-up pants tucked under his arm, but the screen was stuck. It wouldn't budge. A surge of panic washed through him. He had to get rid of the screen somehow. It had to be collapsed—there was nowhere to hide it, and it wouldn't fit through the narrow stairwell door unless it was closed.

The guard stirred; he was starting to wake. Sweat broke out on the back of Ethan's neck. He tugged again.

Nothing.

He dropped his rolled-up pants on the corner of the security desk, and put more muscle into the effort. The thought of messing with Cat's op, with compromising her in any way with sloppy evidence, was intolerable to him. The guard shifted in his chair and his breathing changed. He was coming to.

With one final heave, the screen collapsed.

Ethan exhaled. He folded the screen in a second, and darted out of view, into the stairwell. A warm feeling of relief flooded his limbs. He opened his mouth to tell Felix he was clear . . . and then, he remembered.

His rolled-up pants.

Fuck. They were still sitting on the corner of the guard's desk. He had to go back and get them. "Felix, don't turn the lights back on yet," he whispered harshly.

If the guard awoke and saw a strange pair of men's trousers sitting on his desk, he'd be more than a little suspicious. Not to mention the DNA traces that might be on them.

Ethan opened the steel door a crack, and peered out. The guard was shifting, breathing in an irregular way. He'd open his eyes any moment. Ethan glanced at the elevator doors. Still closed. For now.

Ethan had no time to think about it.

He darted out to grab the pants, heart thundering. He kept his gaze locked on the guard the entire, heart-stopping stretch of time—a total of three and a half seconds—but the man's eyes stayed mercifully closed. Ethan's hands closed around the cloth of his trousers and he darted back into the stairwell.

The instant the door closed behind him, Felix's voice hissed in his ear. "The guard just woke up," he said. "He missed you by a hair."

And then, from the other side of the stairwell door, Ethan heard the *ding* of the elevator car arriving. Hendrickx was there. Ethan closed his eyes and paused, breathing hard. Way too close.

He swiveled and began quickly descending the stairs. He still had one thing to do before he could help Cat get out of there. They weren't in the clear yet.

Chapter Fifty-One

I opened the door to the rooftop. It was well past midnight, and the SkyPark was deserted, closed to the public at this hour. I jogged along the viewing boardwalk that ran the length of the platform, past the floodlit pool and the empty sushi restaurant and the deserted gardens lush with ornamental ferns. I paused twice, frozen in the shadows and listening, making sure no stray custodial staff were up here, or that I'd been followed. It was as quiet as a church. After a few minutes I reached the far end—the cantilevered observation deck that curved out over the Singapore skyline.

I kept my breathing steady. I had a very specific exit route from here and I needed to focus.

Just outside the entrance to the women's restroom, I crouched down and reached behind a large potted palm tree. My hand closed around the backpack Ethan had stashed there earlier, our escape contingency plan. I unzipped it and pulled out a harness and ropes, checked to make sure everything else was in order, flung it on my back, and cinched the straps.

I moved swiftly across the platform to the outer edge. The entire perimeter was covered with a Plexiglas wall, reinforced by steel. It curved high above my head; it was designed to keep people from falling over the edge, obviously. I headed to one specific spot; the place where the Plexiglas had a seam that was designed to come apart for service and repair access. Within minutes I found the panel and quickly removed it, revealing a three-foot-wide gap in the perimeter. A breeze floated up, hot and tropical, and there was nothing between the edge and me but the Singapore night air. I turned to find attachment points for my ropes.

There was Hendrickx, standing directly in front of me, a gun in his hand.

"Stop," he said simply.

I froze, with my back to the edge. My head spun. How was it possible he'd gotten up here so fast? He must have come directly here, not bothering with the vault. Had someone tipped him off?

He couldn't possibly know what I had done, not yet. There hadn't been enough time for him to discover the Lionheart was missing. Besides, someone would have told me that through my earpiece. I had to play that bluff.

"Hendrickx, what's your problem? I haven't done anything wrong."

"I don't believe you. I think something happened in Walker's vault tonight. Why else would you be up here on this rooftop?" With the hand not holding the gun he lifted his walkie-talkie. "Check the vault," he said calmly. I suppressed a satisfied smile. I knew he hadn't inspected it yet. He was going on a hunch.

A damn good hunch it was, though.

There was silence as we faced each other in a standoff. "What are you doing up here, if you didn't take anything?" he demanded.

"I'm a thrill seeker, Hendrickx," I said, shrugging. "Haven't you seen pictures of people rappelling from skyscrapers and structures like this? Well, that's what I'm doing. It's not exactly allowed, of course, which is why I'm doing it at night."

His face contorted. He knew it was bullshit, but he struggled to come up with an argument that would poke holes in my explanation. He didn't believe me for a second, but he was an officer of the law, and he did things by the book. He couldn't accuse me of anything specific, without a good reason. And a little evidence.

We both knew he couldn't lay a hand on me, couldn't search me or force me to empty the contents of my bag without some sort of just cause. I could see the frustration mounting in his face, in the curl of his lip.

And then, a voice came through on the walkie-talkie. "Everything is in order," said the guy on the other end. "We haven't gone right into the safe yet—we're still waiting on the combination code from Walker. But there's no sign of tampering, no sign of forced entry into the vault. None of the security systems were breached."

Hendrickx's nostrils flared.

"Okay, then," I said brightly. "You know, I think I'm going to go down the regular way. I've lost my taste for adventure tonight." I started to move away from the edge.

Hendrickx said nothing. His fist tightened around his weapon and his knuckles went white on the walkie-talkie. He was practically shaking with impotent, pent-up rage. But there was nothing more he could say or do.

He began to lower his gun, when the voice came through on the walkie-talkie again. "Uh, boss? There's something you're gonna want to see."

"What is it?" Hendrickx said, eyes narrowing, holding his weapon steady.

"Well, everything is intact. Except . . . for something on the CCTV camera . . . seems kind of like . . . lipstick?"

My mouth went dry. Hendrickx's eyes sharpened their focus on me and he showed his teeth. "You *did* take it." He took a step toward me. "Don't move or I swear to God I'll shoot."

His gun, steady and unwavering, was pointed straight at my chest. My heart pummeled against my rib cage. It was over. I was going to be captured, or I was going to be shot. That was it. Those were my two options here. I didn't doubt for a second that he would shoot. His rage alone would drive him to it.

I had one chance.

I dropped straight back, right off the edge of the platform, falling fast through the night sky.

Chapter Fifty-Two

A few seconds into my fall, the BASE chute opened.

It flipped out of my parachute pack automatically, unfurling with a snap, and slowing my free fall to a gentle float. My heart pounded in my chest, the image of my near escape from Hendrickx fresh in my mind. The wind rushed through my ears as I spiraled downward. After several seconds, my feet landed on the street below.

The instant I touched down, a black BMW roared up to me. The passenger door flung open and Ethan leaned across from the driver's side. "Get in!" he shouted.

I wrapped up the chute in a matter of seconds and lunged inside the car. I glanced over my shoulder and out the window, as Ethan peeled away from the curb, to see a platoon of security guards bursting through the front door of the Marina Bay Sands. They'd been alerted by Hendrickx, no doubt. Cars and the local police would soon follow—but we would be long gone.

I made a quick change of disguise as we drove, racing to the airport, pulling on a blond wig and tortoiseshell glasses.

"Everyone out?" I said urgently through our communication channel.

"I just cashed in my chips," Gladys said. "And I'm walking out right now."

"I'm off, too," Templeton said. I could picture him innocently making his way to the front exit and simply strolling out the front door. I knew he'd be climbing onto a bicycle stashed in the back alley and pedaling away.

"Gladys is getting into the van right now," Felix said. "We're pulling away. No sign of anybody on our tail."

I felt a tingling up my spine, the first sensation of relief. Things were coming together.

"Jack—what's your status?" I held my breath and waited to hear from him.

"Just reached underground parking. I'll be on my way in a sec," Jack said.

Then, "Shit," he hissed under his breath. "They're all over the Volvo." That was his getaway car. "Looks like Interpol. And local police, too. I'm turning around. I'll try the back alley instead, but I'm on foot now."

I chewed my lip and glanced at Ethan. "We have to go back. We have to get Jack."

Ethan glanced in the rearview mirror. "Montgomery—they're right behind us. We'll be screwed if we turn around. We'll be lucky to get away as it is." He looked at me. "*You* have the ring. We have to get you out of here."

I heard Jack's breathing in my earpiece, and his quick footsteps, heading out to the alley. And then I heard a car screeching to a stop. "Jack—get in," said a woman's voice, muffled in the feed. I strained to hear more clearly. The voice was familiar. Was it—

"*Brooke?* What the hell are you doing?" Jack demanded.

"Helping you get away. What does it look like?"

Ethan and I exchanged bewildered glances. He'd heard the conversation in his earpiece, too.

Was it a trap? There was no way of knowing. Trouble was, Jack didn't have much choice. He had to get away, and this might be his best chance.

Jack obviously came to the same conclusion, because at that moment I heard him climb in Brooke's car and slam the door. Next second the engine roared as they sped away.

I let out the breath I'd been holding. That was everyone. We weren't in the clear yet, not by a long shot, but we were on our way. We would now make our separate ways to the rendezvous spot, the safe house. I glanced down, checking my waistband and feeling the small bulge of the Lionheart Ring in its pouch. A warm feeling spread through my chest. I had it.

We had done it.

I looked forward again, facing the freeway that led to the airport. Ethan reached his hand across and squeezed my knee, sending a shiver through my body. "Almost there, Montgomery."

Chapter Fifty-Three

Bali, Indonesia

The airport taxi carrying Ethan and Cat pulled up to the resort. It was six thirty in the morning, and the sun was peeking above the horizon, washing the sky with pink and lemon watercolors. On the drive here, Ethan had gazed at the dim outlines of lush hills and terraced rice fields, catching glimpses of white, sugary beaches. He'd rolled the window down and breathed deeply: warm air, rich with the smells of fruit and flowers and the sea.

Even though it was only three hours away, Bali couldn't be more different from the bright lights and concrete bustle of Singapore. It was like time was suspended here, hovering in place like a hummingbird dipping its beak in nectar.

When the cab came to a stop in front of the sprawling, grassy-roofed resort, Ethan looked down at Cat, asleep on his shoulder. They had journeyed through the early hours of the morning, flying directly here from Singapore. Everyone on the team was making their way here by different means; they had scattered for security purposes, keeping to small groups. Getting out of the country together would have been stupid and risky. Gladys and Felix had gone by train, through Malaysia to the north, then by bus. Templeton had traveled by boat, and Jack had flown on his jet, but indirectly, via Kuala Lumpur.

If everything had gone according to plan, that is.

They were out of range from one another for their earpieces to work now. So he'd have to wait to rendezvous with everyone to find out if there had been any hitches. But there was no indication that anything had gone awry.

Ethan allowed a small thrill of celebration in the pit of his stomach. They had done it. They had the Lionheart Ring. He glanced down at Cat and knew she had it tucked tightly around herself, safe inside her pouch. They still had to make it back to Yorkshire, take the ring back to its homeland, but for now, they were good.

They were safe.

A porter came out to the car to carry their bags into the resort, although they had none. The driver opened the door and Ethan climbed out, leaving Cat sleeping, for the moment, in the backseat. He stretched and gazed at the resort.

There was an overwhelming feeling of peace here. A fountain splashed gently near the entrance. A flock of birds rose up from the front lawn, and Ethan heard the more distant sounds of tropical birds in the jungle behind him. He felt the last remnants of tension in his shoulders dissolve. It was one of the most spectacularly beautiful places Ethan had ever seen.

The driver agreed to wait while Ethan went to check in and get keys. When he returned he lifted a still sleeping Cat from the car and carried her to her room. He didn't have the heart to wake her so he placed her gently on the bed and left her there, alone.

As he walked to his own room, past the mirrored reflecting pools and manicured gardens of the resort complex, he became lost in thought. Now that the job was done, what was he going to do about Cat? More specifically, what was he going to do with his feelings for her?

He flipped back through the events of the past several hours. He turned to that moment of danger, when he'd been trapped at the security desk, ready to sacrifice everything for her. He closed his eyes at the memory.

What more did he need to know? He had clearly surrendered himself to her.

Only one question remained: how did she feel about him?

Ethan's heart twisted. Could she ever truly be his? Even if they found a way to be together, would a part of her always belong to Jack?

He didn't know if he could live his life in love with a woman who was in love with someone else. But . . . what choice did he have?

Chapter Fifty-Four

I woke up alone in a strange bed, surrounded by white feather pillows and crisp sheets. Sunlight was spilling in through the blinds. It took me several seconds to clear the cobwebs from my mind and remember what had happened. Vague images soon filtered through the fog—our escape, Ethan carrying me out of the cab then tiptoeing from the room, trying to be quiet. I had slept like the dead ever since.

I turned to the clock beside the bed. It read 4:08 p.m. I had slept most of the day.

Memories of last night's heist came flooding back to me, sharp and visceral. The vault, the rooftop, flying through the air. Reflexively, I felt for the pouch inside my suit—there it was, the outline of the Lionheart Ring.

I got out of bed, stretched, and took a deep breath—the scent of flowers and sea air filled my nostrils. The beach. I needed to go down to the beach. I quickly changed into a cotton skirt and tank top, grabbed a towel, and tucked the pouch carrying the ring around my waist.

As I walked down the pebbled pathways and bamboo boardwalks to the beach, I thought I should probably find the others; we would need to debrief. But there would be time for that later. For now, I needed to clear my head about everything that had happened, and be alone for a few minutes. Besides, now that the job was done, I had to deal with an issue that was even more complicated, in many ways. I wasn't ready to face Jack and Ethan yet.

The tiny path I followed opened out into a secluded lagoon. I stepped onto sand like talcum powder, cool and white, and as I looked around my breath caught in my throat. I gazed in awe at the gently curving shoreline and jewel-like turquoise water. Lush palms and coconut trees rustled gently in the breeze, fringing the beach.

After finding a shady spot under a palm tree I spread out my towel and sat down in the cool sand. I reached into my pouch and pulled out the Lionheart Ring to inspect it carefully. I'd only had a moment to look at it in the vault. There was no rush this time.

I had done it. Which meant many things, not the least of which was: *I was in*. I had passed the test put forth by Felix and the League. If I wanted to, I could join them. It was my way out of this illegal life. It was my way to a more honorable path.

It felt completely right.

I gazed at the ring in my hand, my key to a better life. Then, I noticed carvings around the band. I brought the ring closer to my face and squinted. They were letters, a word. Was it . . . Latin? My father had insisted I take Latin in high school—in case I ever decided to go into medicine ("keep your options open, kiddo")—but I remembered very few words from that class.

I did, however, recognize the single word inscribed on the band: *Vigilate.* Something tugged at my brain, something I was supposed to be remembering. I stared more deeply at the ring.

Then I heard a sound in the jungle behind me.

I crouched lower and turned my head in the direction of the sound, a blast of adrenaline signaling danger. I cursed myself for being so careless and stupid.

Ethan stepped out of the trees. "Montgomery, it's okay. It's just me." He strolled toward me, looking refreshed and relaxed in linen trousers and a white T-shirt. He gave me a huge grin.

I sat up again and shrugged. "I knew that," I said casually.

"Did you?" he asked with a raised eyebrow.

I scowled and tossed a handful of sand at him. "Oh, give me a break. It was a long night. Maybe I haven't quite recovered yet."

He nodded and his forehead knotted in concern. "Well, that's why I came to find you. You deserved your rest today. Are you feeling better?" He kneeled down beside me in the soft sand.

"Like a new woman," I said. I gazed at our surroundings and took a deep breath. "This place is amazing."

He sat back. "It sure is." I watched him as he looked away over the water. The sight of him, the wind ruffling his hair, his forearms flexing under him as he shifted his weight back to recline, stretching his legs out in front of him in the sand, sent a warm tingling through my body.

He turned to me then, pinning me with those deep green eyes. "So, can I see . . . the ring?"

I held it out for him and he leaned closer. He took it in his hand and I watched him turn it over, staring at it carefully. My insides continued to melt, a side effect of his closeness.

"We did it, Montgomery," he said, lifting his head again.

"I know."

"Against all odds."

I nodded solemnly. Tears began to spring to my eyes and then I laughed, unexpectedly. He smiled, evidently not confused by my emotional flip-flop. "The victory feels good," I said. "But it's more than that . . ."

"It feels good to do the right thing *and* get away with something highly devious, at the same time," he said.

"Exactly."

The breeze stirred, warm and fragrant. The late-afternoon sun had begun its descent, hovering languidly in the sky, like low-hanging fruit. I dug my bare toes into the soft sand. The air felt heavy and sweet.

"You were amazing, by the way," he said.

A flush warmed my cheeks. "Thanks, Ethan. You weren't too shabby yourself."

There was a pause. Then he said, "We make an incredible team, you and me. You know that, right?" I nodded. It was true.

The air felt charged, like it does just before a lightning storm. In an instant, Ethan leaned forward and kissed me. His hand went up and tangled in my hair and he pulled me closer, kissing me more deeply. His scent filled my brain and the warmth of his mouth became the entire world. The beach, the jungle, the lagoon—everything else faded to a blur.

He pulled away from my mouth and began kissing my neck, traveling in a line down my throat. I let out a soft moan. We were all alone on the beach, tucked away in a deserted lagoon.

In one swift movement, he pulled my top off over my head, then I did the same to him. He kissed me again, and I ran my hands over the bare skin of his shoulders and chest. His strong arms went around me and he rolled me back, pressing me into the beach. The sand felt cool under my hot skin. I pulled him down onto me with a desperate urge to be even closer. His kisses grew more urgent.

He pulled away from me slightly and nuzzled my ear, nibbled at my neck. "You are going to be the death of me, Montgomery," he murmured. I laughed softly.

He propped himself up on one arm then, and gazed deeply into my face. "It's true. Not only do I want you . . . I also *need* you, here." At this, he pointed to his chest. Something flickered across his face. Was it—sadness? "I've never felt like this about anyone before. It's like I can't get enough of you. Even though I always seem to get crushed in one way or another, I always want to come back for more."

I didn't know what to say. His words took my breath away. I felt a spasm of sadness and guilt—I knew I had hurt him. I didn't want to do that ever again.

"You're intoxicating. You're like a drug." His eyes glimmered as he said, "It's almost like you're doing something illegal to me." He looked at me with a wry smile then and a wicked tilt to his eyebrow. "But that's not like you. You would never do anything . . . *criminal*, now, would you? A nice, innocent girl like you . . ."

I laughed again and he did, too. A moment later he tugged my skirt down, slipping it right off my legs. I felt a tremendous need to rip off all his clothes, too. My fingers tugged gently on the waistband of his pants, and with a wink he nudged my hand aside and took care of them for me, pulling his pants off and tossing them aside.

He rolled on top of me and kissed me deeply, pressing me farther into the sand. I was down to just my bra and underwear, and he only wore his boxers.

I arched toward him. We moved in perfect sync. He deftly unhooked my bra with one hand. Now there was nothing between us, and the feel of his hot skin on mine quickened my breath. I thought of nothing but Ethan, and all the amazing things he was doing to me.

This felt so right. Completely and entirely perfect.

Later, we lay together on the sand in afterglow, and watched as the sun dipped below the horizon. I was stretched out along the length of Ethan's body, both of us naked. Our skin glistened faintly with sweat and the beach shone with burnished light.

"I could really get used to that," Ethan said. "A lot more of that, in the future."

I smiled and drew a lazy finger over his bare chest. "What do you see in the future? You know, for us?" I glanced up at his face.

The sun was setting but it wasn't yet dark and I could still make out his features. A cocktail of emotions crossed his face.

I tried to laugh it off, suddenly realizing how ridiculous and clingy I sounded. "I'm sure you don't think about that—"

"No. I've thought about it a lot, actually," he said. "I see an amazing future together for us, Montgomery." It was the most serious I'd ever heard him.

"And?"

"Well, like I said—I see there being a whole lot of . . . *this*." He raised an eyebrow meaningfully. "But what else . . ." He sighed and put his hands behind his head, gazing up to the sky. "We could travel the world. We would learn new things together and have all kinds of adventures. We would eat all the best food, and drink wine, and explore . . ."

I closed my eyes and exhaled. It sounded incredible. Although I felt a small twinge of concern. How would that jibe with the idea of having a family? "And what about work? Do you see us continuing . . . the profession?"

"Of course," he said. Then he hesitated. "Well, I suspect things wouldn't stay the *exact* same. We'd have to adapt our routines a little. Other things might become a priority. But . . . you know, while we're scaling buildings I'll be sure to carry the baby nice and safe in one of those Baby Bjorn things. And, let's face it, a lot of surveillance can be done while pushing a stroller. You know?"

I opened my eyes and gave him a look. In the last rays of the setting sun I could see his characteristic smirk. I laughed and swatted at him.

But I knew what his words meant. I blinked, not daring to believe what I thought he was telling me underneath all the joking.

Ethan propped himself up on one arm, facing me. "Bali looks good on you, Montgomery. Have I mentioned that?" His eyes focused on my naked body and I felt beautiful under his gaze. Warmth rushed through me and I stopped thinking about anything other than Ethan, and how I was feeling.

Under a sky on fire, we joined together again. The urgency had melted away this time, and there was no hurry whatsoever.

Chapter Fifty-Five

Much later, Ethan and I awoke on the beach, in the darkness. We had gone for a swim in the ocean then fallen asleep on the sand, and now the moonlit sky was sprinkled with stars.

My stomach let me know, loudly, how excruciatingly hungry I was. I shook Ethan more fully awake and we both dressed. I checked my phone for the time but the battery was dead.

"It must be close to nine p.m.," Ethan guessed.

"Do you have an undeclared skill for reading the stars, Jones?"

"I have all *kinds* of skills you have yet to learn about, babe," he said.

I laughed.

"I think there's food in the common room," Ethan said. "I saw a sign last night."

"Oh, thank God. I could eat a horse."

"I'm not sure they serve horse in Bali. But we could check . . ."

I looped my arm around Ethan's and we made our way back to the central part of the resort. Indeed, we followed the heavenly scent of cooking food straight to the main grass hut. I imagined everyone else was still in their rooms, sleeping off our escapades. We stumbled into the common room, me giggling and both of us looking rather tousled, our hair still wet.

I stiffened at the sight of the team in the common room: Felix, Gladys, and . . . what the hell was Brooke doing here? Atworthy was here, too, which was almost as bizarre. I hadn't realized he'd come with us to Bali. Jack, I noticed, was not present. I exhaled quietly in silent thanks for that.

"Cat, Ethan, where *were* you?" demanded Felix. "We've been looking for you all day. And neither of you were answering your phones."

I flushed. I wanted to crawl out of my skin with the awkwardness. Ethan looked cool and unperturbed, as per usual.

"My phone battery died," I said quickly, knowing this fell well short of a sufficient explanation for our disappearance. "And . . . we had some business to discuss," I offered. It was a pathetic lie. Normally I was better at thinking on my feet, but my recent activities on the beach must have muddled my head.

Then I noticed, with growing alarm, that everyone looked extremely concerned. Something was wrong.

"What's going on?" I said quickly, a prickle of warning moving up my neck.

Gladys looked at me with worried eyes. "Templeton is missing."

"What?" My heart raced, and I felt Ethan tense beside me.

"He never arrived. Nobody has seen him. And he never checked in to his room."

I swallowed, thinking it through. "I'm sure he's on his way. He'll be here any second."

"Yes, but his journey, by boat, was the most direct one. He should have been here before any of us," Brooke said.

I frowned and turned on her. "Brooke, what the hell are you doing here, anyway? The last time I saw you, you were decidedly *not* on my side."

"I came with Jack," she said plainly, ignoring my tone. "I helped him escape, you might be aware."

I narrowed my eyes. "And what does that mean—you've abandoned Caliga entirely?"

She shrugged. "I wasn't really on board in the first place. It seemed a good idea at the time." A whisper of something crossed her face—remorse, sadness, possibly a touch of repulsion. It was similar to the look I'd seen right after Caliga had killed Esmerelda.

I couldn't spare any additional worry for her now. I'd deal with Brooke later. For now, I needed to focus my attention on locating Templeton. I chewed a fingernail and tried to ignore the twisting sensation in my stomach.

"How can nobody have seen him?" said Ethan.

"He was the only one who was supposed to journey here alone, remember?" Felix said.

Damn. That was right. "Where's Jack?" I asked. I realized I'd been expecting him to burst through the door at any second, ready to save the day.

"He's been missing for most of the day, too. Somebody thought he'd gone into the village for some reason, but we haven't heard from him in a few hours. He left just before we realized Templeton was missing," Atworthy said. I turned to him abruptly; I'd forgotten he was there.

"Atworthy, how did *you* get here? I didn't realize you knew where we were headed," Ethan said.

"I took a flight from Singapore. Once I knew you were all in the clear."

"Professor Atworthy was the one who raised the alarm about Templeton," Felix said. "He was the first to notice he was missing."

I looked at my professor with gratitude. "It seems like I have a lot to thank you for these days, Atworthy." He nodded graciously.

"There has to be an explanation," Ethan said, reaching for Felix's phone, starting to make a call. "Maybe Templeton got lost leaving Singapore. He's not used to field duty, right?"

"Okay, well, you guys keep trying to contact him. I'm going to talk to the front desk," I said. "Somebody must have seen him or talked to him."

I walked briskly out of the grass hut, wanting to believe Ethan's simple explanation but not being able to ignore the growing feeling of dread in my gut. I was also concerned about Jack. Where was he?

I followed the winding garden pathway to the main office, to see if they had any information on Templeton's whereabouts. I was worried, and I didn't like the anxiety swirling in my stomach, telling me this wasn't simply Templeton getting lost. I glanced up at the stars pinpricking the dark sky. Only minutes before, I'd been on the beach with Ethan, gazing at this very same sky, not a care in my mind. How quickly things had changed.

I had to find Templeton. I felt a wave of nausea at the idea that I'd failed him.

Then, I heard someone behind me.

"You probably shouldn't waste your time going to the front desk, Catherine." I spun. Professor Atworthy was there in the pathway. There was something odd about his voice. "Templeton won't be coming."

I frowned. "What do you mean? He went straight home?"

"Not exactly," he said. I didn't know if it was a trick of the light, if I couldn't see clearly in the dim glow offered by the garden lanterns, but there seemed to be something completely transformed about Atworthy. His eyes were different. His face.

My skin chilled.

"Templeton is in prison," he said flatly.

"What?" I choked.

"He was caught. He didn't make it out of there. And now, he's going to be facing the death penalty. In Singapore, they do not look kindly upon armed robbery. Particularly conspiracy with a group. The police, well, they wish they had caught everyone, but they only have Templeton. And they will make an example of him."

I grew still, watching Atworthy very closely. I was afraid to ask my next question. "How do you know all this?"

"I know, because we know everything. There are no secrets from Caliga."

My mouth went dry. It felt like an eternity before I said anything. "You—you're working for Caliga?"

"No," he said. "I'm not working for Caliga. I am Caliga." He smiled, a serpentine expression. "I'm the man in charge."

My head spun. I could not believe what I was hearing.

"Pay attention here, Catherine. Because I am the only person who can get Templeton out of that Singapore prison. So I recommend you listen carefully to what I have to say."

Chapter Fifty-Six

Atworthy didn't have to issue the warning. Although I was horrified, reeling from the shock and betrayal, I was not about to miss a single word he was saying.

"What do you want, Atworthy? I suppose you want the ring back?"

"Yes, that goes without saying. But there's much more."

I cringed at everything about this new, transformed Atworthy, and resisted the urge to take a step back. We stood in the darkened gardens of the resort, surrounded by bamboo and abundant rhododendrons—a beautiful setting for a very ugly conversation.

"We also want you. Joining our team is your only way of getting what you want now. Deep down, I think you know you're a part of Caliga, Cat. You've always been one of us. I knew it right from the beginning, when I first met you." His voice was warm, gently cajoling, yet it sent chills up my back.

It was fascinating, in a bizarre way, to watch him. There was so much about Atworthy's manner that hadn't changed. He wasn't unrecognizable, not Jekyll and Hyde . . . he was just clearly, and quietly, on the side of darkness now.

I struggled to piece everything together. If I could stay on top, stay clear, I had a chance of saving Templeton.

"You were giving information to Hendrickx, weren't you?" I said. "That's how he knew where to go. You were helping us and hindering us, at the same time." It wasn't really a question. He merely smiled.

I dug my nails into my palm. "Atworthy, I'm not joining Caliga."

"That would be a grave error. Besides Templeton, and what might happen to him, you have to know that AB&T is finished, anyway, Catherine. They have not kept up with the times. They cannot protect their assets. They cannot protect their people. Look at what happened to you last year, with Faulkner and the Hope Diamond. Look at what's happening to Templeton right now. If you want to continue being a thief, if you want to save Templeton, you'll need to join us. Really, it's win-win."

I struggled to not reach out and strangle him. "If I cooperate with you, you will arrange for Templeton to be released?"

"I will."

"How do I even know that's possible? You're not the police or the justice system."

"No, we're not. But we *are* Caliga, and you should know, by now, that our reach is far and deep."

Unfortunately, I did know that. "And if I don't go along with whatever you've got in mind—what happens to Templeton?"

"He will be executed in a Singapore prison. If he doesn't die before then."

My stomach twisted in horror. Executed? "They don't execute people for robbery," I said. "You're bluffing."

"They do if it's armed robbery, enacted by five or more people. Singapore is particularly displeased with that sort of crime, and they put it in a class of its own. The death penalty is expected."

"But—it wasn't armed robbery. None of us pulled a weapon. None of us even *had* a weapon."

"No?"

At this point, he handed me his phone. On the screen played a recording of a CCTV feed. It was time-stamped—twenty minutes past midnight, last night. In the Marina Sands, outside the high-stakes poker room, a man with a full face mask was holding a gun to Chips Walker's head.

I blinked at the condemning images. It must have happened after Gladys had left the poker room. After we had all begun our getaway. The video looped and I watched it again. The masked man—his height, weight, and frame were familiar. I could tell it was Atworthy. And this video was the reason they were calling our heist an armed robbery.

The realization slammed into me. He had screwed us.

Atworthy read my expression. "You could interpret this as me working against you," he said. "Or you could see that I helped you. I stopped you from getting caught, Catherine. I allowed you to get the ring. I allowed you all to get away."

"Except Templeton."

"Every gambler keeps a chip or two for himself."

A wave of nausea flooded through me. This was my fault.

"Here, you can read about it yourself," he said, handing me a newspaper. "I'm sure you'll find it fascinating."

I scanned the page in the dim garden lantern light. It confirmed everything Atworthy had said. A "dangerous criminal" was behind bars, charged with armed robbery and facing the death penalty. I pictured Templeton in a grimy Singapore prison, demoralized in a convict's jumpsuit. Would they torture him for information on his co-conspirators?

"Okay, Atworthy—what do you want? What will it take for you to arrange Templeton's release? You must have something specific in mind."

He smiled. "Indeed I do."

"Tell me what you need. I will tell you if I can do it," I said, trying to hold it all together. I wasn't sure I'd ever hated anyone as much as I despised Atworthy at that moment, but I had to remain calm.

"It's heartwarming to hear you being so reasonable, Catherine. First, I need you to fly back to the States. Here is your ticket; you leave tonight. When you get there, I will give you further details. I really think you're going to like what we're cooking up. It's quite a good one—quite exciting."

I heard a car pull onto the nearby service road, on the other side of the garden's entrance. Atworthy lifted his head. "Ah, there's my ride."

"You're leaving?"

"I'm flying back to the United States. You are to make your excuses to the group and find your way to the airport." He handed me a flight itinerary. I glanced at the destination. JFK Airport, New York.

"And the ring?" I asked him. The Lionheart was still burning in my pocket.

"Keep it for now. But bring it with you to New York. We'll need it there. I trust you'll be able to transport it safely."

I thought of a hundred ways I could make the Lionheart Ring disappear between now and my arrival in New York. But each and every scenario ended with Templeton hanging to death in Singapore.

Atworthy watched me carefully. "Catherine, it is no use telling your friends what I just told you. They can do nothing. Your charming little AB&T team does not have the sort of reach Caliga does. Your washed-up FBI agent and his sidekick brother who tends to get himself kidnapped, your charming but ultimately useless art thief, that bitch of a traitor, and . . . a sweet old grandmother. Face it, Catherine, your team is cute, and clearly devoted to you, but toothless. Your only hope of getting Templeton rescued is by cooperating with me."

I seethed inside at his condescending criticism, but said nothing.

"If you were to tell Jack or Ethan," he continued, "I have no doubt they would attempt to intervene. You do seem to have surrounded yourself with idealistic heroes. But let me assure you, this would be a bad idea. They would fail. And if I receive any sort of interference from those two, I will arrange for Templeton's execution to happen right away. Caliga has deep connections in the Singapore justice system. It's a very easy thing to reschedule an execution, move it up by a day or two, for example."

I didn't know if he had the authority to actually make good on this threat. But it was not worth testing. Not right now, not before I knew more.

It meant I couldn't tell either Jack or Ethan. Atworthy was right—they would try to stop me. Or they would try to help, and that could end up costing Templeton his life. I couldn't let that happen.

As Atworthy strode away and climbed into the waiting airport car, I replayed his words. In particular I thought about what Atworthy had said about Felix. Or, more to the point, what he hadn't said.

There was zero mention made of Felix's involvement with the Global Protection League. Was it possible Atworthy had no idea about that? I sifted carefully through our conversation. No, there was no way he knew about Felix and the League.

It was the only card I had. And I was going to have to play it.

Chapter Fifty-Seven

I had the front desk send a quick, urgent message to Felix: "Meet me at the pool, in the southernmost cabana. Come alone." I made my way to the rendezvous spot, an enormous square pool around which were arranged luxurious grass-roofed cabanas, each furnished with cushions and chaise lounges and surrounded by linen curtains shifting gently in the breeze. The far side of the pool was an infinity edge overlooking the Balinese jungle. Ceramic lanterns and three round firepits glowed against the night sky. The pool was closed for the night and the entire area was deserted.

Several minutes later Felix entered the cabana where I waited, looking cautious. "What's going on, Cat?"

"I've got a problem."

I shifted my glance around the pool area. Did Atworthy have some way of watching me, even now? His deception had been so complete anything seemed possible now.

It was a chance I would have to take. I described the situation to Felix, telling him everything that had just happened with Atworthy. When I finished, I took a deep breath and watched him carefully. "So? Can you stop them?"

Felix had been very quiet while I spoke, and he remained so for several moments. Finally he spoke. "Yes, we can stop them. If you give us all your evidence, right now. That flight ticket, your testimony, everything you can think of to nail Atworthy and Caliga. And when Atworthy gives you the details—all that, too. Then the League can take them down."

I exhaled with relief. Then hesitated. "But can you save Templeton?"

"We . . . can try. But to be honest, I'm not one hundred percent sure. I can't make any kind of guarantee."

I frowned and gazed through the open walls of the cabana, across the smooth water of the pool. I swallowed and said, "That's not good enough, Felix. I *have* to save Templeton."

"I'm sorry, Cat. It's the best I can do."

I nodded. "I understand. But it means I'm going to have to hold off telling you everything. I can't have the League getting involved with this and messing up my chance of rescuing Templeton. "

I would have to continue being a double agent. I would have to go along with Atworthy for a little while until I could figure another way out of this.

Felix shifted on his feet, looking even more uncomfortable. "I have to say, Cat, my supervisor isn't sure he can trust you. If you're seen to be working with Caliga, it's going to be hard for me to convince them you're on the right side. And . . . if it doesn't work out, you will be a person of target for us."

I nodded. "That's a risk I'm going to have to take."

Just like that, all my hopes—of changing my life, of working for the League, of finding a way out of my life of crime—simply dissolved into the salty Indonesian night air. A lump formed in my throat. I tried to swallow against it.

Felix looked at me with anguish in his eyes. "Listen, I'll talk to my supervisor. I'll see what I can do to convince him to save Templeton. But Templeton is not on our list of target recruits. I know my superiors won't want to sacrifice any personnel for a rescue mission. But I'll try . . ."

"Okay, the minute you find out, tell me," I said. In the meantime, I knew I had no choice but to go along with Atworthy. I was going to join Caliga.

Felix left me standing beside the pool. I stared at the flickering light reflected on the water's surface from the lanterns.

I could practically taste the irony. After all these years, the exact job that was supposed to bring me freedom had snared me like a bear trap. On the verge of finding a way to use my skills and live an honorable life at the same time—I had to throw it all away.

And Atworthy's betrayal—my head was still spinning at the deception. Atworthy was the top man in Caliga. He'd made it sound like he'd been watching me all this time, grooming me, waiting for the perfect opportunity to bring me over to the dark side. It was almost impossible to believe.

Then I remembered Venice. He had helped us. He had *saved* me. Why had he done that?

I heard someone approach behind me. I swiveled and saw Jack walking up the steps to the cabana.

"Jack! There you are. Has anyone told you? Templeton—" I stopped then. What could I tell him? If I explained about Templeton's imprisonment and Atworthy's ultimatum . . . well, he might be in a position to help. Or, more likely, he would make things much, much worse, by interfering and ensuring Templeton's death sentence.

"Cat, I need to talk to you," Jack said. He was looking at me in a very strange way. I wasn't even sure he'd heard what I said. "I mean, I know Templeton hasn't turned up yet, and I'm sure you're concerned . . . but I really need to get this out. It can't wait any longer."

Nerves twisted in the base of my stomach. I really did not need more bad news. "What's wrong?"

He rubbed the back of his neck and hesitated, seemingly gathering his thoughts. "I'll tell you what's wrong. I am completely in love with you, Cat. I have been fighting it and resisting it—do you have any idea how *bad* you are for me? But I can't fight it anymore. The truth is, I don't want to be without you anymore."

I opened my mouth to say something but no sound came out. It was the last thing I expected to hear right now.

Jack looked away and stared at the water's edge. "Lord knows I have tried to live without you," he continued. "But it cannot be done, Cat. I need you."

This was not a conversation I could handle right now. "But—we've been through this before, Jack," I said gently. "And every time we try . . . well, you know—we're like sparks in a powder keg."

"Yes, but I realized: all that's changing. We're not on opposite sides anymore. Everything that was black and white is in shades of gray now. And then there's the future."

This stopped me short. "What about the future?"

"You know, Cat," he said in a low voice, looking at me deeply. "We've talked about it. You told me what changed for you, what you realized you wanted, after your mom was shot. And the fact is, I want all that, too. I'm ready to settle down. I want a family, Cat. And I want that with you."

"You—what?"

He smiled. A warm, heart-melting expression that made my knees go weak. "You don't plan on scaling buildings forever, do you? Why don't we start that future sooner, rather than later? In fact, why don't we start that future right now?"

I heard a sudden sound behind me—a faint scraping. A footstep? I turned and squinted into the darkness but there was nobody there. When I turned back to Jack, he was down on one knee. I froze as he reached into his pocket and pulled out a small box.

"I know the timing is insane, Cat, but I really need to ask you and I don't want to wait any longer: will you marry me?"

I could not speak for several seconds. Jack opened the box to reveal a ring. A gorgeous gold ring with an enormous white diamond. A fairy-tale ring, a ring fit for a princess.

"Jack, I—I don't know what to say. I'm completely shocked . . . I need some time . . ."

A brief flash of disappointment flickered across Jack's features. My heart twisted painfully as he looked down at his hands. "I know, it was a crazy thing to ask," he said. "I just thought—"

I squeezed my eyes shut. "I really can't think about anything else right now, with Templeton missing and everything . . ."

"Okay," he said, standing up. "I understand. Take—as much time as you need, all right?"

He still held the ring awkwardly. I felt breathless, but I had to fill the awful silence with something. "It—it's a beautiful ring," I said. "Really . . . um, beautiful." In spite of my pathetic babblings, it was true. I wondered where he'd got it anyway. Then I remembered. He'd been in the village today.

His jaw flexed. "Why don't you hold on to it, Cat? You can wear it on your other hand for now, while you're thinking about it . . ."

I chewed my lip and considered. "Okay. I can do that." I shrugged. "The hand of a jewel thief is probably the safest place for a diamond to be, anyway . . ."

He tried for a smile and failed. I took the ring and slid it onto my right hand. With no other words, I walked out of the cabana, back toward my room. My head was spinning with conflicting emotions and I hated thinking of him standing there, alone, in the darkness. But I had to get away.

Chapter Fifty-Eight

Bali, 11 p.m.

Jack stood alone by the pool. He stared at the shimmering surface of the water, not sure what to think. Cat's response had been . . . confusing. She had been caught by surprise, of course. But there was something else.

Maybe she was distracted. He'd chosen a bad moment. *Stupid move, Barlow*. There was too much going on, with Templeton possibly missing.

But even still, he had expected a different response. Had he completely misread her on the terrace in Singapore? Jack cracked his knuckles, hesitating by the water's edge. It had been a mistake to propose. What the hell had he been thinking? He'd let Brooke, of all people, actually plant this toxic seed in his brain. It served him right for listening to her.

He'd go find Cat right now, tell her he'd been too hasty . . .

His phone rang.

"Jack, I need you," Wesley said through the line. "We found it. We know exactly where the Fabergé egg is. And this time it's going to be out in the open, on public display. *We can get it this time, Jack*. Can you make it back to the States? Fast?"

Jack's eyebrows raised. The States? On public display? He hadn't heard Wesley sound this excited, this certain about the whereabouts of the Fabergé since . . . well, since they'd started searching for it.

What had Evelyn, his housekeeper, said to him? What had Templeton said to him? *You need purpose*.

Here it was. There was nothing for him here in Bali. He wasn't worried about Templeton—there were plenty of people looking for him, and that man would surely land on his feet; he was like a cat. And Felix—he was safe now. Hadn't that been Jack's purpose in coming overseas in the first place? Well, mission accomplished.

Besides, the last thing he wanted to do was hang around here in this romantic resort after having proposed to Cat and receiving that lukewarm response. He'd buggered things up, but there was little he could do about it now. Making a clean exit would be much better.

"I can be in the air later tonight," Jack said. "Do I get any more details?"

Jack's private jet was still parked at the airport in Bali. He could pack a bag and make a quick exit. He wouldn't have to talk to anyone; he could simply disappear into the night. That would be best for everyone. His conversation with Cat would have to wait a little longer.

"I'll explain everything to you en route," Wesley said. "It's important that you get wheels up as soon as possible. Call me from the plane and I'll tell you everything you need to know."

"My pilot is going to need a destination, at least."

"All right, tell him to fly to New York."

Chapter Fifty-Nine

It was just past midnight in Bali, and Ethan tossed and turned in his bed. After what he had witnessed by the pool earlier that evening—Jack on one knee, proposing to Cat—sleep had been impossible. He'd been staring at the clock restlessly for the past hour.

He'd felt like an asshole, stumbling across them like that. He hadn't done it intentionally, hadn't been stalking Cat or spying on Jack, but he hated that it had felt like that. As soon as he'd realized what he was witnessing, he'd instantly made himself scarce. He couldn't be sure, but he didn't think either of them had seen him. With a little luck neither of them would ever know.

But he knew.

His chest ached at the memory. The feeling was too close to the way he'd felt years ago when he'd discovered his ex-wife sleeping with his best friend. He wanted to scrub all those images from his brain. A reprise of that—the shocked expressions at being caught, the requests for forgiveness—was the last thing he wanted.

But another image flashed in Ethan's mind: he and Cat on the beach, earlier that day. What about that? How could he possibly have interpreted that wrong? Unless . . . it had meant a whole lot more to him than it had to Cat.

There had to be a reason Jack proposed, Ethan thought bitterly. Guys didn't propose unless they had a damn good inkling they weren't going to get rejected. He must have received some kind of encouragement.

Ethan wanted to forget the whole mess. Turn his back on the lot of them, take some perverse satisfaction that he'd been right all along, and get the hell out of there first thing tomorrow.

But there was one thing he didn't know and it was gnawing at his brain like a worm: *what had Cat's answer to Jack's proposal been?*

After another hour of twisting in the bedsheets, he couldn't stand it any longer. He threw on a pair of jeans and crept outside. He moved through the shadowy garden courtyard to Cat's suite and raised his hand to knock on her door. Then it occurred to him, in a horrible rush of reality, that she and Jack were probably in there together. *Shit.* Why the hell hadn't he considered that before? He abruptly backed away, but then noticed something.

Her door was ajar.

Alarm bells clanged in his ears. Was she okay? Had someone attacked her? Without thinking, Ethan burst into her room, heart pounding, ready to do whatever was required.

The suite was empty. Nothing was out of place. And Cat's bed had not been slept in.

Oh. Ethan felt a wave of nausea. Nobody was here, because they must have been together in Jack's room, instead.

On his way back to his own suite, Ethan shoved his hands into his jean pockets. A piece of paper crinkled in there. He pulled it out, about to throw it in the trash, but then caught a glimpse of handwriting. He unfolded the paper; it was a note from Cat.

I'm sorry I had to leave suddenly, Ethan. There's something I have to do.

He frowned. Leave? He rubbed the back of his neck, totally unsure what to make of this. Instead of going to his room, he changed direction, heading for the bar he knew was still open at this time of night. It was time for a drink.

Under the grassy roof of the resort bar, he ordered a whiskey from the bartender. His mood lightened a notch as he thought things through. If Cat had gone off alone—called away on some kind of assignment—well, that had nothing to do with Jack, right? Perhaps there was still hope. Although, why the secrecy?

As the first sip of whiskey slid down Ethan's throat—smooth, smoky burning—Felix walked up to the bar. "Hey, Ethan, do you have any idea where Jack went?" He hopped onto a bar stool beside Ethan. "I went to his room and it seems like he's gone. Front desk says he checked out a couple of hours ago."

Ethan's hand froze. Jack had slipped out secretly, too? The burning mouthful of whiskey turned sour in his stomach.

Chapter Sixty

My body pressed firmly back in the seat as the plane lifted off the runway in Bali. Partway through the climb I felt the pilot turn, adjusting to a westerly heading back to the United States. It would be a long journey to New York, with stopovers in Jakarta and Abu Dhabi. I stared out the window into the blackness; a few shimmering lights winked at me from the villages far below. My heart ached. How wonderful it would have been to stay there a little longer. But it wasn't to be.

My head was still reeling from everything that had happened in the past few hours. Jack's proposal. Atworthy's betrayal. Being with Ethan on that secluded white sand beach . . .

Had that actually happened? Or had it just been a dream? The flight attendant came by with the drink cart and I knocked back a vodka, then asked for another. I was a mess. But I did know one thing: I had to save Templeton. I clung to that goal like it was a life raft.

I had left the resort quietly, sneaking away from everyone under the cover of darkness. And if there was one thing I was good at, it was sneaking away.

Bitterness flooded my mouth, and it had nothing to do with the vodka. I closed my eyes briefly and allowed a moment of frustration to wash over me at the fact that I had come so close. I had found it—my way out. I could have signed on with the League. They would have taken me. I could have used all my skills and talents for a good purpose.

And now, I was going to have to let all that go.

I stared at my reflection in the tiny oval window. What had made me think I deserved a respectable path, anyway? I wasn't Richard the

Lionheart. I wasn't even Robin Hood. The cold truth: I was just a filthy thief. I was a criminal, and that was all I'd ever be.

No tears fell from the reflected face in the airplane window. I was finally seeing things as they were, and there was a certain amount of peace in that.

I thought about Templeton in prison. I could barely stand thinking about him being there, wasting away even now, while I was being served a packet of crackers and the evening newspaper.

I shut the thought out. It wasn't going to help me do what needed to be done. I simply needed to focus on the job ahead of me. Whatever it entailed.

The pilot came on to announce our flight time and cruising altitude. At the end of this journey I'd be in New York. It was the city where I had first gone to college, where I had first honed my skills and become a professional thief under the tutelage of Brooke Sinclair. Until I had fled after her betrayal.

And now I was heading back, to betray everyone I cared about.

Chapter Sixty-One

Atworthy sat across from me in the limo as we drove away from JFK Airport. I had landed as the sun was peeking over the horizon, filling the sky with the pale sherbet colors of early morning. I shifted in the leather seat and stared at him, trying to understand how I could have been so utterly duped.

"Do you have the ring, Catherine?" he asked. He had the tone of someone asking for a spare pen, not a priceless gold and ruby ring. The arrogant bastard.

I said nothing but removed the Lionheart from my purse and handed it to him. He nodded and tucked it swiftly away.

"I don't understand," I said. "Why did you help us get away in Venice? Why didn't you kill us all then?"

"Big picture, Catherine. The goal has never been to simply stop you and your team. I wanted more than that. I wanted *you*."

"So . . . you were just trying to gain my trust?"

"You could say that."

"And you helped me steal the ring in Singapore—"

"Because I needed leverage. I knew I would get the Lionheart back from you eventually. I also knew you wouldn't willingly come over to our side. I needed to make you an offer you couldn't refuse."

"So this was all an elaborate plan? Everything you did was to get me into this position, to put Templeton in danger, to force me to join Caliga?"

He smiled. "You should be flattered."

"Surprisingly, I'm not."

He chuckled briefly. "Are you ready to hear about your assignment?"

I wasn't. The last thing I wanted to do was work for Caliga. But it was the only way to save Templeton. "Yes," I said. I prayed it would be a straightforward job, an in-and-out that would be over with quickly. Once Templeton was free, and safe, I would somehow sever all ties with Caliga.

He handed me a tablet and tapped open a file. "The job will happen here."

I stared at the screen showing a photograph of a midtown high-rise beside Central Park, topped with a spectacular roof garden. The next pages contained blueprints and schematics.

"And what will I be taking?"

He watched me carefully. "It's . . . complicated." He twisted the watch on his wrist, choosing his words. "To understand this assignment, you need to know what's at stake."

In spite of myself, I felt a prickle of curiosity at the base of my skull.

"You see, Catherine, Caliga has one large enemy we need to get rid of. Can you think who it is?"

"AB&T?" I offered.

He laughed. "Sweet, Catherine. But no. I'm talking about someone with true power to stop us."

"The CIA? The FBI?"

"Think bigger."

"Interpol."

"Bigger. And not so . . . organizational. A country."

"A country? I don't know." I was impatient. "North Korea. Iran. I have no idea. It might as well be the United States." I flung this last one out with exasperation.

His eyes gleamed.

I stared at him in disbelief. "You want to take down the United States?"

Well, that clinched it. They were completely insane.

"Of course it won't be easy," he continued, uttering the understatement of the decade. "So to do it, we need to use its oldest opponent."

"Russia?"

"Older."

I thought. "Britain?"

He put his finger on his nose. "You've heard of the deputy prime minister, Duncan Wakefield?"

The name tickled a memory. Then it flooded into my mind—Duncan Wakefield had been in the center of that whole Succession Bill controversy, the one that had recently been passed, the one the locals had been arguing over in Harrow Hall Pub.

"Duncan Wakefield is one of us," Atworthy said.

I struggled not to let my mouth drop open. "So you—Caliga—did you fix the vote? The Succession Bill—was that you?"

He nodded smugly.

"So if he gets into power, what would he do?"

"A few things. But eventually . . . declare war against America."

"That's completely ridiculous. It would never fly. The people of Britain would never stand for that."

He shrugged. "You'd be surprised. With the right proof, the right people behind the cause, it would take less than you'd think. And you're underestimating the degree to which Caliga has infiltrated the system. We've been planting the evidence for years now. Evidence of Americans spying on British citizens. Evidence of crimes against the British government. Evidence of plots to invade, reviving the old War Plan Red."

The old War Plan Red? "What's that?" I asked.

"In the nineteen-thirties, the US government drew up a plan to invade Britain. It's fact. Look it up. They just never acted on it. But if the British government had evidence the Americans were planning it again . . ."

"The Brits would be entering a war they couldn't win."

"Probably. Although it's a debatable point. But even if they lost they'd cause a mountain of destruction in the process."

I didn't know what to believe. It seemed impossible, but I remembered reading an article somewhere, the *New Yorker* maybe, a hypothetical discussion about who would win—Britain or the United States—if the two powers came to blows. It wasn't as clear-cut as you'd think. The United States had greater numbers, but the article argued that Britain had a more sophisticated military intelligence and a more powerful navy. Numbers don't always dictate. Take Vietnam. War is a complicated thing.

"The UK would be crazy to enter into war with the States."

"Maybe not so crazy. Especially if they had allies."

"What kind of allies?"

"Eastern ones." His eyes glittered.

"Why would the East join Britain against the United States?"

"Because of this," he said, holding up the Lionheart Ring. "Well, not only this. This, plus the other items in the Fabergé egg. I'm sure you know this ring was made with the lost Gold. With it, we now have all three Gifts of the Magi."

"The Gifts of the Magi are part of *Christian* legend," I said confidently. Another hole in his plot.

"Are they?" His triumphant smile caused a fluttering doubt in my chest. "The Gifts are from Eastern kings. The three Magi were from Africa, Asia, and Europe, according to the ancient legends, the old paintings. The power is Zoroastrian, and has nothing to do with Christ. He just happened to be the recipient. Plus—and this is where things get really beautiful—the Lionheart has the additional benefit of being a gift from an Eastern king—the sultan Saladin—to the king of England, Richard. It's the perfect symbol of the joining of East and West."

A wave of nausea curled in my stomach. It made some sense, in a very twisted way.

"Don't you see, Catherine? This is the way to reunite the old countries of the world. We have the Gifts; we are the old power. We need to take back the power from the new dragon."

"Like the American Revolution in reverse."

He nodded.

"But what you're really talking about is World War Three," I said.

"Indeed."

"You're insane. Like Sandor was. He believed the Gifts had some kind of special power. Do you believe that, too? Is that why you're doing this? Do you think the power of the Gifts will assure your success?"

He shrugged. With that gesture, I knew he didn't believe the metaphysical bullshit any more than I did. "Either way, the ring is crucial for getting the other countries on our side. They know the value of talismans in the East."

It was incredible. The depth, the layers of this plan made my brain spin. But I still found it hard to believe that Atworthy and Caliga would be able to catalyze war between Britain and America.

"And how do you plan to actually put this insanity into play? The deputy prime minister is just that. He's not in power."

Atworthy watched me carefully, waiting for me to piece it together. In the next second, I did. "Oh my God, you're going to assassinate the prime minister of Britain."

"And this is what we need you for."

I choked. "I'm not an assassin. That's not what I do—"

"Not to kill him. But because of what we need you to take, right before we kill him."

"And that is?"

He pulled up a second file. It contained information on the prime minister. "The current PM has suspicions. He has, for a while. But he hasn't dared to raise them publicly, as the deputy is too well-regarded. Duncan Wakefield is a very charismatic leader."

"And?"

"The PM is old school. He has kept copious notes and lines of evidence, everything against the deputy PM. Things that would get him kicked out, if he ever did gain power."

"And those files—they are what you want me to take?"

"Bingo."

I frowned.

"He carries his files with him," Atworthy said. "He locks them in a safe wherever he goes. But like I said, he's old-fashioned, and he doesn't save things electronically. Once the files are gone, our way is clear. Of course, accessing the private quarters of the PM would be exceedingly difficult. For anyone . . . except you."

He flipped a page in the dossier for me, revealing an invitation. "There will be a gala at the PM's residence in New York." He pointed to the rooftop garden of the midtown high-rise. "You will be in attendance, and during the party you will sneak away and into the suite. You will take the files, and bring them to me. We will take care of the rest."

I was quiet a while, staring out the window. "So if I get you those files, you will release Templeton."

"Yes."

"And you'll also assassinate the prime minister of Britain?"

He shrugged. "Catherine, it's a tough world out there. Bad things happen to people. You have been searching for a purpose. This is a very singular purpose. You would be instrumental in reshaping the world, the political planet."

It was a purpose, that was certain. But it was not something I believed in, not even a little. It was abhorrent; it was ridiculous. I was signing the death warrant of the British PM, and initiating all the repercussions. Did I really believe all this World War Three bullshit would actually happen? No. But—did it matter? Caliga believed it. Atworthy believed it. And they were prepared to do horrendous things to attempt to make it happen.

It occurred to me then—they would never let me live after this. I knew way too much.

I only had one choice. Agreeing to do this would be a play for time. There had to be some way I could stop their plans while appearing to go along with everything. Maybe there was a way out of this. I held on to a thin thread of hope.

In the back of my mind I knew if I didn't find a way to stop them, I would be part of the plot to assassinate the British PM, and possibly start a war. It would forever make me an enemy of the League.

I was trapped. "Okay, Atworthy. Looks like you leave me no choice."

His face beamed triumphantly.

I felt an immediate urge to negotiate the terms. To bargain, using the leverage I knew I had. *He needed me;* we wouldn't be here if he didn't. But I held my tongue. Better to play along for now.

We drove in silence for a while as I scanned the files. Questions exploded like grenades in my brain. The more information I could get, the better I could understand all the factors at play, and the more likely I could come up with a plan. I tried to ignore the weight of despair that pressed down on me.

"Why me, Atworthy? Why do you need me, exactly?"

He smiled. "I was hoping you'd ask."

I put down the file in my lap and waited.

"You must have noticed that everything about our plan has meaning. For Caliga, heritage, ancestry, and history plays a role. And that's true for you, too."

He handed me one final dossier. This time, it was a folder on . . . *me.*

"Can you guess what it is, about your ancestry, that intrigues me?"

I looked at him blankly. I had no idea. I opened the folder and stared at pages about myself. My history, my stats, my family . . .

"You are descended from thieves, Catherine. In fact, you are descended from the greatest thief of them all."

I froze. I searched his face and saw that he looked . . . proud to be telling me this. I turned a page in the folder and stared at a list of names, a family tree with dates, an insignia, and family crest.

At the top: *The House of Loxley.*

"My mother's family . . ." I whispered. My vision swam.

"No," Atworthy said. "Not your mother." I glanced at him sharply, knowing what was coming now. "*Your father.*"

"You're lying," I said.

He shook his head. "I assure you, I'm not." He reached across and turned the page over. There was a crest for Clan Montgomery. "Here. All the proof you need."

Underneath the crest for Clan Montgomery was the phrase *Garde Bien,* the official motto for the ancient Norman family. French for *Watch Well.* And the Latin translation of that was *Vigilate.*

I grabbed the Lionheart Ring from Atworthy. The inscription on it, the word I'd read on the beach that had felt so familiar: *Vigilate.*

"It's one of the reasons Caliga targeted you years ago. It's the reason I assigned myself to you at the University of Washington."

Atworthy went on to explain the legend. It was told that when Richard the Lionheart gave Robin of Loxley his ring, Robin brought it home to England, and it became the motto under which he toiled, ever loyal to his king. Robin and his true love, Marian, had married, and when Robin had died she had been pregnant. Marian buried him with the ring. To honor him, and to keep his child safe and secret, she adopted the old name Montgomery for her own protection.

I scanned through the family tree in the dossier. Marian Montgomery was on my father's tree, far, far back.

My hand dropped like a weight in my lap, loosely holding the ring. Atworthy reached across and plucked it from me; I did nothing to resist.

My father?

"This may help explain a few things," Atworthy said, turning the page. I stared at a document about my father, with details of his early life. He had grown up under a professional thief. And after dabbling in it as an adolescent, he had ultimately rejected the calling himself. *Just like Jack*, I thought.

The world tilted. My dad's father had been a thief. My grandfather had been one of us. All this time, I'd thought my father had been hurt and betrayed by my choice of profession because it went against his straitlaced upbringing and values. But it must have been because he grew up in that environment and rejected it. That was why my choice gave him so much difficulty.

Had he ever planned to tell me the truth? My heart ached, and I felt a fierce urge to confront my dad.

"I'm not surprised your parents never told you," he said. "Your ancestor, Robin of Loxley, was one of the most infamous villains to ever live. The most devious thief of all."

I blinked, looking at Atworthy, and realized: he saw Robin Hood as a common criminal. A thief and a scoundrel. His tone was smug. I realized something else. Atworthy thought, with this revelation, he owned me now.

But what he didn't count on was the fact that I saw Robin Hood quite differently. I wasn't ashamed of my newly revealed heritage. In fact, the effect this news was having on me was quite the opposite of what Atworthy seemed to expect. A burning ember of determination sparked to life inside me.

I was part of a legendary lineage. Robin of Loxley had possessed a higher purpose. He had helped the king. He had fought against insurmountable odds, under the motto on the Lionheart Ring: *Vigilate*. This was my family's crest, too. Montgomery. *Garde Bien.*

There had to be another way through this. In a flash of clarity, I thought about the ace Atworthy possessed, the whole reason he had me in a noose: Templeton. But what if Templeton wasn't in danger? Atworthy's trap over me would fall apart. If someone could bust Templeton out of prison, Atworthy wouldn't have anything over me.

It all depended on how much time I had. I calmly closed the dossier about my heritage and reopened the folder of blueprints, struggling to keep a neutral face. I couldn't let Atworthy see the change. "When is this all supposed to happen?"

"The party is happening tonight. You'll do the job then."

"*Tonight?* It's impossible—"

"Here's the agenda for the evening, and your invitation. You have the schematics and security details in that folder; it should provide everything you need. I recommend you stay in your hotel room and study up. I will be back to pick you up this evening."

Atworthy's phone rang. He took the call and spoke briefly.

"Is everything in place?" he said. "You have cleared the location, your post?" He listened, then nodded. "Good. We're a go from here. At my signal, you take the shot."

I kept my face impassive, concealing my glee at this. I had clearly done an excellent job convincing Atworthy I was on board, because he'd just been incredibly sloppy and revealed much more than he seemed to realize. It might give me the chance I needed. I surreptitiously glanced at my watch and marked the exact time. We arrived at the hotel where he was dropping me off. I had enough time—barely—but I would have to be quick.

"I expect you downstairs, in the lobby, at eight sharp," he said. I climbed from the limo and he watched me go through into the lobby. I checked in, but instead of going to my room, I walked straight back through the hotel and out the back entrance, then doubled back through the alley and out to the cross street.

I hailed a cab and pulled out my phone. I had two very important calls to make. I punched in the first number and put the handset to my ear, staring out the window with determination as I waited for the call to connect.

Chapter Sixty-Two

I used an encryption code to place the call. I had to assume Atworthy was monitoring my every move. I looked at my watch, and after a quick calculation knew it would be about six o'clock in the evening in Bali. It took a few rings, and then he answered the phone.

I breathed a sigh of relief at the sound of Ethan's voice. "It's me," I said. "Listen, I'm sorry I had to sneak away. I couldn't tell you why."

Ethan said nothing, so I continued speaking. "Ethan, I need you to do something. But it's not for me. It's for Templeton."

There was a brief hesitation, and then he said, "Felix told us Templeton is in a prison in Singapore. Did you know that?"

"Yes."

"Well, what do you need?" He sounded odd. Was something wrong? Trouble was, I didn't have time to deal with it at the moment.

"I need you to rescue him," I said.

There was another pause. "I'm sorry, Montgomery, this connection must be bad. It sounded like you just asked me to bust Templeton out of a Singapore prison."

"I did."

Silence.

"I know it's a big job," I continued. "But you've got Jack. And Felix. And Gladys . . ."

"Wait," Ethan interrupted. "What do you mean, I've got Jack? Isn't he with you?"

I frowned. "No, what are you talking about? I left the resort alone."

I sat back in the cab and thought for a second. If Jack wasn't with Ethan—where was he? Not knowing Jack's location left me feeling unsettled. With him out there, like a wild card, he could mess everything up. There was nothing I could do about it, though; I'd have to keep moving forward with my plan.

"I don't have much time to explain," I said to Ethan. "Atworthy is—well, he's in charge of Caliga. And if I don't do what he says, here in New York, he's going to ensure Templeton's execution." I quickly described what was going on, and exactly what I needed him to do.

Ethan listened quietly throughout. When I was finished, he said, "Montgomery, this is crazy. I need to go there to New York. I need to help you."

"No. That's the last thing that would help. If Atworthy knows I've told you, he'll make a call and have Templeton's execution expedited. I have to stay the course. But it's okay, Ethan, I have a plan. And it entirely depends on you being able to bust Templeton out."

"A prison breakout? I'm not sure it's something I can do—"

"You're amazing at getting precious works of art out of secure settings. Think of this like that."

There was quiet on the line while he considered. "Okay, Montgomery. I'll try. But I'm not sure it's going to work."

"That's all I'm asking. I just need you to try."

"I don't suppose you're going to tell me what your plan is? What Atworthy is making you do?"

"No. I can't. If I did, you guys would try to stop me. And if this gets messed up, then Templeton dies. I need you to get him out."

He sighed heavily on the other line, clearly unhappy with my secrecy. But he didn't object. I squeezed a fist tightly in my lap. *Good.* He would try.

"Okay, so Ethan, the next thing I need is for you to find Gladys and put her on the line. There's something I need from her."

I had a few more puzzle pieces to connect. But I was getting there.

"Sure, Montgomery. But before I go, there's one more thing."

"Okay, but can you make it quick? I'm on a tight schedule here—"

"I know Jack proposed to you."

My words died in my throat.

"I saw you," Ethan said.

So I *had* heard someone behind us by the pool in Bali. I still couldn't find any words.

"I don't know what you said to him, Montgomery, and it doesn't really matter. I just need you to know that I can't do this anymore. I won't be second fiddle, and I'm not going to get all tangled up in this again. No more ups and downs, because I'm getting off this ride. There won't be any more *us*."

A raw ache formed in my chest.

Chapter Sixty-Three

I was in the Holland Tunnel, deep underneath the Hudson River, waiting in the darkness. I had slipped down here through one of the ventilation tubes, and was now tucked into a service alcove, trying to be patient. The air was cold and damp, and the fluorescent lights that lit the road didn't penetrate into my small hiding spot. Deafening sounds of the constant flow of traffic did, however.

It was good to have something concrete to focus on. After Ethan had gotten off the phone, I'd forced myself to suppress the tangle of emotions threatening to derail my mission. I didn't know what to think—much less what to feel—but I knew I didn't have any spare moments. I'd have to deal with it all later.

For now, I was tracking the assassin's cell phone. Technically, Gladys was tracking it, and informing me of his progress. He was on his way to Manhattan; he'd be entering the tunnel any minute. When Atworthy had fielded that phone call in the limo, he'd told me everything I needed to know. *Take the shot* had revealed the method of assassination. *Clear your post* meant the assassin would be operating from a remote location. Which could only mean one thing: the assassin was a sniper.

Making note of the exact moment of the call had meant Gladys could trace it on the network and identify the caller's number. From there, we could track his vehicle, cross-checked with car registration. And now I had a plan for when he reached the tunnel. Atworthy was keeping me mostly in the dark regarding the details of the assassination plot. After all, I was only a pawn in his machinations.

But a pawn can bring down a king.

"Okay, Cat," Gladys said, "you're looking for a blue Prius. He just entered Boyle Plaza."

Perfect. The Jersey City entrance to the tunnel. I smiled a little at the fact it was a Prius. An assassin with an environmental conscience? Nice one.

Gladys was back in Singapore now, having traveled there with Ethan and the remaining team. I knew they were holed up in a hotel there, plotting Templeton's rescue, and I wanted to let her get back to that task. I would only need her assistance for a few more minutes, if everything went according to plan.

"Okay, Gladys, make it happen," I said.

In the next instant, there was a broken water main spraying everywhere. Cars came to an abrupt halt. It wouldn't be long before service vehicles and emergency response vehicles would come flying through.

I held my breath and scanned the rows of blocked vehicles. Blue Prius . . .

There. From my hiding place I spotted the car, although it was too dark to see the driver's face. I waited.

I knew the profile of an assassin. He wouldn't be content to sit there for long without knowing what was happening. Especially a sniper on the job, on the clock. It would only be a matter of time before he got out of his car to see for himself what was going on and insist they let him through.

I watched. And tapped my fingers. And as I was about to despair that he wasn't going to get out, the driver's side door opened. Out stepped a man.

He had short brown hair shot through with gray. His face was square and hard, and he gazed straight ahead with a cold, steely look. If I hadn't been completely sure before, the chills prickling my neck removed all doubt. This was the right man.

I surveyed the scene from my hiding spot. I knew the other drivers would be looking at the commotion, if they weren't already out of their vehicles. I needed to pick my moment.

Sabotage was my only hope at this point. It was the only thing that could buy me time and save the prime minister, without tipping my hand to Atworthy. For Templeton's life, I had to appear like I was still going ahead with the plan.

Like a shadow, I slipped through the darkened tunnel, knowing the focus would be at the emergency, the broken water main. I would be essentially invisible.

When I reached the Prius, I glanced briefly around, then slipped into the backseat. I looked around the interior of the car, hoping the briefcase would be in the front seat or the backseat.

Nothing.

Shit. He must have locked it in the trunk. I glanced up. There was still plenty of fuss over the water main. I had time.

I wiped the sweat out of my eyes and took a close look at the rear seat. Good. It was the kind I could access the trunk through. I unlatched and flopped the seat forward and reached into the assassin's trunk, praying my fingers would meet the hard surface of a briefcase and not the cold lumpiness of a dead body.

My gloved hand closed around a solid case. I exhaled with relief and slid it forward onto my lap. I focused on my next few steps, trying to stay calm. I had to get this job done in a matter of seconds.

Heart pounding, I opened the case and stared at the black rifle resting inside. I gingerly lifted it out and turned the adjustment on the scope by the tiniest amount. I knew he must have already zeroed his scope, and would have tested it before coming. As a sniper, he wouldn't have a chance to recalibrate the sight. Snipers had one shot, and the scope couldn't be off by even the slightest degree. A more obvious sabotage might be noticed by him. A subtle shift would be overlooked.

I replaced the rifle in its case, closed it, and slid it back into the trunk, terrified of the sniper's return. But nothing happened. I relatched the backseat and instantly slipped out of the vehicle. I walked quickly away across the rows of vehicles.

My ears were pricked for any suggestion I had been spotted. But there were no alarms, no shouts. Nobody had seen me climb in and out of a stranger's car. When I got several cars lengths away, I tucked into my alcove again, melting into the shadows.

I peered into the tunnel and saw the assassin returning to his car. He climbed into the driver's seat and I stared at the silhouette of his head. He didn't turn, didn't look behind him into the backseat. Within moments, traffic began to move again.

There was no sign he was suspicious of anything. I allowed a small flutter of triumph in my chest. It was done.

I began climbing back up through the ventilation tower. I had a gala to attend.

Chapter Sixty-Four

Ethan glanced at Brooke in the passenger's seat as he drove the team toward the Singapore prison in the surveillance van. Brooke was staring out the window at the skyline—a forest of skyscrapers with sunlight singing off their mirrored towers—as the van sped along the freeway. He hadn't intended for her to come.

But as he'd been packing his bags and preparing to leave the resort in Bali, Brooke had appeared in the doorway, dressed for a journey.

"Brooke, what are you doing here?"

"I'm coming with you."

"Why would you do that? It's going to be dangerous."

"Oh, is it? You mean I might chip a nail?" Her mocking look transformed into something more serious. "I'm aware of the danger factor, Jones. Obviously. But this is for Templeton. He doesn't deserve to be in there. He's the best one of all of us."

Now Ethan pulled the van off the freeway, where Brooke would take the car that was waiting for her. They would continue the journey to the prison separately.

Before leaving the van, Brooke applied a final layer of deep red lipstick. She checked her reflection in the mirror and smoothed her hair. Ethan caught sight of Felix gaping at her from the backseat, and he chuckled lightly to himself. Brooke was in her element—she was going in disguised as Templeton's lover. And she was relishing the role.

Ethan adjusted his white lab coat. For his part, he would be playing a doctor.

Gladys had discovered, by combing through the hacked e-mail system, that a visit had been arranged for one of the high-profile prisoners to be seen by a prominent cardiovascular surgeon. Ethan would be posing as that guy. Just arriving a day early.

Ethan cracked his knuckles. This was way, way out of his comfort zone. A high-security prison? Gladys had furnished them with a full set of blueprints and security details, but even still. He was going to have to pull off the con job of his life, with equal parts charm and deception. With a quick prayer to the patron saint of hustlers, he put the van in gear and drove on to the prison.

He was determined, and he wasn't going to back down now. Like Brooke said, Templeton was a good man. He did not deserve to be in this prison. He certainly didn't deserve to be on the death row of this prison. He was the sacrificial lamb in Atworthy's filthy game, and that was all kinds of wrong.

In spite of himself, Ethan wished Jack were there. The man was irritating, but he might have been of assistance. When they'd still been in Bali, Felix had tried calling him. "Jack, we need your help," he'd said, after finally getting through. "Where are you?"

There had been a pause. "I'm in New York."

"And what are you doing there?"

"We've located the Fabergé," he'd said. "This is big, Felix. I have to see this through."

Felix had disconnected the call and looked at Ethan, shaking his head. It wasn't going to happen. *Fine.* They'd do it without Jack's help.

After learning Jack's location, Ethan had hesitated a moment, then fired off a quick encrypted message to Cat. If Jack was in New York, maybe he could help her, somehow. Then it was immediately back to the planning of their own mission impossible.

At the prison, Brooke went in first. She approached the guard office while Ethan, Gladys, and Felix watched from the van just outside the parking lot, staring at the CCTV feeds they'd hacked into. Ethan tightened a fist; he wondered what state Templeton would be in. Would he realize what was happening and play along? Would he say something to blow Brooke's cover?

At the front desk, the guard shook his head firmly when Brooke said she was there to visit Templeton. "No visitors."

Brooke cocked her head, and arranged her mouth in the subtlest of pouts. She ran a hand through her hair, ostensibly trying to figure out what to do next . . .

The other guards in the office turned their heads toward her. Ethan smiled knowingly. It was impressive, the way she carefully amped up the sex appeal. He watched the guards' response.

Come on, Ethan thought. Were they really going to turn her away? Wouldn't they want to let her in so they could watch her a little longer? They were well-trained, clearly. It was the only explanation for their refusal.

And then, after a few brief words among them, they let her in. Ethan exhaled. *Good.*

And now it was his turn.

Ethan left the van and climbed into the driver's seat of the Mercedes that was waiting for him. He drove through the entrance to the prison parking lot, knowing they would be following in the van shortly. He parked in a VIP spot and walked to the guards' office, his breathing loud in his ears. Like flipping a switch, he centered himself and gathered his composure. He knew Cat had always marveled at his effortless ability to appear cool under pressure—she'd told him many times. But it wasn't effortless; it was a skill, like any other.

"You aren't on the schedule until tomorrow," the guard said in British-accented English, inspecting Ethan's ID.

"My surgical schedule got rearranged, and I had a block of time available this morning. My assistant was supposed to contact you with that information."

The guard scrutinized him, his deliberation stretching out agonizingly. Finally, he buzzed Ethan through. "Feng will inspect your belongings. You will have time to set up; your patient will not be here for a few minutes as we need to arrange his transit."

As Ethan waited in the visitors' area for his arrival to be stamped and approved, Feng, a larger, meaner-looking guard, rifled through Ethan's black doctor's bag. Then Ethan saw guards leading Templeton to his visitor, Brooke.

He didn't look good. Ashen, hunched, and much older than his years. Ethan fought to keep the shock from his face—only a few days' detention had done this to Templeton?

Ethan was then taken away by Feng, buzzed through the entry doors, and marched down a long corridor. But he could still hear Brooke through his earpiece.

There were murmurs of the sorts of words a lover and a prisoner would exchange. Ethan was impressed; Templeton was playing right along without missing a beat.

"Sugar, are you okay? You don't look so good. Maybe you need to see . . . a doctor."

"To be honest, darling, I'm not feeling at all well, suddenly . . ."

Good, Ethan thought. He'd taken the hint.

And then things got a little more agitated. "Oh honey, please stay calm," Brooke said. "I don't want you to have another heart attack, like last time. I couldn't stand that. If you had a heart attack. I'll never forget how you looked last time, the way you clutched your chest, started breathing heavily . . . it would be awful if that happened RIGHT NOW . . . Baby. I'm just so worried."

"Guard?" Brooke was saying. "I think he's having a heart attack! Help him!"

The only part of the gamble was this: how much would they care if Templeton dropped dead right there? He was on death row. It would save them the trouble.

But Ethan hoped the Singaporean sensibility would not allow something messy like that to happen. They valued control and order. A prisoner dying a few weeks before it was scheduled would not be looked upon favorably.

There were shuffling sounds and some discussion, and Ethan heard a guard's voice say, "Sir, sit down here, we're taking you to the infirmary."

Another guard said, "Your lucky day, old man. There's a famous heart doctor working there today. You picked a good day to have a heart attack."

At this point, Ethan had reached the infirmary. The regular doctor who worked there was on a tea break, he was told. Ethan began setting up the room and arranging his equipment on a tray—faking it utterly, but making it look good, Ethan hoped. A guard came in then and asked Ethan if he could see another patient first. He briefly described the situation.

"Fine," Ethan said. "Bring him right in."

While Ethan waited for his patient, part of his "setting up" process was to disable the CCTV in the room, which he did in short order.

In another minute they wheeled Templeton inside, seated in a wheelchair. He was clutching the center of his chest, hunched over. The room was suddenly crowded, with Ethan, Templeton, and one guard standing right behind Ethan. Ethan was unsurprised that Brooke was not with them.

"If they don't let you in," Ethan had said when they'd been planning this part of the op, "you still need to hang around. You need to look like you're waiting for news. What you're really doing is causing more of a distraction for the guards in the main office."

"You know I object to this role, on one level," Brooke had said. "I would rather be doing the interesting stuff."

"I know. But this particular world is male-dominated and sexist. We're just using that against them." She had seemed somewhat satisfied with this.

The guard was standing close, right off Ethan's shoulder, but his gaze was pinned on the prisoner. It was with a quick, smooth action that Ethan reached over and attacked the guard, pulling him into a strong headlock. The man had no idea what hit him, and then Ethan plunged a syringe in his neck, injecting him with the fast-acting tranquilizer he'd brought in his doctor's kit.

Templeton took it all in stride, as if he'd been in on the plan, and waited for instruction from Ethan. Even as a trampled prisoner, Templeton still managed to remain unflappable. It was an awe-inspiring sight. Ethan flashed Templeton a grim smile, and together they set to work.

They hauled the unconscious guard to the infirmary bathroom and stripped him of his uniform. They were going to disguise Templeton as the guard, switch their identities. They would only have moments in which to work; another guard could enter the infirmary at any time.

They shaved Templeton's face and eyebrows, and he inserted brown contact lenses. Ethan handed him a pot of cream to apply to his face—Brooke's secret weapon. "It's an irritant," she'd explained. "It'll plump the skin up, fill out the wrinkles. It'll take years off, within a minute. It doesn't last, and it burns like a son of a bitch. But if you really want to look younger, this will do the trick." Next came a tinted cream that gave Templeton the proper Asian coloring, and the finishing touch: a black wig.

The disguise didn't need to be perfect. It just needed to be good enough to give them a way out.

Templeton uttered quick pointers on the guards as he pulled on the uniform. "They'll send a second guard here in a minute. We won't have long." Ethan nodded. Templeton had obviously been monitoring the guards' habits and movements while he'd been inside the institution.

Working together, they dressed the unconscious guard in Templeton's prisoner uniform, and placed him on a gurney, rolling him over so he was facing away from the door. Then Ethan and Templeton quickly left the infirmary.

They marched down the corridor and reached the front security checkpoint. "This guard is escorting me to my vehicle," Ethan said in his most important and impatient tone, while Templeton stood behind him, pretending to be busily adjusting his walkie-talkie. "I need some further equipment." He waited for the guards to clear their exit.

"Where's the prisoner? The one having a heart attack."

Ethan glanced past them at the CCTV screens behind them. The screen under the label "INFIRMARY" was black. "We've left him in the infirmary. Another guard is there with him."

Ethan stared at the office guards and they stared back. A trickle of sweat rolled down Ethan's neck.

And then they buzzed him through.

Ethan and Templeton kept their eyes up, straight ahead, as they walked through multiple sets of doors and out into the parking lot. Ethan could see the van, waiting. They were almost there.

And then, Ethan heard Felix's voice in his ear. "Another guard just disappeared into the infirmary. He'll see the guard on the gurney. Any second—"

Ethan swallowed uncomfortably but they kept walking straight for the van.

"Guys, you need to move. *Now.*"

Chapter Sixty-Five

I stepped out onto the rooftop patio on Atworthy's arm and took in the sight that greeted me. Surrounded by Manhattan skyscrapers, with a twilit summer sky arching overhead, the rooftop gardens shimmered with a thousand twinkle lights. Marble sculptures gleamed among deep green yew hedges carved in whimsical shapes. Men in black tie strolled with women in couture, while a chamber orchestra sent music up to the heavens. A warm breeze rose up from the street, twenty-five stories below.

Thick, luxurious turf sank underneath my Louboutins as I walked. I accepted a flute of champagne from a waiter in white tie. Not that I was going to drink it; I needed to be sharper than that tonight. Atworthy was posing as a diplomat from a tiny country in Europe that nobody had heard of, and I was posing as his wife. The top floor of this building, an old art deco masterpiece from New York's golden age, had recently been renovated and converted into a luxurious private residence where guests of the US government would stay when visiting New York. Specifically, it was functioning as the official residence of the prime minister of Britain and his entourage.

And this was a party to celebrate the long and illustrious period of harmony between the two nations.

I wore a midnight blue gown, a floor-length column of silk—red carpet suitable. Which was appropriate, as I would be giving the performance of my life tonight.

My role on Atworthy's arm suited my purpose perfectly. Nobody ever paid the wife of a diplomat much attention, much less suspected her of doing anything duplicitous. Like breaking into the private rooms downstairs and stealing sensitive documents that would affect international security, for example.

I looked like myself; there was no need for a disguise. Nobody was looking for me here. And even if they were, it would be all over before they figured out who I was and what I was really doing.

Atworthy led me out to the dance floor. I could barely stand to look at him, but I had to keep up the charade.

"Are you enjoying yourself?" I asked through my teeth. It was a sentence that could have many meanings.

He merely smiled.

"Are you ready?" he asked me.

I nodded pleasantly. I was ready. But not, perhaps, in the way Atworthy intended. A steely resolve hardened inside me as I thought through my plan.

And then, a feeling of emptiness took over. I would be doing this whole thing alone. I thought of the Singapore heist. A true team effort; we'd had each other's backs. This couldn't be more different.

When I had been getting dressed in the hotel to come here tonight, I'd received a brief text message from Ethan. *Jack is in New York. Looking for Fabergé.*

I'd thought long and hard about how to handle that piece of information. But however I looked at it, it meant only one thing: Jack could mess everything up. And I couldn't risk that.

I'd gone down to the pay phone on the street outside the hotel, and placed an anonymous call to Wesley's boss, Oliver Cole, left a message, and hung up. Then I'd returned to my suite and applied one last coat of hair spray before Atworthy arrived to take me to the gala.

Atworthy spun me around the dance floor as the sky continued to darken. I glanced at his hand—the one holding mine. He was wearing the Lionheart Ring on his middle finger.

It was bold of him to wear it. But then again, nobody here knew it was stolen. Hell, nobody even knew of its existence.

My gaze slid over to the corner, where the Fabergé egg was on display in a bulletproof case. A mere party decoration out in plain view. Just another beautiful piece of art among the other riches on display. The origin of this particular Fabergé had been such a secret I knew nobody else there would understand the significance.

But I did. It was a test, for me. Atworthy knew I could make a try for it. And if I attempted to take it, he would order Templeton's execution.

I tilted my head and looked up at the buildings that loomed all around us. In one of them—I didn't know which—the sniper would be setting up. My palms went sweaty at the thought. Had I sabotaged his rifle enough? I could only hope I had.

The song ended and we separated. "There's someone here I'd like to introduce you to, Catherine," Atworthy said. "He's going to accompany you . . . should you need to attend the ladies' room, or if you feel unwell, or . . . well, anything like that."

I knew by "attend," he meant this would be the lackey who would go with me when I made the play for the papers. Someone posing as Secret Service perhaps, some henchman who would ostensibly protect me, but more accurately would protect Atworthy's interests.

"He's also here as backup. And a little bit of insurance," Atworthy said.

A man's footsteps approached behind me and I turned with a smile, ready to be introduced to the underling I would need to outsmart. And stared into the face of Sean Reilly.

Chapter Sixty-Six

Jack and Wesley stepped from their cab onto Fifth Avenue. They entered the lobby of the grand old hotel and crossed the busy, bustling lobby, Jack dressed as a white-jacketed waiter, Wesley as a guest of the gala upstairs, in a tux.

They rode the elevator together, all the way to the top, but separated after that. Jack would enter through the top floor kitchen, but Wesley would enter the party from the guests' entrance. They'd mocked up a fake invitation, once they'd received the tip the Fabergé was there.

Jack carried a tray, making sure he looked busy—lest he get roped into some menial task or other—as he walked by sous chefs preparing caviar and lobster, and porters carrying crates of champagne bottles.

Once he got inside the party, Jack would need to first locate Cat, and make sure she was safe. He knew she was there somewhere—that was the other piece of intel from the tip. Once he'd found her, his next job would be to find the Fabergé.

Why, exactly, the Fabergé was there tonight, Jack had no idea. Was it being watched? Being dangled? Being used as mere decoration—or as a demonstration of the prowess of the United States?

Jack wished he knew more about the particulars. He also wished he knew why Cat was tangled up with this again. Last he'd seen her (*had that really been only two days ago?*), she'd been in the paradise of Bali, at the resort. And he'd just proposed.

His gut tightened at the memory. God . . . what was he going to do about that?

Jack attempted to push all that out of his mind. He had a job to do. He did briefly wonder how Cat was going to feel once he and Wesley crashed this gala. Would she be pissed at them for messing with this little side operation she'd been working on?

She'd get over it.

Jack made his way toward the service entrance that led out to the gala. Before going further he straightened his jacket and pulled himself up to his full height. He pushed the door open and walked through.

He took two steps forward and found himself standing in a perfectly empty ballroom.

Jack stood there, stunned. Then the door opened on the far side of the ballroom and in walked Wesley. His bewildered expression matched Jack's exactly.

Jack instantly scanned the space, looking for dangers or signs of an ambush. Nothing. They were entirely alone. He crossed the floor quickly and approached Wesley.

"A trap?" Wesley hissed, looking around warily, exactly as Jack had.

Jack shook his head. "There's no evidence of that." No evidence of anything happening there at all.

Wesley pulled out his phone and double-checked the intel. But it was quite clear; this was the location. It soon became obvious what had happened: this was a wild goose chase. They'd been fed incorrect information, to keep them away from the real location of the Fabergé, the real operation, whatever it was.

And although it was possible Caliga themselves had set up this decoy, Jack had a likelier candidate. This trap hadn't really been a trap at all. There was no danger, no harm. If Caliga had set this up, they would likely be dead by now. No, the whole purpose of this ruse was to keep Jack and Wesley out of the way.

It had Cat's name written all over it.

Which meant one thing: Cat was in trouble. A prickle of dread walked up Jack's spine. How could he help her if he didn't even know where she was? A name immediately flashed into his mind—one person who might be able to help. He closed his eyes and thought it through, making sure it was his only option.

Jack turned on his phone and dialed Ludolf Hendrickx's number.

Chapter Sixty-Seven

Reilly twirled me around the dance floor of the rooftop patio; for a sociopathic son of a bitch he was a surprisingly good dancer. He was posing as an undercover Secret Service agent, but my mind raced as I wondered what role he was actually playing in Atworthy's plans. It couldn't only be to keep tabs on me. There had to be something more.

Atworthy had ordered us to dance, ostensibly so Reilly could issue some last-minute instructions. No doubt he was also going to assess how well I was falling into line.

"So, Cat Montgomery," Reilly said. "It seems we're working together on the same side, at last."

"Why doesn't it surprise me that you're part of this?"

He shrugged, smiling. "I'm part of whatever side is going to win. Anyway, do you think I care what happens to the British PM? I'm Irish, remember?"

"Don't worry, Reilly," I said through my teeth. "I would never have thought you might have cared about anyone. British, Irish, or anything else."

I started to pull away, but he held me tight. "Not just yet, lass."

He grinned, apparently not offended in the least by my attempt to get away from him. He pulled me closer, proving his point.

As offensive as it was to be embraced by this man and forced to dance with him, it did glean me a few interesting pieces of information. For one thing, as I began to pull away, my hand had dropped down his back a little. And what I felt there was a slender pack strapped around his waist, rising up under his jacket.

It was a microlight BASE jump parachute, in a slim backpack. I could tell because I'd been coveting one myself, although they were considered "experimental," only available as top-secret military issue.

So. Reilly was preparing to jump from this rooftop. But what was his intention? Was it merely a contingency plan? I thought back to dancing with Atworthy—I hadn't felt a similar pack on Atworthy's body. Reilly must have a special assignment.

The other thing I'd detected, when Reilly had pulled me tighter, was the edge of a firearm tucked in his holster. I wasn't terribly surprised he was armed, but it raised another question: was he planning to shoot someone?

And then I remembered something Atworthy had said, moments ago. He'd said Reilly was here as backup. As *a little bit of insurance*. My heart dropped into my stomach. Reilly was here as backup for the sniper, if the sniper failed.

Which I knew he would. Or at least I hoped he would, if my sabotage efforts had been a success.

This gave me a whole new problem. Now I was going to have to find a way to neutralize Reilly.

I remembered the gun Reilly had used in Paris. A Walther P99. It was a good weapon. It also happened to be my choice of firearm, too. Not that I usually carried a weapon, but when I did, it was always a Walther P99. It was the weapon I'd trained with. It had always bothered me that we had this similarity, but here it might work to my advantage. I knew that gun inside out. If I could get it from him, I could remove the firing pin, completely disabling it. The job could be done in less than a minute using little more than a pair of tweezers—something I had in my purse even now.

If I were to take his gun, however, it would have to be now. On the dance floor. This was as close as I was going to get. But was it even possible? My pickpocketing skills were solid, but Reilly was a seasoned thief, a professional. He'd know.

Unless I distracted him. It was time to use the other tools I had at my disposal. I commanded my muscles to relax, to soften into his arms a little. "Truthfully, Sean, I've been hoping we'd have the chance to work together someday," I said, my voice pitched a little lower.

I tried to keep things subtle; I couldn't lay it on too thick or he wouldn't believe me. I leaned in a bit closer, and let him feel the length of me pressed up against him. He was a man. On average men might be stronger than women, but they all had one major weakness.

He had always seemed disinterested in me on a personal level. Tonight was going to have to be different. I held my breath and gingerly moved my fingertips underneath his jacket, toward his holster.

This was multitasking at its best. Reaching in to his weapon, yet pretending to be calmly seducing him, all at the same time. I was close, and then I looked up into his eyes. What I saw there stopped me in my tracks.

He was not buying it. His gaze hadn't softened one iota; he was not being pulled in by my femme fatale routine. He hadn't detected my play for his gun yet, but if I went any further, he would.

I gingerly withdrew my hand.

The song ended and he nodded at me brusquely as we went our separate ways. That had been close. I had narrowly avoided disaster, but I was still left with a major problem: how was I going to disarm Reilly now?

Chapter Sixty-Eight

I strolled back toward the party, away from the ladies' room. It hadn't taken me long to pickpocket a woman's cell phone as she stood in front of the mirror applying lipstick. A phone was a critical part of my plan, and Atworthy's security assistants had confiscated mine when he'd picked me up.

I tucked into an alcove and sent Ethan a text on the stolen phone. "Send a message as soon as you have him." I hadn't heard whether Templeton was safe. I needed to know.

I then jotted a quick e-mail to the NYPD, with a critical piece of information I thought they could use. But I didn't send it. Instead, I scheduled it to send twenty minutes from now. I hoped my timing would be right.

The phone slid into my purse. I would have one more use for it.

I took a deep breath. A big task loomed ahead of me. Briefly, I considered an entirely different course of action. All it would take would be a word in the ear of the Secret Service guys at the gala.

I quickly dismissed the idea. For one thing, I didn't know which Secret Service guys were actually working for Atworthy and which ones were there to protect the prime minister. Even if I did manage to choose wisely, tipping them off about Atworthy's plan would effectively be giving the go-ahead on Templeton's execution order.

Until I got confirmation from Ethan, I needed to keep moving forward with my plan. There was always the chance Ethan would fail. A wave of queasiness passed over me at the thought.

Reilly and I met in the foyer outside the elevators, as arranged. When nobody was watching, we took the staircase down one floor, turned sharply to the left, and continued down a corridor—the one that led to the prime minister's private quarters.

The hallway was dim and our feet sank deeply into the plush carpet as we moved. There were no guards to overcome here; all the security staff were at the party protecting the prime minister. The belongings were entrusted to barriers and technology.

Always a mistake.

As we crept along the hallway toward the east wing, a plan formulated in my mind. I had to get that firearm away from Reilly.

When we reached the doorway that separated us from the east wing, where the prime minister's quarters were, I held my hand out to stop him. "There's a metal detector here," I said.

Reilly looked at me sharply. "Bullshit," he said.

"I'm serious, Reilly, I saw it on the blueprints. If you go across that threshold, your gun will set it off."

"How do you know I have a gun?"

"I assumed. You're posing as Secret Service, right?"

He narrowed his eyes at me. "I need to go through to disable the entry panel. Only my irises are coded for the scanner." I tried not to smile. I'd hoped this was true; there was mention of this arrangement made in the security dossier Atworthy had given me, although the name had been omitted. It had been a tricky maneuver on his part, and one he was proud of, no doubt. And now I was using it against him.

"Listen, I'll hold the gun," I said. "You go through and disable the door, then come back."

Reilly made no move to give me his weapon. He watched me with extreme suspicion.

I rolled my eyes. "Reilly, how stupid do you think I am? If I shot you, how would that help me? Atworthy would kill me, he would kill Templeton—and that's the whole reason he got me on board anyway, right?"

Reilly flicked on his phone and spoke into it. "Atworthy, I'm disabling the door. Montgomery is holding my firearm out of range of the metal detector. If you hear anything, come and kill her immediately."

I crossed my arms. "Feel better?"

Reilly, with a twist of his mouth, removed his Walther P99 from his holster and handed it to me.

"How suicidal do you think I am, Reilly? Come on, let's get on with this."

Reilly smirked at me, then walked through the archway, through the imaginary metal detector, and then several more feet down the corridor. There, he set to work on the security panel.

I waited, holding the handgun behind my back. In a second I had my tweezers out of my purse. With a few flicks of the wrist I had the slide removed. In another several seconds, and some deft tweezer work, I had flipped out the firing pin.

Reilly finished unlocking the iris scanner and returned through the doorway. I slowed my breathing and held out his gun for him, a pleasant smile on my face.

"Your turn," he said, stepping out of the way. This was why Atworthy had forced me to join them. This was where my skills were needed. Reilly had many talents, but advanced safecracking was not one of them. Neither was maneuvering through a laser grid.

I carefully pushed open the door to the prime minister's suite. The rooms were hushed and dark, apart from the glowing red lights of the laser web, blocking the way. The laser grid proved to be more of a deterrent than an actual barrier; I barely broke a sweat getting through it.

Within minutes I reached the safe on the far side of the living room, and started the process of cracking into it.

To my surprise, I cracked it much sooner than I expected. All those acrobatics must have warmed me up and centered my mind. I smiled; things were going much smoother than I'd hoped.

But that was good because I needed a little extra time to enact the plan I'd concocted.

I reached into the safe and pulled out a sheaf of papers. It was an odd feeling for me, to be stealing paper. It wasn't shiny or sparkly, but without question, valuable.

I flipped through the pages and snapped pictures of them on the stolen phone. I was going to send copies of all these documents to Felix, who could forward them to the League, before I handed them over to Atworthy. It would be the insurance policy, the only way I could be certain the right thing would be done. The only way I could stop Atworthy—even if all else failed. I felt a rueful glow of pride at that. I needed to do the right thing here. I needed to know I wasn't going to be the catalyst to all-out war.

I typed Felix's number and pushed SEND.

Nothing happened. *Searching for network. . . .*

All the air left my lungs. There was no network. I kept trying but I soon realized the Wi-Fi was down and there was no other way to connect. I couldn't complete the one task that would make this all okay.

What was I going to do now?

Chapter Sixty-Nine

I tried again to connect, sweat forming on the back of my neck. A copy of these papers had to get sent out without Reilly or Atworthy knowing I had done it. But it was simply not working.

I glanced around the room in desperation and spotted a framed photograph of the prime minister with his family. They were at a park together—smiling in the sunshine. I gritted my teeth. There had to be a way. I took a deep breath and mentally called up the blueprints of the east wing. Then I remembered there was an office in the next room, like a business center. Offices almost always contained a fax machine. It was old school, but it just might work.

Then Reilly's voice came through my earpiece. "Are you in the safe yet?"

"Um, no. Not yet." I needed to buy myself some time. "I'm still working my way through the laser grid," I lied.

How was I going to get to the office next door? There was no internal connection between the rooms. I'd have to climb outside on the window ledge.

I made my way to the window and slipped off my shoes. There was nothing I could do about the gown. I'd have to make it work. The stone of the ledge felt rough as I climbed out into the cool night air. I found my balance and began making my way, seeking stable handholds and footholds as I went.

"Okay, I'm almost through the grid, Reilly."

"What's taking so long? Do you need me to come in—"

"No! You'll ruin everything. Besides, I need you outside the room, to make sure nobody interrupts. And don't forget the metal detector. You can't leave your gun behind."

My mouth went dry at the thought of what would happen if Reilly discovered what I was up to.

"Fine. Hurry up," he said. "I thought you were supposed to be good at this."

"I have to do it right, Reilly."

At last, I slipped inside the window of the neighboring office. I quickly spotted the fax machine and exhaled with relief. I hadn't used one of these things for ages but how hard could it be?

"Okay, starting to crack into the safe now," I said to Reilly, trying to stretch things out as long as possible.

I pushed a few buttons and got the fax machine going. My heart seized for a second as I realized I had no idea where to send it to. And then I remembered the only fax number I knew: the queen's. From the pub at Harrow Hall, the business card the man had shown me. It was really simple . . . what was it? Right. 01234-QUEEN1.

I punched in the number and sent the pages through. They fed into the machine agonizingly slowly. I wanted to jump out of my skin as I waited.

At last, the whole batch went through, spitting out copies on the other end. I pulled out the copies and stared at the two sheafs of paper in my hands—what was I going to do with the duplicates?

I made a quick decision, and pushed them through the shredder that sat under the desk.

In an instant I was back out on the window ledge, picking my way to the prime minister's suite. "All right, Reilly, I'm getting close. I should have this combination cracked in a few more minutes."

A trickle of sweat dripped between my shoulder blades. I had almost done it. I was so close to pulling it off; I just needed to hang in there a little longer.

Chapter Seventy

I continued on my way back to the prime minister's suite, balancing on the ledge, staying focused on my breathing and my foot placement. The sounds from the Manhattan streets, twenty-four stories down, rose up and surrounded me—rushing traffic, honking yellow cabs. I glanced down; I was plenty high for a fatal fall. But instead of feeling afraid . . . I felt exhilarated. I felt alive.

Not for the first time, I realized: *this was truly my calling.*

An image popped into my mind—me doing this with a Baby Bjorn strapped to my chest, soothing an infant as I went, trying to keep him quiet. It was the image Ethan had put in my brain.

Despite my precarious position at the moment and the situation at hand, I smiled at the thought.

It was totally absurd. And yet—it was closer to the sort of reality I envisioned than the future Jack had in mind for us. *You're not planning on scaling buildings forever, are you?* he'd said.

At that moment—at that highly inconvenient moment—I understood something I hadn't been able to articulate before.

Ethan got me, in a way Jack never truly would. He just understood. There were so many things that could go unspoken between us. It was easy.

I remembered, then, what he'd said to me the first day I'd met him. *We're the same, babe.*

Opposites attract, sure, but they don't always make the best life partners. When Jack spoke of our future, when he was proposing, he'd used the words "settling down." When Ethan spoke of our future, he envisioned everything we had right now—just a whole lot more of it, with a few alterations in place. And that was what I wanted. It was a connection that would never need explaining.

The hot breeze rising off the street ruffled my hair. The problem was, it felt like I was too late with Ethan. After what he'd said on the phone . . .

No. It couldn't be too late. Nerves twisted in my stomach at the idea of being so close, at knowing exactly what I wanted at the worst possible moment.

One step at a time, Cat. I had to get out of here first, and that was no small thing.

"Cat, where the hell are you? What's going on in there?"

"I'm getting close, Reilly, almost into the safe . . ."

At last, I reached the window to the prime minister's suite. I climbed back in through the window and picked up my shoes. I wove my way through the laser grid, on my way back to the front door.

Reilly's voice pierced through. "That's it, Cat, I'm stashing the gun on this side and I'm coming in."

"Wait, I'm almost done—"

Reilly flung the suite door open the moment I reached the foyer. "There," I said, breathing heavily. "It's done. I have them." I patted the outside of my purse, indicating where I'd stashed the papers. Reilly stared at me with extreme suspicion. Then he exhaled, satisfied. "All right, let's get back to the party."

"My pleasure," I said with a smile.

Then he turned away and I fought every instinct to slump against the wall with relief. One step closer.

Chapter Seventy-One

Ethan knew they had detected Templeton's escape. Which meant one thing—Brooke was in immediate danger.

She was still in the waiting room—she'd had no choice but to stay there, even after they had wheeled Templeton away to the infirmary. It would have looked very odd indeed if she had bailed immediately following that turn of events.

But now she had to get out of there. "Brooke, you need to go. Now," Ethan said through the communicator as he and Templeton were walking as quickly as they could toward the parking lot.

"Working on it," she said quietly.

Ethan knew she'd had to park very far away that morning in the full lot. Visitors parked on another side of a dividing wall. Even if she were on the move right now, she would never make it. "Come straight to the van," Ethan said. "You're not going to make it to your car." Ethan, posing as the cardiovascular surgeon, had parked his Mercedes up front in the VIP spot. The van, where Gladys and Felix were stationed, was parked off to the side, pulled over near the lot exit.

Ethan bleeped the car doors unlocked with the keyless entry, and he and Templeton quickly climbed in. He expected to hear the sound of the prison break alarm any second.

"We'll wait for you," Ethan said.

"No," Brooke said. "They're watching. It'll be too suspicious. I can do it. I'll make it to my car. Go, Ethan. Get Templeton out of here."

Ethan gave Templeton a grim look, then started to drive. The alarm hadn't sounded yet. Maybe he could pick her up partway. Maybe he could get Templeton into the van, then double back to pick her up. Either way, Ethan wasn't leaving without her.

They reached the van, and Ethan pulled up beside it. "Get him out of here, before the shit hits the fan," he said to Felix and Gladys. Templeton quickly transferred vehicles, and Ethan watched the van head toward the exit.

"Brooke, I'm coming back for you," Ethan said. He squinted through his windshield into the sunlight and saw her striding purposefully toward the far parking lot.

"No, I'll be fine. I can make it."

And then the alarm sounded, an earsplitting howling of a siren.

Brooke leaned down, almost casually, and removed her shoes. She was going to run for it. But she was going to run the wrong way. He could see where her sight line went—she was going to try to make it to her own car, not backtrack to where Ethan was waiting near the exit.

"Brooke, this way," Ethan shouted through the communicator. "The west side. The exit!"

"Is he clear?" Brooke said. "Is Templeton out?" Her voice was amazingly steady.

The van had just cleared the exit tower, right before the siren sounded, and it was nearly out of sight.

"Almost."

Brooke started running. Ethan heard Felix's voice then, in his ear. "Ethan, they're looking for her. I can hear them shouting to each other. They're saying—*shoot her if you have to*."

Guards burst out onto the parking lot. They looked around and immediately spotted Brooke. "Stop!" they shouted.

She didn't turn, didn't break her stride. She was leading them away, Ethan could see that. He knew she was giving everyone else a chance to get away.

But he was not leaving her behind. He put the car into gear and pressed the accelerator. "I'm coming for you, Brooke."

"We're clear. We're out," came Felix's voice. "Get her, Ethan."

The Mercedes flew through the parking lot in a direct line toward the fleeing Brooke. The guards were growing closer, sprinting toward her.

Then, Ethan watched in horror as a guard withdrew his weapon and pointed it in Brooke's direction. Ethan had almost reached her.

The lead guard issued one further warning to Brooke. "Stop!" But she didn't stop. The guard pulled his trigger.

A loud *crack* echoed through the parking lot and Ethan watched in horror, helpless, as Brooke fell. He couldn't tell where she'd been hit.

In the next second he reached her in the Mercedes, slamming the brakes and squealing the car around, putting the vehicle between the guards and Brooke. More shots were fired, but Ethan barely heard them. In a heartbeat Ethan leaped from the Mercedes, lifted her unconscious, bleeding body, and shoved her in the backseat. More shouting, more bullets pinging off the body of the car, as Ethan leaped behind the wheel again and peeled away.

As Ethan raced toward the closed gate—the only thing blocking his way out now—he kept his foot heavily on the accelerator pedal, barrelling forward at full speed. Whatever it took, he was getting them out of here.

Chapter Seventy-Two

Reilly escorted me away from the prime minister's private rooms and back toward the gala. When we stepped out to the rooftop party, it was like nothing had changed. The chamber orchestra was playing; the VIPs were sipping champagne. All told, we'd only been gone about thirty minutes. I tried to quiet my pounding heart.

When we reached Atworthy, Reilly gave him a barely perceptible nod. Atworthy offered his arm to me, continuing the charade that we were married, and he guided me to a more private alcove, tucked away from the rest of the party. It was a small area adjacent to the chimney and ventilation tower, hidden from view of most of the party. He stared at me expectantly.

This was the moment I was supposed to produce the papers. The moment Atworthy would give the go-ahead to the sniper.

I felt a wave of nausea. I touched my purse reflexively, willing the phone inside to vibrate with a message that Ethan had succeeded in rescuing Templeton. If only Ethan would send me word—something to let me know Templeton was safe. I wouldn't have to go through with any of this. But I hadn't heard a thing.

There was applause from the party. I glanced over to see the prime minister walking up to a small podium by the orchestra stage. He was going to give a speech. I turned back to see Atworthy waiting for me to give him the pages.

I had no choice. I pulled out the sheaf of papers and Atworthy's eyes flashed. I held the papers tightly, not handing them over just yet. "Okay, Atworthy, now you have to live up to your side of the bargain. You said you would give the order to release Templeton. I need to see you do that."

"I will. But I need to see the papers first. I'm not an idiot, Catherine. You could be holding anything in your hand right there."

I struggled. But I had very little to bargain with.

"Fine. Once I give you these, you'll call off Templeton's execution, right? You'll do whatever you have to do to get him out of there?"

He gave a brisk nod, and held out his hand. I took a deep breath and gave him the pages. I was faintly aware of the sound of microphone feedback as the prime minister began addressing the partygoers.

Atworthy quickly glanced at the papers, flipping through each page, then looked up and smiled. "You have done well." He began to put them in his inside jacket pocket. But then he froze; darkness spread over his features.

"Wait." He pulled them back out and scanned them once more.

I followed his eyes. My mouth went dry as I immediately saw what he was looking at. In tiny print at the bottom of the page, a fax stamp. Dated today, time-stamped for eight minutes ago.

Oh my God. I had grabbed the fax copies, not the originals. In the rush, and my unfamiliarity with that fax machine, I had grabbed the wrong pages. I had shredded the originals.

I dragged my eyes up to his. He was staring at me, eyes burning with rage.

"What have you done?" he growled.

A choking sensation clawed up my throat. I knew exactly what I had done: I had killed Templeton. And probably myself.

Atworthy would never release Templeton, and I was trapped. How would I get away from Caliga now? How could I have been so stupid? I had one consolation: there was no way Atworthy would give the go-ahead for the assassination now.

"I'm very disappointed, Catherine," he said with an arctic chill to his voice. "I really had high hopes."

Then I watched as Atworthy pulled out his phone, pushed a speed-dial button and said, "Go. Do it now." I gaped at him in horror as I realized what was happening. He was going ahead with the assassination anyway.

Chapter Seventy-Three

Everything went into slow motion as Atworthy pushed DISCONNECT on his phone. I turned, desperate to alert everyone. I had to get out of this alcove, into view, where I could scream a warning. There was nothing left to lose.

But the moment I took a step and opened my mouth, I found myself tightly wrapped and gagged by the enormous arms and hands of one of Atworthy's men who had been standing beside the alcove.

Applause for the PM's speech drowned out my muffled shouts. Nobody noticed the scuffle because we were so snugly tucked away. All eyes were looking in the opposite direction, up toward the podium.

I could only watch, helplessly, eyes wide. And then, there was a zinging sound as a bullet ripped into the banner above the prime minister's head, shredding it into two pieces.

It had worked. My manipulation of the sniper's sight had worked. For a suspended second, the world was frozen. Then chaos erupted as the crowd realized what had just happened.

The Secret Service team instantly fell upon the PM to protect him. People screamed and scrambled for the exits. And then, at the edges of the crowd, I saw Reilly moving toward the prime minister. I struggled against my captor, and found my defense moves anticipated. I could only watch.

Within the maelstrom, Reilly withdrew his gun smoothly and took aim. It was a suicide mission, but he looked cold as a glacier. My heart thundered.

He pulled the trigger and . . . nothing.

Reilly blinked. Removing the firing pin had done the trick. He had no way of knowing what I'd done. He tried once more, to no effect.

I turned to see Atworthy's face contorted with rage and frustration. His carefully executed plan, even his backup plan, was crumbling to pieces. I wanted to smile triumphantly, but the fact was, I was still in extreme danger.

Atworthy pressed a gun to my spine.

I turned back as Reilly lunged for the edge of the terrace, only a few feet from us. I knew what he was going to do. In another heartbeat, he leaped straight over the side. His BASE chute opened instantly, from under his jacket, and he sailed down.

I craned my neck over the edge of the patio. When Reilly was halfway down, the cars parked on both sides of the street suddenly flared with lights and sirens, and several officers leaped to position. All they had to do was wait for Reilly to drop right into their arms.

I smiled. So they'd taken my anonymous tip seriously.

Atworthy looked like his head might explode. But there was also a small tinge of fear in his eyes now. This was very bad news for me; desperate people were the most dangerous of all.

He yanked my wrists together in front of my body and cinched a zip cord around them. He flopped a coat over them, concealing the ties. It was subtle enough that nobody would comment, at least for the first minute or so. But I wouldn't be here that long. "Say a word and I will shoot you without a second thought," he hissed in my ear.

I might have been able to neutralize the weapons of two of his team members, but I hadn't done a thing to Atworthy's gun. It was a fully functioning weapon and I had no doubt he would hold to his word.

He hustled me, alone, away from the party and down the service elevator. My mind raced—what could I do? He was more than my physical match. He was a trained assassin. I had no chance against him.

The prime minister was safe from assassination tonight. But I wasn't.

Atworthy pushed me out a side door and we slipped out onto street level, unseen in the turmoil.

I had no idea where Atworthy was taking me. If this were anyone else, I might have been able to execute an escape maneuver. Plus, there was the zip cord around my wrists—a very tricky thing to remove.

I thought about screaming for help, creating a scene. But I was fairly certain he would shoot, just as he said. You can stall in certain situations by creating a diversion, but not with a stone-cold killer. Besides, I was of minimal use to him now. There was no choice but to go along with him . . . for now.

He barked an order into his phone. "I need an extraction, now." He listened to the instructions, then disconnected.

He marched me down the brightly lit streets, blending into the busy Manhattan sidewalk crowds. If I was going to attempt an escape, I'd have to choose my moment carefully. Then I realized where we were headed: in a straight line toward Central Park.

Oh God. I couldn't let myself get taken into the park. It would be all over if that happened.

Then I saw my salvation. Hendrickx pulled up in a car. He was alone.

He spotted us immediately. His eyes flicked down to my wrists, noting their awkward angle, the coat covering them, Atworthy standing too close. Hendrickx might be many things—cold fish, son of a bitch, heartless bastard—but he was not stupid.

I saw the realization of truth kindle in his eyes. I could tell he knew what side I was on in that instant.

I felt a flutter in my chest. My life was about to be saved by the most unexpected person I could think of.

"Atworthy," Hendrickx said flatly, "stop right there."

We were half a block from the park's entrance, on the corner of the hotel block. There were no other agents or officers with him—thanks to my tip, everyone was around on the opposite side to retrieve Reilly. Atworthy positioned me between himself and Hendrickx. Smart. Signaling my hostage status to the Interpol officer so he wouldn't shoot.

This was my last chance. Together with Hendrickx, we could take Atworthy down. A blast of adrenaline shot to my muscles. I was ready. I could throw myself off balance, bring him down with me, and Hendrickx could cuff him—

What I didn't count on was Atworthy simply lifting his hand and firing a bullet into Hendrickx's chest, point-blank. Hendrickx fell.

In the next instant Atworthy was dragging me away from the scene, forcing me to run with him straight into the park.

Chapter Seventy-Four

Atworthy had me in an unbreakable hold as we raced through the park entrance. My head spun with disbelief. The image of Hendrickx falling, dead in the street, flashed horribly in my mind.

Atworthy pushed me forward with an economy of movement. He obviously knew my strengths and weaknesses. Hell, he'd practically trained me. He'd taught me how to get out of most sticky situations. This situation—one-on-one with your physical better, who also possessed the only weapon and had your hands bound—I knew was virtually impossible to get out of.

It was over.

"What are you going to do, Atworthy?" I asked, trying to keep my voice steady as we moved farther into the darkness of the park.

He flicked a glance at me. "You know I can't let you walk around, Catherine. I can't let you go free."

I had served my usefulness to him. I heard the faint chopping sound of helicopter blades in the distance. This must be his extraction.

We arrived at a deserted clearing among the trees, beside a small concrete pavilion. A dry breeze rustled the leaves. He pushed me down on a park bench and tied a second zip cord around my ankle, securing me to the leg of the bench. He stood two paces back and aimed his gun at me, waiting for the helicopter. The distance was smart. I could no longer do anything to him.

I had been the hostage, but I had no further purpose. This was the place where Atworthy would kill me.

"Atworthy, you don't have to do this," I said, breathing heavily. I cast around our immediate surroundings for anything that might help.

The concrete pavilion held a steel door labeled: *Service Access. Authorized Entry Only. Tunnel No. 3.*

"I do, in fact," he said. "It's a shame because you would have been a great asset to our cause. But I can see, now, that you would never have joined our side. You believe yourself to be a thief with ethics."

"I don't just *believe* it, Atworthy."

He laughed without humor. "And there's your error. You don't realize that when it comes right down to it, you're nothing but a common criminal. Doing people's dirty work for them. Replaceable."

I tried to ignore his words, tried to focus on getting out of this. I had only minutes. He wouldn't risk being caught by shooting me before the helicopter arrived, but the moment it was here . . .

Then, there was a voice in my ear. The earpiece I had put in there, that I had been using to communicate with Reilly—suddenly I heard a very familiar voice coming through it.

"We're coming, Cat," Jack said urgently. "We're on the ground. We'll be there in a minute. Keep him there."

I said nothing, concentrating on keeping my face unreadable. *Where are they?*

"We have the park surrounded, and we're closing in on your exact location," Jack said, reading my mind. "We have a beacon on you, but not Atworthy. Whatever you do, don't let him bolt into the tunnel."

I flicked a glance at the door that led to Tunnel Number 3. I knew it was the water tunnel, the mega engineering project that crisscrossed underneath Manhattan. If he bolted down the stairs, they would lose him.

The chopper, his escape, was approaching, but it was far enough away to buy us that precious minute. Would Jack and his team get here before Atworthy shot me?

Then I watched Atworthy's face change. He indicated my ear with a flick of his gun barrel and an even more terrifying level of anger. "What are they saying?" he said, biting off his words in a low, cold voice.

He'd realized they were speaking to me. He'd heard the buzz through the earpiece, or he'd read it on my face, maybe. He was, and always had been, a step ahead of me.

He glanced around for escape options and then squinted up into the sky. Did he know thc helicopter was still too far away? I had to keep him from fleeing through the tunnel. It all came down to me. But if I told him they were approaching through the tunnel he wouldn't believe me. He'd think I was bluffing.

And then, in a blast of clarity, I knew what to do. I would tell him the truth.

I lifted my chin. "They've got the park surrounded. They're going to get here before the helicopter does. Your only escape is down that staircase into the tunnels."

I held my breath as my heart beat furiously against my rib cage. Atworthy had always had the upper hand because he'd lied and deceived and tricked. We were both part of the criminal world, and in that world, nobody ever told the truth.

Atworthy narrowed his eyes. "Yes, I'm sure they said that. How stupid do you think I am? Let me guess—they're approaching through the tunnel. They're waiting for me to go down there this very minute. Am I right?"

"No. You're wrong. Your only escape is through the tunnel."

He let out a bark of a laugh.

Part of me wanted him to go, to flee, to get away from me. The longer he stayed there, the more likely he would shoot me after all. The stronger part of me stayed firm. I had to keep him there.

"Fine. Don't believe me."

"I don't. Face it, Catherine, you're a crook. Just like me. No better. You will always be a filthy liar. I'm not falling into your trap."

I swallowed. It was working. But how much longer would it take before Jack arrived?

"Unfortunately, it also means your time is up," he said. He leveled his gun at my chest. And without any further hesitation, he pulled the trigger.

At that exact moment, Jack plowed into him, a football tackle. I felt a searing, ripping pain in my left shoulder and I fell off the bench, my ankle still tethered.

Through the fog of the pain, I could see uniformed officers—FBI, NYPD—surrounding Atworthy. They were handcuffing him. It was over.

I looked down and saw blood blooming out onto the fabric of my gown. I glanced up at Atworthy, to see an expression of utter shock on his face. "You were telling the truth."

My head was spinning, but I managed to spit out a few words. "The only filthy liar here is you, Atworthy. My hands may not be lily white, but you . . . there isn't even a *sliver* of goodness in you."

I had beaten him by refusing to lie. I had defeated Atworthy by turning my back on the habits of my profession. By simply telling the truth.

Jack was at my side then. I glanced at him. "Jack—Atworthy has the Lionheart Ring. He's wearing it . . ."

And then, everything faded to black.

Chapter Seventy-Five

I woke up and things came into fuzzy focus. I was in a hospital bed under starched sheets, my head resting on a plastic pillow. I became aware of a dull throbbing in my left shoulder.

I heard something beside the bed and turned to see Jack sitting there.

He gazed at me with extreme concern. "Hey there, sleepyhead. You okay?"

I nodded. "I'm not sure . . . but I think so."

His face softened. "Cat—you have no idea. I was so worried."

"I know. I was worried, too." I licked my lips, trying to get moisture into my mouth. A thousand questions crashed into my consciousness. "Is Atworthy in custody?"

Jack nodded and his face turned grim. "He won't be going anywhere for a long time."

"And the helicopter? What happened?" I asked Jack.

"It buggered off, once the pilot saw we had surrounded Atworthy. Cowards."

"How did you guys know where to find us?"

Jack told me he and Wesley had gone to the Plaza Hotel on the wild goose chase I'd sent them on—I cringed at this—and how he'd called Hendrickx right away after.

"Oh God. Hendrickx," I said, closing my eyes at the memory.

"He's okay, Cat. He was wearing a flak jacket."

Relief flooded around me like a warm bath. I kept listening.

"Hendrickx called the troops—Interpol and FBI and even the NYPD. They had already taken care of Reilly—thanks to your anonymous tip. And then they realized that Atworthy had you. They were able to track you because you were still carrying the phone you'd used to send the tips."

I nodded. Everything had worked out. From that end of things, anyway.

"Do you know anything about Templeton—is he okay?"

He shook his head. "I haven't heard a word yet. But it's still early. It's barely morning."

I fidgeted with the bedsheets and tried to put Templeton out of my mind. There was nothing I could do until I heard from Ethan.

"Cat . . . I noticed you're not wearing the ring I gave you."

I looked down at my hand and then up at him. Truth was, I had never really put it on. I could have given him an excuse about being on the job, not being able to wear an identifying ring . . .

But I didn't say any of those things. Because they weren't the real reason I wasn't wearing his ring. Still, I struggled in the face of his question.

"It's okay," he said. "You don't have to explain."

He held my gaze. A lesser man might have looked away. But not Jack.

"Cat, you know I love you. More than I ever thought possible. And—I wish . . . I wish you could be mine. Forever. But it's just not meant to be."

"Jack—I—" My voice caught in my throat. I wasn't ready for this conversation.

"Cat, you know what I'm saying. We've had a wonderful history together. Unforgettable, really." He smiled here, but there was deep sadness in his eyes. "But—well, I saw your face when I was talking about our future, when I was talking about having a family, and settling down. Maybe that kind of future is in the cards for you, and maybe it's not. But I can see we're not headed there together. There's so much that's right between us. But there's a lot that isn't."

I couldn't make any words come out of my mouth.

"I know there's a lot between you and Ethan. It's undeniable, anyone can see it. And the fact is, as much as I can't believe I'm admitting this, I think he's your best chance at lifelong happiness. He can give you what you need." His voice caught on these words.

A lump formed in my throat.

"So I'm letting you go, Cat. I'm letting you follow your heart. Because as much as I might wish your heart would lead you back to me, I know it won't. So I'm giving you your freedom, and letting you go."

My chest ached. We had so much history together, so many memories. But I knew we would only have the past now. It was over between us. And this time, it was forever. "Jack, you know I will always love you." My voice was ragged.

He smiled again, though it was a sad smile. "I know." His face grew serious. "I'm going back to the FBI, Cat, and I'm accepting a transfer to Washington, D.C. It's who I am. You don't need me, hanging around, making it hard for you to be who you are."

There was nothing more to say. Jack leaned down and kissed me then, and there was no mistaking it as a good-bye kiss. Tears streamed down my face, turning the kiss to salt.

Jack stood up. His eyes were full of heartache and determination, but as he turned to walk out, I thought I saw in his expression a glimmer of peace.

Chapter Seventy-Six

I must have dozed off after Jack left, because much later that morning I woke up to find a nurse changing my IV. She looked at me as I opened my eyes. "Oh good. You're awake," she said kindly. "There's someone here who wants to see you."

She disappeared and two minutes later, Felix poked his head around the doorframe. "Up for a visitor?"

"Felix. Oh, thank God," I breathed out deeply. "Is Templeton out? Is he okay? What happened?"

He walked into the room and broke into a grin. "We did it, Cat. Templeton is out. He's safe."

Relief filled me. "Where is he?"

"He's back in Seattle, in a private hospital—the ultra-discreet kind, if you know what I mean."

My relief was immediately replaced by despair. Templeton would be a fugitive from now on. Singapore would want him back. He would be a wanted man, on the run.

"And so you know," Felix said, reading my mind, "Interpol has worked everything out with the Singaporean government. The charges have been washed. He doesn't have anything more to worry about."

My eyebrows lifted. Then I understood. By *Interpol*, he meant Ludolf Hendrickx.

I smiled at that, then grew uneasy once more. I wanted to know where everyone else was, whether everyone else was safe. If Felix was here . . . where was Ethan? I felt desperate to talk to him, to see him.

I opened my mouth to ask Felix, but he cut me off. "Listen, Cat, I know you're processing a lot," he said, pouring me a glass of water from the pitcher on a table at the end of the bed. "And the timing may be less than ideal at the moment, but my superiors at the League want me to offer you an official position."

I almost dropped the glass of water he handed me. "What?" I shifted in the hospital bed to face him more fully, wincing with pain at the movement.

"The board knows everything you did, and they are beyond impressed," he said. "You're in. We'll give you more details . . . in time. But your training will start soon. As soon as you heal up." He gestured to my heavily bandaged shoulder. "If you want to do it, that is."

"I do," I said quickly.

Excitement fluttered in my belly. I lifted the glass of water to my mouth with a shaking hand. My future was going to begin. With the League, I'd be able to do what I loved, what I was good at, and make the world a better place at the same time.

Felix was quiet as I turned everything over in my mind, and then he held an envelope out to me.

"Listen, I'm supposed to give this to you," he said.

I searched Felix's face for an explanation but there was none. "What's this?" I asked.

"Just open it."

I took the envelope and unfolded the letter inside. I immediately recognized the handwriting.

Dearest Catherine, the letter began. I could practically hear Templeton's voice. My eyes stung. I looked up at Felix and he shrugged. "He wrote it in the hospital. He said he wasn't up to a telephone conversation yet, but there were things he wanted to say."

I continued reading.

Catherine, I don't believe I will ever be able to thank you sufficiently, for everything. And before you start blaming yourself for what happened I have one thing to say:

The decision to come to Singapore was mine, and I would do it again.

Now, a little business. Your payment will be transferred shortly. Even though the job didn't exactly come off as expected, the sheriff was happy you two were able to save the ring.

Finally, a little bird told me you're going to be moving on, Petal. I can't say I'm happy about it—for my sake. But . . . I am happy for you.

I bit my lip. I would no longer be working with Templeton. It was possible this would be the last I would hear from him. I forced myself to read his final words. *I want you to know, Catherine, that you are the best of us. It has been an honor and a pleasure.*

My throat constricted in a painful lump. The honor had been all mine. One day I would find a way to tell him that.

I folded the envelope and put it on the tray beside my hospital bed. I turned to Felix. I wanted to ask him about Ethan, where he was, why he hadn't come . . . but I was afraid of what he'd tell me. I grasped at a different subject.

"Templeton mentioned the sheriff," I said. "Is he pissed about the truth about Robin Hood? That he was a Yorkshireman?"

"Well, it's not so simple. The fact is, he was both. He was born in Nottingham, and died in Yorkshire. They both have a claim to him. At any rate, it's an area of ongoing research and controversy."

I was happy to let the academics duke this one out. As for my little secret about my own connection to Robin Hood . . . well, I wasn't quite ready to share it yet. Someday, perhaps.

"So what happens to the Gifts, now? And the Lionheart Ring?"

"The DOA obtained the Fabergé from the gala, and the Lionheart from Atworthy," he said. "They will soon be installed in a permanent place in the British Museum."

"On display?" It didn't sound like a good idea. They would just be stolen again.

"Their replicas, sure."

"And where will the originals be kept?"

"Well, let's just say . . . you know that warehouse they show at the end of *Indiana Jones and the Raiders of the Lost Ark*? Well, think of that. And then double it."

I smiled. It was a fitting end.

Atworthy was finished. He'd be locked up for a long time, after shooting Hendrickx and all the conspiracies and organized crime they'd be able to pin on him. And Interpol was busy rounding up the rest of Caliga.

I, for one, was happy to let it all go. It was time to move on.

Felix was quiet a moment and then he pulled out his phone. "Cat, there's someone else who wants to talk to you." He held the phone out to me, then slipped out of the room to give me privacy.

I held the phone to my ear. "Montgomery? How are you feeling? Are you okay?" My heart skittered at the sound of Ethan's voice.

"Ethan, it's . . . good to hear your voice," I said, then cleared my throat. "I'm getting better. They're going to let me out of here in another day or so."

There was a pause. "I heard about everything," he said quietly. "And I wanted to be there. It's . . . there's something I have to deal with here."

I swallowed. His voice sounded tense, worried for me. But distracted, somehow. "Where are you?" I asked.

"I—I'm still in Singapore."

Something was wrong.

"Montgomery, I have to tell you something. Not all of us made it out of the prison escape okay."

My stomach dropped. Ethan was in trouble. He was hurt. Or he'd been caught. I tried to ask, but I couldn't form the words.

"It's Brooke," he said. "She didn't make it."

Didn't make it? Was she stuck in prison, or . . . did he mean something worse?

My mouth went dry as Ethan described in a few brief, agonizing sentences, what had happened. She'd been shot. Ethan had gotten to her, and they had managed to escape. But it had been too late. Brooke was dead.

I let out an anguished cry. The truth slammed into me. *She had sacrificed herself so Templeton could get away.*

Brooke, who had always looked out for number one, had always taken care of herself—in the end, she'd been the true hero. It was more than I could stand. I gripped the phone in my fist and squeezed my eyes tight. And then, anguish mixed with guilt. I realized part of me felt relieved that it wasn't Ethan who was hurt.

"I have to stay here," Ethan said, "to take care of getting Brooke's body back home. It's tricky, but I've managed to get an alternate identity . . ."

"Of course," I said hoarsely, nodding. He was staying to do the right thing. He wasn't leaving her behind.

I glanced out the hospital window. The Hudson River sparkled, reflecting the brilliant July sun. I thought—*Brooke will never see that again. She'll never see anything again.*

"It's my fault," I said, barely a whisper.

"If you think of it like that, then you are detracting from Brooke's final act," Ethan said. "You are taking the burden—and the glory—of her sacrifice away from her. She chose to help, she chose to be part of the team, she *chose* to make that one final decision that ensured our getaway. It was her choice, completely."

I hoped someday I could fully believe those words. They had a core of truth to them.

There was silence on the line for several seconds. I took a deep breath. There was something I needed to tell him. I knew the timing was all wrong, but I couldn't hold it in.

"Ethan, I want you to know . . . it's over with Jack. For good."

He was quiet. "Why are you telling me that?"

"Because I realized, at last, that my future isn't with him. It's . . . with you." I swallowed. "If that's what you want, too," I added.

He said nothing for a moment, during which time my chest began to ache. "Montgomery, I really can't talk about this right now." His voice sounded distant. "I have to go and handle things with Brooke. I'll call you when I get back home. Okay?"

"Sure. Okay, I understand," I managed to say.

I disconnected the call and placed Felix's phone on my bedside tray. It was over with Ethan. His silence at my declaration confirmed that. There would be no future for us. My insides felt hollow. Somehow, I was going to have to find a way of accepting I had lost him for good.

Chapter Seventy-Seven

The next morning, my parents walked into my room just as the nurse was about to disconnect my IV. "All ready?" my mother said brightly, bustling in and sweeping open the curtains. "It's a gorgeous day out there, maybe we can enjoy it before heading home. Go out for lunch, perhaps?"

They had arrived late last night, and were here to collect me when the hospital discharged me. We would head home together tomorrow as planned, as long as the doctors said I was okay to fly.

I squinted against the sunlight that streamed into the room. The very last thing I felt like doing was going out for lunch with my parents. My mother turned from the window and glanced down at me in the bed. I winced as the nurse briskly removed the IV from my hand and pressed a cotton swab against my stinging skin.

"Or perhaps we should go back to the hotel," my mother said, her voice softer, her face gazing at me with concern. "You can rest, Catherine. We'll take care of everything."

The nurse made a note on a clipboard and then walked out, shoes squeaking faintly on the polished floor.

My dad came to stand beside me. "Feeling a little better, Kit Kat?"

I shrugged. "A little." Truth was, my shoulder was healing well, and I was regaining my strength. But it wasn't the physical pain that would be a problem.

I turned to him then, finally ready to talk about what I had learned. "Dad, I know about our family's connection to Robin of Loxley. I know the . . . *profession* has been in our family for countless generations. Why didn't you ever tell me?"

He glanced up at my mother, standing on the opposite side of the bed, then looked at me for a long time before answering, shock and indecision mingling on his face. “I couldn’t, Cat. I was afraid I would lose you further, that you would see it as validation. And you would never stop doing what you were doing.”

“I know about your own father. What he did.”

My mother was watching us carefully. There was no surprise on her face; she’d clearly known his history. But I could see she was worried about his reaction to all this. He nodded. “It tore our family apart. It’s why I had so much difficulty with your, um, career choice.”

I understood. And I didn’t blame him. None of us mentioned my sister Penny. But she was, and always would be, in all our thoughts.

I took a deep breath. The air in the hospital smelled of bleach and freshly starched sheets, with a faint odor of breakfast being served down the hall. “Well, I have news. Good news,” I added, seeing my mother’s expression. “I’ve been recruited . . . and I’ve chosen to go to the right side of the law. I can’t tell you exactly what it means—you don’t have the security clearance for that,” I said with a wry grin. “But you can be assured I’m telling you the truth when I say I’m not a criminal anymore.”

My father stared at me and his eyes grew glassy. He said nothing, but I knew what this news meant to him. He had always been a man of few words. My mother, on the other hand, had plenty of words. She peppered me with questions about job security, work conditions, maternity pay . . .

I deflected it all. I was finally getting good at that.

One thing she said was a little trickier to deflect, though. “I’m happy for you, Cat. It sounds like an exciting move. And I’m glad you won’t be in quite so much danger.” I wasn’t sure about that, but I didn’t say anything. “But I must confess, I’m still waiting for you to find someone you can share your life with.” A wistful expression crossed her face. “I want grandbabies, damn it,” she added with a teasing tone. But there was heartfelt sincerity under her teasing.

Though it had taken me awhile to realize it, this was my wish, too. Before I could stop myself, I thought back to my conversation yesterday with Ethan, and my wounded emotions throbbed again, raw and fresh.

At last, my father found the words he wanted to say. “Penny would be happy, Cat. And she’d be proud of you. Like I am.”

I managed a smile. Although my love life was in tatters, at least this was something I could find comfort in. A feeling of peace curled around my heart at his words.

I glanced at my mother. She looked more content than I'd seen her in a long time. She'd obviously recovered well from her own stint in the hospital. And although I couldn't erase the fact that she'd been shot, my decision to leave the criminal world went a long way to soothing my guilt over her injury.

That evening, after I'd been discharged from the hospital, I decided a walk around the city was in order. My parents had protested my request to go alone, but I'd assured them I'd be okay. I couldn't sit still at the hotel any longer, watching television and killing time before the doctor cleared me for our flight tomorrow. Too many thoughts swirled around in my head. I needed to keep moving.

The day had been gorgeous and sunshiny, the heat of the city wrapping around me like a favorite sweater, but it was growing later now. The sun slipped lower and the full heat settled a bit. My thoughts kept drifting to Brooke. It was going to take some time to come to terms with what had happened to her. It was going to take time to come to terms with everything, actually.

I grabbed a coffee at Dean & DeLuca and hopped in a cab down to the Brooklyn Bridge. When I'd lived in New York, this was one of my favorite places to watch the sun set over the city.

I was in the cab when my phone rang. "Hello, darling," my mom said when I answered. "I was just checking us in to our flight tomorrow. Would you like a window or aisle seat?"

I sighed. It was a thinly veiled excuse. I could hear the worry and the unspoken questions in her voice. "Window," I said. "And, Mom? I'm fine."

She gave a short laugh. "Of course you are. So . . . where are you, anyway?"

"On my way to the Brooklyn Bridge. I'm going to watch the sunset with my coffee. I'll be back in a little while."

"Oh. Well, that sounds nice. Catherine, will you please call if you need anything?"

"Sure," I said. "But don't worry, Mom. I'm okay."

As I said the words, I realized I meant it.

Several minutes later, the cabbie dropped me at the Brooklyn Bridge. As the sun began to dip low toward the horizon, filling the sky with a golden glow, I made my way along the pedestrian walkway to a spot near the center. While traffic roared beneath me and suspension ropes soared overhead, I leaned on the railing and took a deep breath.

A few tourists strolled behind me, snapping photographs, sighing over the sight of the sun setting through the stone archways of the bridge. I lost track of the passage of time. I lifted my coffee cup to my lips and took a sip—*ugh*. Stone-cold. Oh well.

I fiddled with the paper cup, and looked out over the water. It was fitting, really, for me to be alone. I had chosen an unconventional path, and a journey like that was always destined to be taken alone.

Someone cleared his throat beside me.

"Need a warm-up on that coffee? I can help with that."

Chapter Seventy-Eight

I turned my head to see Ethan standing a few paces away, holding a coffee cup in each hand.

It was a miracle just to see him. There had been a moment when I didn't think I ever would. He didn't need to offer me anything more than a coffee. My heart expanded at the sight of him.

"Ethan—"

He strolled toward me and handed me one of the coffees. He was wearing a T-shirt, jeans, and Ray-Ban sunglasses that suited him so perfectly, he looked like he'd been born wearing them. A characteristic crooked smile played on his face. It was the best thing I'd seen all week.

I was suddenly flooded with emotion. "Thank you," I blurted out. "For the coffee . . . and for Templeton. Everything," I said breathlessly, stumbling over my words, sounding like an idiot. My face flushed and I took a deep breath. "I mean, how can I ever thank you enough?"

He shrugged. "I'm sure we can come up with something."

I turned to him with a mock look of shock on my face. "Mr. Jones, I'm not sure I like the suggestion in your voice."

He grinned. "I'm pretty sure you do."

He put his coffee down on the railing. I took a sip of mine and placed it on the railing beside his. He turned to face me, more serious now. "How are you feeling, Montgomery? I mean—are you okay?" He looked me over carefully, his brow creasing with worry.

I nodded. "I'm okay. No permanent damage."

He tried to smile through a pained expression. "That's good."

Then something occurred to me and I raised an eyebrow. "How did you know I was here, anyway?"

"Your mother," he said, with a guilty expression.

Ah. So that had been the purpose of her call. She must have sent him to check up on me. We stood in silence a little while, watching the sun melt down below the horizon. I thought of the last sunset we had shared—the one on the beach in Bali. My face flushed at the memory.

We'd had fun on that beach. But the truth was, I wanted more than that. I needed Ethan in my future. I wanted . . . *everything* with him. But my head filled with the echo of his last words on the phone when I'd asked him to rescue Templeton. *I can't do this anymore*, he'd said. *There won't be any more* us.

"I guess we won't be working together anymore," I said. "It was a good last job." I tried hard to keep my voice upbeat.

"You're not getting rid of me that easily."

"I'm not?" Hope bubbled up inside me.

"Didn't Felix tell you? He offered me a position with the League, also."

My eyebrows lifted. It was good news. A twinge of disappointment told me it wasn't exactly what I'd hoped he was going to say. But it was still good news. "That's wonderful, Ethan. Are you going to take it?" Of course, if we were working together, maybe there would be a chance to rekindle things again, someday . . .

"I need a little time to think about it," he said, shrugging. "But I gotta say, doing the mission in Singapore—the black op to help Templeton—it made me realize that my skills could really make a difference. I could make the world a better place. I've never thought about that before."

I knew exactly what he meant. I lifted my coffee and took another sip; it was still hot. No matter what happened, I would always remember drinking this coffee with Ethan on this bridge.

"I heard you gave your money to your NGO, Global Life," I said, smiling. At least some genuine good would come out of this whole mess.

He nodded. "I did. I guess I've already started on my do-gooding."

"They're lucky to have you," I said.

"You know, if I accept Felix's offer, we'll be working closely together again," he said. He watched me carefully, gauging my response to this. Was he worried our history would mess with our ability to work together? Would he want to keep things professional?

"There's something I need to tell you," he said. I tried to read the expression on his face, but it was impossible. "You know I've always been content with the idea of being a bachelor forever," he began.

I looked away. This had the sound of a breakup speech. But he'd already told me it was over—did he really think I needed to hear it again? I took a deep breath and struggled to gather my emotions. I stared at the sunset, barely hearing his words, trying to keep my breathing even and stop the tears from coming.

". . . the fact is, you have changed my life in ways I can hardly put into words. I never imagined meeting anyone like you. I thought I wanted to be the lone wolf. Nobody to pin me down. But you changed all that. Freedom means nothing if it means I can't be with you."

Wait—what was he saying? I turned then, to see Ethan down on one knee.

"Catherine Montgomery, I love you. I want to spend the rest of my life with you. And . . . I'm hoping, with every fiber in me, that you want the same thing."

He held a ring in his hand. "It's not the Lionheart," he said, "and it's not the Hope Diamond, but I'm hoping you like it all the same."

I stared at the ring. It was the exact one I'd described when we had been on the Orient Express: a red diamond surrounded by a halo of tiny white diamonds.

"How did you . . . ?"

He winked. "I have skills, Montgomery."

"Not stolen?"

He shook his head firmly. "Nope."

As Ethan held the ring out to me, his hand trembled—something I had never seen in all our escapades together. At that moment a kaleidoscope of images flashed through my head, my future life with Ethan. There were adventures, travel, laughter, the excitement of doing missions together. It was all wonderful and thrilling. But the most wonderful of those images was the last one: the two of us cuddled by a fire on a rainy Sunday afternoon. Me reading a good book, Ethan watching the football game on TV and rubbing my feet as they rested in his lap. I could almost smell the coffee brewing in the kitchen.

It was perfect.

"Yes, Ethan. *Yes*. I want to marry you. I want to spend the rest of my life with you."

My eyes burned and I was helpless to stop the tears that flooded them. I smiled through it. Ethan exhaled with relief and his eyes turned glassy. I stared at the ring as he placed it on my finger. It was impossible not to think of the Lionheart, looking at the ring now. Equally impossible was not thinking of the ring I used to wear. Penny's ring.

Then he stood and in one fluid movement lifted me up, right off my feet. He laughed and let out a loud whoop, and—heedless of the tourists all around us—murmured sweet words as his mouth found mine. We kissed for a long, long time.

I knew the adventures we'd been through together, as crazy as they'd been, were nothing compared to what would come.

"What is it with us and bridges?" Ethan murmured. I smiled. We stood there, arms around each other, and gazed back toward the city as the sky filled with fire. I glanced down at the ring; it was spectacular. Truly a jewel thief's ring . . . worn by a woman who was finished being a jewel thief.

For the first time in a long time, there was no struggle inside me. Just peace. I would still go on scaling buildings and sneaking around and doing things most people—wisely, I might add—were unwilling to do. But now I would be doing those things for all the right reasons.

I'd always known that everyone broke the rules eventually . . . and some of us even made a career out of it.

But what I'd learned was this: there was good and bad inside everyone. Which side would win? Well, that was in our own hands.

Even if those hands happened to be exceptionally talented at pickpocketing.

Acknowledgments

First, heartfelt thanks go to my agent, Sandy Lu. Without her vision and tenacity, these books would never have been.

Thank you to my editor, Peter Senftleben, for bringing my books to life (and also for taking me out for my first publishing lunch in Manhattan). And thank you to the whole amazing team at Kensington and Lyrical.

An enormous hug of gratitude goes to Karma Brown for being a rock-star critique partner. Thank you to my writing support group on Facebook, the International Thriller Writers, the wonderful SIWC community, and my sister-wives at YMC.

I will be forever indebted to *Writer's Digest* for awarding me second place for one of my first stories in their annual competition many years ago. Second place, of course, being the perfect place for a budding writer: high enough to be validating, not so high to make me think I knew it all.

Thank you to my parents for so many things. Life, mostly.

Kudos to my sisters for their never-ending support of their big sis and for letting me boss them around as we were growing up . . . and not holding it against me later.

Hugs and kisses to my boys—for many things, but mostly for their patience. Although I suspect a lot of that patience had to do with knowing there was another book launch party coming. My boys—always looking for an excuse to party. They're not teenagers yet. I'm in trouble.

Thank you to my husband, Ken, for so much: for listening and brainstorming and not batting an eye when I burst from my writing room to announce random questions ("Would you expect to be served filet mignon on the Orient Express?"). Also for indulging me when I want to do things like go inside the Beverly Hills Hotel when we have no business being there. ("Yes, honey, *inside*. It's for research.") But most of all, for having the superpower of coming up with kick-ass book titles.

Thank you to the people of Yorkshire and Nottinghamshire for feuding and providing this writer with a germ of an idea.

And thank you, Robin Hood . . . whoever you really were.

About the Author

Kim Foster is the author of the Agency of Burglary & Theft Series, a series of novels about a professional female jewel thief. Prior to writing thrillers about thieves and spies, Kim obtained her degree in medicine, and she has been a practicing family doctor for sixteen years. (Don't worry, it doesn't make much sense to her friends and family, either.) Online, you can find her blogging about her left-brain, right-brain mash-up on www.kimfoster.com. Kim lives with her husband and their two young boys in Victoria, British Columbia, where she's hard at work on her next book. And drinking a ridiculous amount of coffee.

AN AB&T NOVEL

The only crime is getting caught…

A Beautiful HEIST

KIM FOSTER

AN AB&T NOVEL 

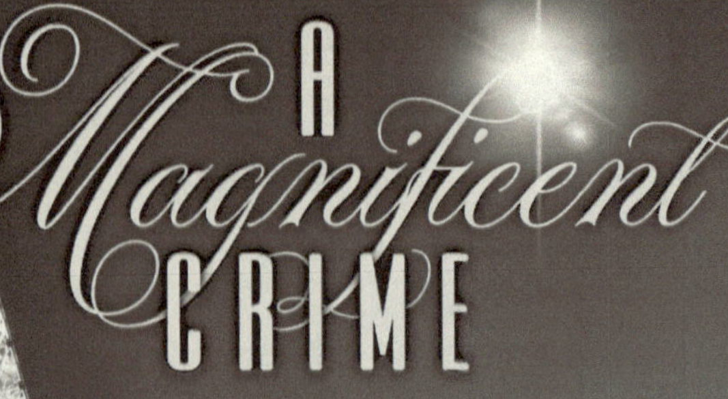

Diamonds are a thief's best friend...

KIM FOSTER

www.ingramcontent.com/pod-product-compliance
Lightning Source LLC
LaVergne TN
LVHW091020080826
845145LV00002B/302

9781601834850